Lar Redmond grew up in Emerald Square, on the edge of the Liberties in Dublin. He was educated at Rialto School and James's Street Christian Brothers. At the outbreak of war he joined the Irish Army, and in 1941 he went to England to work as a carpenter. He later returned to Ireland with his wife and child, and worked as a foreman for his father's building company.

Lar emigrated to Australia in the 1950s after the collapse of his own building firm. He worked for many years as a foreman and builder. He won two bursaries to the University of Adelaide for writing, and had his first short story published in Australia in 1963.

In 1967, Lar returned to Ireland. Since then he has appeared many times on television and radio, and has had several short stories and articles published. *Emerald Square* is his first novel.

Emerald Square

Lar Redmond

EMERALD SQUARE

A CORGI BOOK 0 552 13036 2

First publication in Great Britain

PRINTING HISTORY

Corgi edition published 1987

This book is set in 10/11 pt Cheltenham
by Colset Private Limited, Singapore.

Corgi Books are published by Transworld Publishers Ltd.,
61–63 Uxbridge Road, Ealing, London W5 5SA, in Australia by
Transworld Publishers (Australia) Pty. Ltd., 15–23 Helles
Avenue, Moorebank, NSW 2170, and in New Zealand by
Transworld Publishers (N.Z.) Ltd., Cnr. Moselle and Waipareira
Avenues, Henderson, Auckland.

Made and printed in Great Britain by
Cox & Wyman Ltd., Reading, Berks.

Contents

1 82 Lower Gardiner Street

I was born with a caul in a second floor back room of a respectable tenement house in Lower Gardiner Street. The house is still there, though I have no need to go back to remember every tiny detail of it.

Perhaps it was the terrifying period and surroundings that branded events on my childish mind, but I can recall with clarity every single thing that happened there, as far back as when I was eighteen months old. To draw your first breath in the middle of a revolution, smack in the centre of the capital city was a good start. And, if your father was 'doing time' for taking on the forces of the Crown, here was an additional bonus. He was a member of the guerrilla force that broke the power of the British in the twenty-six counties, a 'Shinner'.

'Sinn Fein' is the Gaelic for 'Ourselves Alone', and by God, in Gardiner Street we were very much alone, Mam, Sean and me. Dad was on official hunger strike in Dundalk jail and we three were on unofficial hunger strike in Gardiner Street. There was only one important difference. We had no choice in the matter – he had!

Every other night, when the shooting got too heavy and explosions, shouts and the thunder of army boots were all about us, I would be bundled out of bed, falling with sleep as we headed for the safety of the basement, where a drunken old crone lived with the rats. My mother's fear would communicate itself to us. Me, she frightened. My brother she drove to such a frenzy, that he was scarred for life and would never walk willingly in the dark again.

For me, the nightmare ended when we left that accursed

Georgian house, but while in it, my mother's constant emotional ferment got to me, so that Gardiner Street was branded on my mind in black and smoking letters. Gardiner Street was a six letter word – *terror*!

High ceilings in a cavernous house and an elegant, bare, echoing staircase went past our room, where Mount Everest-like, 'that one' squatted on high in the attic. Sunshine through tall windows, dust motes floating over bare poverty and a bluebottle buzzing frantically against dirty glass. A Georgian house, almost anywhere in Dublin, where each resident had their own personal key to poverty.

On the bottom floor of our house, lived a drunken old West Britainer, Mokeler by name, hated as a suspected informer, who staggered in and out of the place with a motley collection of whores. Down the stairs, towards the terrifying darkness of the basement, lived an unfortunate wine-soaked creature, female, one supposed, by the attire worn.

We lived on the second floor. My mother, small, plump and pretty, was twenty-two. Sean was going on four and I was two and a half years old. Mrs O'Hara lived on the same floor as us, though in a much grander room at the front. The rest of the tenement was occupied by vague ghosts I never came to know. It was 1920 – twenty small, terrible deposits on a brutal and pitiful century.

'Come away from that window,' snapped my mother. 'Didn't I tell yeh before.' She gave me a sharp slap on the leg and I immediately started bawling. Not having much interest displayed in this performance, I really let go, for I was a delicate child and played on it. She would not belt me the way she belted Sean. This time, however, I was likely to be wrong.

'If yeh don't stop that racket,' said my mother, viciously setting her lips, 'I'll beat the bloody daylight out of yeh.' I took one look at her strained white face and finished off quickly, with a few piteous sobs.

It had been interesting looking out of the window, for a lot of soldiers with black leggings and tan uniforms had been assembling outside. The Crossley Tenders, big lorries that had seen service on the Western Front, were arriving one after the other, and from each about twenty soldiers came down. I had been enjoying the spectacle of women being searched and molested on the pavement. Their screams of outrage floated up to me and I, a little savage as all children are, had been innocently enjoying the sight. The savages below were all half-drunk and enjoying it, too. A big raid was being mounted. Michael Collins, leader of the Sinn Feiners, was supposed to be hiding somewhere in our street.

We had been in our room until a few minutes before, until Mrs O'Hara ran across the landing and knocked on our door.

'Mrs Redmond,' she gasped, 'Mick says yeh better come across to our room. You'll be safer with us.' She was a fine, handsome Tipperary woman, no longer young. 'Thanks,' said my mother and grabbed a comb.

A thunderous noise reverberated through the echoing Georgian house, as the front door panels gave way to brass-shod rifle butts. The 'Tans' were coming.

'Jesus . . . hurry,' said Mrs O'Hara, begining to panic. 'I'll take the childer.' And we ran across the landing, my mother combing her long hair as she went.

Mrs O'Hara's husband, Mick, was clamly reading the *Evening Mail* in the sunlight that poured in through the open window. He smiled and took my brother up on his knee as the door below crashed open. The raid for 'The Big Fella' was on in earnest.

'Don't forget, Mrs Redmond,' said Mr O'Hara, 'that you're supposed to be me daughter; I'm the kids' grandfather.'

'Suppose they ask after Laddie?'

'Say he's workin' in England.'

Mr O'Hara was a fine looking man in his late fifties, who had served with the British Army in India and South Africa and had got a Boer bullet for his trouble. He still walked with a slight limp from a smashed ankle. After his discharge from the army, he had been found a small job as a civil servant in the Customs House. He was a product of the times, a mercenary Irish soldier, who had taken the Queen's shilling because it was the only one he could get. He had done what he was told to do in far away places, where no one at home would ever know. Smart and soldierly, with kind brown eyes, it was difficult to imagine him doing anything wrong. His eyes and his Kitchener moustache had won him Mrs O'Hara late in life. To her, whom he had rescued from domestic service, he was Jesus Christ, the Pope and the twelve apostles rolled into one. She patently adored him and spoiled him like an only child. Anyway, he was the only child she would ever have.

Mick rose, and carrying Sean, went across to the door and opened it.

'It'll save them from kicking it in,' he said and left it swinging open.

As he turned back, the clatter of shoes on bare boards came to us and 'that one' appeared in the doorway. It was the prostitute, who lived above us in the attic. Her name was Ada, I knew, but my mother never used it. 'That one' was good enough for her. Her lovely golden hair was uncombed and last night's make-up clung flakily to her face. With her smudged mascara, she looked like a pretty clown.

'Jasus, Mr O'Hara,' she gulped, 'that's the Tans. Will yeh let me stop wit yeh until they go? Christ only knows what they'll do to me, an' me on me own.'

'A lot you have to fear,' hissed Mam. My mother, trembling, could still find time to hate.

'I'm a woman, anyway, the same as you,' said Ada.

From the hall below came the heavy tramp of army boots and, for the first time in my life, I heard foreigners speaking English. It sounded strange and unnatural to my ears and I could only make out the half of it.

'Will yeh, Mr O'Hara . . . Jasus, will yeh? Will yeh let me stay?'

'Just a minute,' said Mrs O'Hara, standing up. 'I have a say in that!'

'Sit down Rose,' said Mick firmly. 'How would *you* like to be alone with that lot? We all know what she is, God help her.' He placed my brother gently on the floor and indicated a chair to the prostitute.

'Sit there,' he told her kindly, 'and don't make a sound.'

Thundering up the stairs came a dozen Tans. Some of them ran past up to the floor above. They crowded into the room.

'Good evening, boys,' said Mr O'Hara. 'What can I do for you?'

'You can shut yer fuckin' mouf' until you're spoken to, Paddy . . . that's what you can do,' said the Sergeant.

Beside me, I heard my mother's sharp intake of breath, ending on a sob. I had heard her before, speaking of this Tan. Of all the thugs in uniform, who swaggered through inner Dublin, this one was the most feared. His appearance was guaranteed to put the fear of Christ into any man. His effect on women was truly horrific, for he had been born with a head like a pig. Little beady eyes set under a sloping forehead, a pig-like snout, for in no way could it be described as a nose, thrust forward, the black nostrils staring, like his eyes. A slit mouth set in a sloping chin completed the picture. He rammed a Woodbine into the slit, lit it and, belching smoke, swaggered towards the wardrobe. It was an old fashioned piece of furniture, beautifully carved by a master craftsman.

He placed the barrel of his rifle under the handle, exerted pressure and the door flew open, the small brass lock dangling by one screw.

Facing him, immaculately pressed, was Mick O'Hara's best suit with its row of service medals pinned under the breast pocket.

'Who owns this?' said the Tan.

'Me, Sergeant,' said Mr O'Hara carefully. 'I gave thirty years of me life to the old Queen.'

'Where?'

'In India, Quetta. I was in it for the earthquake. I did fourteen years there alone, an' afterwards in South Africa. That's where I got shot up . . . an' out of the Army.'

'You're all right, Paddy,' said the other. Turning, he addressed the others.

'Scarper round the 'ouse an' see if you can find that fucking Shinner, 'ee's about 'ere somewhere.'

'Now,' he said, turning back to us, 'who 'ave we 'ere? Who are you?' he said to my petrified mother.

'Mrs Redmond,' she said faintly.

'That's one of the bastards on our list. Where is he?' he roared.

'Workin' in Liverpool, I think.'

'You think? Where in Liverpool?'

'I'm not sure,' she said, starting to whimper. 'He's findin' work hard to get . . . him bein' Irish an' . . .'

'Bein' a fuckin' Shinner an' all,' the Sergeant completed for her. 'What do you know about him?' he said, turning to Mick. 'Is he a Shinner?'

He carefully stubbed out his Woodbine on Mrs O'Hara's polished mahogany table and regarded him balefully.

Mr O'Hara proffered another cigarette.

'Sergeant,' he said, 'they'd never let an ex-British Army soldier know that, not with my record,' he added placatingly.

Across the street, the kindly sun of a summer's day was sinking behind the tall houses, turning their roofs to gold, and I saw distinctly silhouetted against the evening sky, the form of a man with a rifle, settling himself behind a chimney. I wondered what he was doing there, but I knew what the rifle was for. Children of a revolution learn fast.

The Tan took the cigarette and the light that went with it. Then he walked to the door.

'C'mon back down,' he roared, 'the bastard ain't here.' And with a thunder of boots on the echoing staircase, they were with us once more.

'Stick around, boys,' said Pig Head. 'We got a couple a 'nice little fillies 'ere.' Grinning, he turned to the prostitute. 'Who are you?'

The prostitute regarded him with hate. 'The girl whose room them bastards are afther wreckin' up the stairs.'

'Stow that,' warned one of the soldiers, 'an' answer the Sergeant properly.'

'I'll only ask you once more,' said Pig Head ominously. 'What's yer name?'

'Ada . . . Ada Addy,' she said defiantly. Somehow, she had managed to tidy her hair and wipe some of the cosmetics off her face, though the dark smudges of mascara still lay under her eyes, making her look fragile. Standing with her back to the sun, her golden hair ablaze, she must have appeared eminently desirable to the men.

'I know 'er,' said one of the soldiers. 'She's on the town, hangs round McDaids, she does . . . in the lounge.'

'Not for the likes of you,' she said furiously. 'I'm particular.'

'Sooner 'ave a length of Irish,' said Pig Head chattily. He grinned at my mother. 'How about you? You got any preferance?'

Mam took a step backwards. 'Get out of here, ye dirty get and wash your mouth out with carbolic soap,' she hissed.

Grinning, the Sergeant turned to the others.

'Any of you fancy a bit of this one?'

'Might be all right, Sarge,' one of them agreed. 'I'll chance 'er, if someone holds 'er down.' He spoke with a thick Yorkshire accent.

Like lightning, my mother shot across the room to the dresser, tore open a drawer and turned to face them with a long, shining carving knife.

'I swear to Jesus,' she cried, 'that the first one of youse that touches me 'll get this!'

Standing there, with her bloodless face and bared teeth, she was enough to daunt even the Tans at least for a while.

Ada regarded her with compassion and made her decision. She stepped forward and pirouetted flirtatiously, her skirt flying high.

'How about me, Sarge?' she said. 'Would you fancy a bit of me?'

'Thought you were strictly for the Pads?'

'Oh,' she said smilingly, 'I'd make an exception for a good lookin' bloke like you.'

'Would you now!' The Sergeant was plainly pleased.

'Yes,' she said, on a rising inflection. 'I'd like teh have the pleasure of givin' yeh the finest dose a' the clap ever a man had, yeh dirty, pig-headed English bastard!'

The Sergeant's rifle left the floor and in one blinding movement connected with the prostitute's head. She collapsed without a sound, rolled over on the floor and a small pool of blood began to form under the golden hair. There was a long silence, while we listened to the hollow beat of footsteps climbing the stairs. Presently a British officer from the regular army stood in the doorway. British officers, the Sandhurst type as this one obviously was, hated the Black and Tan scum that they had to deal with.

'What's going on here?' he demanded.

Pig Head jumped to attention and saluted.

'Routine check, sir,' he said. 'We 'ave information that a Shinner lives 'ere.'

'You're information was a little tardy, Sergeant,' said the officer contemptuously. 'We caught him this morning. But . . .' He directed his tired gaze to the woman on the floor. 'Was this absolutely necessary?'

'Yes, sir,' said Pig Head eagerly, thrusting his snout forward. 'She tried to stab one of the men.'

The officer turned wearily to Mick O'Hara. 'Is that correct?'

'Yes, sir,' Mr O'Hara lied.

'I take it then,' said the officer, turning to Pig Head, 'that you and your men were about to leave?'

'Yes, sir,' Pig Head barked. He saluted again and marched his men smartly out of the room. They went down the stairs with a rumble like thunder.

'Mind if I sit down for a minute?' the officer said to Mick. 'I'm very tired.'

Mick O'Hara grabbed a chair. 'Sit down here, sir, as long as yeh like, an' welcome.'

'How is she coming along?' the officer asked Mrs O'Hara, who was bathing the prostitute's head from a basin of water.

Mrs O'Hara's kind, brown eyes were full of tears.

'She has a bad cut over her ear, sir, but I think she's comin' around . . . she never deserved this anyway,' she burst out.

'Did she try to stab one of the soldiers?'

'No,' said my mother from the window where she had joined me. 'I was the one who threatened to stab them. They were talkin' a' . . . rapin' me, sir.'

'Oh.' The officer drew tiredly on his cigarette and sighed. The only sound in the room was the sloshing of water, as Mrs

O'Hara kept bathing the injured woman's head.

Across the street the roofs had turned dark blue, as the sun went down. I was interested to see that the man was still behind the chimney. There was a sickly privet growing on the ornate wrought-iron balcony, and I watched him through the branches.

I pulled tentatively at my mother's skirt.

'What is it?' she asked, stooping down. 'What is it, child?'

'Mammy,' I whispered, 'there's a man over there with a gun, on the roof.' I pointed across the street and heard the sharp intake of her breath.

Downstairs, the old West Britainer Mokeler had staggered in with a bag of booze and walked into the Tans. They had delayed to relieve him of it and drink it for him. We could all hear them effing and blinding in the hall. My mother stole a sidelong glance at the officer. He was talking quietly to Mrs O'Hara and had his back turned. I watched as my mother quietly took off her kitchen apron and, holding it out of the window, waved to the man on the roof. Then she deliberately pointed down!

The Tans were leaving. I saw then, in silhouette, the man slide down on to the ridge tiles and settle himself comfortably.

I heard the Tans slam the big door of our house. I saw them swagger on to the road in front of the house. Three shots rang out in rapid succession and three of the soldiers did ridiculous little turns and twitches before falling on the road.

Pig Head, roaring, started to run. A single, fourth shot rang out.

He stumbled along and kept on stumbling until he fell on the road. The man on the roof waved to my mother and disappeared from view.

At the first shot, the officer had jumped up. My mother waved him away. 'Don't come near the window,' she warned. 'There's a sniper out there.'

It had all happened in seconds.

'Anybody shot?' said the officer.

'Yes,' said my mother, who was watching all. 'There's four of them shot. They're helping three into the trucks, but that

Sergeant fella is still lyin' in the gutter. He's dead, I'm sure . . . and I'm glad,' she added venomously.

The officer sighed again. 'Let's hope so,' he added unexpectedly. 'For this kind are a disgrace to the British Army.'

Ada Addy rolled over on the floor and sat up. She looked dazed, stupid, seeing nothing.

'Are yeh all right, love?' asked Mrs O'Hara.

'Yes, Ma'am,' she replied in a slurred voice. 'Thanks, I'll go up teh me room now.'

The officer stood up quickly and went across to her. He stared intently into her eyes.

'Stay where you are, my dear,' he said. 'You're far from well. Mrs O'Hara, don't let her move. This young woman is a hospital case.' He turned to Mick O'Hara. 'Concussion, old chap. Run and fetch a doctor, will you?'

'I will,' said Mick, and slipping on his jacket, he left the room.

Ada Addy's eyes opened, wide with fright. She tried to speak but stumbled over the words.

'Jasus, sir,' she said, 'don't send me to the hospital, don't. Me room'll be took be the time I come out.' She slumped forward and lapsed into unconsciousness.

'That Sergeant hit her harder than I thought,' said the officer. He had been kneeling before the prostitute but now he stood up.

'Mrs O'Hara,' said this kindly man, taking a five pound note from his wallet, 'see that this unfortunate's rent is paid while she is away. I will drop by again in a couple of weeks.'

Mrs O'Hara gave him a penetrating stare. 'Oh,' was all she said, as she took the money.

The golden-haired prostitute snored gently in Mrs O'Hara's lap. She wore a deadly pallor and her eyelids fluttered faintly.

'Concussion, all right,' muttered the officer. 'If that girl dies, I'll have that Sergeant on a murder charge.'

'You can't,' said my mother. 'The dirty get is still lyin' where they left him. Here's an ambulance now. Yes,' she added with satisfaction, 'he's dead all right.' She blessed herself hurriedly while the officer looked on in wonder. 'May

God forgive me,' she whispered to herself, 'me cursin' him an' he standin' before his Maker, this very minute.'

'Mrs Redmond,' said the officer, 'could I have a word with you in private? That's what has brought me to this house.'

She glanced at him sharply. 'Is it about Laddie? Me husband?'

'It is. Where can we speak alone?'

'In my room, across the landing. Excuse me, Mrs O'Hara,' she said to her neighbour, 'I'll be back in a minute.'

In our room it was almost dark. Our old brass knobbed bed shone dully in the twilight. We lived at the back of the house and night came earlier here than in Mrs O'Hara's. I glanced up fearfully at our large statue of the Blessed Virgin, standing over our hand basin, on the washstand. It was an old fashioned timber affair with a hole in it to hold our enamel basin, where we washed every morning. The Blessed Virgin presided over this ritual, reflected in the clear water at first and her sweet expression did not change when we dirtied it.

But I could not see her face tonight and was afraid of her. She looked ethereal and ghostly in the near dark.

'Mrs Redmond,' said the officer, 'your husband was arrested this morning.' He produced a letter from his pocket while my mother lit the gas light and turned it up.

'This is from him,' he added and gave it to her.

Squinting at the familiar writing in the flickering gaslight, for the mantle was damaged, she began to cry.

'Please,' said the officer, 'no need to cry. He is quite safe. A damn sight safer than he has been for a long time.'

'Where is he?'

'In Dundalk jail.'

'Who caught him? I hope it wasn't the Tans.' In the jumping light her face looked as white and ghostly as the Virgin's.

'No,' the officer assured her, 'the Tans didn't catch him, I did.'

'You!'

'Yes, me. We got a tip-off that a train load of our boys were going to be blown up on the Bray side of Dalkey station. They were being transferred back to Blighty, so you see Mrs Redmond, given the time and the place it was easy.'

'Did . . . did Laddie make a run for it?'

'No . . . none of them did. They had too much sense. They didn't stand a chance!'

Many years afterwards, my father pointed out the exact spot where the ambush had taken place and he was taken prisoner. It has always been easy since then to imagine the scene.

The sun rising out of the Irish Sea and the early morning mist fleeing before it. The silent, intent group surrounding my father, who was laying the charge under the railway line. Old Bray Head, with its feet in the ocean, coming slowly into view, and the magnificent carpet that was Killiney beach. On the other side, Dalkey Island and, across Dublin Bay, Howth Head with Ireland's Eye steadfastly regarding the sky.

Blue sea and yellow sands, hillsides golden with spendthrift gorse and the quiet splash of little waves. Heaven all on a summer's morning and white gulls wheeling in the sun. And all hell about to break loose, coming from the dexterous fingers of my father, while minute by minute a trainload of young men was drawing nearer and nearer!

'I'm glad you caught Laddie,' said my mother slowly, 'before the thing went off.'

'Why?' The officer was plainly taken aback.

'Because,' she answered, 'them soldiers are some mothers' sons, an' I wouldn't want me husband to have a thing like that on his conscience.'

The officer stood there, smiling wryly.

'He'd never be able to forget it,' Mam added. 'I know what killin' does to a man. I haven't been married to a Shinner without knowin'. I've met some a' them, either broken . . . or animals. They were never the same.'

The officer slowly shook his head. 'You're a strange, kindly, fighting, bitter race of people,' he said.

This was all very boring to me, after the excitement of the evening, for my father I did not remember and it made no difference to me where he was. I started inching towards the door.

'Come back here, you,' said my mother absent-mindedly.

I stood still for a couple of seconds, then continued on to the door. In Mrs O'Hara's room the doctor had arrived, and two ambulance men were lifting Ada on to a stretcher.

I was not yet three years of age and that afternoon I had seen a prostitute's head nearly stove in. I had watched Pig Head die on the road and three of his men lying in their own gore. I had heard an officer tell my mother that her husband was doing time in jail. And learnt enough curses to last me a lifetime.

About a week after this I awoke one morning to the sound of my mother crying, a hopeless keening sound that had gone on for some time.

'What's wrong, Mam?' I said sleepily.

For answer she stirred a cup of cocoa, split it by pouring half into another cup, one to Sean and one to me. We got half a slice of bread and butter too.

Sean wolfed his down first. 'Any more bread, Mam?'

'Jesus, child,' she said half demented and beginning to cry again. 'I haven't a thing in the room. What in the name of the Holy Mother of Jesus are we goin' teh do . . . an' the Boys must think we live on fresh air.'

The 'boys' referred to were the Shinners, and it was through their help that we stayed alive. Just barely. They gave us what they could and that was not much. Only too many of them were locked up, like my father. And Mam was too proud to ask help of anyone, even Mrs O'Hara.

I got hungrily through my half slice of bread but knew better than to ask for more. My mother was lightning quick with a slap these days. She cried a little more, sitting in the sagging old cane chair, then suddenly rose and got the two of us out of bed. The Blessed Virgin stood serenely on our wash-stand, while my mother knelt down before her.

'Kneel down, children,' she whispered as if we were in Chapel, 'and say a prayer with me this day for a miracle . . . we haven't a crust in the place. Repeat the prayer after me:

Hail Mary, full of Grace
The Lord is with Thee . . .'

'Thee,' said my brother, 'not *me*.'

'I didn't say me.'

'Yeh did!'

'I didn't.'

'Stop that!' my mother screamed. 'Yez pair of gets. An' you,' she snapped at Sean. 'Don't be so bloody smart with the child. He's younger than you. Now pray after me!'

It was on the third 'Hailer' that a knock came on the door. A very special knock. My mother gave a small gasp and clapped her hand over her mouth. Soundlessly she stole across the room and opened the door. A big man in a trench-type raincoat slipped inside.

'Dolly,' he said, 'this is from the boys and this . . .' he handed her another envelope, 'this is from Laddie. He's well and sends his love.'

My mother nodded. 'Thanks very much, Paddy,' she whispered.

So I thought, here was another one who called her Dolly. I'd call her that in the future.

'Look out the door Dolly an' see the coast is clear. I'm always afraid that oul' informin' bastard downstairs'll spot me.'

'Hold on, Paddy.'

She slipped through the door, over to Mrs O'Hara's room, to look down the street. She was back in thirty seconds, white faced.

'Jesus, Paddy,' she said. 'That oul' Mokeler is talkin' to some Tans on the steps.'

'Can I slip out the back?'

'Not without going through the hall. You'd never manage the drop from this window. You'd be killed.'

'Here,' said Paddy, 'take this. I can't be found in this room anyway.' 'This' was a revolver, shining and deadly, a Colt .45. My mother could act quickly and courageously when she was up against it.

She took the weapon, pulled up a bit of the slate hearth stone, for it was cracked in a dozen places, and put the revolver underneath. A small cavity was there and it had been used before for this purpose.

'They'll hardly hang *me* if they find it, Paddy,' she said.

'Them bastards 'ud hang their own mother, Dolly, so don't count on it.' He grinned. 'Best of luck, Dolly,' he said. 'Don't worry about Laddie. He's fine.' And then he was gone, a good-looking Dubliner with a head of wavy, black hair and a strong manly face.

Three minutes afterwards we watched him being arrested and beaten up by a lorryload of Tans. Mam was crying and so was Mrs O'Hara.

'The Blessed Virgin Mary sent him with this to me,' she wept, holding out a few pound notes. 'An' I'm the cause of the beatin' he's gettin'.'

'No,' said Mrs O'Hara, with glittering eye, 'it was oul' Mokeler downstairs that got him caught. Didn't he run out an' stop the lorry when Paddy Doyle came to the house.'

The penalty for carrying a gun was death by hanging. He had no gun, but they hanged him anyway, for they found a bullet in his pocket.

His wife stood outside Mountjoy Jail in a November snow-storm, holding three-day-old twin boys in her arms while her husband was hanged. Afterwards, demented, she came to our room, for she had been one of my mother's bridesmaids.

That night, when she had gone on her way, my mother's nerve finally broke, and to the rattle of gunfire and the deadly chatter of a machine gun, we fled Gardiner Street, never to return.

On the way out, Oul' Mokeler opened the hall door in front of us and came in. Without a second's pause, my mother snatched a milk bottle from the pram and smashed it into his face. He screamed one long scream and his blood spurted as high as the fan-light. I can still see my mother's bitter, vengeful, satisfied face as we hurried past Morans Hotel.

I lay in the pram, nearly smothered by bedclothes, sheets and blankets while she ran up Talbot Street. My brother had been left with Mrs O'Hara. No street lights shone. It was dark, the city lit fitfully by a clouded moon. Bullets sang through the air like angry wasps, the night was full of explosions and the desolate tinkle of broken glass.

Once or twice, an angry voice roared at my mother. 'Get the bejasus out of it . . .' 'Lie down, yeh stupid bitch . . . Yeh'll be killed . . .' but she was frantic, past caring, panting and pushing, sobbing with fright.

Along O'Connell Street – at that time Sackville Street – over the wide bridge, through Westmoreland Street we went. Into the comparative quiet of Dame Street. We were leaving the battle zone behind. Up Cork Hill and soon we were on the top, beside old Christ Church, magnificent in the fitful light.

The firing was dying away now and she stood for a while, gasping, trying to get her breath. Presently, she rummaged in the pram and found me, half suffocated.

'Are yeh all right?' she said anxiously.

'Yes, Dolly,' I replied stoutly.

I can still see the look of shock on her face, her reprimand struggling with laughter.

'Dolly it is,' she said to herself and gave a little laugh. And for the first time it came to me, that she was not old, but very pretty, lovely really, especially when she smiled. Strangely, she never afterwards looked old to me. Not even when she was getting old.

She reached into the pram and kissed me, half laughing, half crying. Below us, the spire of St Patrick's stood out against the moonlit sky, a winter sky with glittering stars reflected in the puddles of the potholed road. Below us, Patrick's Street and the Coombe, the heart of the Liberties, the place where I would live for the next fourteen years, the crucible that would mould me, temper me, make me or break me.

2 *A Liberties Prairie*

And that was the way we came to Clanbrassil Street, running the gauntlet, soon to be joined by my father, who, with the signing of the Treaty, was released from jail.

It was like heaven at first, like coming out of the dark. To wake up there, on a sunny morning in November, away from the tall menace of the Georgian houses, was the same as coming up to the morning light from the rat infested cellar. I had reached an oasis in the desert of my childhood. I had come in from the cold and my little heart rejoiced.

I loved the narrow streets and the low roofed houses. They were close together, cosy and warm to the heart of a child, who had been intimidated by the vast houses. Here, all was on a smaller scale. The people were not dwarfed by their surroundings, the roads and pavements were narrower by far, teeming with life.

My Granny's house, old as the district, vibrated from the turmoil of steel-shod wheels on flint-like cobbles. Herds of cattle stampeded through the narrow streets on their way to the cattle market. Flocks of sheep bleating pitifully, scuttered along the paths on their last journey to the abbatoir. All the comings and goings of animals and goods came through this street, one of the city's main arteries.

I quickly found out, somehow, that among the society that comprised the Liberties, my mother came from one of the 'superior' families. Her father was a post man, a British civil servant, who loved the shining Crown on his brass buttons. The transition to a Harp, after the British were slung out, nearly killed him. He never got over it and took an early retirement.

He never fogave my mother, either, for marrying a Shinner, one of the back stabbers who had fought his employers implacably, while his own heroic son Jack was holding back the savage Hun with fixed bayonet in Flanders.

I was aware of a dangerous and civil animosity between my Grandad and my father, and between my mother and the Granny things were no better.

I was a sensitive child and I knew this. In consequence, I was very subdued while in Clanbrassil Street.

The Grandad wasn't a bad old devil, I decided, when he was sober and he often slipped me the odd penny with instructions to keep quiet about it. He never went out in the dark winter mornings without slipping me a half slice of bread and butter, country butter, with sugar grains so large on it that they felt like pebbles in my mouth, and an oul' moustachey kiss. And the sweet bottom of his mug of tea.

But I knew we were not wanted here. Although my father adored my mother and never even *saw* another woman all his days, he had married beneath him and he could not get her away from her family, who were often coarse of tongue, fast enough.

He had been the scion of a Georgian house. It had been upstairs for him and downstairs for the likes of my mother. But for the robbery of his patrimony, he would never have met her. Even though he had had to leave his big house and had joined the faceless working class, a mere carpenter, some of the aloofness of the aristocratic houses clung to him.

He was a gentleman, come down in life. Even when he consciously tried to mix with his fellows, on an equal footing, he was accepted with reserve. The inclination of the people he found himself among, was to call him 'Mister' or 'Sir'. He was not tall, but people made room for him. He was a Norman, deprived of his castle, yet one knew he had been used to one.

It was around this time, that we took to spending whole days over in Auntie Nelly's, my mother's sister, who lived just across the road in a single storey, two roomed Artisan dwelling. She was even better looking than my mother with delicate features and pale, porcelain skin, like a beautiful Korean. And she was infinitely more gentle, though a hopeless housekeeper, or so said my mother. She had none of old Granny's steely hardness. She was no match for her mother. But my mother was, every inch of the way. It was a facet of her character that, strangely, I knew she regretted.

Somehow, it had suddenly become summer, and my çousins and I played in this traffic-free cul-de-sac, where we took refuge from the gathering storm in the Granny's.

We were taking too long to find a place of our own. Our welcome, never cordial, was worn out. My parents were frantic, but houses were almost impossible to get.

There would be sudden flurries of excitement and off Dad would dash, on the strength of some rumour, usually another fruitless errand. The endless summer was coming to a close, the longest summer of my life. Autumn was here, and still no house. One morning towards its end, I woke up to find I had a baby sister. I had been waiting for Mam all week, for she was gone to look for a baby. She had a long way to go and now she was back.

Privately, I thought she had wasted her time, getting an ugly little bitch, red-faced and angry, who screamed for nothing.

After this event, my parent's anxiety reached fever pitch, with my mother doing Novenas to the Blessed Virgin Mary, Auntie Nelly reminding me to say prayers for my mother's 'Special Intention'. I did, for I knew after the way she had brought the fiver in single pound notes to our room in Gardiner Street, that a miracle was no bother to her since she stood on the right hand of God himself. But I often wondered what was keeping the pair of them. Mam was always busy, taking little notice of me, for ugly and all as the small bitch was, she had the power to consign me to the oblivion of just another child.

When the move came, there was little warning. A lot of whispering had been going on between Mam and Dad, and one night I found myself walking up the South Circular Road, holding the family alarm clock, wrapped in tea towels in case I dropped it.

Beside me, pushing his bike, came my father loaded like a

pack horse. It was about eight o'clock, gone dark and nearly winter. Behind the facade of red-bricked houses on the far side of the road lay the Canal. There was a tang in the wind, that tasted different, I could not figure it out. But I found out soon enough. It was the smell of open fields and cabbage, and manure and hay, for behind the houses and over the Canal, it was country all the way to Cork.

Mam had gone to the new house before us, to be there when the furniture van came. Our bits and pieces from Gardiner Street had been stored somewhere, against the time we got a house. And now we had one. It was a few days afterwards before I realised why we had moved in the dark, like fugitives.

It was because the landlord did not know we were moving in. The former tenant had given my father the key of the front door in exchange for twelve pounds, more than a month's wages for a carpenter then. We were taking a chance, squatting. We could be pitched out in the morning.

Although I understood only some of this, fear was abroad and alive in our home again, and I felt it. The guarded tension of the Granny's was gone, but real fear like that experienced in Gardiner Street was back. I felt it in the way my father left the house the following morning, kissing my mother, arms around her to comfort her.

'Don't let the kids out today, Doll' . . . not until we see how the land lies.' Then quickly he cycled off into the morning darkness.

All that day my mother was in a fever of anxiety, whispering to me, making Sean and I play quietly, for we were in a terrace of artisan dwellings and the next door neighbours would hear. We were afraid to cough. The former tenant had had no right to sell us the key. It should have gone back to the landlord when he left. We had taken a mad chance, and if it did not come off it was the street for us.

That day passed, an endless day with the shopping done at night, and the next night too . . . and the next.

We had moved in on a Monday and on Thursday night the expected blow fell. The neighbours, of course, had found out there were strangers in the house and now the landlord knew too. The note dropped through the letter box told all.

Dear Sir,

Please report to number 17, three doors above you, to explain your presence in the house. I will expect you at ten sharp tomorrow morning.

Signed: A. McKay
Official Rent Collector.

'You'll have to lose time at work, Laddie,' said Mam anxiously.

'No matter, Doll', it'll be worth it if I get on all right.'

'Jesus, Laddie . . . he wouldn't throw us out, would he?'

'He might, if he had a friend lined up for the house.'

'But if we paid the rent, Lad', he couldn't . . .'

'Doll,' said Dad gently, 'the man I gave the key money to had no right to sell me the key at all. He was telling lies.'

'Then you've been had?'

'No . . . I knew he was telling lies, I'm not a bloody fool altogether. But I know something else, too. Possession is nine tenths of the law. He'll have a job to put us out.'

'But surely if we pay the rent?'

'He doesn't have to accept the rent. If he refuses to issue us with a rent book, we're in trouble. He'll be able to enforce the law that much quicker. Don't worry, Doll'. We won't be put out that easy.'

For all his brave words, he was grey of face when he went to see the landlord the following morning. He was soon back, still grey of face. We had spent the time praying to the Blessed Virgin Mary and I was sick of this occupation. It seemed, she was very humoursome about granting favours and took her time. And there was all that praying and beseeching to be done. Why could not she just give a straight 'yes' or 'no' and be done with it.

'How was he, Laddie?'

'Abrupt . . . a little old man, Mr McKay. Told me I had no right to be in the house. Said we were trepassers.'

'Jesus, Mary and Joseph!' My mother's face was drained of all colour. 'He'll put us out then?'

'Maybe. He wouldn't take the rent. Said he'd give the matter some thought over the weekend. He also said Monday was rent day. Not Friday. He'll make up his mind by then.'

'Do you think there is any hope for us?'

'Somehow, Doll', I think so. He was very rusty at first but he thawed out a bit before I left. He said "you seem to be a decent enough man, Mr Redmond, but I can't help feeling you were in no way taken in by the former tenant, who you say sold you the key in good faith. However, I'll see you again on Monday morning".'

He did not see him on Monday morning. He saw me. I was the one who took the rent up, rolled in a note from my mother. I had been told to say please and thank you and mind my manners, to be careful, all the other guff, for my mother was frantic with worry. She communicated her fear to me again, and in the end I had to be coaxed to go up. No knight ever went forth to kill a dragon with more trepidation than me.

I knocked timidly on the door, four or five times before I was heard. A sweet, little old lady with lace or something on her head opened the door.

'Please, Missus, me mammy sent me up with the rent money.'

'Come in, child. Who are you? I don't remember ever seeing you before.'

'Mrs Redmond's Lar.'

'Indeed,' she said smiling, 'Mrs Redmond's Lar is a good-looking boy, isn't he?'

Their place, although only a two storey artisan dwelling like our own, seemed very posh to me. Gleaming lino in the hall, with a coat and umbrella stand behind the door. In it there were two umbrellas and a walking stick, all with ivory handles and banded six inches from the top with gold! There were thick woollen mats on the floor and the door to the kitchen was hidden by a heavy green curtain. Just to the right, Mrs McKay opened another door and ushered me into the small parlour. The window, like our own, looked on to the Square. At that point, all resemblance between the two homes ceased. Their house seemed terribly rich to me.

An ornate overmantle, glittering with bevelled mirrors, each shelf laden with porcelain ornaments, the same as my Granny's. A little shepherdess, smiling, patted a laughing sheep dog forever. A glazed organ-grinder played the organ, while his monkey begged, and behind them the music notes flew all over a porcelain sky. There was a glass case on the sideboard, exactly the same as Granny's, full of stuffed birds. Goldfinches, and scarlet jays, blackbirds and rainbow coloured kingfishers, brilliant survivors from some long gone tropical Ireland, forever frozen in flight. Swallows that had returned all the way from Africa to reside in the glass case forever.

On the opposite wall hung a picture of Queen Victoria, crown and all, with the Prince Consort, bug-eyed with mutton chop whiskers, beside her, though a pace to the rear. There was a beautiful, circular mahogany table that almost filled the room and in the corner by the firebreast, was a leather-covered roll-top desk. One could hardly move in the room with such wealth.

'Sit down here, child,' said Mrs McKay and I sat down on a horse hair sofa, that prickled my legs.

She left. I was terribly impressed. It was obvious to me that the McKays were very wealthy. He came in then, the spectre that hung over our house like a thundercloud.

He was a little man. Small and all as I was, even to me he seemed tiny. He was dressed in a black morning coat with old-fashioned swallow tails, striped trousers and wearing slippers. They made no sound on the heavy carpet, as he slipped easily through the room, looking perfectly in place among the knick-knacks, a small piece of Victoriana himself, miraculously preserved for a twentieth century boy to remember. With his bloodless face and shining bald head, tinted yellow like old ivory, he put the fear of Christ in me.

I handed him the rent money, folded up in an ill-scrawled note from my panic stricken mother. I sat and watched with bated breath as he read. I knew the importance of this moment for our family. Presently he sighed, went to his desk, put the money in a drawer and came back with a shining red rent book. He wrote in it a little, then reaching over to the mantlepiece, which was as high as himself, he found a tin, opened it and handed me two chocolate biscuits. Then he smiled and I wondered why I had ever been afraid of him. His bloodless old face grew warm, his pale eyes sparkled and on the instant, I loved old Baldy McKay. That was what he was called behind his back and well out of earshot.

'Tell your mammy to send you again, next week,' he said. 'Tell me, what is your name?'

'Lar . . . Lar Redmond, Mr McKay.'

'Well, Lar,' said old Baldy, 'here's twopence for yourself and give your mammy this book.'

'Thank you, Mr McKay.'

Two whole pennies. Here was unexpected wealth indeed, for the most I ever got at home was a penny and sometimes not even that. He ushered me out through the tiny hall and warned me not to go to the shops.

'Your mammy will be waiting for you,' he said.

He must have known, God love him, how it was with her, but he had no need to worry. I knew exactly how it was with my mother. I was advanced far beyond my years and in my short life had come up against more stark reality, than a wealthy family might have encountered in a lifetime.

So I gravely walked back the few doors to our house, circumspectly, like Old Baldy McKay whom I was imitating, and my heart was singing. Mam would nearly go mad, she'd squeeze me to death, she had a lovely voice and she'd sing all day, she'd buy us ice-cream, she'd make coconut cakes for tea, she'd . . . I had reached the door by now, it flew open and I was jerked inside, the door quickly slamming behind me.

'Well?' panted Mam. She was very pale and her blue eyes looked enormous with dark shadows under them. Her mouth was tightly set against the bad news. To me, she looked deadly sick. Primly I took the rent book from behind my back and handed it to her.

'Mr McKay said I'm to come with the rent next week as

well.' Her hand moved out slowly and she took the book.

'Thank you, child,' she said with great composure. No smiles, no tears, no thanking the Sacred Heart of Jesus . . . Nothing!

'Mr McKay gave me tuppence as well. An' two chocolate biscuits. I like Mr McKay. He's nice.'

'You'll share that money with your brother,' she decided.

'But Mr McKay gave it to *me*.'

'You'll share it with your brother, I said. Give it here.' I handed over the money with rage in my heart. It was not that I begrudged sharing the money, it was that I begrudged sharing it with *him*. He had always got more than me, especially in Gardiner Street when Mrs O'Hara lived next door. She would have adopted him if she could, and he loved her far more than he ever loved his mother. Another thing, my father favoured him, the eldest son and doted on his first daughter. I was Mister-in-Between and only Mam loved me.

One other thing. He had, on countless occasions, given me one sweet and hidden the rest in his pocket, eating them on the sly. I thought he was mean and selfish and I knew to my sorrow, that he could knock hell out of me. On such things are built the lifetime of warfare between two brothers, quarter neither given nor asked for.

I grudgingly handed over the money. 'He never shares with me,' I said.

'He will from now on,' said my mother placidly. 'He's not with Mrs O'Hara now. He won't do as he likes here!'

My brother was wild and a natural scrapper, and while we had lived with the Granny he had been sent back to Mrs O'Hara for long spells to save him from the wrath in Clanbrassil Street. The Granny couldn't stand him and made no bones about it.

'That's a bloddy get, if I ever saw one.' So for peace sake, he had been sent away.

'We have our own home here now,' said my mother coolly. 'I'm the boss here. I'll tell you both what to do and when to do it.'

She helped us into our jackets, put on her own coat and

marched us out the door, with her head held high. She had completely altered since I had handed her the rent book. One minute, wide eyed with fear, the next minute transformed! I know now what brought the metamorphosis about. She was the queen bee in her own hive, nobody shoved her around any more. She was the proud tenant of 20 Emerald Square and the rent was paid. Her children could be as noisy as they liked. It was *her* house!

Proudly she walked across the Square, holding each of us by the hand and out into Dolphins Barn Street. It was even better than Clanbrassil Street, narrower, noisier, with the same low double storey houses, the bottom portion of each one a shop. It had a forage stores, where the hay and oats spilled out on to the pavement. It had a cobbled street for iron-shod wheels to bounce off. Half way up, it had a real forge and you could smell the burning hooves as the Smithy shod the horses with hot iron shoes.

It had Blanchardstown Mills Shop, with sacks of flour and bran and bruised oats for pampered ponies, with sacks of biscuits for dogs that lived on the South Circular Road, where they *ate* soup, I learnt afterwards, and did not slurp it up, like 'The Barn' crowd.

In the middle of this turbulent street, stood a dreadful old tenement with hardly one window intact, though still lived in, and a gaping hole where the hall door used to be. It seemed to sway above the milling traffic. We went into a hardware shop, and my new mother, for she was hardly recognisable as the one who had sent me up with the rent an hour ago, selected a sweeping brush and a handle and coaxed the assistant into fitting it to the head which, discreetly wrapped up in a brown paper bag, she carried home.

On the way, we went to the sweet shop and munching away, my brother and I had no time to quarrel. A truce had been declared in the face of the new parent we had. It was half-time.

In this strange atmosphere, Mam calmly walked us home. All of a sudden, she was very sure of herself. When she opened the door of Number 20, she left it open and told us we could play outside. She seemed sublimely unconscious of half the Square peering from behind their curtains or the covert glances of the neighbours, going shopping. She went into the house and came out again in a sparkling, brand new apron. God love her, she must have kept it for this occasion. And she was carrying her brush.

Years later, I learnt that wild animals mark out their territory by leaving their mark or scent. The fox urinates against a rock. The mighty grizzly leaves his claw marks twelve feet up a tree. My mother marked her new territory by sweeping the pavement outside our door.

And I, who had expected a delirious welcome with the rent book had learnt something about the ways of women, though what the hell it was, I have never been able to figure out.

Just then, the woman next door came out. She was small, like most Dublin women of those days. She was pretty and fair haired, and friendly too.

'Good morning,' she said. 'My name is Mrs Keirsey. Welcome to the Square.'

Mam's face flushed with pleasure. 'I'm Mrs Redmond,' she replied. 'Would you like to come in for a cup of tea?'

My brother had gone off in his usual independent fashion. He did not want me. I was too young and, anyway, I did not want his company either. I was never happy around him and was content to explore this new world on my own. Mam was occupied with Mrs Keirsey, so I wandered away on my first inspection.

The Square, I found, was not a square, being shaped more like a boomerang. It was a cul-de-sac, as far as heavy traffic went. Bicycles and pedestrians could go through on to the walled right-of-way, known all over Dublin as 'The Back of the Pipes', always to be known to me as the 'Backers'.

The end of the Square was partly blocked off by an old stable yard and a little river flowed past. This was a branch of the ancient Poddle, and on the far side was a real farm with green fields, with hedges and trees and an orchard a couple of acres away, just now loaded with russet apples and old breeds of pear that required a frost to ripen them. It was a big orchard with perhaps a couple of hundred trees and a beautiful old Tudor house, with high gables and dormer windows in the roof, the walls covered now with a scarlet creeper, leaves turned red before falling.

A couple of horses and donkeys were grazing in the field before me and on my right a smaller field had been let out into plots, or allotments as the English call them. A few men were working them. Potato drills were being broached, and two boys were hanking onions, dried by the wind and sun. There was cabbage everywhere and lots of birds, free and uncaged. And this incredible farm hid behind the festering slum that was Cork Street. Just behind the tenement houses, on the edge of the Liberties, lay virgin ground where the shamrock grew.

Sometime in the past, when the old Huguenot silk masters had fled persecution in their own country and had come here, they had brought wealth with them. Their knowledge of the silk industry assured that and the Liberties, in a wealthy convulsion, had jerked this far into the fields. Over the years, the trade had died and the whole area, once prosperous, had degenerated into a slum, a slum with its feet in the country.

I was getting on for five years of age now and every Saturday my brother and I were given the money to go to the pic's, the matinee, with my mother's youngest sister, a lovable bitch, who would hit you as quick as light, then smother you with kisses and sweet bribes, not to tell on her.

I was mad about the Horse Opera. Buck Jones and Richard Dix, all the big fellows saying that Tom Mix was the best of them all, but I do not remember him. He was before my time. But I was mad about cowboy pictures anyway. It was the roaring twenties and jazz and the silver screen had come in time to heal the minds of half a world of war shattered peoples.

There were no Georgian houses here. I could get lost and forget, enter a new world for twopence on a Saturday afternoon. It was here I began to read. I could make out . . . 'yeah . . . nope . . . gone thattaway . . .' for the movies were of course silent, with the script printed at the bottom.

Most of all, the endless prairies, with their savage canyons in the background, and the attendant tribes of pitiless painted warriors had captured my imagination. Now, looking across the vast expanse of green grass, the first real open space I had seen in my young life, I felt a savage wave of exultation and I came into possession of my own. I stood there, watching the mighty herds of bison thundering past. For how long I do not know. Presently, Mam found me and stood beside me, silent.

'This is better for the children,' she said to herself and squeezed my hand.

'Are you not hungry, child?' she said at length.

I nodded. I was starving. A good buffalo steak was what I needed. But the Irish stew she dished up was all right, too. It would do for the present. At least, until I rode west.

3 *Rialto School*

Shortly after we moved into Emerald Square I was enrolled as a pupil in Rialto School. Miss Kennedy, who looked after the infants, was gentle and kind. We played with plasticine, made mats with raffia, learnt the alphabet and how to count up to twenty. I loved school, right from the start. As we were the 'babies', we played at different times to the older boys and only heard them shouting in the distance. We were let off earlier too, so we had no contact with them.

Always a sickly child, I became ill quite early in the term, attending at intervals but somehow managing to keep up with the others without much trouble. I finished off the term with another illness, which merged into the summer holidays and one day found myself back at school, but with a difference. I had been passed into first class, I was finished with the infants forever and was now among the mainstream of boys. Gone was the sweet faced Miss Kennedy, to be replaced by a tall, black-haired man, who was destined to play a major role in my life. The best school master, who ever stood in shoe leather, Vincent Ahearne, cadaverous Wicklow intellectual, who was to teach us and form us and belt us and help us over the next five years.

He carried a black leather strap sometimes, which he called 'Towser' and was merciful in its use. He put up money, considerable sums by the standards of the day, for the boys who came first, second and third in his exams. I was quick to learn and came first and second every time. Looking back now, I regard these boyhood days, for all the poverty that went with them, as the brightest in my life.

* * *

Gradually, as I progressed I became a part of the Liberties, so close at hand. For the Square was not considered to be in the Liberties, though the Back of the Pipes, notorious for fornication and the like after dark, lay over our back wall. Running its length, one could be in James's Street in five minutes and that *was* the heart of the Liberties. And then, my mother's sister, gentle Auntie Nelly and her mother, lived in still another heart of the Liberties, for where *is* the heart of the Liberties?

It was originally a small area around St Patrick's Cathedral, the Huguenots came, bringing their expertise in weaving with them, built their Dutch Billys on the banks of the Poddle and soon covered the green hills around with their dwellings and looms. High Street, Francis Street, Meath Street, Patrick Street, Black Pitts, New Street, Clanbrassil Street, Cork Street and even Dolphins Barn became enveloped by the developing industry and absorbed into the Liberties scene, as I was being absorbed into its seething life.

I joined Thomas Street library and twice a week ran down Marrowbone Lane to swop books in the shadow of Catherine's Church, where poor Robert Emmet was hanged, drawn and quartered. I was the courier of many messages between Auntie Nelly and my mother and the Granny. I went with Mam every weekend to help carry the shopping we bought from the dealers in Thomas Street and Meath Street, for with our growing brood, Mam counted her pennies and shopped frugally where the goods were cheapest.

In short, I was enveloped by the seething life around me and marked by it.

Old, congested, filthy, poverty stricken, this area nevertheless sent out grand tradesmen, who built the Georgian squares of Dublin, while their own ancient part of the city was falling apart at the seams, a teeming down-at-heel Irish Casbah on the Poddle, the river responsible for its being. One day, at the bottom of Cork Street, I had come across a great bit of excitement and had squeezed through the crowd to see what was going on. 'What's wrong, mister?' I said to a man. In the middle of the road a big Leyland truck with solid tyres was tipped over on its side, the driving side wheels having gone stright through the cobbles.

'It'd be around here,' the man told the crowd, ignoring me, 'that the bed a' the Poddle'd be. Me grandfather told me that he remembered it flowin' through here before it was bricked up.'

And, as the crane winched the lorry out of the hole, it was only too clear that he was right.

The arched culvert over the little river had collapsed and a black and turgid stream flowed past, from which came a poisonous, sulphuric smell. The breach in the culvert was quickly repaired and the next day, when I went to have another look, they were filling in the road.

But the memory of that defiled trout stream stayed with me and my boyish imagination, of which I always had too much, suggested terrible retribution if ever the Poddle got out again into the Coombe. Some day, in roaring flood, it would burst its banks, lift the roof of its containing brick prison and, blowing like an oil well, inundate the place all the way from the bottom of Cork Street to St Patrick's Cathedral, filling up the tarmacadam valley that lay between with unspeakable filth, unleashing a cholera that would make the Black Death of the Middle Ages seem trivial by comparison.

And the tumbrils would roll once more and some scrawny scavenger's cry would be heard again in the stricken city . . . 'Bring out your dead . . . bring out your dead!' as had been heard so often before down the centuries. And a frightful horde of obscene rats, that lived and bred under the Liberties would swarm out, red-eyed, ferocious and starving, and grow fat on the pale corpses of the Pale!

It was a love-hate relationship between me and the Liberties. I hated the poverty, the squalor, the bare feet, patched trousers and bare arses. I hated the pinched and peaky faces of these children of hardship. The seamed, lined faces of women, who were prematurely old from hard work and harder child bearing. Small, tough women who had been dragged up in frightful conditions and had been exposed to every known disease before they could walk.

The dealers, shoulder to shoulder in Thomas Street and Francis Street. 'Thruppence a dozen th'apples, fourpence a poun' th' grapes, tuppence a poun' th'onions, lovvely Dubilin Bay herrin's.' How did they know they came from Dublin Bay?

The process of natural selection still operated in the brick jungle that was the oldest part of Dublin. These ladies of the trading fraternity were as cagey as monkeys and would slip a couple of damaged tomatoes or bananas into the bag with the dexterity of a conjuror and defy you with a brazen stare to examine the contents.

'Robbers, the lot of them,' said my mother. Robbers they may have been, but they were hardworking robbers and the latent kindness that lay behind the trading instinct was never more evident than when a misfortune took place beside their stall. Perhaps some poor creature, undernourished and dawny, dragging a couple of heavy shopping bags, buying thriftily for a large brood, would faint in the street and right then and there was the heart for all to see.

Stalls were left unwatched, as she would be seated on an orange box, cradled in the arms of a dealer. 'Mary,' she would screech to the next stall, 'get inteh the pub . . . hurry an' get a small whiskey on me book . . . this woman has done a sevener' – the Liberties equivalent of a lady out the Ballsbridge way having the vapours. At times like this I loved my native place, but mostly I hated it.

The diabolical Dublin wit, that could demolish man, woman or child in a second. I remember in Meath Street one night, I watched a lady, probably from Rathgar from her 'refained' speech, pawing disdainfully through a dealer's tired vegetables, one by one, critically assessing their quality. It was the end of a Saturday's trading and in normal circumstances the dealer would have been glad to strike a bargain and clear her stall. However, the Rathgar one had roused her ire and it was obvious from her glittering eyes and rising complexion, that this was not about to happen.

Oblivious of her impending doom, the lady kept on turning over the vegetables. She was a thinfaced woman with a slight body, whose bottom could only be described as plenteous, a woman shaped exactly like an electric light bulb.

She held up a couple of large onions and said: 'How much?' The dealer told her, tightlipped. 'Then,' said the bulb-shaped lady, 'Ai shan't be wanting any.' She put the stuff back and was some distance away, when retribution caught up with her.

'T'anks . . . t'anks ferry much Ma'm,' screeched the dealer the length of the street. 'T'anks ferry much . . . *scallion arse!*'

This was my Liberties. Nobody ever spent a childhood here without being branded. You could adopt a new way of speaking, go to another place, even adopt a new country, but the thinking remained Liberties' thinking and you would always be indelibly Dublin to the core. This place, if it owned you, never let you go and those who came from here, even when very old, returned if they could.

Striding through the concrete canyons of New York, muffled against the winter cold, or shuffling through the stinking heat and red talcum powder dust that is the Australian desert, this place could come at you with shattering impact, for, while your legs were mechanically finding their way along, you were not there and to save your sanity, would dart down Thomas Street or High Street to buy a mouth organ, or a Jew's Harp from Johnny Fox's, keeping an eye out for Johnny Forty Coats or poor Tom the Moon, ancient, ragged, wearing his indestructible grin. The kids dancing around him, screaming while he mumbled some forgotten ballad, old as himself . . . 'Tom . . Tom . . show us the mewin.' And when he took off his greasy cap to collect a few ha'pence, there was, 'the Moon', shining and hairless for all to see and the delighted squeals of the urchins raining down around him like stardust from heaven.

Or, if you were lucky, a running gunfight with that famous gunslinger from the Liberties, Bang-Bang, who, imaginary gun smoking, would shoot it out with half a hundred kids and the street would be in uproar, oul' fellas laughing, pulling a gun themselves and the dealers in fits.

'Ah Jasus, sure there's no harm in him.'

And down the lost alleys of the Liberties and the lost years of your life, the acrid smoke and gunfire of the Coombe's only cowboy could bring tears to your eyes.

Years after I had left this place, back from abroad with a couple of school pals, we encountered Bang-Bang again in Dame Street. We were in great form after a half dozen bottles of stout and a couple of balls of malt. It was Christmas. We were all exiles home for a week's holiday and this brief escape from rationing and the black-out was heaven to us. Back from the air raids and worse, the unceasing hostility, for the Irish from neutral Eire were not popular. There was no work in Ireland and we had to suffer it.

Colin saw him first and slapped leather. 'Bang . . . bang . . . bang!' Three rapid shots fired from the hip at Bang-Bang, who was swinging out of the landing pole of a double decker bus, riding side saddle and firing with deadly accuracy from his four wheeled bronc. We were sent staggering, dying, against the railings of the Bank of Ireland. This was our beloved cowboy, having forded the raging Rio Poddle, come to town for a showdown. Dame Street was full of gunfire as Dubliners, too slow on the draw, collapsed laughing before his ferocious door key, and two old tweedy types with monocles dangling and well nourished like ourselves, threw lead and whinnying in high British upper class accents 'Beng . . . beng . . .!' fell through the swing doors of Jury's hotel. The dignified commissionaire with rolled umbrella, forgot himself so far as to drop on one knee and to rake the bus with rifle fire.

On another day on top of a double-decker, we were stalled in Nicholas Street, when the familiar sound of shooting reached my ears. It was Bang-Bang, fighting his corner against terrific odds. A big copper stood majestically against a lamp post, watching with studied gravity. Bang-Bang had been dry gulched by bounty hunters and was fighting grimly. He was holding his own, when a sly tribe of Liberties Indians nearly cut him off. He flung himself into the jammed herd of lorries, and ran head first into the copper. He fired at once, the big door key he carried, pressed into the officer's stomach and then stood stock still as the row of silver buttons sank in. A Sheriff!

Poor Bang-Bang looked up slowly, the big copper looking down, all the outraged dignity of the law struggling with his desire to keep a straight face. They stood thus, polarised and then the cowboy took off, running low around the Lord Edward Hostelry, headed for the little known canyons off Bull Alley.

Another Liberties character was Damn the Weather, who had been effing the Irish climate for years. He was a small, comfortably dressed man in sensible, heardwearing clothes, who walked around, innocently damning the weather. It was the frightening manner in which he damned it, that brought him fame.

He would be quietly walking along, when a sudden impulse would take him. His arms would fly open as far as they would go and then he crashed them together again, with a report like a rifle shot. Women out shopping would scream and scatter like a covey of partridges and Damn the Weather would roar above the noise. The man must have developed hands like saddle leather, for the report would carry the length of the street. His irritation with the Irish weather temporarily over, he would quietly resume his stroll until the next time.

In the Liberties of those days, many of the men, returned soldiers from the sustained lunacy of Flanders, were shell-shock cases. Some were as nutty as a fruit cake *all* the time, some a ha'penny short of a shilling some of the time and all of them half mad most of the time. These men were not dangerous in the accepted sense of the word, but sometimes they constituted a real danger as they walked, head down, under the hoof of a horse or the wheels of a lorry. The coppers kept an eye on them and were gentle.

There was one fine soldierly figure, who used to stride the streets. Nobody seemed to know where he was from, but he became another legend from his habit of bombing Kevin Street police station. For some unknown reason, when he saw the station, something inside him would snap. He would step straight off the pavement into the traffic, ignoring the screech of brakes and the curses of cabbies trying to hold their plunging horses and, standing four square on the cobbles, the police station would come under assault. The attack would be sustained until some copper came and led poor Shellshock away and all would be well until the next time.

On one unforgettable day, Damn the Weather, Bang-Bang and Shellshock Joe were all in the same street at the same time, the weather man damning a sunny day with a lovely blue sky, Shellshock standing on some Vimy Ridge of his mind, shrapnel tearing up the cobbles around him while, with dauntless courage he slowly and accurately lobbed hand grenades into the station.

Just down the road, Bang-Bang had bailed up a dude gambler from Rathgar against the trees outside the public lavvo in New Street and it was a case of 'Claw sky, hombre' or be ventilated. Dealers screeched with laughter, as a red faced young copper, just up from the country and not used to Liberties ways, prevented Shellshock Joe from earning another Victoria Cross and roared encouragement to Bang-Bang to shoot it out.

The unfortunate gentleman from Rathgar, who found himself in this menagerie was transfixed to a tree, but made a run for it as the cowboy threw lead, 'bang . . . bang', and the whole street went mad as men, women and children went for their shooting irons and dry gulched each other in the dusty ravine at the bottom of New Street.

The Liberties, where beshawled women, too broken for barrow work, could be seen any day in the chapel, rosary beads in hand, praying to St Joseph or St Francis, or if things were desperately bad, to the Blessed Virgin herself, to intercede through her Son, for a little miracle that would put a bit of pig's cheek into their mouths or made frantic by the want of another, would boldly beseech:

> 'the makin's of a Coddle . . . for the daughter, Sweet Mother a' Jesus, her fella is out of a job, an' she has six childer, an' the eldest is makin' her first Commyewinyon seuin' . . .'

And throwing discretion to the winds, would promise to do a 'Special Novena, dear Mother a' Jesus, an' y'll get her a new Commyewinyon frock, won't yeh?'

The crazy, heartwarming, drunken, poverty-stricken give-yeh-the-bit-out-a-their-mouths-Liberties of my boyhood.

The brutal, consumption ridden, bare-arsed, bare-footed, thieving, kind Liberties of my youth. No wonder, it was love-hate with me. No wonder I could never outlive it!

So much viciousness, so much gentleness, so much loving and caring, that Jesus would have felt at home here. If fortitude and Christian charity was the climate necessary to His love, surely then, on His second coming He would be reborn again in the Coombe, a Jesus with a Dublin accent!

Dolphins Barn Street and Clanbrassil Street were great gas, I thought. It was through here, that half the fragrant meadows of Leinster came, the low carts piled high with plunder running the gauntlet. For it was fair play to attack the hay bogeys and exact tribute to feed the baker's or the milkman's horse or get a bit of free bedding for your dog.

Down they came, horses steaming in the frosty morning air, littering the cobbles with seed and hay, bringing for a while a whiff of broad acres to the mean streets. An invading army of mobile hay tanks, rumbling over the sets in an unending line, assaulting the decadent and greedy city. All the way from the top of Dolphins Barn to Catherine's Church, the joyous countryside like some fair slave in chains, graced the smelling city, scattering largesse as she went.

It was such a morning, when Jinny Lynch emigrated to England. Leaning out of my Granny's window, I watched her go. She had captured my boyish heart and I was hopelessly in love with her. I thought her the prettiest thing God had ever made.

She slipped gracefully between the rumbling hay bogeys, a slight girl of seventeen, carrying her small suitcase, due now for export, with eighteen hundred heads of prime Irish cattle from the North Wall in Dublin.

'Me sister, over there, is afther gettin' her a great job, in great big Britain, an' she's goin' teh live in a hostel, like a great big hotel, wit' great big wages . . .'

My resentful heart had heard this from Jinny's younger sister and my mind went back to when my own father, released from jail, had come home to our backroom in Gardiner Street. I had watched my young mother embrace him and had listened to her bitter tears of joy. For my father, the war was over. He had never taught me hatred of England and I had never felt it until now – until I watched young Jinny trip away to sell her golden youth on the dusty floor of some cotton purgatory in Lancashire.

'An',' said Trisha, the younger sister, 'she'll be sendin' me mammy home money, an' we'll all be rich.' And the little bitch stuck out her tongue at me.

I watched Jinny's saucy green hat until it was lost in the flood of hay and soon I had forgotten her, in the excitement of hanging out of a hay bogey.

This was the highest point of joy a slum child could ever hope to reach, to go to the hay market before the auctions started. Here, the shorn meadows were offered for sale and the huge cobble stone square became one big farm for the day, with real grass and real horses and real countrymen; men smelling of cows and milk and fields and manure. They lacked the reek of city poverty.

Here, in the huge square that is Smithfield Market, a child could wander at will among the pyramids of hay, all noise and sight of Dublin gone.

It did not last very long. Soon the auctions got under way and the top heavy meadows began to thin out and the dirty outlines of the square began to appear. It was time to go home, and sadly home.

No more climbing of golden hills, no more running under a horse's belly. Any boy with sense went home then. The desolation of an Australian desert was nothing compared to the draughty square without its meadows.

Thus it was the morning Jinny went away – thus it was when she came back. This time she did not carry her suitcase, but came home in style in a hansom cab, trotting smartly against the tide of hay. She had come up in the world, it seemed, while where she lived had gone down even further.

Her tenement had possessed a hall door when she went away. Now, after a hard winter, there was none.

'Eee,' said Jinny in an affected accent, 'this place is werse than I remembah.'

The cabbie pocketed the few shillings she gave him and eyed her sardonically while he handed down her suitcase from the roof.

'Why, miss,' he grated, 'did yeh expect the Liberties teh change while yeh were over beyond teh see the time? Yup!' he finished contemptuously and drove away.

So Jinny came back. Ah yes, sure Jinny came back, with her nice little red consumptive complexion and her nice little red cough. She came home to die and die she did. But in her own brave little way. She stood on her feet, plastered with cosmetics and boasted, English accent and all, of a 'bettah' life where she had been. She did not say that she had been *sent* home, after she was discovered vomiting blood in the toilet.

Very soon she had to take to her bed and it was in that room that I, a child, happened to be when Jinny Lynch died. Nobody expected her to go so quickly. We all knew she had a touch of 'the Con', but everybody expected that she would get all right again, when she had had a good rest. What we did not know was that she had galloping consumption.

Her father was a bird fancier and the huge roses of the Victorian wall paper were almost obliterated with bird cages. Urban canaries, wild linnets, goldfinches, blackbirds and sweet thrushes, all in fetters like their owners, slaves of the bird market and sold for a song. They were singing on this sunny Sunday afternoon, when Jinny suddenly sat up in the bed.

'Mother,' she said, 'it's gettin' dark.'

'Hush now, daughter,' said her frightened mother. 'Hush now, love, it's only your own foolishness.'

'Is it?' gulped Jinny, and a little trickle of blood came out of her mouth . 'I'm tellin' yeh mother, it's night.'

I watched her die, with her eyes wide open on that summer afternoon in Clanbrassil Street and all around the captives were singing their little hearts out. Requiem to another little bird, Jinny Lynch. She was dying and she was too young to die, so she could not go gracefully. But as the hot afternoon started to fade, Jinny started to fade too.

'Mother,' she gulped and with no trace of English accent left now, 'Jasus, Mother, it's gettin' darker . . . Mother . . . Mother it's night . . . I'm dyin', mother, I'm dyin' . . .'

'Hush, daughter,' whispered her frantic mother.

'I'm not goin' teh die,' Jinny screamed, 'I won't die . . . I'm too young . . . I'm not . . .'

And while her mother held her hand, Jinny had her last haemorrhage and with the birds singing and the blood pouring down her nightdress and shouting defiance to the last, she died.

Her oul' fella came in shortly afterwards. Half gargled, he found a few blankets and doggedly started to cover the cages. And the birds fell silent.

He went to the window, waved across the road to his friend, made the sign of the cross and pulled down the blind. The gramophone that was playing 'When I first fell in love with you, Maggie', was abruptly knocked off and except for the quiet keening of Mrs Lynch, all was quiet.

Two days later, the body of Jinny Lynch was interred with due ceremony in the graveyard at Mount Jerome. She went off in great style, for her mother had been to see the money-lender and money was no object.

It was the first time I had ever been to a funeral, the first time I had ever ridden in a hansom cab, so my sorrow was not unmixed with joy.

We were third in line behind the hearse, my mother being slightly related, and we sedately clip-clopped up Clanbrassil Street, across the South Circular Road, over Harolds Cross Bridge and all too soon we were at the graveyard gate.

Here the hearse halted and the small coffin was placed on a low handcart to be trundled the rest of the way. After the majesty of the hearse, it seemed a poor and commonplace way to go. The four black horses pawed the ground disdainfully, their feathered plumes tossing in the sunlight, behind them the ornate hearse, beautifully handcarved and lightly floating on its springs, black as anthracite coal, terrifying as a nightmare.

George Lamb sat up there, the reins firmly held in his hands, red, drunken face set in lines of mock sorrow. It was his nine-to-five face, six-days-a-week face and his kind had been described by another Lamb in another age, as an 'excellent tosspot'. Which he was.

Our drunken faced cabbie, Keegan, was even more florid of face by the time we came out of the graveyard. He had been having a drop on the sly.

'Hurry up out a' that,' he snapped. 'I've plenty more teh do.'

Mrs Lynch eyed him hard. 'I know the work you'll do for the balance a' the day, George,' she said, 'an yiv plenty a' time for it.'

'I've no time teh waste on gabbin' oul wans, anyway,' said Keegan furiously.

Mrs Lynch sniffed contemptuously. 'Thry actin' the gentleman, George,' she told him loftily, 'an' nobody'll know yer not.'

It was hard to recognise the keening Mrs Lynch now. She had been reared in a hard school, the one I was going to . . . Life and death, birth and marriage, drunkenness and brutality were commonplace to her. Life went on. So did Mrs Lynch, a daughter of this place and I, a son.

This was my inheritance. I could never change either, hallmarked for life, made in the Liberties, a Dubliner forever. In hindsight, I could have fared worse.

4 *Dreaming Again*

At school, under the kindly tutelage of Mr Ahearne, my real boyhood began. Three years flew by like a dream, I was quick to learn and had no real worries or traumatic events to disturb my mind. Mr Ahearne, pronounced 'A'herrin' in the Liberties, became the beloved 'Kipper', for after all, a kipper is a smoked herring. And the dear old 'Kipper' he remained in my mind forever.

Nevertheless, I was absorbing impressions, being branded, for to grow up in the teeming Liberties of my boyhood was to know the urgency of the present amid the debris of the past. The whole place was falling down. Only the breweries, the distilleries and the churches were sound. The tenement houses, like drunkards, stood up by leaning against each other, welded together by time.

There were two kinds of bells that were clamorous here, the bells of the churches and the Liberty belles. The quaint musical cadences of a feminine voice, half jeering, half coaxing, infinitely alluring, 'aye, young fellas, . . . here's young ones'. The pavement-walking, hipswinging, bauble-flashing Colleens of the Coombe. If you stayed on here, you had no chance of avoiding one bell or the other. They married young in slumland, mad for loveland and, having nothing to lose, were foreigners to fear.

The death rate was frightening and already these teenage girls were survivors, for frequent epidemics closed all the schools, diphtheria and scarlet fever raged through the streets and the black death crepes, sinister asphodel, bloomed on every second door. And consumption, the 'oul'

Con' never let up and picked his victims at will.

Before I was ten, I could tell at a glance if a girl was infected. In its early stages, it showed in a delicate transparency of the cheeks and clear, limpid eyes. I often watched them, when coming out of the library.

Here, in Thomas Street's Garbos and Tallulah Bankheads, lay the urgent present, impossible to resist and some little gurrier was Rudolf Valentino up the dark lanes in Crumlin for a night and a hasty wedding followed. Reproduce, said imperious nature, before it is too late. They did.

Except when it was a 'shotgunner', many of the girls were virgins. With the young men it was different, the vast majority having bought sex at the Back of the Pipes or up against the towering walls of Guiness's Brewery. Running back from Thomas Street library, with perhaps Stevenson's *Treasure Island* tucked under your arm, you got your sex education young, any night when it was dark enough. Especially on Friday night when the few bob were stirring. You always kept to the centre of the road, mid-way between the towering brick canyons.

'Run all the way,' your mother had warned you, 'and stop for nobody . . . *nobody*.' And you did that. You would have done it instinctively anyway, for terrible things were going on in the shadows of the brewery walls.

The lone electric light, fixed high on a corner only made the darkness around more obscure, and the shabby, shuffling figures on the perimeter, waiting with their fourpence in their hands and further back, out of sight, some unfortunate whore, an ageing reject of Leeson Street, dispensed sin and sex at a very reasonable price, and the dose of the clap was on the house.

And while all this was going on, the bells of James Street Chapel might start up, then John's Lane would join in, then Meath Street and High Street would add their carillion and if it was a special night, you would get the added benefit of St Patrick's and Christ Church, friendly Protestant rivals, and the very air would tremble.

On a stormy night, running fast, you could jump high and

almost ride the wind and the sound, like Quasimodo in the belfry of Notre Dame.

It was such a night, when having secured my reading for the week, I headed for home. I had become a devourer of books, most of which I succeeded in digesting. Comic cuts were still acceptable, but they had become lavatory reading. It was Dickens, Somerset Maugham and Robert Louis Stevenson for me. With no one to show the way I was, in an indiscriminate way, becoming discriminate.

It was late autumn and over Pimlico ragged clouds were scudding across the sky, tearing across the moon's face and with the wind screaming behind me, I fled the sterile streets of the brewery. My metal tipped boots rang loud and hollow on the little iron bridge, that used to span the canal. From here the grain barges went out, and came back laden. The little bridge swung aside to admit them to James's Gate basin, the small harbour that lapped the walls of the brewery. Here it was off-loaded to begin the long process and journey that might end up as vomit against the walls where it had been made.

Suddenly, eerily, the wind dropped, ceased. In the glassy water of the harbour, the moon rose a second time and a dead pup, past all care, floated serenely. With the cessation of the storm the bells ceased too, though I thought I could still hear them faintly, from somewhere.

I looked into the water and a boy looked back, then suddenly was beside me, sitting on a metal bollard, shining from many a Dublin arse.

'You haven't grown much,' he said.

I regarded him with rage. 'There's a fella in our class an' he's two months older than me an' he's an inch smaller.'

'I know all about him,' he said indifferently. 'He'll be a big fella yet. You won't, ever.'

'Yeh think yeh know everything,' I snarled.

'I know plenty, Lar,' he said seriously, 'more than you'll ever know in your little earthly lifetime.'

It was probably true, I thought. Despite his boyishness, an aura of incredible age hung about him.

'How old are you?' I shot the question at him, hoping to catch him off guard.

He looked at me calmly and smiled. 'I was born not far from here about eight hundred years ago,' he said softly. 'About the same time as your Norman gang invaded this country.'

Overhead, the moon had gone behind a cloud and now it reemerged turning the little harbour into a sheet of silver. A shoal of rudd nosing half a loaf floating on the surface made a circle of sequins around it and two swans glided in from the main canal, pale, ghostly daughters of Lir. It was vacuum quiet now between the warehouses and malt houses of James's Gate. It was light years away from the clamorous bells and even more clamorous people of the Liberties.

'Do you know what a "coombe" is?'

'Of course! You mean *the* Coombe,' I said distinctly. 'It's the road from the bottom of Cork Street to St Patrick's. Everybody knows that!'

'Then everybody is wrong,' said the boy. 'It's an old English word, meaning a small valley between little hills. Sometimes it has a stream running through. Now you know.'

And standing there, I thought it all out and it was true. All the way from the top of Dolphins Barn, Clanbrassil Street and Thomas Street, the little roads descend into a valley. The small hills that had become Meath Street, Francis Street and the rest, all went down to the Coombe and my imagination started to run riot. For surely then at one time, sheep and cattle had grazed these slopes and the monks who tended them had sought mushrooms in late summer. But I had to be sure.

'What was it like when you first came here?'

The boy sighed. 'Lovely and green,' he said. 'Peaceful with hawthorn and blackberry bushes and buttercups and cowslips. The cows had to share the pasture with rabbits and hares and deer, fine Irish Red Deer, not like the little Sika deer they imported from Japan. They looked grand, drinking their fill from the little river that ran through the Coombe . . . the Poddle.' He fell silent, still remembering.

'That must have been lovely, all right,' I said wistfully.

'Ah, Lar, it was. The river was clear then with bags of brown trout and sea trout, and believe it or not, the odd salmon ran up from the Liffey. The monks used to watch for them, looking for a change in their diet. I suppose . . .' His voice tailed off, as he walked back into the past.

'I wish I could have been there,' I said enviously.

'Actually,' said the boy, 'you are far more suited to what has gone than you are to this.' He waved his arm towards the tall buildings, embracing the turbulent city.

'What did Dublin look like in those days? From the Coombe, I mean?'

'There wasn't too much of it,' the boy said. 'Just a small town by today's standards, with high stone walls around it but bloody old Dublin Castle was there, eyeing the country around with suspicion. You'd see the Normans in armour on top of it, watching out for the O'Byrnes and the O'Tooles, for they never knew when those fellas would come on the rampage.'

'Did you ever see them fighting?' I asked excitedly.

'I wish I had a quid for every O'Byrne, O'Toole or Norman I've seen with his guts hanging out, dying in the Coombe. The O'Tooles came most often and you couldn't blame them looking for a bit of their own back. I'll tell you, Lar, something for nothing! The same Normans had beaten the O'Tooles off the plains of north Kildare, beat them off some of the best land in Ireland, and drove them up the mountains. And they had to fight their corner there too, for the O'Byrnes didn't want them either. But they were able to hold their own with them. It was the Norman iron mail that beat them.'

'Imagine,' I said in wonder, knowing the filth and squalor that lay just behind the brewery, 'The Coombe once being a lovely valley with a trout stream.'

'Yes,' agreed the boy, 'but I'm used to the city now. Looking back on it, it was a bit lonely in the old days, although there was always the odd bit of savagery to keep you from falling asleep. Not,' he hastened to add, 'as much as now, but still enough.'

He paused, remembering. 'I've seen scores of men die in

that little valley and die hard . . . there has never been much shortage, really, of killing.'

'No,' I fervently agreed, remembering the terror of Gardiner Street, blood all over the road and Pig Head lying in the gutter.

'I've seen the Poddle run red with blood.'

The swans, ghostly in the moonlight, glided across the little harbour and disdainfully scattered the school of rudd, as they shared the bread between them. The rudd, commoners all, put in their place by royalty, swam deeper and ate the crumbs that fell from the royal table.

From a great distance off, perhaps in another world, I thought I could faintly hear the howling of the wind and the clanging of bells, though all was quiet here.

'That must have been a terrible thing to see,' I said.

'Bad, all right,' the boy agreed. 'But they were savage men on both sides . . . they gave no quarter and expected none! Savages,' he added. 'Wolves . . . as bad as the bastards, the fourlegged ones, that used to eat the liver out of a living animal.'

'Janey,' I said involuntarily, 'the wolves didn't do that, did they!'

'They did. That's the one thing I'm glad died out in Ireland. The bloody wolves . . . The only good thing the English ever did here, put a ten pound bounty on the sconce of a wolf and wiped them out.'

He paused, spat accurately onto a water spider, innocently skating in the moonlight and minding no one.

'That was one good thing they did anyway,' I said.

'Ah,' he said savagely, 'they couldn't even do that right. They had to spoil that too.'

'How?'

'They put ten pounds on the head of a priest at the same time. *That's* what they did.'

'Oh,' I said and fell silent.

The harbour grew dark now, as a black cloud raced across the moon and I did not think it my fancy that the storm still raged and bells clamoured somewhere. I could see it all, now that it had been pointed out to me. The fine red buck, antlers aloft like some fossilised sea plant, charging through the scrub, then headed off by the snarling pack, backed up against an ancient oak, the green grass, soon to turn red with blood and gore, trampled underfoot. And I could hear the gulping wolves swallowing the living flesh. I shivered.

'I'm glad they're gone too,' I said.

'There were worse things than that, though,' said the boy.

'Worse! What could be worse than that?'

'It was worse to see the priests and the monks on the run, coursed for fun like a hare. I saw one at the botton of New Street once, it was all open grassland then, and a dozen Roundheads had picked him up about where Leonard's Corner is now. They had great sport between them, knocking him down with the shoulder of their horses or a belt on the head with a brass knobbed riding crop, sending him flying . . . him trying to run.' He paused then for a long time, gazing down the centuries.

'Go on,' I said at length, 'finish it.'

'Anyway,' he resumed, 'they coursed him to the edge of the Poddle, where he collapsed. He was done! He could run no further. He was covered with muck and blood and lay gasping on the bank like a grassed trout.'

'What happened then?'

'The Roundheads stood around for a while, laughing and talking, letting him recover a bit. They didn't want to kill him without having some more sport. Then they asked him to renounce the Catholic religion and of course he wouldn't. So they tied him between the two heaviest horses they had, feet tied to one, hands tied to the other.'

'Jesus,' I whispered, shocked.

'Well you may say that, Lar. Then the whole lot of them laid into the horses with the whip, slaughtering them and they whinnying and squealing, trying to get away, and the screams of a man torn in two . . .'

'God Almighty, is that true?'

'True as I am looking at you. That was just after Cromwell beat us and the monastery lands forfeit to the Crown. Along with the gas they were having, they'd share a tenner, a lot then, for killing him and with the money went the glory of ridding the earth of another Papist.'

The clouds had passed across the face of the moon at last and now it sent out its counterfeit light once more to illuminate the harbour. The swans were preening themselves, and the school of rudd were dabbling on the surface again. In the bright light, a tiny, almost imperceptible V was moving across to the fish.

'Watch this,' said the boy, 'you'll see a queer sport now. That's a pike. That fella has been here many a day.' The swans must have seen the dark submarine that was the pike, for with a screech and a water churning beating of wings, they tore across the harbour before taking off. And yet no sound of beating wings came. The ghostly silence still prevailed. Then, suddenly, the moonlight was full of flashing rudd, as they desperately flung themselves out of the water to avoid the pike.

'Look at that, Lar,' said the boy as the monster fish had his supper, and he pointed towards the sky. Silhouetted against the moon, necks stretched out, wings gently paddling, the swans swam across the night in slow motion.

The boy shivered. 'That's something I don't like to see,' he said, 'a swan flying by night.'

'Why, is it unlucky?'

'I always think so. I regard it as an ill omen. I hope, Lar, no bad luck is going to come your way.'

'And, why,' I jeered, for he had frightened me, 'why should bad luck come to me?'

'No reason, Lar, no reason.'

'Then why should swans flying in the moonlight make you feel that way?' I persisted.

He squinted at me, reflecting. 'The first time I ever saw a swan fly by night,' he answered, 'or land on anything except water was after poor Robert Emmet was butchered. One of them flew in fast, circling St Catherine's Church and finally landed on the scaffold, that was still standing after the afternoon's entertainment. The people, who had all seen him carved up, fell on their knees and started to pray. They said that it was his soul come back. And that old corpse,' he said, pointing at the moon, 'was shining as now.'

'The scaffold,' I told him, 'was level with the top of the door portal.'

The boy gave me a quick, hard stare. 'How do you know that?' he said.

'I saw an old print of the execution once,' I told him. 'Tom Horan and I found it, but Tom kept it.'

It was a graphic and explicit drawing in colour of the execution of Robert Emmet. It had been drawn from an upstairs room on the corner of Thomas Street and Marrowbone Lane. From that angle, the artist had sketched hundreds of frightened Hogarthian faces jammed into the street, spilling down Bridgefoot Street until lost on the slope. It was like something out of a nightmare, the native Irish with eyes wide apart, staring in terror, little cock-a-snoot noses and long upper lips, wide mouths open and, as depicted, more like animals than people. The square in front of the church had been kept clear of the rabble and shoulder to shoulder the Red Coats stood with fixed bayonets, while British justice prevailed.

Ghoulish work completed, the executioner was shown holding the head aloft, blood splashing down on to the door below. The print had been intended to strike terror into the Irish, and certainly the headless, legless trunk, lying in its own gore, had struck terror into me. I never passed the church without glancing fearfully at the portal and the door.

'I know all about Robert Emmet,' I told the boy and sang:

'Bold Robert Emmet, the darlin' of Erin
Bold Robert Emmet, who died with a smile . . .'

'You've a nice voice, Lar,' the boy interrupted, 'but that's bloody rubbish they're teaching you at school. The poor man was pissing himself with fright.'

'What . . . Robert Emmet! I don't believe it!'

'I don't care what you believe,' the boy snapped, 'he was and do you blame him?'

'I know,' I said, 'hanged, drawn and quartered. It must be an awful way to die.'

'Yes, a great deal more awful than you think, for first they hung him a little and let him choke, then dropped him and did it again and when they got tired, they spilled his guts out before his living eyes. He was dead before they beheaded and quartered him.'

He glanced at my horrified face, staring at the harbour in all its quiet delight. The boy suddenly gave a sharp cry of warning, as a sudden, vicious gust of wind ruffled the water and had it churning in a second. And truly the storm was back, shrieking around us though the bells had ceased. It must be very late.

'Run,' shouted the boy, 'you should have been home hours ago. So should I.'

'What time is it?' I shouted above the gale. But he had gone.

I had been warned not to be late. Mam worried about me if I was and she would give me the handle of the sweeping brush tonight. I started to run, along Marrowbone Lane, for I was afraid to take the short cut along the Back of the Pipes. I had a crazy hope that Mam would be in bed, but no such luck. She was seated in front of the kitchen range, with a good fire on. She was in her night dress with a white shawl around her shoulders, which had held only too many babies.

I came in quietly, prepared for another storm that night.

'Where have you been, child?' she said softly.

'Nowhere, Mam, I was just standing on the bank of James's Street harbour and I never felt the time passing.'

There was a sharp intake of breath and a fretful sigh. 'Dreamin' again, child,' she whispered and started to cry. 'Christ, Lar, you'll be the death of me with your dreaming . . . I suppose I'll have you sick again on my hands. Where do you go, child, when you get like that? Jesus, you frighten me . . .'

Seeing that she was not going to slap me and that I had caused her such distress, I stole over and put my arms around her.

'I'm sorry, Mam,' I said.

'There, child,' she said, kissing me briefly on the cheek, 'as long as you're back home safe.' She kissed me again, took the singing kettle off the fire and regarded the glowing coals wistfully.

'I'd love a roasted Spanish onion,' she sighed. She had these sudden longings sometimes, especially when she was getting fat. Although I did not know why, I had come to realise this. And here was my moment! A few days before, I had dropped a big Spanish onion behind the gas stove. Being too busy reading a comic cut, I had forgotten all about it. I found it now and presented it to her with glowing face. It was a great fire for roasting onions. My sisters and brothers were all in bed and I had her completely to myself. I loved her and she loved me, though sometimes I frightened her. I knew that. Very soon now, I would discover the word for the thing about me that frightened her. It was a Scottish word – fey!

But there was nothing fey about the way I tucked into the delicious onion, swimming in butter, the fresh loaf and the strong tea.

'Your little face is gettin' a bit of colour back,' she said presently. 'Now, finish your tea and off to bed. And don't forget to say your prayers. Good night, love.'

'Good night, Mam.' I kissed her and gave her a squeeze. I was halfway up the stairs when she spoke again.

'Try not to dream anymore, child,' she said. 'You've school in the morning and you mustn't be late.'

'OK. Good night, Mam, good night.'

'Good night, Lar.'

5 *Say Balloon*

The following morning I slept it out. Mam had been vomiting again and had forgotten to call me a second time and now I was running up Dolphins Barn, trying to beat the clock.

It was a fine, sunny, frosty morning in 1928, the age of Jazz and from a room overhead in a tenement, a Red Red Robin was sent bob bob a-bobbin' down the street, via the tinny horn of a gramophone. The street was full of horses and carts, all headed back from the Dublin vegetable market and making an appalling row, as their iron shod wheels bounced off the cobble stones. Piles of dung on the road and the acrid smell of men, horses and urine was in the air.

'Janey,' I panted to Dessy Duffy, who joined me at this point every morning, 'there's the chapel bell!'

'It might be only a quarter to ten,' Dessy panted hopefully. 'Sometimes he's early ringin' it for Mass.'

'Yes,' I panted back grimly, 'but it might be five to ten, more like. That fella that rings it 'id be late for his own funeral.' I glanced sideways at Dessy. He was looking sicker than usual this morning and although he had only covered a few hundred yards, was gasping like a broken winded horse.

'What time is it, mister?' I shouted to a passing cabby. The cabby grinned and took out a solid gold Hunter watch.

'Five teh ten,' he shouted. 'Get the lead out a' yer arse an' start runnin' or the school master 'ill kill yeh.'

'Feck you, y'oul get,' I shouted and jumped into a tenement halldoorway to avoid the whip slash he aimed at me. He was gone then and the horse got the slash that was meant for me, to brighten him up.

I resumed the race against the clock and soon caught up with poor Dessy, who had stopped running and was holding his side.

'Janey, Des,' I said frantically, 'c'mon. Y'll get the pair of us killed!' He started to run beside me, but before we reached South Circular Road he stopped again.

'Come on, Dessy,' I shouted, 'you're like an oul' wan.' He was green about the gills and shook his head. 'Go on, Lar,' he panted gallantly, 'or you'll get worse than me. You were late yesterday morning too.'

'All right, then, Des,' I shouted and sped off. As I ran into the school yard I heard the whistle shrill out. Ten O'Clock! I had barely made it. They were already lining up and I jumped in beside Ernie, who made room for me.

'Thanks, Ern,' I panted.

He was a pal of mine, though not as close as Dessy. Ernie and I were good scrappers and about the same size, so we respected each other, carefully avoiding a fight, although the rest of the class were always 'gettin' it up for us.' This boy came from the same small, shabby Artisan dwelling streets and rejoiced in the aristocratic surname of Montaigne, though everybody called him Ernie Mountain.

'Lar,' Ernie whispered, 'our teacher is out sick. "Yella' Man" is takin' us tehday.'

I felt my heart give a sick lurch. 'He'll murder poor Dessy for being late,' I whispered back.

'SILENCE!' roared Yella' Man and gave the whistle another blast. He gazed along the lines of scared boys, looking for a chance to lace one of them, a Kerry expression we had come to understand without the aid of a dictionary. It simply meant that he would beat the daylights out of you.

He had two classes to take today and it was clear that the prospect did not please him. On the other hand, there was the consoling factor that he had twice as many Jackeens to beat if they gave him a chance. He hated Dublin kids, who jeered him behind his back, imitating his country accent, thick as pig's muck when he was aroused and he liked to tell his Dublin class, that he would 'bate the Jackeen' out of them yet.

Yella' Man! He had been well named by the school, a small, skinny Kerry man with a mouth like a closed trap and I was terrified of him. It is only in retrospect, that I can describe him as small, for five feet, four inches can be as tall as a grizzly bear to a four feet nothing boy. He suffered from some ailment of the kidneys, which dyed his face a sickly yellow and about him a smell of stale urine fouled the air.

He had small, discoloured rather pointed teeth and his temper, not improved by illness, was as vicious as a starving stoat's. In the distance, the Barn chapel spire stood out against the blue winter sky, as he kept us there, shivering, tapping his leather strap against the palm of his hand, balefully surveying the double line of boys, who were class three and four. We were class four.

Behind us, a green field stretched across to the Grand Canal and beyond lay fields and villages, all the way to Cork and Kerry, to where I fervently hoped this evil little bastard would return.

The other classes had long gone in, but he kept us there for a good five minutes longer, while the heat died in undernourished little bodies and a cold foreboding came in. At length, tiring of his game, he marched us into the school. His classroom adjoined ours and this morning the folding doors between had been opened to enable the two rooms to be turned into one. His own class, long since cowed, got quickly down to work.

In palpitating silence, he came into our room and went to the blackboard. Using two different colours of chalk, he skilfully drew an air balloon, even showing up two tiny figures in the basket that swung below.

'Jasus,' whispered Ernie Mountain, 'he's out for blood!'

We had often heard of this practice of his and what it led up to, and now we trembled with fear. Out for blood he was! He was putting the final flourishes to an excellent drawing, when the door slowly opened. Dessy Duffy had arrived!

Yella' Man turned slowly and surveyed the small figure of Dessy *kindly*.

'And what's your name, my little man?' he inquired pleasantly.

'Dessy Duffy, sir,' the child panted.

'That is to say, Desmond Duffy, is it not?' said Yella' Man encouragingly.

'Yes, sir, Desmond, sir, Duffy, sir.' Relief flooded poor Dessy's face.

'Well, Desmond, come in and find your place like a good boy,' said the teacher softly. 'He's making us all cold, isn't he boys?'

A fawning chorus of 'yes, sirs' answered him. He finished the drawing, placing a pink cloud over it. It was finished and so were we. The excellence and skill of execution boded ill for us. He had drawn it many times, a fiendish plan that could not fail. It must, by the very accent they possessed, end up in a beating for Dublin Jackeens. Yella' Man faced the class.

'Well, now,' he said, 'will master Dessy, or Desmond Duffy, stand up?' His voice was soft and kindly and he was looking out the window at the sunny winter sky. Dessy clattered to his feet. The class held its breath.

'Now, Desmond,' he said coaxingly, 'would you mind telling me and, of course, your class mates why you were ten minutes late for school this morning. I don't really care, but your friends would like to know, wouldn't you boys?'

A frightened titter ran around the room and a few less 'yes sirs.' I said nothing. I was not going to help this country man make a laugh of poor Dessy and, anyway, I wanted to keep low. This Yella' Man bastard was always on the watch for me.

From his own class came not a sound. He had given them a composition and an hour to do it in. He could give us his undivided attention and a change of Jackeens was always welcome. Give this palefaced rabble from the Pale some exposure to a *real* Irishman.

'Please, sir,' said Dessy. 'I don't feel well, sir. I got a stitch in me side runnin'. I couldn't keep up wit' Lar.'

Janey, what was he saying, why was he dragging me into it!

'Running,' said Yella' Man, vastly puzzled. 'Running? Could you not have started out ten minutes earlier? Surely, if running gives you a stitch in your side, surely you can avoid it by getting up earlier?'

Dessy gulped. He was terrified. 'Please, sir, me mother knocked over the tea an' she wouldn't let me come to school until she made some more.'

'Well, now,' said Yella' Man, reaching for his strap and slowly hefting it. 'That sounds perfectly reasonable to me. Does it not class?'

Not a sound came from the class.

'Answer me!' roared Yella' Man, his face suddenly suffused with rage.

'Yes, sir,' the class said. I said nothing.

'I suppose your mother upset your tea as well,' said the teacher, turning to me with a wolfish grin. 'You didn't think I spotted you bolting into the yard after the whistle went, did you? Stand up, boy.'

I stumbled to my feet with sinking heart and remained silent.

'I asked you a question, boy,' said Yella' Man on a rising inflection.

'No, sir.'

'And now you are surprised, no doubt?'

'No, sir . . . I mean, yes sir . . .' I didn't know which way to answer the Yella' bastard. Either way I was in trouble.

'Did your mother spill your tea? I'm still waiting for your answer!'

'No, sir, she didn't spill me tea. She never has the breakfast ready in time, these mornings.'

'Indeed?' said the Kerryman loftily. 'And, pray, why not?'

'She's always sick in the mornings, sir. She does be vomitin'.' Yella' Man smiled. 'She does *be* vomitin', eh?' he said slowly. 'Well, Redmond, if your mother's complaint was a valid reason for being late for school, I'm sure I don't know how any of you Barn crowd are ever here on time.'

He paced up and down the floor for a minute, chuckling at some private joke he thought, but I knew what it was, the dirty oul' bastard.

'I don't live in the Barn, sir,' I said.

Yella' Man gave me a hard stare. I looked straight back at him. If he killed me, he was not going to jeer my Mam.

'I heard tell yeh were a smart boy, all right,' he said, his accent beginning to thicken. 'A bit too smart for yer own good. I heard yeh were a good runner too?'

'I don't know, sir.'

'Well, we can always find out, can't we? By a run around the yard.'

His voice hardened. 'Now let me see yeh run around it, fast. We might enther ye for the Tailteann games yet.' Fury was taking him over and his voice and pronunciation were reverting to his native bog.

'Move, boy,' he roared, 'and run round the school yard until I tell ye teh shtop.'

He aimed a swipe of the leather at me on my way out, but I was too quick for him and he missed. I went down the passage and entered the school yard, running. It was about forty yards square and after a couple of turns I was licked. I had already had a hard run against the clock on the way to school and now the stitch in my side grew worse with every step. My legs were like lead and I stumbled around the yard, blinded with sweat. Yella' Man stood with the classroom window open, giving an occasional savage roar to speed me on my way.

I fell a couple of times, before he gave the order to stop and I staggered into the classroom, saturated with sweat. On the way past, the bastard caught me with a well directed blow, full force across the back so hard that I gagged and nearly vomited. His strap was half an inch thick, one layer of leather upon another, eighteen inches long with a well shaped handle. There were few boys in Rialto school, who had not felt it at one time or another. Rumour said that the belt had coins or flat lead weights sown into the leather, in the middle, and my aching back said this was true.

'That'll help ye on yer way,' he grinned.

I sat in my desk, crying with weakness and pain, effing and blinding the Kerryman as hard as I could under my breath. I'd have to confess my terrible language in confession, I knew, but that was another day's work. And, anyway, I was fed up with the bloody priests. When they came to our school, they never had much to say to me even though I was Dux of class. Oh no! A nod was good enough for Emerald Square.

It was different for the South Circular gang or the ones who lived in Mount Shannon Road.

They were merely spending three or four years in the national school, before going on to Synge Street to get their Leaving Certificate. The education the Barn lot got here was all they were ever going to get, no secondary school for them. Out to work, when you were fourteen, with or without the primary school certificate. It made little difference. They were going to work in overalls, hewers of wood and drawers of water for all their days.

The boys from South Circular Road and the prosperous places over Rialto Bridge always stuck out a mile away among the poverty of us others. No secondhand books for them! No cheap canvas school bags. And, to add insult to injury, they were usually bigger, cleaner and better dressed, though they were not as clever. I could beat them every time, my special pal Colin, the only smart one among them. His end of the South Circular Road was very near the Barn and he identified with us. Ernie Mountain would walk all over them, when he put his mind to it.

The bright winter sunshine was pouring through the windows when I looked up, wiping my eyes on the cuff of my jersey. Yella' Man was pacing slowly through the desks, up and down, up and down, a tigerish look on his face. The room was growing warm now and dust motes sailed gaily over the terror stricken boys. Eventually, having come to a decision, he mounted the rostrum and pointed the leather strap at the blackboard.

'Now, Desmond Duffy,' he said encouragingly, 'would you be good enough to tell the class what that object is . . . The drawing I have made.'

Dessy jumped up. 'A balewin, sir,' he said eagerly.

'Jasus,' whispered Ernie. 'He's in for it.'

'A BAL-EW-IN, is it,' said Yella' Man softly. 'Caaan't ye seah it prroperrly?' Bad sign. He was reverting again into his Kerry accent.

'Thry agin!'

With difficulty, for his voice was trembling, Dessy tried again. He *knew* what was coming. We all did.

'Balewin, sir,' he said shakily.

'Balewin, sir,' Yella' Man whispered to himself. He shook his head, rage making him more yellow of face than usual.

'BALLOON,' he roared, choking with fury. 'BALLOON! Now . . . try again, Duffy!'

'Balewin, sir,' said Dessy faintly.

Yella' Man left the rostrum and coming down among the desks, stood behind Dessy's back.

'Now, boy,' he whispered sibilantly, 'thry again, wance more.'

'Ba . . . ba . . . balewin, sir,' Dessy quavered and screamed as the heavy strap thudded across his skinny shoulders: 'BALEWIN!' The heavy leather found its mark on his back again and a hard box in the ear sent him flying into the aisle between the desks. Yella' Man pounced on him then and grabbed him by the scruff of the neck, the heavy leather strap flailing off the boy's arse – and suddenly a terrible stench invaded the classroom. Yella' Man looked disgusted, but I, observing him with hate, thought it put on. Ernie evidently thought so too, for he whispered to me, 'He's afraid of what he's after doin'. Look at him!'

The school master retreated to the rostum. 'You, boy,' he snarled at me. 'Take that thing out to the toilet and get it cleaned up.'

'He's bet the shite out of him,' Ernie whispered. I had often heard the expression used before, 'I'll bate the shite out a' you', but I had never seen it actually done until now.

And one day, I swore, when I grew up, I would beat the shite out of Yella' Man.

Outside in the toilet, despite the bright sunshine, it was east wind cold and Dessy shivered uncontrollably as he tried to clean himself. I found some newspaper and he did the best he could with that, but I could not bear to go near him. He was sobbing weakly all the time and we were about to enter the classroom, when the master came out.

'You, boy,' he said between his teeth, 'take that object home and report straight back here. Don't get any bright ideas of takin' the day off . . . or I'll *lace ye* tomorra'.'

'Like hell,' I said under my breath. I had made up my mind that I *was* staying at home.

'What did you say? Did ye say something?'

'No, sir.'

'Off wid ye then!'

He had little fear of the consequences, for besides being poor, Mrs Duffy was a widow. The two of us went slowly homewards. Dessy could hardly walk and I, for a different reason, could hardly walk either. At Dessy's home in Dolphins Barn Street, Mrs Duffy, seeing the condition of her lone chick, gave a loud wail. I spoke for Dessy.

'Yella' Man is after murderin' him, Missus Duffy,' I said, 'he's after beatin' the shi . . . after killin' him.'

'May the curse a' God light on him, the dirty Kerry bastard,' said Mrs Duffy, her lower jaw coming forward, her teeth resting against her upper lip. 'But if anything happens to my boy, by Jasus, he'll live teh rue the day.'

Well, something *did* happen to her boy, for Dessy never came to school again. I went to see him often at first before he became too ill. From what Dessy told me, when they put him in a wheelchair, his sickness was something to do with one's bones. We used to sit in front of the fire that winter, playing Ludo and Snakes and Ladders, but after a few weeks Dessy became too ill to play and I used to tell him all the news from school, especially if I had any bad news about Yella' Man. And sometimes just made it up, just to bring a smile to his face.

He could no longer walk at all and his poor mother hovered over him constantly, as if by her very presence she could defy the old Reaper, drawing nearer day by day.

Then, my mother heard something about Dessy and I was forbidden to go there any more. I defied her once, when I was sure she would not find out, but she did and that evening, when Dad came home from work she told him.

'Look, Lar,' said my father kindly, 'I know you are very fond of Dessy, but we are fond of *you*. Dessy has consumption and that means it is catching and you could end up in Dessy's wheelchair when he doesn't need it any more! And that, poor lad, will be soon from what I hear.'

He frightened me, and I went to Dessy's house no more.

In early summer, less than a year after Yella' Man had beaten the boy, the traditional black crepe with mourning card appeared on the widow's door and Dessy was dead.

'We should go to see him before he's buried,' Ernie told me and so, on a summer day, we went to Mrs Duffy's to have a last look at Dessy. He lay still and shrunken with two pennies on his eyes, black against his waxlike face, and suddenly I was terrified. Mrs Duffy, distraught and wild, made us kneel beside the coffin and we began to pray. When we had said ten Our Fathers and ten Hail Marys, we both made to go, but Mrs Duffy, with a rolling glance stuck us to the floor and began the Rosary.

Ernie glanced at me and for once I could see that he was frightened. I was scared stiff. We prayed . . . and prayed . . . and prayed, the cold sweat of fear running down my back. In the end, it was quick-thinking Ernie who saved the day and provided our salvation.

'Missus Duffy,' said Ernie, 'if yeh had another prayer book for Lar, we could say more prayers together for another couple a' hours.' When she shot off to get same, Ernie and I shot off too, and escaped. Mrs Duffy was clearly mad.

Ernie, I had noticed, was a thrifty boy. His school books, at end of term, looked still new, unlike mine. He was a natural conservationist and hated waste. He resented sending Dessy off overloaded with prayers, in no way commensurate with his sins.

'For,' said Ernie, as we sped down Dolphins Barn, 'poor oul' Des didn't need all them prayers . . . ridiculous. A few Our Fathers an' a half a dozen Hailers would a' done just as well. Enough is enough!' shouted Ernie as we split for home. As for me, I would never again look willingly at a corpse. Not even on Mam, God forbid, would I look if she died. As regards prayers, I felt I had said enough Hailers to last me many a long day.

6 *Class of '26*

Just before Easter, Mrs Duffy paid her first visit to the school. I had seen her a few times since the death of my friend and she was obviously insane. Mr Ahearne, my school master, met her at our classroom door, but she was not looking for him. I heard him tell her how sorry he was about the death of her only son, but she was not listening to him. She closed the door in his face, without a word. He opened it again and stood watching her go down the passage, a worried look on his face.

She was looking for Yella' Man and she found him next door. In the sudden electric silence that had fallen, we distinctly heard her open the door of the Kerryman's classroom. Then, after a full minute, with not a sound, her footsteps were heard coming back along the passage and I caught a fleeting glimpse of her, as she passed the door on the way out. Gradually her footsteps died away and we could all breathe again. For a few minutes, an incalculable terror had menaced us all, made worse because it was indefinable.

A few minutes later, Yella' Man came into our room, green in the face, trembling. Even though he tried to hide them, I could see his hands shaking behind his back. As Dux of the class, I occupied desk one, in row one and he stood a short distance in front of me. I got the familiar stench of urine, but today it seemed to have magnified itself and he stank like the lion house at the zoo.

'That was Missus Duffy, wasn't it, Mister Joyce,' said Mr Ahearne, our master.

'T'was,' said Yella' Man, gulping.

'What did she want?'

'I don't know.' The Kerryman's voice was trembling. 'She just stood there, moving her lips . . . layin' a curse on me, I think.' His voice tailed off and I thought he was going to faint.

Mr Ahearne managed a smile. 'Don't let it trouble you, Mr Joyce,' he said without conviction. 'Missus Duffy was always a little odd. I knew her fairly well.'

He offered the other a cigarette and the two of them moved off into the corridor, smoking, a thing that was rarely done during class time.

That was the start. This incident happened on Friday morning and was forgotten over the weekend. On Monday, she called at precisely the same time again.

I had been sent upstairs to see the Headmaster with a note and coming back along the passage, saw Mrs Duffy in front of me. She stopped at Yella' Man's door, opened it and stood there, a mad glare in her eyes, lips moving in some soundless malediction. For a full minute, there was dead silence. The class had been repeating a poem after the master, but all sound had stopped the moment Mrs Duffy opened the door. Then she turned and like some evil spirit came towards me. I shot into my own classroom before she passed me.

'What's wrong, Redmond?' said Mr Ahearne sharply.

'Please, sir, I got out of Missus Duffy's way. She's after visitin' Mr Joyce again.'

'She has visited . . . not *is after visiting*. I am surprised at you.'

So would my father have been, had he heard me speak like that, but it happened when I was excited. Liberties speech came naturally to me.

'Has she gone?'

'Yes, sir.'

Mr Ahearne made no reply, but frowning anxiously, he left the classroom. He left the door ajar and from the vantage point of the first row I saw him talking to a shaking Mr Joyce in the corridor.

My heart was singing. Mrs Duffy was making the bastard pay for the terrible going over he had given both of us. Excitedly, I sent the news around the class.

'Missus Duffy is after visitin' Yella' Man again an' he's afraid of his shite of her . . .'

Oh joy, oh bliss, Oh Sacred Heart of Jesus who loves little children, send her again! Send her in spring and summer, grant her the strength to come in autumn and the black days of winter too. Sick, well or dying, send her, Dear Lamb of Jesus, who takes away the sins of the world. Let his days be numbered and a burden to him.

Let him shit himself, as he pisses himself now. Take the shadow of him, Dear Lord, from this school. Shame him, fracture him, curse him, kill him, lurry him up, he's no relation . . .

There was almost a festive air in the school the following day. Word had gone around, that Dessy Duffy's mother was terrorising Yella' Man and four hundred Liberties lads lifted up their little hearts in thanksgiving. For our class, it was God's blessing strengthening our faith in the awesome rite of being Confirmed in our religion. It was a positive sign, that prayer, if persisted in long enough would be answered. God was good. And certainly every boy in the school, at one time or another, had stormed heaven with prayer for the demise of the Kerryman. We had often thought up tortures for Yella' Man. Such things as hanging him up on a butcher's hook by the nakers had been bruited about, or shoving the rough end of a pineapple up his kite – but we had never thought up a torture as good as this.

On Tuesday, she varied the time and struck again at half past two, just as the Kerryman was heaving a sigh of relief, the day almost over. We were made aware of it, by the scream from next door.

'Away wid ye . . . . Away wid ye!' Yella' Man's voice cracked with fright, then the noise of a small scuffle and the slam of the door in the adjoining room. And the quiet, slow slither of Mrs Duffy's feet along the corridor.

After this, the visits abruptly ceased for three days until we found the reason why. On the orders of the Headmaster, all outside doors in the school were to be kept bolted from the inside. Every morning now, the Head walked around, inspecting each door. Mrs Duffy was locked out. But not for long.

When the reason for her absence was discovered, the whole school, as one man, entered a silent conspiracy. Opening move?

Get permission to go to the toilet, then run like hell and make time to slip the bolts on the front door. Sometimes, some other kid had got there before you and dear Mrs Duffy could enter the school unimpeded.

In the face of this conspiracy, the Headmaster was helpless. But not quite. He would turn the key in each mortise-lock personally. Nobody else carried keys. He had beaten us! Then, fate stepped in and gave us a hand. The very first day he tried this was a disaster. Our overworked Head had to take a class himself on the second floor and a long trip to the front doors. The first day he locked them was spent going up and down the stairs. He was a portly man, very much out of condition and he nearly had a heart attack.

'Sir . . . sir, the coal man is outside.' The coal had arrived for the school boiler. A trip downstairs.

'Sir . . . sir . . . the Canon is wavin' from the far side a' the road!' Another trip downstairs and a very irate Canon admitted. And just after that, the dreaded school inspector was locked out for nearly half an hour before anyone noticed and he came in in a fury and took it out on the masters, grilling their classes one by one, the whole school one and a half hours late home. That finished the door thing. And left us free to slip back the bolts again.

It was a fiendish and terrible retribution on Yella' Man, who grew visibly weaker. His flogging days were done, it seemed, and the noise from his class, formerly as silent as the grave except when he laced some unfortunate, grew louder by the day. And Mrs Duffy kept calling. But never at the same time. The teacher could never be sure, from one moment to the next, when his door would slowly open and he would be transfixed by her mad glare, wild eyes under an uncombed mass of grey hair, bloodless lips silently whispering their venomous curses.

Easter came and went that year in a blaze of sunshine and a powdering of petals. Lilac, apple and pear blossoms, wild cherries, in the groves outside Crumlin village. Hawthorn in the hedges, fat as cauliflowers, dandelions, daisies and daffodils, like the old song. The sudden onslaught of warm weather after a cold spring was nearly too much and all nature, drunk with joy, went on a spree that ended in a riot of colour.

Girls, like the flowers, appeared from nowhere, gaily dressed in print pinafores, dancing, singing, mincing past the boys in the square, and street games were in full swing-skipping-ropes and spinning-tops and once again, time to go fishing in the quarry.

It was the day after the long Easter weekend, that Mr Ahearne called me. 'Here, Labhras,' he said, 'take this book in to Mr Joyce and tell him I enjoyed it.'

I ran down the corridor quickly, slipped the bolts on the door and ran back. I knocked fearfully on Yella' Man's door as he glanced up and beckoned me in. All the class doors had three glass panes in them, so the Head could see in as he walked past.

'Well, boy,' said the teacher. 'What is it?' He had his strap in his hand and several boys, standing against the wall, were wringing their hands.

'The oul' bastard is gettin' better,' I thought viciously, but I glanced up at the school master humbly enough.

'Please, sir,' I said politely, 'Mr Ahearne sent in your book and told me to say that he enjoyed it.' I placed it on the table and turned to go, for I had a very good reason to be in a hurry. As I had slipped the bolts, Mrs Duffy had entered. She must have been waiting outside. She would be here any second now.

Yella' Man regarded me with hate. Knowing that I was Dux of class and rarely felt the leather seemed to increase his anxiety to lace me.

'Did I give ye permission teh go, boy?' he snarled.

'No, sir. I thought you were finished with me, sir.'

'I'll tell ye when teh go. Mind yer manners and hand me that book.'

'Yes, sir,' I said and retrieving the book, extended it to the master. He did not see it. He was gazing over my shoulder and a look of complete terror was spreading over his face. It seemed to grow smaller, to shrivel, the cheeks sucked in with fright. I was looking at death's head, so frightful an apparition that I threw the book on the table again and turned to flee.

Mrs Duffy had arrived and was standing in the doorway, lips moving in what had come to be known as 'the Divil's Litany', soundlessly cursing the school master. Then, for the first and last time, she broke her silence.

'Murderer!' she screamed, 'MUUUURRRRDERERRRRRR!'

The terrible accusation echoed through every classroom in the school. It even penetrated to the Head's room upstairs, and for a minute one could have heard a pin drop, as she shuffled away, in that school that housed four hundred noisy youngsters.

The next day Yella' Man was absent from school. He never came again. Mrs Duffy had avenged her son. After about a week, we heard he was desperately ill. No word came by way of our superiors, but Joe Donoughue's mother was in the ward next door in the Meath Hospital. He kept us well informed and every morning before school, we would gather round him to hear the latest good news.

'He's vewwy bad,' Joe would tell us with a grin, 'Vewwy bad! He's gettin' wowse!'

He made my days happy, for I carried a bitter and terrible rancour against Yella' Man, born by the death of my friend and the punishment he had given me.

One day, the Canon arrived with news of grave import. Mr Joyce's condition had deteriorated, he was near death. We were exhorted to pray for him, to beseech God to spare him for us for many a day, that he might continue with the onerous task of trying to instill a little education and manners into a crowd of slumbirds.

It was not expressed in exactly those terms, but we were left with the firm impression that he had not earned his money easily and had deserved a better fate. At five minutes to three, just before we went home, it became our duty to pray for the soul of Mr Joyce, who lingered with one foot in the grave.

'I'd help him with a shove,' said Ernie.

We stood behind our desks, mumbling the prayers with reluctance. In no way could any enthusiasm be instilled in to us for the task. Every boy in the class had suffered assault at the unmerciful hands of Yella' Man, and we prayed because we were compelled to pray. Ernie treasured a special hatred against him over the beating of his little brother and had his own prayer made up and said no other.

'Our Father, Who art in heaven, have yeh got his name?
It's oul' Yella' Man, whether he is on earth or down under,
Give him his daily dose, beat him up, break his glasses,
As we would give them who trespass,
And lead us not into his classroom, but deliver us from evil. Amen.'

He took delight in saying this, his masterpiece, and the kids around him would be in fits of laughing and trying to hide it.

'That he may die woawin' like Dow'ins ass,' said Joe Donoughue. Whether he did or not, we never found out, but one early summer's day with the sun splitting the trees and the scent of flowers and grass heavy on the breeze from across the canal, word came to school that Mr Joyce was dead.

Rialto school was closed for the day and four hundred boys were marched to Dolphins Barn chapel, where the mortal remains of oul' Yella' Man lay, to pray for his soul. Never, in the history of the world, could there have been a more cheerful funeral procession.

In the chapel, however, the Canon got down to the serious business of the day. Endless prayers were offered up for the repose of his soul. I thought they would never end, spoiling an unexpected day off school. But remembering my mother's words, never to speak evil of the dead, I said a couple of grudging Hailers and let it go at that. And I only went that far, because I was afraid of ghosts.

We were made to sing a hymn, too, with gusto, and then the Canon told us from the pulpit that Mr Joyce had gone on his last, happy journey to his Maker and was now looking down on earth with love . . .

'Lookin' up, he means,' said Ernie loudly and there was an

explosion of muffled laughter from the pews around.

We were to pray for the repose of his soul this day . . . nay, every day when we said our prayers. Mr Joyce's full and useful, not to say dedicated, life had come to a premature end . . .

'Thanks be teh Jasus,' said O'Connor nearby and another burst of laughter ran round the chapel.

His work on this earth was done, we were all to pray for him . . .

'Me arse, like,' said Ernie.

The school would be closed tomorrow, the Canon continued sadly, and the day was to be kept as a day of mourning. Every boy was to attend ten o'clock Mass and follow the funeral cortege to Mount Jerome afterwards.

'And how the hell does he expect us teh keep up with the feckin' horses?'

'If th' oul' Yella' bastard was here, he'd show yeh . . .'

'He'd *lace* you, boy,' said O'Connor in a thick country accent.

'The divil 'ill have a good fire banked up for him,' said I, not wanting to be left behind by the hard chaws.

Two school masters, further up the chapel, stood up and looked pointedly in our direction, where the noise was becoming audible. We all ducked our heads. They were trying to memorise faces for punishment, when we went back to school.

Though tomorrow, the lemon faced oul' Canon told us, was a school holiday, it was not to be regarded as a joyful occasion. We were to keep this in mind, he warned, his well developed lower, disapproving Catholic lip stuck out, and offer up prayers throughout the day for the repose of the soul of our late friend and benefactor. We were to dwell on his death . . .

'Not feckin' half,' said Ernie in a loud whisper. 'I'm shaggin' gloatin' over it.'

'Yes, dwell on death, so soon to come to us all . . .'

'He didn't die any too fuckin' soon,' said Deasy, a big stupid clod who rarely said anything. The remark came from such an unexpected quarter, that it unleashed another small gale of laughter.

Ernie nudged me. 'Ay . . . Lar . . . will yeh look at that little bastard Branwell. Bejasus . . . I'll Mount Shannon Road him when we get out.'

I glanced over nudgewards. Branwell was kneeling bolt upright, hands joined, thumbs under his chin, eyes fixed in piety on the priest, a perfect example of what we all could be, if by any chance we had come from Mount Shannon Road instead of the rowdy Barn. By his attitude, without saying a word, he was screaming all over the chapel that he was not one of the malcontents and 'Please, sir, don't slap me . . . I wasn't with them!'

I whispered viciously to Ernie: 'I'll feckin' guzzle him.' At length, the service came to an end and we were allowed to go home, it being the Canon's opinion that no useful purpose would be served by marching us back to school, being, as we were, too upset by the death of Mr Joyce, unable to concentrate on our lessons.

Ernie and I put the plan we had made in the chapel into action right away. Branwell, who had seen Ernie's baleful glance in his direction accompanied by a dumb show of a punch in the eye, another on the nose and six in the face, was off like a hare. And here was another thing about these 'better off' boys. We could outrun them any time, which was easy to understand if you thought about it, for they got no training whereas we were always at concert pitch from being chased by young country coppers and shop keepers.

Neither of us made any attempt to follow him and strolled casually towards the Barn until he disappeared down the South Circular Road. Then we took to our heels, flying across a field behind the houses and parallel to Branwell's course. We tore along Reubens Street and came out running at St Andrew's Protestant church. Our quarry was casually strolling along, seeing as there was no pursuit. He turned green as we fell in on each side of him.

There were a few people around and we were afraid for a minute that he would yell out for help, but we treated him real pally-like, until we had him alone, then I gave him an ill dig in the ribs with a bony elbow that made him yelp.

'Now,' said Ernie, 'you're either goin' teh fight Lar or me. Which is it goin' teh be?'

'I don't want to fight either of you,' said Branwell nervously. 'I'll tell the master when we go back . . .'

'What'll yeh tell the master, this?' said Ernie, giving him another vicious elbow in the side. 'Is that what you're goin' teh tell him?'

'Or this!' I said, punching him in the back, hard.

'Now, will yeh fight?' said Ernie venomously.

'No,' said poor Branwell, starting to cry. 'You'd only murder me.'

'Give him the coward's blow,' I said.

'Right,' said Ernie, and did.

It was a formula as old as the Liberties itself. One boy, in this case me, held the victim while the other administered the coward's blow.

'Wan . . . two . . . three . . . Y'll never bate me!' intoned Ernie, each word accompaied by a vicious blow, full force, on the back. Seven blows in all, one more telling than the other.

Branwell was hurt – and badly hurt. But he stood there, sobbing, taking them, a thing you never did if you came from the Barn. Not even if you got killed, never!

'Now, you,' said Ernie, grabbing Branwell.

I glanced at Branwell with assumed contempt. 'He's not worth it,' I said. But secretly, I was ashamed of myself. And, looking at Branwell, I felt like crying with him.

'C'mon,' I said roughly. 'Leave him alone, Ernie, he's not worth it.'

'Bejasus,' said Ernie between his teeth, 'if you split to the feckin' master, I'll bloody well kill yeh . . . An' don't forget it.'

But the shame of the thing lingered with me and I was withdrawn and sullen for the rest of the day. So much so, that I got several boxes on the ear from Mam, for various causes.

But I did not care and in some queer fashion welcomed the punishment, I would not give her the satisfaction of crying. At the back of my mind was the thought of my father. He would never have done a thing like I had done! But then, of course, he had not been dragged up in the Liberties. It had been somewhere on the north side of Dublin for him, with a Georgian house and servants before he had had his patrimony stolen by his eldest sister and her husband. His family had had a governess and he a pony until he was twelve years old and suddenly came down in the world.

Apprenticed to be a carpenter, he and his brother, two years younger and in due course sent to be an electrician, were kept in lodgings until they could fend for themselves. But he had never lost sight of the fact that he was a gentleman. For all the crude talk around him and the hardship of the building game, calculated to turn any man into an animal, he had not given way. He had ingested gentility with his first breath, marked for life with the indelible stamp of a gentleman. He tried to pass it on to his sons, but the little they acquired did not stand up to the crucible of the Liberties.

And here was I, the son of a gentleman, born out of his proper environment and saving up to be numbered among the best bowsies the Liberties could produce. I felt, that after the low thing I had helped do to Branwell, that I had let my father down.

I was confused and torn between the two sets of boxing rules: my father's, strictly Marquis of Queensbury, and the Liberties, the boot and the head.

'Shake hands like gentlemen, and come out fighting' as opposed to 'lurry him up, he's no relation'. 'Put the boot in'. 'Give him the Ringsend shake hands'. A knee in the balls.

Jesus help me, I thought, being undersized like me one had to resort to the Liberties rules or go under. You had no choice. But a small, still voice at the back of my mind that could not be silenced said there was no need to go out of your way to *prove* you were a bowsie and that was exactly what I had done.

The real reason for my attack on Branwell was that he came from a better home, wore better clothes and, I felt vaguely, deep inside me, that he was destined for a better future. He would go on to secondary school, he was not going to be a carpenter, a blue collar worker with dirty finger nails.

I hated and envied boys like him, with their leather school bags, their school caps and the way they never had to suffer the crucificion of being paraded, day after day, because their mothers could not afford the year's school books at the start of term. The bastards would sit there, straight faced but grinning inside, while you stood before them.

But the handicap of late school books did us little harm when it came to exam time. I took savage delight in winning. Branwell and Colin disputed first place with me every time, the only ones of the well-off families who had any brains. But after them, it was all Liberties. Ernie, Matchbox, Bock, Spider – small, tough, quickwitted, some of whom could make up a cross double or treble in the bookies like a flash. Branwell and Colin, like myself, had no knowledge of that department. It was not done in our families.

In Dolphins Barn Street we parted. Ernie was excited over the demise of Yella' Man.

'Look, Lar,' he said, 'bring your fishing rod up to the chapel in the mornin'. Have plenty a' worms.'

'But we have to go to the chapel. An' then we're supposed to go to Mount Jerome.'

Ernie grinned. 'Chapel, me arse,' he said bluntly. 'Not for that oul' get. I wouldn't mind seein' him buried, but it's too much trouble.'

'Janey, Ern,' I said, genuinely shocked, 'that's terrible talk.'

'Just because the oul' bastard is dead?' Ernie brushed my words aside contemptuously.

'Listen, Lar,' he said, 'we'll hide our rods in the bushes at the back of the chapel. Make sure that the master sees you. Then start inching to the door.'

The following morning we both did this and met outside. None of the masters had observed our departure and, anyway, we didn't care.

We found our fishing canes, got a free ride up the hill to the Barn on the back axel of a cab, until some louser shouted: 'Scut the whip!' and we had to jump off in a hurry to avoid the cabby's lash, and ran up Rutland Avenue to the quarry.

The Ramparts was the Liberties' name for this place. It gave refuge to hundreds of courting couples in the summer and the quarry was home to a million perch and an unknown number of huge trout.

A branch of the ancient Poddle, the Cut, divided further up by a granite construction, called the 'Stone Boat', which split the river in two, sent one branch alongside the quarry. Only a narrow bank separated the two and in times of flood, the river trout got into the deep water. These fish, although they could never breed due to lack of running water, grew huge, for they had an unlimited supply of small perch to feed on and frogs and tadpoles in season. The shallow pools about the quarry made us change our minds about the bait. From them, we got a rusty tin full of tadpoles and threw away the worms, for they were useless today. This was the annual Carnival of the Tadpoles and the perch turned up for the banquet with ravenous appetite.

The quarry lay sparkling before us. Dragonflies skated on the small waves and the swans swam belligerently up and down, guarding their nests in the bullrushes. It was a great day to be alive.

'All the same,' said Ernie philosophically, baiting up his hook, 'he did good afther all, be dyin' . . . oul' Yella' Man, I mean.'

'How's that?' I was busy sliding a split cork onto the line.

'Got us the day off, didn't it?'

There was no disputing that, so I just nodded and watched Ernie impale a tadpole through the side of the mouth and deftly cast into the water. At once his cork went under and he jerked a fine pound weight perch onto the bank.

'Janey, Lar,' he roared happily, 'get in quick! They're goin' mad tehday!'

I walked away a couple of paces and cast in. Immediately, my cork started to bob, moving away unlike any perch I had ever caught. Just before my line gave out, it suddenly went under.

'Stick it inteh him!' roared Ernie. I did and nearly went arse over kick into the quarry. The strong cane I held bent over, as one of the cannibal trout fought for his life. But the fishing tackle was coarse and strong and the old cannibal lost the day. It took me ten minutes to land him and with him came a memory that would last for a lifetime, and sometimes be remembered in tears.

Hours afterwards, starving but triumphant, we headed for home. Between us we carried, threaded through the gills, the day's total catch for all to see. Thirty-one fine perch and, holding pride of place in the centre of the cord we picked up, the trout, which turned the scales at seven pounds.

All the kids in the square came thronging around us and some of their fathers and mothers too. It had been a day never to forget for, as Ernie commented, it had started off well with oul Yella' Man getting buried. It was a day in which we had been closer than brothers, for we had shared a great victory. But it marked the end of our friendship for a time, for that night Ernie learnt something of grave import and passed this information on to me the following day at school.

In succinct and explicit terms, he told me what was wrong with my mother, how she got her belly swelled and what my father did to her in bed. And outraged and shocked, I struck him, calling him a fucking liar and the school had their long awaited fight. Half the school surrounded us, as we fought like two Kerry Blues from the pavement on to the tram lines, both bleeding from a dozen places.

They had all agreed, that since Ernie had started going to the Andrews Boxing Club and was learning pugilistic skills that he would beat me now. But it took all he had learnt and all his strength to stop me from beating him into a pulp. I had gone berserk.

My mother . . . *My* lovely mother, to do a thing like that. Impossible! And I fought on, until some men, idly watching, became concerned over two kids who were really hurting each other and tore us apart. For what boy could believe a thing like that about his mother? Especially, if that boy told his brothers and sisters fairy stories and sometimes, gazing into the canal, went to fairy land?

7 *The Kipper*

After the death of oul' Yella' Man, the school became a more cheerful place. Although not in his class, his shadow had lain heavily on me. In the school yard, at play, his bloodshot eye had seemed always upon me and if the horseplay got a bit rough, it was me he singled out for a blow. He always kept his leather with him and if he were where I wished him to be the devil was using it to good purpose now – on him!

I was ten years old, under instruction to make my Confirmation, a milestone in the academic career of a boy, whose education was destined to end at fourteen. When you came to this point, you were on your way out. Only three more years to go. If your father was a tradesman, you followed in his foot-steps. If he worked in the Post Office or the railway, or in the Dublin Corporation, you went on to secondary school for a couple of more years in preparation for the stiff exam that the post required. But if your father worked in Guinness's you were sweet – and sweet for life at that. The Primary Certificate was good enough for Catholics, for few boys, however brilliant, who came from a Catholic home, ever made it to office level.

A Guinness-owned house or flat went with the job when you married. The firm had a clinic, where employees and their families were entitled to free medicine, malt extract for anaemic kids, lovely stuff, like toffee, not like the Parrishe's Food and codliver oil mixed, that boys like me had to gag over. Free hospitalisation and a convalescent home afterwards. They had a concert party, that they alone could join. No matter how well you sang, like me, a soloist in Clarendon

Street Choir, you were out. And above all, they had job security, God's blessing in the hungry thirties. They qualified as drivers of horse and dray, or lorry, for the war was on in earnest between animal and machine. The huge Clydesdales were on the way out. These boys were sweet, all right.

But if your father did not work in Guinness's, you did not either. The system was inflexible. As employers, Guinness's were streets ahead of most in the days when the sweat shop was the rule. Maybe it was a bad conscience, that made them better than others. They got their money easy and caused misery all over Ireland, not least in the Liberties. Powers, Jameson's and the Dublin Whiskey Distillers, all sited in the Liberties, were good employers too, and wreaked even more havoc in Irish homes.

But in all four firms, jobs for Catholics ceased at office level. From there on, it was jobs for the other side, the Prods, and I never met a Catholic boy, who made the clerical staff. This was the only discrimination I ever knew in the Irish Free State.

When the British had been beaten out, Guinness's, bastion of the Empire, had been left behind, alone, like a shag on a rock. If it had been possible to do so, they would immediately have shipped their factory over to England with the first boatload of returning Black and Tans.

Their recognition of the Irish Government had been bitter and sullen, much like the reaction of American companies in Cuba, until Castro clipped their wings. Guinness's would have changed the harp on their label to a crown with delight. They had come down in the world. Anglo-Irish firms no longer had the dubious respectability that comes from belonging to an empire, withal, a bit tatty now. Guinness's the monolith, at that time the largest brewery in the world had to get along as best they could in a poverty stricken belligerent kind of banana republic. It would never have done for his lordship . . . it would never have done for his grace!

The categories mentioned, were the jobs open to our school, but in the main, the vast majority of boys came from the homes of casually employed labourers and tradesmen.

Work was scarce, hunger was plentiful, and a dozen boys in our class were barefoot and in rags. They could not afford to buy school books. The Masters got tired of caning them for this. They never submitted any exercise as they had no exercise book. They got slapped every day for this. They failed every exam and remained in the one class for two or three years, or until they were fourteen. They were better starved than fed. They were stupid, dispirited, hungry and despised, the scrapings of the Liberties, on whose outer perimeter this school had been built. Unwelcome because of their poverty, dirt and lice, miserable in winter beyond description.

They disappeared into alleys and tenement houses after school, never seen anywhere at play, frequently being absent from school for weeks at a time. Harried by the School Attendance Officer, most of them were gone by fourth class. A few died, I know. The rest simply disappeared into some limbo and were never seen again. And some of the poor little bastards, captives of the law, were sent as 'incorrigibles' to places of correction, Artane, bad enough, or Jesus help them, Glencree! They paid dearly for their poverty.

Throwing Christians to the lions was a kindly act compared with sending these boys to the Celtic Inquisition of those days. For the Roman captives it was soon over. For these boys, it was a never ending nightmare, a protracted hell of beatings and floggings so that many of them came back to 'civvy' street, like some shell shocked veterans of the Western Front, cowed, fumbling, destined to move from dosshouse to jail all their lives.

'Suffer the little children to come unto me, for theirs is the Kingdom of the Lord'. The Christian Brothers, who ran these places of correction were the Instruments of the Lord, but my viewpoint was similar to the drunken lady of easy virtue I heard in McDaid's years later. 'Fuck them!' she shouted, 'And up the stallion!' (Stalin) and this because they had nearly killed her young brother.

But, of course, school had its lighter moments, even though from reading, I realised that we had been born

degraded. For instance, we were *in* school, whereas Harr
Wharton and Co. of Greyfriars were *at* school. There were n
Billy Bunters in Rialto school. The Liberties' diet in no wa
contributed towards manufacturing baby elephants. Rathe
the reverse. In the animal world, a famine stricken gazell
would be a fairer comparison.

In one respect though, there was a likeness between Rialt
school and the English Greyfriars. Our master, Mr Ahearn
(A Herrin') The Kipper – was a genuine Irish reproduction c
English Mr Quelch, though younger. Quick-tempered, can
wielding, kind, eccentric, both were dedicated teachers. Th
Kipper's punishments, though severe on occasion, were mil
by comparison with other teachers'. He dealt with tough kid
and he had to be tough with them. But he took no pleasure i
punishment. The Kipper was all right.

He was the only school master I ever heard of, who put u
money prizes, and good prizes, out of his own pocket. Te
shillings was a lot of money in 1927, but that is what he gav
to the boy who headed the class, ten bob for first, five shilling
for second and two-and-six for third. Two years later, th
prizes soared to fifteen shillings, ten and five, princely sum
for in those days a carpenter's pay for eight hours sloggin
was fifteen bob and The Kipper received little more.

Time after time, I stood at the head of the line, first in th
class and sent home for the day with fifteen bob, a Godsend i
our home in the middle of the week.

Leaping like a gazelle, mad with joy, along the South Circu
lar Road to stop at Stewart's, the Scottish confectioner. It i
almost worth being born poor, to know such joy. To stan
before a counter and grandly order and select six assorte
fancy cakes, six cream buns and a very special chocolate one
with four cherries on it, for Mam alone.

It was Monday morning, black Monday for her, for this wa
wash day. She had five kids now and was in the puddin' clu
again. No more quarrels or fights on that issue. She was i
the puddin' club, fair and square. You had seen a man and
woman up the dark lanes. Ernie had been right and I ha
fought for nothing.

But she was *my* Mam, my own, very special one and between us there was that love that sometimes exists between a boy and his mother. She gave me no quarter if I was bold. She never favoured me above the others. But I knew, and she knew, that it was special between us and would always be.

I can still see the small kitchen, heaped with dirty clothes, the black metal kettle on the fire, all the jets on the gas stove going, each with a pot full of water on it, and she bending down over the wooden wash board, sweat streaming down her face, brown hair stuck to her forehead. And me, coming in like a sunburst, carefully placing my treasures on the table, thirteen cakes, six on one plate, six on another and her special cake on a nice plate with a willow pattern. And eight shillings beside them!

'God Almighty, child,' she said. 'What are you doing home? Did you rob a bank?'

'I won the exam, Mam! I came first in Irish and English and singing . . . I won the singing easy . . .' the words tumbling out.

'The singing doesn't surprise me, Lar. You've a lovely voice. But I didn't think you were *that* good at school. You don't study much at home. Anyway . . .'

She wiped the sweat off her forehead with a towel and combed her thick, lovely brown hair in the mirror over the mantlepiece.

'That Mr Ahearne must be a grand master, Lar. I hope you appreciate him and never give him any trouble.'

I could have told her that I did, plenty. More than any other boy in the class, but I kept my mouth shut. Learning came easy to me in the early years and I had loads of time to make trouble. For myself and for others.

'Chuck in the washing for now, Mam, an' we'll have a feast. I'll make a lovely cup of tea.'

The last baby was asleep in the pram. Rory, two and a half, was playing next door and the two others were at school. I had her all to myself. I gave her seven bob and kept a shilling for myself. Her eyes filled up.

'There, child,' she said and gave me a clumsy hug, on account of her stomach being so big, and a rough kiss.

'Make the tea . . . this is a Godsend on a Monday morning.' So Mam and I had our feast, a leisurely half hour gorge. She must have had one of her longings for sweet stuff, for she mentioned nothing about saving some. We just tucked in until we were bursting, six cakes each and her special one kept for four o'clock tea.

By that time, I had gone up to the South Circular Road to collect Colin, my friend, who also had a day off. He was a gentle boy, with none of the tiger in him that was in me. Smart, too, for I had only beaten him in the singing. We shared a love of reading, writing, poetry and fields and rivers. We could get lost for hours at a time in the green fields over Dolphins Barn bridge. Sometimes, we would take a couple of slices of bread with us and walk all the way up to the seventh lock, the ultimate journey, ending in deep countryside and the never ending spell of the quiet, clear water of the Grand Canal. In short, we were a couple of dreamers, inoffensive boys, who found pleasure in each other's company.

Being from the South Circular Road, his parents frowned on his association with anything from the Barn direction so although we never mentioned it, we always met away from his house and split when we got back near it.

On this magical day, being off school early and loaded with money, we filled our pockets with sweets in Miss Pringle's shop. Bars of chocolate, sweets and I bought as well a cigarette and a match for a penny.

Colin, who had kept all his ten bob, bought a kingly packet of Goldflake, loaded up with sweets and away we went. We were over Dolphins Barn bridge and passing the dark lanes in ten minutes, already in unspoilt countryside. Two miles up the Crumlin Road lay Crumlin village, a place we took care to avoid, for there were a few County Dublin tykes, who lived there and who picked on stray travellers and Colin and myself were both small. And he could not fight very well.

So, we always went up Windmill Lane, which almost missed the village entirely. There was an estate just outside with high stone walls and there lay all the treasures of the countryside. There were blackberry bushes that covered the ground and were easy to get at, beech mast in season and close to the old mansion, walnut trees, that carried a heavy load in autumn. If you were daring enough, you snaked through the grass on your belly and in the shadow of the house got as many as you could in a hurry.

Behind the mansion was a long reed fringed lake, more like a crooked canal than anything else and sometimes we fished there, furtively, for it was alive with perch and rudd. Sitting quietly, watching our split corkfloats, we saw a great deal of wild life. Brown water rats, squirrels, swans, water-hens, bald coots, crows, magpies – all the birds that lived in Ireland were here, even a couple of dazzling kingfishers, that lived on the pinkeens and minnow.

We were both mad about nature and it was around the green fields of Crumlin, so near the slums, that we came by considerable knowledge of the wild life of our land. There were plenty of foxes, badgers and hedgehogs about, though these were rarely seen alive. The Crumlin Road had lately been tarmacadammed, to facilitate the evil-smelling motor car and to provide some work for the hungry. The roads the British left behind had no equal in Europe, with perhaps the exception of Poland, being for the most part mud tracks and now a native government was trying to bring Ireland into the twentieth century via tarmacadammed roads and the Gaelic language . . . a quare mixture. But the slaughter had begun. Animals, like the badger and the hedgehog, shortsighted creatures of the night, easily dazzled by the headlights of a car, were increasingly found lying still at the sides of the road.

Foxes shot in summer with pelts of no value, were hung on barbed wire fences. There was little we did not know, at first hand, about the country, an astonishing accomplishment for city kids. But then we came from a city like no other. I have never since come across any metropolis, where the evil-smelling slums terminated in the fragrant countryside. The thin, red-bricked line, that was the South Circular Road had confronted the slums and contained them for fifty years, their back gardens running right down to the Grand Canal. And the canal, like the English Channel, had repelled all invaders for a century.

Poor though I was, I was growing up in an extraordinary environment. No wonder this area was so rich in 'characters', not all of them savoury.

'Mad Alick', the tramp, roamed hereabouts. There was something about him and little boys that parents hinted at, but whatever it was, it was all the more terrifying because it remained unspecified. No boy ever went near him, even when he coaxed and held out an apple. What Mad Alick could do to boys remained a mystery to me for a while. When I finally found out, I suffered the same shock as Ernie Mountain had given me, but was too wise to fight over it. It was possible, so if it was possible, I supposed some dirty bugger would do it. My education was proceeding rapidly.

'Kit Watts' was another tramp, a rather heroic figure, with his wild head of red, curling hair and red beard. Sometimes, he marched down Dolphins Barn Street dressed only in a singlet, trousers and split canvas shoes, an iron bar over his shoulder and the women, who envied his glorious mop of hair, scattered before him like a gaggle of squawking geese. He was, of course, quite mad and killed himself in his prime, by staunching a cut knee with red lead he had found on the city dump.

Mad Aleck and Kit Watts, unlike the legion of other characters, lived in and off the fields and were not often found in the streets.

On this magical day, we had seen neither and about six o'clock, bloated with sweets and blackberries, and each puffing a Goldflake, we took a chance and came back through Crumlin village. It was a bit shorter than going by Windmill Lane and that was the one mistake of our day. Hurrying through the village, for we had suddenly a sense of disaster, a shower of stones, dancing on the road around us, announced the presence of the village gang. They had never numbered many and, today, there were only five of them. Being such a small gang, they relied on ambush and a quick get-away, for when the Barn bowsies swaggered through they kept out of the way. Any one of them who got caught were due for a 'lurrying up' they did not forget. And now, here was their chance.

Two city kids and small ones, at that. Running, we were quickly brought to a halt. Three of them appeared in front of us, all big ones and when we turned and ran for Windmill Lane, two more were there to cut us off. Both Colin and myself had sticks for slashing weeds and now I made my decision. Two were less odds than three.

'C'mon, Col',' I yelled and charged at the two big tykes, trying to get around them. They were twice our size and stood there, confidently grinning. We could not get past and came to a halt, panting. The others were rapidly closing the gap behind us . . .

'Got yez,' said the biggest one, who sported a mouthful of black, rotten teeth. The other one grinned. He had good teeth but too many of them. His mouth bulged with them, a buck-toothed bastard with an ill streak in him.

'Why are yez runnin' away,' he grinned, 'sure we're not mindin' yez.'

'They must have done something,' said his mate.

And now it was time to play my trick. Colin knew it and was ready.

'But we didn't, did we?' I said to someone supposed to be behind him. The two eejits whipped around and in a split second we were past. Rotten teeth managed to grab Colin by the jersey and swung out of him, but I smashed my stick across the back of his head with such force that I split his skull and the blood spurted down his neck. Squealing with fright, Colin got by and then the second one was on me. I had no room to swing the stick and jammed the jagged edge, torn from a hedge, in his face. He screamed as his face opened up and then I was free, running like a hare, passing Colin easily.

'Janey,' panted Colin, 'Thanks . . . but that was a terrible belt you gave him.'

'Nothin' teh what I gev' the other bastard,' I replied speaking gurrier style, the way my father hated. 'I split his face open . . . the buck-toothed one. He'll get about seven stitches in it.'

'Will he?' said Colin and I could see he was shocked.

But then he came from the South Circular Road. There was only about four hundred yards between our two homes, but they might as well have been four hundred miles. He did not have to run the gauntlet of the Barn bowsies. The square was a separate little entity of its own, very respectable with hard working people and the slum birds, as we called them, hated us. I knew Colin was shocked at the ferocity of my defence and my apparent disregard of the consequences, but then Colin was not often attacked. I was. And Colin had known nothing of the central city struggle between the Black and Tans and the Sinn Feiners . . . would never know what it was like to lie, at two years of age, in a blanket in a wet basement with the bullets screaming and whining through the house.

And the rats doing a rallentando on the bed. He had not lived with terror and did not know, as I did, that there is nothing crueller on this earth than panic.

He could not be expected to know that it was not savagery that made me strike so hard, but panic, sheer animal panic that sparked me off and turned me into a cornered rat. A dangerous little beast. And he was not permitted to see that was quaking inside.

Already, in my imagination, policemen all over Ireland were searching for me. One of the boys had died from the blow I gave him . . . the other, Scarface, marked for life and in the nightmare that was taking place in my mind, I ran faster and faster. Glencree, that terrible, granite built institution with granite built priests to match, was waiting for me with all its attendant pain. Flogged bloody and stood in a barrel of brine to heal my wounds . . . Oh my Jesus . . . faster and faster until I heard Colin's footsteps no more.

At length, gasping, I came to a halt and threw myself down on the bank. When I looked back, there was Colin, cool as a cucumber, strolling along with his gob full of sweets, puffing on a Goldflake. He was a terrible smoker, really hooked before he was fourteen, whereas I only smoked for bravado.

'You're a gas man,' he said when he finally caught up. 'After bursting two Crumlin villagers, an' you'd think, to see you running that you were afraid of your own shadow.'

Grinning, I brazened it out.

'Just thought they might have sent a copper after us, that's all.'

'Why should a copper bother? They started it, didn't they?' Cool and logical, our Colin.

'Thought maybe one of their oul' fellas might follow us on a bike.'

'Janey,' said Colin startled, looking over his shoulder, 'I never thought of that.'

And sure enough, one of their oul' fellas *was* coming along, at speed.

'C'mon Col,' I screamed, as the man threw his bike into the ditch and, face suffused with fury, made for us unbuckling a brass studded belt as he ran. A two inch belt with a huge brass buckle.

Through the small opening in the hedge the pair of us shot. Your man took a little longer, not much. We had half a field lead over him, but the bastard could run and we were already tired. He was a dogged looking brute, not old, probably with drink on him for I had a vague recollection of seeing a man come out of a pub as we fled. He came at us like a tank. He ran us through hedges, panic stricken and torn with Colin starting to cry and the pair of us just barely ahead of the lethal belt.

Poor Colin had gone completely berserk with fear and was making little sounds, like a rabbit makes when a stoat is after it. My side had a stitch in it, so bad, I thought I was going to die. But I had been through this before and in a flash, as we came to a worked-out old sand pit, I got my second wind and ran free. Not Colin! He was a gonner. Too much smoking and soft South Circular Road living.

At least three times a week the 'square gang' got a chase. It was the highlight of our lives. To wait, with a pile of sods, for some grown up 'jazzers' at the Back of the Pipes, who, all blemmed up, were heading for the Fountain Picture House in James Street for a session of cinema and sex and an exercise in 'grope therapy', belting them around the ears with wet sods of grass and the resulting chase. We never got caught. We were too fast and knew all the bolt holes, but this was a more serious matter. We were lost now and had a ferocious adversary. He would exact terrible retribution for my acts in the village.

Squealing, Colin ran straight into the sand pit, a cul-de-sac with high stony walls. Then, your man with the belt slowed down and grinned. When I saw the teeth my heart dropped. The buck-toothed bastard in the village. This was his father, teeth and all and, as the saying goes, the boy did not lick the likeness off a stone.

The old sand pit was nearly a perfect circle, with a narrow entrance for horse drawn carts, like a small Roman coliseum. Poor Colin, weakly trying to climb the sliding-gravel and stones, the man advancing slowly on him, sure of his prey. Like his son, he was savouring the moment, licking his ivories with anticipation. His freckled face was streaming with sweat and in the late evening, turning cold, the steam rose off him like a horse.

I had no fear of him now. I could run forever and now I dodged around him, effing him, Barn style, trying to get him off Colin, but he was too wily for me. He was mad with rage when I let him have a particularly good mouthful of filth which included a reference to his teeth, but he was not to be deflected. He would have given anything to get *me*, but he was going to get one of us, anyway. He was almost on Colin now and judging the distance nicely, let fly with his belt. Only luck saved my pal. He slipped and fell down the sliding incline and the big brass buckle missed and struck sparks out of a stone. Buck Teeth swung again, this time at the helpless boy on the ground and missed again, for I ran near and hit him fair and square between the two eyes, blinding him, with sand.

Well, that was the end of our day. We got away, it grew dark quickly and some time about nine o'clock we staggered out onto Dark Lane. We had been lost, but we knew where we were now. We split at the top of the Barn, Colin down the

South Circular Road, me down the Back of the Pipes, sneaking home quietly, utterly exhausted. There was no way I could risk Dolphins Barn Street tonight.

There were half a dozen boys, who had felt my fist one time or another, who would be only too glad to find me in my present state. So I tottered down the Backers, too worn out to be afraid of the dark and the terrible things that went on in it.

Wearily I climbed over our back wall, dropped down on Murphy's shed, onto the division wall and into our yard. I pressed the back door latch and went in.

'Christ!' said my father.

'Oh, my Jesus,' said my Mam. 'Where have you been? What in the name of the Holy Father have you been up to!'

I stood there shaking, wanting to boast that I had defeated two big boys today and saved my pal by blinding his pursuer, a thing, if they knew about it, would get me the mother and father of all hidings. Especially from Dad. He simply seemed to be living in another world at times. He did not seem to comprehend that the outside world was a dangerous place, and particularly in the Liberties. And more so for small ones like me!

Whatever I wanted to do, I did not do it. I just stood there sobbing, harder than poor Colin in the sand pit. I was scratched and torn, had dried blood on my face, skin off everywhere and the patch on my trousers hanging off. I was unrecognisable as the boy who had stood at the head of his class that morning.

'Answer your mother, young man,' said my father angrily.

'Leave him alone, Laddie,' said my mother gently. 'He was a good boy this morning. What happened to you, child?'

I tried to tell her some of the events, but I was sobbing too hard and in the end she said:

'All right, Lar. Sit down and I'll make you some tea.' She gave me toast and an egg too, unusual for mid week – the exam money – and afterwards washed the blood off my face and legs. I was asleep on my feet as I stumbled into bed.

The next two or three days are vague. I was very sick. I slept a lot, ate what was given me and slept some more.

By Friday I was up again and went back to school on the Monday, exactly a week from the time of the exam. And here was the funny thing. Colin had not missed a day. After all the running, he was all right the following morning. Not me. And it was always the same. There was some deep delicacy inside me, that came to the surface under stress. I was faster, tougher, more self-reliant than three Colins. I could have beaten him in a fight any day, with one arm kneeling. But in a funny way, he was stronger than me. The day after he came second in the exam, he could have beaten me with his cap without rising a sweat.

So, I returned to school on Monday morning. It was on this day that many of our class felt the first real surge of love for the Gaelic, the tongue of our forefathers.

'Tabhair dūinn, tabhair dūinn teanga na h-Eireann' which translated means 'give to us, give to us, the tongue of Ireland'. However, the sad fact remains that most of the little gets in our class did not give a damn if they never had it. The truth was that most of them hated it and, there again, Colin and I lapped it up and loved to speak it. In this, we were almost alone in a Dublin classroom and both being of Norman descent prided ourselves on being more Irish than the Irish themselves. Stokes and Redmond!

On this day, the Kipper introduced us to a new word in Gaelic. It was Irish language hour, before de Valera introduced the lunacy of teaching English-speaking children all subjects through the medium and turned a couple of generations against our native tongue forever and made them illiterate in two languages. The new word, which we were to incorporate in that day's composition, was the word 'however' – 'áfach' in Gaelic. The Kipper wrote it on the blackboard, then pronounced it.

'Adverb,' said the Kipper, 'however . . . nevertheless . . . all the same. However means all these, but to use it is to be more concise. "However" – pronounced "awfuck".'

He pointedly ignored the sly grin and furtive digs and with a slightly flushed face, he broke class for a break. There was a lot of Irish spoken in our school yard that day and much use of the word 'however'. It was a wonder we had ever communicated successfully before without it.

Awfuck, I mean 'however', the next day's exercise received real application, and I remember Mrs Butler remarking on Bock doing his exercise before going out to play.

'Very studious, that boy . . . all of a sudden,' she told my mother darkly. 'It's a thing I don't like teh see in any boy . . . none of 'is brothers ever showed a streak like that . . . not natcherel . . . Bock!' she screeched into the hall, 'come out here at wanst an' play wit' Lar!'

'Tá mé ag coming', came Bock's voice in bastard Irish, a form much favoured by the class. 'Awfuck nil me finished'. Mrs Butler's eyes opened in disbelief.

'What's that yeh said?' she screamed.

'It's all right,' I reassured her, 'Bock is only speaking Gaelic.'

Her face was flushed with rage and her eyes gleamed.

'He said "awf" . . .'

'Awfuck,' I said deadpan. 'It means "however" in Gaelic!'

'Well,' said Mrs Butler, turning away, 'as if it's not hard enough round here teh bring them up half dacent, without the shaggin' Irish makin' it a bloody sight harder.'

Later I warned Bock about it. 'You'd better watch out, Bock. Next time she'll belt you. She nearly did that time.'

'Awfuck,' said Bock smugly, 'but she didn't.'

At 10.30 the following morning Mr Ahearne finished correcting our exercises. His face was glowing with honest pride.

'A surprisingly good effort, class,' he told us. 'At last we seem to be getting to grips with the language.'

He was mistaken. Between Colin and myself alone we had dictated about ten exercises. The other four stars in Irish had done the same, hence the happy result and the Kipper's temporary residence on cloud lucky seven.

'Deasy,' said the Kipper, 'stand up.' Deasy, the biggest, thickest 'stumer' in class, lurched to his feet.

'Deasy,' said the Kipper kindly, 'you have used the word in your composition and used it correctly, the word "however". Please read out your composition to the class.'

Deasy hardly knew two words in Irish. He hated it. But one word he had come to love. Áfach.

'Do bhi me . . . (Iwas) . . . ag dul abaile . . . (going home) . . . do bhi me . . .' Deasy was starting to stumble. 'Do bhi me . . . ag dul abaile . . .'

'Say it, yeh stupid get,' I whispered. 'Say "go thapaidh" (quickly).'

'Go thapaidh,' said Deasy triumphantly, (he was home now). 'Awfuck . . . do rith me . . . (I ran) . . . awfuck . . .'

'That'll do,' said the Kipper abruptly. 'Sit down.' The class was silent now, watching. The Kipper seemed at a loss, unable to cope with this situation and we were quick to spot it. We would best him, this time. Christ help him, if he lost control of the class. He would be shown no mercy.

'Butler!' shouted the Kipper.

I think the master wanted him to run some errand, but he got no chance to speak. Bock jumped to his feet and began to read his composition. His Gaelic was fluent and rapid and smacked, necessarily, of the Liberties. He would have corrupted the pure speech of the Aran islanders in a couple of weeks. Translated his composition read:

'My mother said it was time to go to school . . . awfuck . . . I did not feel like it . . . awfuck . . . She gave me some medicine . . . awfuck . . .'

'Right,' said the Kipper grimly. 'Out here, Butler. You too, Deasy.'

The rest of us were knotted laughing and trying not to be seen. One boy, Dessy O'Connor in the corner, pissed himself, laughing.

The kipper slowly hefted his cane, then changed his mind and produced 'towser' and gave us his hard smile. We all knew what was coming. A towser march. This was the Kipper's ultimate in punishment and at the same time an expression of his eccentric sense of humour.

'So,' he grinned, 'we are in a jocular mood this morning. Well, we'll see what towser has to say about that.'

In a towser march, the unfortunate victim was led over to the window, the furthest point in the classroom from the door. His wrist was then firmly held, palm outstretched and to the wild whoops of the Kipper, raced across the room, leather slaps raining down at speed on his hand and then raced back again and if the Kipper was feeling fit, another turn or two, the slaps still descending, the Kipper wildly whooping and the outraged roars of the victim.

It was a spectacular exhibition, which to tell the truth hurt nobody very much. No teacher could wield a leather with much force at this speed and I think the Kipper got as many on the back of his own hand as the victim got on the front. But the Kipper pretended and with much success, that a 'towser march' was a frightful thing, a thing to be dreaded.

Now it began with Deasy, roaring like a bull lugged across the room and back, the rest of us on the verge of convulsions from trying not to laugh. Deasy was the heaviest boy in the class. On the second trip he pulled against the master so hard, that the Kipper nearly landed on his arse and for that received another 'towser march'. The Kipper, six feet tall, not a pick on him, jumping across the room, lank, black hair flying . . . whoops, whoops . . . and the roars of the victim.

At this point, the classroom door opened and Gleeson, a cheerful, reckless young school master, Yella' Man's replacement, appeared in the doorway, grinning.

'Towser march on the menu today, Vincent?' he said.

The Kipper sat down on the table. He was easily winded and the nicotine stained fingers told the reaon why.

'Towser is excelling himself today,' he panted. He waved his hand at us.

'We were in the mood for a little frivolity today,' he explained. 'Everything was going splendidly until towser joined in. They don't seem to appreciate his sense of humour, Ned.'

'I wonder why not,' said Gleeson, taking a packet of Goldflake out of his pocket and nodding towards the corridor. The Kipper lowered himself off the table a bit stiffly.

'Open your readers at page thirty seven . . . Clonmacnoise. I'll want to know all about that monastery when I return. Branwell!'

'Yes, sir.'

'Take charge of the class. Report any boy who makes a noise or speaks. I want names. Got that?'

'Yes, sir,' said the snivelling little bastard, taking out his pencil and going up to the rostrum.

'And you,' said the Kipper to Bock, who was still sweating it out, 'I'll deal with you when I come back.'

Clonmacnoise. How solitary now she sits on that great river, that once thronged city. Her streets are silent, her gates are broken, yet in the olden times she was a queen and the children of many lands came to do her homage.

I knew it all. Even today it comes back to me, just like that. Furtively I looked over the top of my reader. The Kipper and Gleeson were strolling in the corridor, smoking and laughing and it came to me, that the Kipper was no older than Gleeson, although he seemed years his senior.

Gleeson wore polonecked pullovers and plus-fours. Gleeson wore oxford bags, trousers with twenty-four inch wide legs, pointed shoes, winkle pickers and jazzy waist-coats. Gleeson also had the unusual distinction, for those days, of being a Dubliner who was also a teacher and he was an unusual teacher as well. He taught his boys to box, prancing on their toes like pugilists. He taught them to dance the charleston and he did it with them. He taught them other things too, for his class was excellent, I knew, and no longer cowed by that unprintable Kerry man. At singing he did not mess around with dirges like *Tabhair dūinn, teanga na h-Eireann*' but taught them *Bye bye blackbird* in Irish and in his class, the Red, red robin went bob, bob, a-bobbing through the desks in Gaelic.

The Kipper was a Wicklow man from around Woodenbridge and was more conservative in dress. A good, old-fashioned tailor made his suits from black broadcloth and the cut had not changed since Grattan's time. He, like the English Mr Quelch, was a genuine throw-back to Victorian times.

When the Kipper came back, he executed a master stroke.

'All exercises back up here again for examination,' he ordered with a grim smile. 'I think I perceive the hand of the few in the work of the many. Proceed with Clonmacnoise. Branwell, sit down.'

'Janey,' whispered Col', who sat with me, 'He's on to us.'

'I know,' I said miserably.

'Devlin!' called the Kipper after a half hour study of the exercises.

'Yes, sir?'

'Devlin, since you've become such an eminent Gaelic scholar perhaps you would be able to explain to me, and I'm sure the class in general would welcome the explanation avid as they are for the old tongue, the meaning of the excellent phrase "tá mo croidhe briste"?* You've used it, and correctly, in your composition. No doubt you will remember?'

Devlin, another thick, stood there, head hanging. As for the Kipper, his face was glowing. He was having the time of his life and we guessed, correctly, that he had figured a way to pay us back.

'Well, Devlin,' said the Kipper delighted, 'we seem to have forgotten our hard-won knowledge, have we not? Sit down, you amadawn. Now, I'm sure,' he said thoughtfully, tapping his teeth with a pencil, 'that Butler or Stokes . . . or our own erudite Lar Redmond, all of Norman stock incidentally, would be able to answer this question. Stokes! Stand up. What does the phrase mean?'

And he had poor Col' by the big brown ones. If he said he did not know, he would be punished for being stupid. If he *did* know, he stood accused of helping Devlin.

'It means,' said Colin in a whisper, 'my heart is broken.'

'Speak up,' roared the Kipper jovially. He was having a ball. He was asserting his superior intelligence over a turbulent Liberties class and his heart rejoiced.

'My heart is broken,' said Colin loudly.

'It will be . . . it will be . . . presently,' agreed the Kipper amiably. 'Stand over against the wall.'

So, Colin was first in line. I joined him next. Montaigne next. Fitzsimonds, Butler and Lacy followed. Quite remarkable. All Norman names. He had found us all. Smiling, the Kipper paced slowly up and down his rostrum before the

* my heart is broken

blackboard. Occasionally he rubbed his blue-black chin, for he had a heavy growth, and grinned. We were only too aware of his eccentric sense of humour and justice and feared the worst. Never had he displayed these qualities to better advantage than today.

'So,' he said at last, 'we have discovered the revolutionaries in the cellar, the Norman intelligentsia. . . . the minds that move the masses . . . We must now mete out justice, tempered with mercy. No doubt,' he added kindly, 'you lads will appreciate this. You may all go to your desks and sit down.'

Dumbly we sat down. What the hell was he playing at? The Kipper was openly grinning, rubbing away at his five o'clock shadow. There was not a sound from the class.

Then the Kipper faced us.

'The rest of you, except Deasy, come out here. Line up against the wall.' He unhooked the long cane from the blackboard and hefted it a couple of times.

'There'll be wigs on the Green,' he said, 'skin and hair flying . . . You are all,' he added chattily, 'being punished for copying your exercises from those six. I saw their trade mark all over the place. So you know who you have to thank. Devlin, hold out your hand!'

They got four strokes each, all except Branwell, who was too smart to have to copy off us. The Kipper took him out of line. Last hope gone. No ray of comfort left. The whinging boys came back, wringing their stinging hands under their armpits, vowing venegance on us, sibilant whispers as to what would happen to us when school was over.

Colin was terrified. So was I, but I would not let on. Colin did not answer the threats. I did and defied them all. I had about eight fights lined up, all from bigger boys, who wanted to beat my brains in. Butler was in the same boat. He would not back down either.

As three o'clock drew near, us six decided to make a concerted break for it after school. We decided to stick together, our only chance. Directly opposite the school, there was a hundred yard break in the red-brick facade of the South Circular Road and behind it a twenty or thirty acre field of cabbage, what was bounded on one side by the Grand Canal, on the other by Rialto buildings and on the last side by a branch of the Poddle, called the 'Slang' and over that wall was home for me.

When the bell went, we made a break for it and together were over the gate just in front of the pack. There were plenty of stones on our side and we belted our would-be attackers with glee, until they had accumulated enough to launch an attack, and then we made off.

We had won. We had defeated the mob and the teacher both and we were sweet.

But the Kipper, God bless him, thought otherwise and had the last word. First thing next morning, we six were lined up before the grinning class.

> Charge: Stone throwing.
> Defence: The others were throwing stones too.
> Verdict: Stones do not grow on tram tracks.
> Punishment: Six hard, each, with the cane.

So, in his own inimitable way, Mr Ahearne, alias the Kipper had bested us and retained our respect. We returned to our desks with smarting hands and with considerably more respect for the Kipper. It would be a long time before we tried to out-smart him again.

'Now,' said he, in the height of good form, 'take out your catechisms and we will see how far you are progressing towards becoming Catholics. Mark you,' he emphasised, grinning, 'I did not say Christians. Towser and the cane seem to be the only things respected here. You have less than three weeks to go before you make your confirmation. You have been studying, or not studying your catechism for two weeks now. I fear, that there will be more work for towser this morning . . . Wigs on the Green, skin and hair flying, towser marches galore. Deasy, stand up.'

Deasy stood up.

'Now,' said the Kipper, 'recite the Ten Commandments.'

The Kipper *was* right. There were wigs on the Green and the rest of it before we went home that day with a new and quickly learnt knowledge of religion.

8 Holy Confirmation

And so, the long awaited day of my confirmation was here at last. Today I would reaffirm my allegiance to the Catholic Church and be confirmed in that allegiance for life. Somehow, money had been found for a new suit, tie, shirt, cap and shoes – and of course my confirmation medal. It looked large and shining with its silk ribbon, pinned over my heart. Some of the boys had smaller medals, the South Circular Road gang for instance, and I soon learnt that these were pure silver. But I did not care. I thought mine looked better.

Going to work, my father put two pence in my hand and gave me a love. I squeezed him back. He felt different from Mam, hard and tough not soft and feminine, but all the same it was nice to be held by him. As the Granny would say, what was seldom was wonderful. My father at this time, scarcely existed in our lives. He was merely a grey or occasionally angry presence, overworked, never seen between seven-thirty in the morning and six at night. A tired workhorse, who went out and made money with great effort.

My mother, with her built-in will to survive, shrewd and thrifty, kept her squad comparatively well fed, where a slut's children went short. And no matter how it was done, we made our confirmation dressed as well as the best. We were blessed with good parents, but only too often it was the angry father I was to know.

We never seemed to communicate, except when I was in trouble. He was too tired. He was a quiet, small, well-knit man, strong-willed more than strong, battling to rear a family already too large for his slim wage packet, harried by broken employment. Jesus, the times I'd seen him come home paid off, and my mother's frightened face, and he off the following morning to search a hungry city for another job.

I remember him cycling from the Barn to Stillorgan and Dollymount in mid-winter, starting out with hope in the rain, to sit all day, soaked in a cold hut until it got too late to start. And then to cycle back in the rain and not one ha'penny earned that day. The good old days!

Nevertheless, he and I did not hit it off too well. It seemed to me that he was partisan in his judgements and that, in any dispute with my brothers or sisters, I came off second best every time. But then, I had always resented him and, I suspect, he me.

It went back a long way. When I was little, I became accustomed to living with my mother alone, he being either in jail or on the run from the forces of the Crown. I would wake up in the morning with Mam beside me and I would snuggle into her and nuzzle her, like the little animal I was. I can still remember the absolute protection and love she gave me and, of course, having her completely to myself.

My brother practically lived next door with Mrs O'Hara, she had taken him over and my mother resented this. But there was little she could do about it, for his temporary adoption left more on the table for us two and that, God knows, was little enough. I would wake up, sure in the knowledge that she was there and roll over sleepily into her arms.

Then one morning I woke to find her back turned to me and a man in the bed. There was a lot of whispering and giggling going on, Mam happier than I had ever known her and this bloody fella making very free, tickling her and kissing her and worst of all, she lapping it up, as if he could never kiss her enough.

I was seething with jealousy in an instant and peevishly gave her a thump on the back. She turned around, kissed me absentmindedly and turned back to the man. She had scarcely seen me! From that moment stemmed the resentment I bore my father. It took many a long year to figure this out, but that was it. I hated him at first and showed it! I would not accept him. I would not go to him. I would not kiss him and he resented that!

As the morning dragged on, my resentment grew worse. Somehow, with his coming, rashers and eggs had come too, both on the same plate.

Such gluttony I had never enjoyed before, but even this did not appease my wrath. Him kissing the back of her neck when she was cooking at the gas stove, and she loving him back!

However, as the morning drew on Mam became very quiet and suddenly turned fretful and weepy. Around mid-day, she made a silent sortie down the wide, carpetless Georgian stairs to the front door to see that all was clear. Dad was on the run. His Majesty's troops were looking for him. She came back then, openly crying.

'You'll take care, won't you Laddie!' she pleaded and clung to him desperately.

'There, there, Doll. The Boys will keep you informed. I'll be all right.' And then, kissing her hard, he was gone. Leaving me with a half demented mother, who seemed to love me no more.

I did not fully understand what was going on, but I was glad he had gone. And I sincerely hoped that he would not come back. But he did!

One morning after the truce with the British he came home and walked into another guerrilla war with me and no truce for many a year.

But on this, the morning of my confirmation I realised for the first time that I really loved him. Had he been more outgoing with his sons and treated them as children, not as men, things would have been better all round. But he suffered from a hang-up of Victorian times, when the father was a figure triple bound with brass and boys were reared in the fierce British tradition of the stiff upper lip. So all his affection – and he had plenty – was given to my mother and her daughters and alienated at least one son.

Another thing that contributed to our mutual animosity, was the fact that he had insisted on me being circumcised.

Mam was reluctant and her ignorant neighbours had never even heard of it. But dad won. My brother had had the operation no bother and so would I. About the actual operation I remember nothing. I suppose they gave me a whiff of gas, but I remember plenty afterwards. For the doctor had used a dirty scalpel which infected me with blood poisoning, so that I became full of running sores all over my skinny little body.

The treatment for this was to sit in a bath of hot water with plenty of Jeyes fluid in it, your arse covered with scabs, the pain intense. Often my mother was not strong enough to force me into it and dad had to do it. Sobbing, resisting, beaten into submission, for my own good. Any way they could do it, it was done. This act of circumcision kept me out of school for over a year. It was the reason for my being eighteen months older than Colin, the season for my unstable health.

One further piece of resentment to nurture. The boys, when we were pissing for height in the school lavatory, a favourite occupation of every normal boy, spotted my unusual penis and started calling me 'Mushroom Mickey'.

I had a long and well exercised string of resentments against my father, but this morning I loved him. I stood at the door of our little home and watched him cycle off to work, me in my best regalia, he, with neat patches on the seat of his trousers, to slog his guts out for another day.

It was the first twinge of conscience I felt towards him, a sign of my early and expected maturity. You got your Primary Certificate at thirteen or fourteen years of age and you went to work, not overburdened with knowledge. At sixteen, you were in your second year of your apprenticeship and handing over every week to your mother. You were expected to be a man before you had ceased to be a child.

The confirmation passed off as expected. Three boys were sent home for having no shoes or confirmation medal.

All of them came from crumbling tenements and were an embarrassment to the school. Soon after this, all three quietly disappeared from class and were not seen again. It was generally supposed they had gone to Artane industrial school where the gentle Christian Brothers would make them regret they had been born poor.

But we did not allow anything to spoil our day. The ritual of being confirmed in the Faith mattered nothing. It was the new clothes and shoes and getting money from all and sundry that mattered. It was the custom. Shopkeepers, where your mother dealt gave you a couple of coppers. The neighbours coughed up, even old Baldy McKay knocked on his window and gave me a sixpence, God love him.

In the afternoon I was allowed to go to Auntie Nelly's and the Granny's. I carried a note, which I was not to read and on account of the day that was in it, I did not. I was to give it to Granny and no one else. Nobody was ever to know about this! Mam was very earnest as she instructed me and seemed a little desperate. Above all, my father was never to know!

I promised all this with a light heart and off I went, bound for Clanbrassil Street and the heart of the Liberties. Going across the square, all the girls surrounded me, ooohing and ahhing with feigned admiration. I tried to get away, but I could not break free without hurting one of them. The girls were off school too, some of them had also made their confirmation. They were all dressed in their Sunday best and the square girls had been joined by a dozen girls from Rialto buildings. Colourful and gay in their printed cotton dresses, like so many tropical parrots, they filled the air with their chatter and singing, hands joined, dancing around me.

'She is handsome, she is pretty
She is the girl from Belfast city
Ethel Miley sez she'll die
If she doesn't get the fella
With the marble eye . . .'

Then, still dancing around me . . .

'Stands a lady on a mountain
Who she is I don't know
All she wants is gold and silver
And a nice young man you know . . .

'Who shall love her?
Who shall love her?
Who shall love her . . . farewell
What'll yeh take love . . .
What'll yeh take love . . .
What'll yeh take love . . . farewell'

The women, all out at the doors wistfully laughing, the girls getting it up for me.

'Go on, Molly, give him a kiss, yeh know yeh love him!' pushing poor blushing Molly at me. Then Fanny Gibbons planted a kiss on my cheek amid roars and cheers. Ethel Dowling followed suit, more cheers and jeers and then Phyllis, the little Protestant girl, who had red hair and delightful tiny freckles on her nose, stepped up to me, smiling, and softly kissed me. Not like the others, wet smacks, but a real soft kiss, which I returned. I forgot all about the crowd, for I was mad about her. And then the screams and cheers, the women calling my mother from their doorways. 'Ye'll have to watch that Lar, they're starting young now!' and the whole square full of laughter on that God given day, that was to haunt me down the years. Innocence!

In the end I broke free and ran for it. 'That's a boyo, that Lar 'ill be one for the mots!' The cries followed me as I ran, but one thing was true anyway. I *was* one for the mots, then and always. I loved girls. I loved their soft skin and pretty legs, their lovely long hair and most of all, their soft lips, made for kissing. In the dark autumn nights, before the cold drove us in, we sat on window sills and most times I was kissing one of the girls. Kathleen and Phyllis I liked best and kissed the most.

I was backward by day, but like the cat in the dairy I was shy, but willing and bolder by night. Now the girls' singing followed me as I fled.

'Halloway sez she'll die
If she doesn't get Larry
with the marble eye . . .'

I took the short cut, running fast down Cork Street to avoid ambush from the Cork Street gang, hated and implacable enemies, up Donore Avenue and down one of the double storied red-brick terraces, which ended at a wire fence. Over this, the first of Dublin Corporation's many schemes for relieving the tenement congestion was under way and, at last, the fields known as the 'Tenters', where the tradesmen used to spread their hides and canvasses to dry long ago, was being built over. It is now called Fairbrothers Fields.

I ran through the half-built houses all the way to Ducker's Lane and so into Clanbrassil Street. But once there, I changed course and went to Auntie Nelly's first. I hated going over to Granny's. I disliked her coarse ways. Also, she had only too many grandchildren and had long ago ceased to give anything for Holy Communions or confirmations. She would hardly give you a kind look.

Auntie Nelly admired me, told me how grateful I should be to have such a good mammy and daddy and found three pence for me. She also gave me a kiss and having been told by me that I had a message to deliver told me not to waste any more time. So, over to Granny's I had to go. Granny greeted me shortly. She was long ago fed up with her family and only wanted to be left alone to go up to the pub and meet her cronies.

'What de yeh want?' she said. I handed her the note.

'Yeh look nice,' she said briefly and read it.

'Hmmmmm,' she mumbled under her breath, looking hard at my new suit. 'She'd be better off puttin' it in her belly . . .' She found a stub of pencil and scrawled another note.

'Take this over teh Missus Byrne, yeh know where she lives.'

I shook my head. I *did* know, but I did not want to go.

'Ye've been there before,' said the Granny. 'Don't tell lies on yer confirmation day!'

She was a thin woman, quite tall for a Dubliner, with hard, good, indestructible features. I had been told that she was a beauty in her day. Maybe, but with her steel grey hair pulled back in a tight bun and her narrowed, suspicious eyes, she was no beauty now. Though when she smiled, one could see something of the woman she had once been. Life in the Liberties had removed all gentleness from her. I caught the smell of whiskey off her as she passed me to the window. She stood beside it and beckoned me over.

'C'mere, you,' she said.

I went over. She pointed to a house a few doors down, on the opposite side. It had a blue door with a shining brass knocker.

'The blue door,' she said. 'Off yeh go . . . an' straight home to yer mother . . . you have to be home before five a'clock, mind. Don't delay.'

'Yes, Granny,' I said and went, glad to be out of her sight. I went across the road and knocked on the blue door. I knocked carefully and just as carefully Nuala Doyle opened it. She was a pale-faced girl of thirteen, who had lost her mother to galloping consumption the year before. By the look of her, she would be going the same road herself soon. Solemn beyond her years, she was not the usual type of slum child – witty, brazen and scornful. She was always silent, surrounded by an aura of doom, or so it seemed to my overfertile imagination. She seemed like a tortured and hunted thing, but then, how could one know anything about her? She never said anything.

The leecher Byrne I hated instinctively. She employed Nuala after school and she worked like a slave for a feed and a penny. 'Get this . . . do that . . . shut the door . . . go to the press . . ..' The leecher Byrne was a fat, tallow-coloured slug, a moneylender crippled by arthritis, who had turned vicious and battened, like some foul parasite, on the poverty stricken people around her.

Things happened to people who tried to diddle her. They got beaten up, rooms went on fire, things like that. She had her racket well organised. She sat now in her comfortable armchair, hands folded, opaque light-blue eyes, like a three-day-old Dublin Bay cod, sizing me up. Presently, she read the note, sniffed disparagingly and made her decision.

'Get the drawer over,' she told Nuala. Nuala obeyed. My

eyes bulged. Never in my life had I seen so much money. Once, the Kipper had sent me to the bank on some errand and I had seen the teller counting heaps of money so I knew that the stuff existed somewhere. I had read of King Midas and I even knew about Fort Knox, but I had never before been so close to so much.

'Filthy lucre' the Greyfriars chaps contemptuously called it, but this was the Liberties; nobody around here had a 'pater' who casually gave you a pound. They had an 'oul' fella' who gave them a thick ear and sometimes a penny. Poor Nuala got more thick ears than pennies. I had heard Auntie Nelly, who lived a few doors from Nuala, talking about her drunken father. 'Yeh know, Dolly,' she had said to my mother. 'Them childer should be in a home. I don't think they ever get a good feed an' that oul' Meddler is mad.' Mam had burst out laughing. 'Jesus, Nelly, don't call him that! Call him Mister Doyle!' 'Well,' said gentle Auntie Nelly, giving her infectious giggle, 'that's what he's called. I didn't christen him.'

I had soon found out why they had called him the 'meddler'. Like most soldiers, who had come through the sustained lunacy of Flanders, he was half mad. Unscarred by bullet or bomb, his mind had been maimed by fear beyond repair. His dole money, his small English pension for shell shock went on drink. Every Friday morning he shuffled back from the Labour Exchange, his few shillings already invested in cheap wine. No sign of the soldier remained about him. His shoulders sagged and his boots scuffled the pavement, the very picture of a broken man.

By Friday evening, drinking all alone at home, the Meddler was *all* mad. He drank anything he could lay his hands on. Methylated spirits and wine was his favourite tipple I was told. It was this rocket fuel, that sent him into orbit. It was then he would appear at the front door, naked as the day he was born and, swinging out of the cross bar below the fanlight, would invite all and sundry to 'look at me medals'. Women screeching and fleeing in all directions, the kids jeering and pointing and laughing until they were belted indoors, the Meddler was left in possession of the street, his testicles swinging to and fro as he swung from the cross bar.

I only saw the performance once and thought it very funny. I also thought that the Meddler, in the parlance of the Liberties, 'was very well hung'. My cousin Paddy, Auntie Nelly's eldest son, endorsed my opinion by informing me that 'his bollix is an unmerciful size'. In general, it was widely accepted that the Meddler had not been behind the door when they were dishing out the 'nackers'.

And this was the father of poor Nuala, who stood so quietly before me. The leecher Byrne shifted her enormous arse and daintily pawed over the money. She folded up a pound note, put it in a piece of newspaper and rolled it into a ball.

'Give this to yer ma,' she told me, 'and don't loose it.'

'No,' I said and made for the hall.

'Come back here,' she shouted, 'yeh unmannerly get, an' say thanks. Have yeh no manners!'

I came back into the room. 'No,' I said, 'none for you!' I would be in trouble over this, but I did not care. It would go back, and swiftly, to my mother but I was completely reckless as always, when I lost my temper. I hated this leech. I would never be sent here again, that was for sure. It was what I wanted. I had heard too many whispered conversations about this woman to have any illusions about her or to pay her any respect. She was a vicious old bitch of a moneylender. My mother was short of money, because I had it on my back and so she had to lower herself to go to this vulture for a loan at scandalous interest. I knew this a long time. As I have said, children of a revolution grow up fast. So do children of poverty. I was a child of both.

Since I was going to be in trouble, I decided I might as well be hung for a sheep as a lamb. I had no pity for this crippled woman, stuck in a chair for life because of arthritis. I was only glad she could not get up and beat the hell out of me. I realised suddenly, like it or not, that there was a lot of the old Granny in me too.

'Say thank you,' she screamed.

'No,' I said as impudently as possible. 'Fat arse.'

That's done it, I thought with satisfaction. She had turned purple at the insult.

'Gimme back the money!' she screamed, 'yeh little bastard.' I was frightened, but I managed to brazen it out and grinned in her face.

'I haven't got it, I threw it in the fire!' I was lying of course and enjoying every second.

'Yeh didn't, yeh lyin' little bastard! Did he, Nuala?'

'I didn't see him if he did,' whispered the girl.

'Where is it?' panted Mrs Byrne. She was going black in the face. I thought she was going to have a stroke. If that was the case, I would help her!

'Up the fat woman's arse in Moore Street,' I said deliberately. She rolled the eyes towards heaven and fell back into the chair.

'The whiskey, Nuala,' she whispered. 'The Jameson . . . top drawer . . .'

She took a long swig and fell back again, panting.

'Oh, that filthy-tongued little fucker. Is he gone yet?'

'No, Missus Byrne, he's still here.'

'Get the police, child, have him arrested,' she said faintly. It was all an act and I knew it.

'I'm going, don't worry,' I said loudly and walked boldly out of the house. To tell the truth, I was frightened. The remark about the police had terrified me and I ran back through the Tenters building site like a deer. What I was going to tell Mam I had not figured out yet. But one thing I did know. I was not handing over the pound. Not today, not any day. Not this time. I had money of my own. I had thirteen and six and Mam could have ten shillings of that. Dad got paid tomorrow. I loved my mother more than anyone in the whole world and instinctively I felt the comedown it was to her, to have to send her son behind her husband's back to a money lender on his confirmation day. Maybe she would not be too hard on me, when she learnt of the language I had used to Byrne. She was waiting at the door for me.

'Well, Lar?' she said anxiously.

'No, Mam,' I lied. 'She wouldn't give it to me.'

Her face blanched.

'Jesus, Mary and Joseph,' she whispered, 'an' me with

nothing for your poor father's dinner. The bloody oul' bitch! Why?'

'Don't bother with her, Mam,' I said grandly. 'I've plenty of money. Here's ten bob . . . Is that enough?' I showed her all the money I had and she agreed to borrow ten bob from me. We both knew I would never get it back, but it saved us from being embarrassed. And it got me a kiss and a hug.

'You're a good boy, sometimes the best of the lot, when yeh like. Now, run up to the butcher's an' get me a half pound of the best surloin steak . . . Hurry!' Dad would dine royally tonight.

The following day was an ordinary school day and with much relief I went. Mam had been lovely to me that morning, giving me a special kiss and a love, squeezing me hard, but I was wondering how long she would feel this way. Especially if she was told – and I was sure she would be – where I had told the money lender to look for the money. 'Up the fat woman's arse in Moore Street' did not sound so funny now.

Calling the leecher 'fat arse' compounded the crime. It was only a matter of waiting for the blow to fall. I was quite sick with worry until I remembered that Dad would never know about this. There would be no leather strap around the legs tonight. She would not dare tell him of my remark to the moneylender. He would go stark staring mad, if he knew his wife had been driven to one like her.

The miracle of providing for a family of eight on the small money he gave her, he left to her. He gave all he had, but it was not enough. He was always saying, that Mam could make a penny go further than anyone else and that was right. But there was a limit to what she could do and first communions and confirmations strained her slender resources beyond the limit. On these desperate occasions she would resort to the moneylender or the pawnshop at the top of Clanbrassil Street, well away from the Barn, where no one would know.

At four o'clock that afternoon, Nuala Doyle knocked on our door. It had not taken the leecher long to find out where we lived and here was the heavy hand of retribution.

'Mammy,' said Mag, my little sister, 'there's a girl at the front door, who wants to see you. She has a note for you.'

Mam glanced up sharply, went to the front door and brought Nuala into our front parlour. In a couple of minutes the summons came for me. I went in and joined them. Mam looked shocked while Nuala, white faced and silent, sat on the sofa.

'Is this true,' said Mam angrily, 'what I see in this note?'

'I don't know . . . I haven't read it.'

'What,' she snapped, 'Yeh cheeky get . . . Did you rob a pound off Missus Byrne?'

'No, Mam.'

'Well, where is it? What have you done with it?' I took the rolled-up newspaper out of my pocket, found the quid and handed it over.

'I told you he had it, Missus Redmond,' said Nuala faintly. My mother glanced sharply at her.

'Are you all right, child?' she said softly, lowering her voice.

'Yes, Missus Redmond. It's just that I feel a bit dizzy.'

'Get her a glass of water, Lar,' commanded my mother. I went to the kitchen and got the water, grateful for any respite. Mam held the glass to the trembling girl's lips while she drank, watching her face through narrowed eyes. I could not fathom her expression. It seemed to me that it was one of horror, unbelieving horror. She had a habit of which she was quite unaware of squinting intently, when she wanted to size someone up. Abruptly she turned to me.

'Now,' she said, 'why did you keep the pound, an' you better have a good excuse. Did you think you could keep the pound an' palm me off with ten bob?' She shook her head. 'No,' she said to herself, 'he wouldn't do a thing like that'. 'Why did you do it?' she said on a softer note.

I hung my head. I did not want to discuss this in front of Nuala Doyle.

'Give her the pound, Mam, and send her back to the oul' bi . . .'

'That will do,' she said sharply.

She went to the sideboard, found an envelope and put the

pound note inside. I noticed that she wrote no note of apology.

'Give this to "that one",' she said to Nuala briefly, 'an' tell her from me, that's the last.'

Nuala nodded dumbly and got shakily to her feet.

'Yes, Missus Redmond,' she said at last. Her voice was barely audible. She started towards the door. Mam caught her arm.

'Are you all right, child?' she said anxiously.

I knew the sight of this wan motherless child tore at her heartstrings, that if she could she would have taken her under our roof. I could see that she was not far off crying. She had a streak of the Granny in her alright, but only a streak. Or maybe I had judged the Granny too harshly. Perhaps there was kindness in her too. Maybe it was just that I had never seen it.

'Yes, Ma'm, I'm all right . . . I'll go now.'

'Wait, Nuala,' said my mother. She rooted in her apron pocket and found a sixpence. She handed it to Nuala.

'Get yourself some fish and chips on the way home, love. Don't spend it on trashy sweets . . . they're no good for you.'

'Thanks . . . thanks very much Missus Redmond.'

I showed Nuala out and went back to the little parlour. Somehow it had got furnished well and a cottage piano stood against the wall. For reasons unknown to me, my terrible sins seemed to have been almost forgotten. Mam took no notice of me, having pulled the lace curtains aside and stood watching Nuala's slow progress across the square.

'Surely to Jesus,' she whispered aloud. 'She couldn't be . . .' She blessed herself, still watching Nuala.

'How old is Nuala Doyle?'

'Just over thirteen, Mam.'

'An' small for her age, half starved . . . the poor little bitch.' She seemed to have forgotten my presence.

'Sacred heart of Jesus,' she whispered. 'Say a prayer that I'm wrong . . . oh Jesus . . . Jesus,' she finished distractedly.

There was a long silence in the little room which I did not

dare to break. Presently she turned to me, coming back from a long way off.

'Now, you,' she said grimly, 'needn't think you're gettin' off scot free. Why did you rob the pound?'

'I told you, Mam, I didn't rob it.'

'Then why didn't you give it to me?'

'Because the oul' cow was going to rob you!'

I noticed the shocked look on her face, but I did not care. 'Cow' was, for reasons unknown, the worst word one could use in our house when applied to a woman, but if I got rattled I spoke Liberties style and just now I did not give a fiddlers.

'She's evil, Mam. I'm learning all about money at school, simple interest and compound interest. She'll want two pounds for that one . . . an' I didn't want you to be in debt.'

So there it was and the defence rested its case. My mother regarded me in some surprise.

'You're really a very clever boy,' she said at last. 'But then, child, I forget you're growing up an' will be off to work in a couple of years.'

Work was coming nearer by the day. My eldest brother Sean had already started as a carpenter's apprentice and was allowed two afternoons a week off work to attend Bolton Street Technical School. He was paid seven and sixpence per week and was given a few coppers from all the men on the job for making tea at lunch hour. He gave up five bob a week to Mam and didn't break himself. He had much more than that for himself and that is who he spent it on. Still thought he had a racing bike to pay for now, having got a racing model with dropped handlebars and a hardboard-like saddle, that would slice your arse in two.

The worst was over for Mam. The first of her brood had gone to work. This was the turning point for every working class family. One by one they went to work after that and for a few years things were easier. Until they went off to England and forgot all about home . . . or got married . . . or got drunk too often . . . turned out bad. I was next on the production belt.

Mam released the curtain as Nuala turned the corner and

sighed. She read the note again and tried not to smile.

'Did you use the language she says you used . . . what it says here?'

'What does it say, Mam?'

'About the fat woman in Moore Street?'

'Yes, an' she is the fat oul' wan of Clanbrassil Street! You should have heard what she called me . . . She said . . . well . . .'

'Don't tell me, I can well imagine. But you're gettin' to be a very impudent boy, d'you know that?' Her voice was trembling, trying to hide her laughter.

'Not really, Mam. It's just that I hate that oul' wan.'

'Woman,' she corrected. 'If your father heard you speaking like that! It's a good job he doesn't know about your carry-on. I don't want him upset. He's not too well.'

He wasn't either, going to work in agony each day with a neck full of suppurating boils, that I now know came from overworking and undernourishment.

'All right, mam.'

'Mind, I don't want any more reports like this one, or he'll be told. I'll have no Dolphins Barn gurrier in *this* family!'

'It won't happen again. I'm sorry, but I'm not sorry about the pound.'

'Nor am I,' she said and came over and kissed me and gave me a love. 'But this is all between you and me, no one else, mind!'

'No, Mam,' I whispered into her lovely brown hair and kissed her back. In an instant she drew away, ruffling my hair as she went and our little moment of closeness had fled, to be remembered for a lifetime, to be remembered with joy and tears not too long away.

And I *had* achieved something after my own wayward fashion. Neither I, nor any member of our family would ever knock on the blue door again. Mam had had her lesson and the message was 'starve before you go to a moneylender'. Let your husband know how it is, let the whole family go on short commons, but never again get into the clutches of a Liberties leech.

Oul' Byrne could shove it, I thought, shove it up her arse sideways from this on. And with this pious thought, the events of the day I had made my confirmation came to an end.

9 The Meddler Doyle

Some time after all this, Marge, Auntie Nelly's daughter, came up to our house. She had a note for Mam, but Mam was not at home. She was up in Meath Street or Thomas Street bargain hunting among the dealers. It was Saturday morning and this was the high point of my mother's week, haggling in the heart of the Liberties. She had been bred in this environment and knew every trick and dodge of the dealers. She could meet a bold stare with one just as bold, reach into a bag, take out a doubtful tomato, place it on the stall and *look*.

'That's the way I have teh buy them, Ma'm, good and bad alike.'

'That's your worry, Missus. My squad only eat good ones.'

I looked at Marge with some concern.

'She won't be back for hours yet,' I told her. 'Will you wait until she comes?'

'No, Lar . . . I'm not too well.'

She was my favourite girl cousin, my ex-playmate from Clanbrassil Street. During that glorious summer of long ago (five years) we had found the Lousy Acre at the bottom of New Street. It was the Liberties name for St Patrick's Park and we had played games among the dusty shrubs, that lived in the shadow of the cathedral with, perhaps, the ghost of the old rancorous Dean Swift looking on.

Today she looked sicker, even more dawny than I remembered her. It was two months since we had last met and she had disimproved a lot in that short time. Two bright spots on her cheeks lit up the rest of her little face, which wore that clear pallor that boded ill, and she had a weak, chesty cough that frightened me.

I had too much experience of the 'con' not to spot it, but I could not bring myself to face the truth that Marge had it. Consumption did not run in my mother's family, nobody of her family had ever died of it, so why should Mam's sister's child have it? I could talk myself into anything and so far I refused to believe the evidence of my own eyes, as my mother had done in the case of Nuala Doyle.

'I'll make you a cup of tea, Marge,' I said, 'and you can have some bread and jam, too.'

'Is it all right?'

'Yes,' I reassured her. 'I'm left in charge of the house.'

Even her voice frightened me, it had grown so soft and timid.

We had tea and bread and jam together. Mam had a couple of the older ones with her, the last baby was asleep in his cot in the hall. I had the front door open and he slept in the sun, as near to the fresh air as I could get him, for the pram had been taken to carry messages, spuds and cabbage having displaced his majesty.

I had little love of babies. There were too many of them. And every one of them that came along, took over the centre of the stage before being consigned to the anonymity of the herd. Like Charles Lamb, writer of another century, I preferred them 'bbbboiled!'

'I'll go now,' said Marge at length, 'I'll have teh leave the note. Auntie Dolly 'ill get it when she comes back.'

'But then she'll send me all the way down to Clanbrassil Street with the answer.'

'Well, I'm sorry, Lar, but I'll have teh go. I don't feel too well . . . I've been off school this three weeks.'

'Why wasn't Paddy or Freddy sent up here?'

'Paddy has started work, the same as Sean. Freddy is sick in bed with the flu' . . . I'm all right again, Lar . . . it's just that I want teh get home . . . I feel awful tired.'

'Yeh should go back teh bed,' I told her.

'I will, Lar, I'm awful tired.'

She walked across the square, a dawny little Dublin child, who lived in overcrowded conditions, her family almost as large as ours with their cottage half the size. We were bad enough with only two bedrooms, but Marge's family had two rooms and a scullery in total. The air was very much rationed at night.

It was the last time I was to see her. Shortly afterwards she was taken to hospital and a year later buried in Mount Jerome, the first culling of the TB crop of that generation. I sensed all this as I watched her and I felt sad. My instinct was sure and I no longer had any doubt about Marge. She had the 'con'!

In the meantime, I read Nelly's note to Mam. Marge had warned me not to read it, but that didn't worry me. I always read their notes. That was how I knew what was going on.

'Dear Dolly', I read, 'I wish you would come down for a bit of a chat. I have not seen you for a while. I am worried about a few things. Freddy is sick and Marge has not been too well. You saw Nuala Doyle a couple of weeks ago . . . we all think she is going to have a baby. Did you notice? Try and get down.

Nelly'

In the afternoon, as I had predicted, I was sent down to Clanbrassil Street with another note. Of course I read that too. It said:

'Dear Nelly,
The baby here is starting 'hooping cough and I can't get down. Try and get up Tuesday morning for a bit. As regards Nuala Doyle . . . I thought that myself . . . she's in the family way all right, I think.

Dolly'

And the response I also read.

'Dear Dolly,
I will get up for an hour on Tuesday morning. I have a lot to tell you.

Nelly'

Monday morning being washday, the meeting had to be on Tuesday, I figured. My mother and aunt had communicated a sense of urgency and disaster and privately I decided I was not going to be left out. 'I have a lot to tell you . . .' On Monday morning I laid the groundwork for being sick on Tuesday, going to bed, complaining about a headache.

On Tuesday morning when I put on the act, Mam swallowed it. It was well known that I loved school and was quick to learn.

'Anyway, child,' said Mam as she gave me my breakfast in bed, 'a day off school won't hurt you an' you can study your books in bed if you like.'

'I'll do that, Mam,' I said and got her to bring me my school bag. I lay in bed in luxury, reading *The Gem* and the latest adventure of Harry Wharton and Co.

It was a great story and I was reading it for the second time, when I heard Auntie Nelly's voice. It was only ten thirty.

'I had teh come early, Dolly, as I have teh get back soon. How are yeh?'

'Fine, Nelly . . . Lar is up in bed with a little bit of a cold, nothing really wrong . . .'

'I was wonderin', Dolly, if yeh could get some a' that extract a' malt off Missus Keirsey . . . Maybe she could spare a bit . . . Marge's chest is very bad an' sore from coughin'.'

'No, I'll give yeh some, Nelly, that I got off her. I wouldn't like teh ask her so soon again.'

Mrs Keirsey was one of the Guinness wives, who got free medicine from the brewery clinic.

'I have some left in a jar somewhere. I'll find it before yeh go.'

'Who's that upstairs, coughin'?'

'Lar . . . in case he'll be left out a' the cup a' tea. There's not much wrong with him . . . that's just a little reminder.'

'I love Lar,' said Auntie Nelly, 'the best a' them all.'

I could hear every word that was spoken, because the bedroom door was open. It would be different, when they got down to 'a bit a' scandal'. The voices would drop, the door would be shut tight and then it was time to use my secret weapon. Under the bed was a cracked floorboard. By the persistent use of a penknife, I had enlarged a crack, enough to form a small hole. If you put your ear to it, you could hear every word that was said in the kitchen. Nobody knew about it except me. It was my defence against adults. It kept me informed against their likely movements. I was an intrusive and curious little bastard, knew it and enjoyed it. I was, of course, imitating Key-Hole Kate, another character from an English comic.

Mam came up the stairs soon, with a cup of tea and a piece of toast.

'Thanks, Mam,' I said, really surprised, like.

She smiled.

'As if you weren't expectin' me,' she said and left, closing the door behind her. I gulped down the tea, took the slice of toast under the bed with me and got my ear to the hole.

'Well, Nelly?' came my mother's voice.

'You were right, Dolly . . . Nuala is up the pole all right!'

'When is the baby due? Does anybody know?'

'The baby is over an' done with, the poor little thing was born dead.'

'What!'

'Yes . . . dead.'

'When?'

'Yesterday mornin', in the Coombe hospital.'

'Jesus!' came my mother's shocked voice. 'An' she only a child herself . . . I can't understand it . . . She's not that kind of child . . . Still with the mother dead . . .'

'No, Dolly,' came Auntie Nelly's lovely, soft voice, 'it wasn't that way at all . . . an' she nearly died havin' it. In fact, she may be dead now for all I know – or anybody else either.'

'Did she know the father?'

'Oh yes she did. But they couldn't get her teh name him. She was under questionin' for a week before the baby came, but she wouldn't split.'

'Surely she told some a' the women in the ward?'

'The women in the ward wouldn't speak teh her, none a' them. They said a young whore shouldn't be mixed up with decent married women.'

'An' what happened?'

'The priest was brought in. He had her behind the blue screen for hours, questionin' her but he did no good. An' she wouldn't have her confession heard either.'

'How do yeh know all this is true, Nelly?'

'Because Missus Dempsey next door is havin' a baby in the same ward. I saw her yesterday.'

'Did you see Nuala? Jesus, the child must be dead with it all.'

'I didn't see her, Dolly. She's been taken away.'

'Where?'

'Nobody knows and them that does aren't sayin'.'

'An' the father is still a mystery?'

'Not any more. They got the bishop for her. He made her tell.'

'Who is it?'

'The Meddler . . . her father.'

There was no sound from below for nearly half a minute and I could picture my mother, mouth open, gazing in horror at her sister.

'Are yeh quite sure a' the facts, Nelly?' came her voice at last. I could barely hear her, for she was whispering.

'Quite sure!'

'Jesus Christ Almighty . . . that's the most terrible sin I've ever heard of in my whole life! Jesus, Mary an' Joseph, that child an' that bloody oul' animal . . .' And my mother burst into tears and her crying came loud and clear through the hole in the floor.

'There, there, Dolly, don't be upsettin' youself. You could do yourself harm . . . in your condition. Hush, Dolly.'

And now it was my turn to be shocked. The terrible story of incest that I had just heard had not fully registered. I was too young to take it all in. But the prospect of another baby in the house!

Under the bed I cursed fiercely to myself, all thoughts of Meddler Doyle gone. The big news for me was that I was going to have another baby sister or brother that I did not want. This would be the eighth. Mam and Dad made it ten. I had a brother or a sister in every second class in the bloody schools, girls' and boys'. The fucking place was bad enough with me having to do my exercise alone in the classroom after school, or after eight o'clock at night, when the others had been put to bed and I was tired. And, in winter the classroom was a cold and lonely place. But this latest was the last straw! The last baby was twenty months old. The new one would be here by the time it was two. That was the way it went. Another mouth to feed every two years.

All the other mothers around seemed to have called it a day. Colin's mother had thrown in the towel at five kids, Ernie's mother had quit long since with four, Tom Horan's mother had jibbed early in the act and had only two, Bay McKays had two older sisters going to work and only one older brother going to secondary school in James's Street; a very nice, small well spaced family. In all the other homes I had access to, the sight of a shitty napkin had long ceased to exist. As long as I could remember, I had lived with them and I hated the dirt and filth that went with babies.

In a house as small and crowded as ours, you could not escape the sight of nappy changes and shitty sheets. Sometimes, one of the younger ones would piss the bed, with you in it. And I hated it. I loved the order of the other boys' homes, where the napkin had long been banned, where the wash line was full only on Monday mornings, where peace reigned and squealing babies were no more.

'Well,' said Auntie Nelly from below, 'I have teh go, Dolly. Get the extract a' malt an' I'll be on my way . . . Sorry the news I brought yeh upset yeh so much.'

'I'd a' heard it anyway, Nelly,' said Mam quietly and her footsteps went across the kitchen to where the jar of malt was.

I got dressed in a flash and went downstairs. Our toilet was in the backyard, a good excuse to get up. I grinned at Auntie Nelly.

'Hello!' I said. She smiled back at me, I knew she loved me.

'How are you feeling now, Lar?' she asked.

'Great, Auntie Nell . . . I feel great all of a sudden. I got up to go to the toilet.'

I told my mother. She did not answer. She did not even seem to hear me, seemed almost in a trance. I could get away with murder this day, I surmised.

'Mam?'

'Yes, child.'

'I feel a lot better now. Can I go a little way with Auntie Nell?' She nodded absent mindedly.

'Where's your man . . . you know who . . . the father?' she said to her sister.

'Nobody knows, he hasn't been seen this two days, not since the news got out.'

Auntie Nelly moved towards the door and I went in front of her, afraid my mother would awake from her reverie.

'I hope the police get him first! Jesus help him, Dolly, if he shows up in the street! Goodbye now. Come an' see me as soon as . . . you know what.'

I shot a quick glance at my mother. Yes, she was getting fat again. Outside in the square, Auntie Nelly took my hand in hers.

'Seein' me safe to the top a' the Barn, are yeh?'

'Maybe a little further than that, Aunt Nell, I'd like to see Marge.'

'An' you just up out a' bed? No, some other day. Anyway, she's not well enough to see anybody, even you.'

'Well, let me see you a little bit down the South Circular Road, then.'

She nodded. She was as far away as my mother and I kept quiet until we came to the top of Clanbrassil Street, Leonard's Corner. Auntie Nelly looked at me.

'You've come further than I intended. Better go back, your Mammy will be worried.'

I squeezed her hand.

'If I go down Clanbrassil Street with you, I can take a short cut home through Duckers Lane and the Tenters. That's just as quick.'

'All right, then . . . But no Marge. Come down this comin' weekend.'

We drew near to where Auntie Nelly lived. The usual

crowd of idlers held up the corner opposite, where the blank wall blocked the wind and held the sun's warmth. There seemed to be more than the usual crowd this day and Auntie Nelly was suddenly flurried and to me seemed frightened. She looked hard down the road.

'Run home now, Lar, before anything starts. This is no place for you.'

Maybe not, but it was exactly the place I wanted to be. My instinct for trouble had been correct, for coming up New Street was the unmistakable figure of the Meddler, shambling along. Auntie Nelly had spotted him before me and that was the reason for her flurried actions. Down a few doors was Granny's house and she made for that. She disappeared inside without even seeing if I had gone off.

Clanbrassil Street, as we came down it, had been its usual bustling self. It had not yet been tarmacammed and although the ironshod wheels that bounced off the cobbles were getting less and the piles of horse dung fewer, it was still a noisy street. There was intense competition between the motor drivers and the men who drove the horses. They hated each other, the same as in the old days when the captains of proud, whitewinged schooners hated their steam driven rivals.

The horse men took full advantage of the rule 'make way for the horse' and most days the street was enlivened with shouting matches between lorry and horse drivers and sometimes a punch-up on the spot.

Today was market day and the cobbles were strewn with hay. The sun was shining and suddenly, unaccountably, the street was empty. It was as if it had cleared itself in order to make way for the Meddler Doyle's crucifixion, the last of the hay bogeys having disappeared over the canal bridge and into the fragrant countryside.

I ran across the road and stood on the opposite corner to the line of shuffling men. They had been told the Meddler was coming and had moved about fifteen feet into Garty Place, so that the Meddler would be well around the corner before they pounced. I counted them. They were eighteen in number, tough, shabby, underprivileged products of the slums. Between them, there were not many crimes they had not committed. Most things they had done from pitch and toss to manslaughter. They drank too much when they could get their hands on money and they got it any way they could. If one of their number disappeared, that meant he was doing time for some theft. Violence rolled off them like water off a duck's back. They would ride anything with a skirt on it. There were many wife beaters among them, but the line was drawn at 'messin' with little kids'. Incest was so dreadful a crime, that not one of them had ever come close to a case of it before. It was beyond their comprehension, a sin so terrible, that no punishment could atone for it.

Towards this implacable jury the Meddler shuffled. No Papist had ever faced a more terrible Cromwellian court, no dissenter a more fiendish inquisition! Had they been permitted, they would after long and searching tortures, have hanged, drawn and quartered him.

'Ay . . . you!'

The biggest of them was shouting at me.

'Jow off!'

'I'm waiting for me mother,' I shouted back.

'Wait somewhere else . . . now fuck off quick or ye'll get me instead!'

I turned away, walked a few paces up Clanbrassil Street and simply came back. The Meddler was turning the corner. Nobody was going to bother with me now.

From where I stood I could see the Granny and Auntie Nelly's white face in the window over the shop. The Granny was settling her black shawl over her silver hair. She had her chair close to the window, so as she would miss nothing. She looked like an implacable Comanche squaw, awaiting the torture of a hated paleface. And the truth was not all that much different. The Meddler's ordeal by fire had begun.

The Meddler, as he shuffled around the corner, spotted the line of men and stepped into the gutter to pass. Bangers Cullen, the first man in line and the biggest, shuffled his greasy cap a couple of times on his head and stepped lazily across. The Meddler never even lifted his head, moving slowly along.

Bangers gave him a left handed swipe with the peak of his cap across the face and, as he looked up, casually hit him. It was the way a man hits a punchbag, no hurry but with terrific force. The Meddler's nose spurted blood, broken sideways, but surprisingly he did not go down.

'OK, Bangers,' said Jemmier Connors, next in line, 'my turn.' He knocked the Meddler's hat off with his right hand, grabbed him by the long, grey hair with the other and belted him behind the ear with the right. As he fell forward, Johnny Cox brought his knee into his face. The Meddler gave a single broken cry and fell forward into the gutter. There was a crash of glass as he hit the road. One of his bottles of wine had smashed.

Bangers moved across and leisurely turned the Meddler over with his boot. He took another bottle of wine, still intact, from the other pocket and uncorked it in a second with the blade of his penknife. He took a long swig and passed it along the line.

After a couple of minutes, the Meddler recovered a bit, and staggered to his feet. The fourth man in the line strolled over, eased his shoulders a bit, spread his arms wide and buried his fist in the Meddler's stomach. As he went down again, the man strolled back to his place.

It was all arranged, I could see that. They were all going to have a piece of him. Nobody was going to hurt him that bad, that he would remain unconscious. He was to be preserved as long as possible. The court of the Liberties had sat and the Meddler found guilty. Now sentence was being carried out, according to the law.

However, the last punch in the stomach had finished the Meddler from walking for a while.

Presently, he rolled over onto his hands and knees, and dripping blood, started to crawl his way through the spilt Old Tawny Port and shattered glass. The men watched with interest.

A couple of policemen on the far side of the road glanced

over, but appeared to see nothing and continued placidly on their way. Number five in line grinned with relief. For a second it had looked as if the sport was over. He danced quickly across the pavement, hopped on the left foot once and drove the right boot into the Meddler's stomach. It was like taking a penalty shot at goal.

The bottle of port, empty now, was flung in front of the Meddler's face, where it broke into a thousand pieces. He could crawl through that as well, while he was at it!

I was trembling like a leaf, sorry now that I had stayed to watch this massacre, but somehow compelled to see it out. I felt like vomiting. The Meddler *was* vomiting. From where I stood, I could hear the terrible gulping retching of a badly injured man.

The line of eighteen waited patiently. They had all day, they were going nowhere. An animal was being dealt with and it was all legal. Had not the coppers passed by? And at the back of it all, it was not all that often they got a chance to exercise their brutal instincts with the tacit approval of society. Sure, wouldn't any decent man do the same?

After a long pause, the Meddler came back on to his hands and knees and painfully crawled a few more feet through the broken glass.

'He's just about fucked,' I heard the Jibber Keegan say. 'But fucked or not, he'll get one from me.' He turned to the man next to him.

'Hold him up for me, will yeh.'

The man he had asked was known to me as well. He was a Meath man, called the 'Very Man Riley'.

'I will, begod,' he replied eagerly, 'an' I'm the *very* man that will!'

The Meddler was dragged to his feet. Blood was pouring from his mouth and nose and he was covered with gore. Jibber tapped him lightly with two fast lefts to get the *feel* of him, and then came across with a terrific right that nearly lifted the Meddler's head off his shoulders. Jibber grabbed him then and held him up while the Very Man gave him the Ringsend shake hands. And then the whole line of men went for him at once, for it was obvious that you got your kick in now – or never. The Meddler disappeared under the mêlée and when they broke up he lay very still in the gutter.

And I was left, shaking, on the corner opposite, the men talking half heartedly, a show of bravado. For I knew every one of them wanted to run like hell from the broken body before them.

It was then Auntie Nelly passed by without seeing me. She was weeping, heading for home and Marge. But she stopped opposite the men and looked down at the body in the gutter.

'Yez are big fellas all right, aren't yez . . . Took the whole crowd a' yez teh beat him up,' she sobbed. 'Yez dirty crowd a' no good bowsies!'

She stood facing them, a small, beautiful woman of the Liberties, unafraid. And in a sudden flash it came to me that she looked down on them. Not just because of what had happened, but because of who she was.

Her family had never lived in a tenement, ten or fifteen to a room. Her father had been a postman, who had never known the Labour Exchange or the dole. She and her family had lived in three rooms over a shop and they had the key to their own hall door. Her family had rated with the shopkeepers and the publicans. She came from the natural aristocracy of the Liberties and it showed in her manner of speaking to them.

'Sure, yeh know what he's afther doin', Missus Barker . . . I'm surprised at yeh standin' up for an animal like that!' Bangers Cullen spoke up.

'An' you an' them bowsies have fixed everything, haven't yez. Yez should be out scoutin' for a job, but no, this is the kind a' work yez prefer, yez dirty, rotten. . . .!'

'G'wan home teh yer kitchen, woman,' growled Bangers, making his voice sound as deep and masculine as possible, 'home teh yer kitchen where yeh belong!'

'I'll go home teh me kitchen when I'm ready, not when you tell me. Thank God I haven't anythin' like that on me conscience.'

'He deserved what he got!'

'Maybe!' she screamed. 'But nobody made you judge an' jury. If was to tell the half of what I know about you lot, the policemen 'id be lookin' for you too.'

She glanced with compassion at the broken body of the Meddler, lying still in his own blood, then fixed her tearfilled eyes on the men. One by one they slunk off, disappearing into the warren of tenements around.

Auntie Nelly walked away as the ambulance turned the corner. The two coppers must have phoned for an ambulance, figuring correctly that one would be needed. Then came the black Maria, loaded with police. They stopped the passers by, asking questions, making little notes in their books, very casual about it all. I knew it was all an act. Nobody would ever do time over the Meddler Doyle. Not even if he died this morning.

I walked slowly home. When my mother saw me, she knew there was no pretence this time, that I *was* sick. She could always tell when I was.

'Yeh bloody little eejit,' she snapped. 'Where have you been? What have yeh been up to . . . Get up to bed at once!'

But later that night, by candle light, I told her of the Meddler's ordeal. She sat there, tightlipped, as her mother had done in the window, listening intently to me, but no shadow of compassion passed over her face. It was the first time I had ever *really* noticed any resemblance between my mother and the Granny. But in the silent, implacable judgement it was plain they were mother and daughter.

Had they been walking the streets of Jerusalem, when the woman taken in adultery had stood before the mob, they would both have felt it their duty to pick up a stone. Black was black with them, white was white! There was no in between. They made life hard for themselves. But at the back of it all, someone like Auntie Nelly cried silently inside and never ceased to reproach.

10 Éileen Alannah

The year was 1930 and I was twelve years old. I was the smallest boy in the class now. A terrible and paralysing inferiority complex was taking me over. Everybody looked *down* on me. I was constantly ribbed on account of my lack of inches and it was warping my nature. And it made life in the Liberties twice as hard and, Jesus knows, it was hard enough without being small.

Although I still stood first or second every time in the school exams, it did nothing to comfort me. The final indignity came in the square one day, when Kevin O'Connell, a big thick, who now outstripped me by five inches in height and a stone in weight, got above himself and warned me if I bumped into him again, I was 'for it'.

'It was an accident,' I said sullenly.

He showed me his fist, waving it an inch from my nose.

'This won't be an accident,' he promised me.

He had waited a long time for this day. He knew I regarded him as a 'stumer', was jealous of my position in class and had taken to jibing at my small stature for some time now. He was growing, like my inferiority complex, at a fearful rate and he was now prepared to put his additional height and poundage to the test. So was I!

'You're lookin' for a fight,' I said.

'I am!'

'Right then . . . here's fight!'

I squared up and O'Connell, grinning, moved in. I picked a spot, just under his left eye, moved in fast, ducking under his guard and let fly with a bony fist on the exact spot I had chosen and danced out again. He blinked and the smile went off his face.

I had chopped sticks for the house as long as I could remember. I had cut hedges for firewood and gone out with my father on some spare time job, nailing down floors for hours. I could use a jackplane, which is the second biggest plane used by a carpenter, not very well, it is true, but I could do it.

My arms were deceptively smooth, like a girl's, but in reality were very strong for a boy so slight. When I hit O'Connell he felt it.

Before he could gather himself, I shot in again and nailed him in the same spot. His enraged panting grew louder and he made a run at me like a bullock. I let him charge past, dancing aside and the second he turned, I gave him another ill dig under the same eye and moved away grinning. It was my turn now. I had him and I knew it. So far, he had not even touched me.

He backed away, taking stock of the situation. I could almost hear his lame brain working, telling him he had all the advantages and that all he had to do was to box cool, stand back and take me apart, using his superior reach. I had other ideas for him. He slowed down and moved forward deliberately, his right fist, the one he was going to bury me with, making threatening, useless little circles.

I shot forward to meet him, ducked under the powerhouse right he threw, I could see it coming a mile off, slipped under his guard and planted another punch on the bright, red spot that had appeared under his eye.

He started to blubber then. After all, for all his size, he was fifteen months younger than me. I could have walked away with honour. I could have shown some mercy, but the way of the Liberties was not the way of the Lord. Turning the other cheek was not in the curriculum. This bloody big softie, the youngest of a family of girls, had looked for a fight and now he would get all he wanted, and more! Besides, if I gave him a real going over, the other big bastards who had been getting cheeky all of a sudden, would back off.

He came at me again, from a new angle, favouring the damaged side of his face and I shot in and gave him a beauty under the other eye. This was more like it.

His face was starting to have a creased look about it, like a crumpled handkerchief, for he was spoilt and overfed, but he had a lovely complexion for hitting. You could see the mark every punch left!

The rest of the square gang had gathered around us. From the first, most of them had been loud in their encouragement of O'Connell. Now they fell silent, as he started to cry. The way I walked from now on depended on the result of this first fight, for many of them had felt my wrath at one time or another and were all, like O'Connell, considerably bigger. I planted another vicious punch on the red spot and he burst into tears. The fight was over. At the same moment, the circle exploded and Linda, his virago of a sister, a skinny bitch of sixteen, fell on me like a rending fury. She gave me no quarter, grabbing me by the hair with one hand and belting me with the other. I could not get near her, so I rushed as far as the grip on my hair would allow and kicked out. She let me go quick enough then, for I got her, solidly, on the knee.

There was a chorus of dismay from the onlookers. Some of the women had come to their doors to watch the mêlée and their outrage was because I had kicked a woman – well, nearly a woman.

Woman or girl, I figured she would have beaten the face off me, had I let her. Nobody, but nobody, laid a finger on 'Son', alias Kevin O'Connell, with impunity. His tribe of Amazon sisters saw to that. Now I stood in a circle of hostility, victorious, while the two O'Connells bawled for sympathy.

'Yeh dirty little maggot,' sobbed Linda, 'teh kick a woman!'

'I'm surprised at you,' said a country woman, who did not like me, 'kicking a woman. Your mother will hear of this.'

At that moment Mam came to our front door.

'Come in here, you,' she called loudly.

'He's after kickin' the legs off me an' murderin' Kevin,' sobbed Linda. 'He should be checked.'

'What did you expect him to do?' said my mother unexpectedly. 'Stand there and let you wool the head off him? An' beatin' him? I saw it all!'

I ran over to our door and squeezed past Mam. It would be over the backyard wall and along the Back of the Pipes for many a long day now. I would be torn to pieces if I was caught crossing the square by the O'Connell sisters.

'That's your rearin', is it?' screamed Linda.

'Get inside, yeh common tinker,' shouted my mother. 'An' advise that brother of yours not teh pick on the Redmonds, we're well able for you!'

With that she closed the door and sailed into me. Then I was sent to bed for the day, sobbing more with temper than with hurt, though like me, she could hit when she wanted to. In the afternoon she got me out of bed and sent me for the messages to our local grocer, one Scuffle by name and often referred to as 'the lightweight champion of Dolphins Barn'. His shop was on the corner of the square, but to get to it now, I had to go over the back wall, all the way up the Pipes to the top of Dolphins Barn and back down again to Scuffle's, from where I could see my own house, but the O'Connell vengeance lay in between. I made the purchases and then had to do the whole thing again, in reverse. When I got back, I got another clout for being so long. This could not go on. Something would have to be done.

In the school yard the following day I did it. O'Connell was there, sporting a beautiful black eye and a smirk. When we were lining up to go back to our classrooms, I made it my business to be next to him.

'Wait 'till Linda gets yeh,' he whispered. 'An' Sis . . . an' Maura . . . an' Rosie . . . they'll flitther yeh. An' me mother sez she'll break yer bloody face!'

'Wait 'till after school,' I promised him, 'an' we'll see whose face gets broken!'

With that dire threat, I left him to ponder until three o'clock, when we left school. He tried to get away from me, but he had no hope. He was a big, flabby baby elephant, pursued by a young jaguar. I caught up with him opposite Reuben Street on the South Circular Road.

'Now, "Son",' I said to him. 'We're going teh get one thing straight an' it's fuckin' this. Every time one of yer sisters hits *me*, I'm goin' teh hit you twice. Linda gev me a hard one yesterday, now here's two for Lyon.'

And I lit into him and hit him twice as hard as I could, but not in the face. I was afraid to mark him again, so I drove my fist into his stomach with vengeance.

'Let him go home an' tell that to his oul' wan and sisters,' I said to Ernie Mountain, who was with me for the occasion. 'I'll give him two boxes for every one they give me.'

'Jasus,' said Ernie, 'the bitches 'ill tear yeh teh pieces.'

'They'll do it one way or the other, unless I fix "Son".'

I left O'Connell holding his guts and bawling like a hungry calf.

I came into our house by way of the Back of the Pipes. Mam was at the front door, quarrelling with some other woman and I knew who – Linda. I had been waiting for this. I dropped my school bag on the floor and instantly my mother called me. She had ears like a fox.

As I expected, Linda was on the doorstep with a tearstained 'Son', still holding his belly. My mother was white in the face, as I was too, when really angry or frightened and this time I knew it would be the handle of the sweeping brush for me. But brush or no brush, the bloody O'Connells were not going to frighten me off the square and double my journey every time I went for a message.

'Did you hit Kevin O'Connell?' asked my mother.

And here goes nothing, I told myself. I would probably get a hiding anyway, so I would be as impudent as possible. I had nothing to lose.

'I did, an' I'll hit him again if she hits *me*.'

'You'll what?'

'I'll burst him if she or the others hit me again.'

'Yeh can hear for yerself,' said Linda sanctimoniously. 'That's the makins' of a cur.'

'Cur or not,' said my mother with surprising venom, 'you've heard what he said. If you or your sisters lay a hand on him, he'll lay his hands on Kevin.'

'Jasus,' screeched Linda outraged, 'if that's your attitude you're worse!'

'That's my attitude, Miss O'Connell and it's fair enough. They had a boys' fight an' Kevin lost. Besides, he started it.'

'He did not!' Linda screamed on a rising note.

'He did so! I was watching the whole thing from the window. An' if yeh think I'm goin' teh beat Lar teh please you, yeh have another think comin'. Now, take yerself off, yeh common hussy!'

And she banged the door in her face. As she turned to come up the tiny hall, two thunderous knocks shook the hall door. She shot back, flung it open, but one look at her face and the tigerish Linda fled.

I went into the kitchen, silent, waiting for her to attack me. She did nothing of the kind.

'Put on the pot for a cup a' tea, Lar,' she said.

I was open mouthed. 'Yes, Mam,' I said eagerly.

'That's run that one,' she said with satisfaction. 'I've been waitin' for a chance teh nail that hussy. Nobody's son is teh defend themselves, we're all teh be walked over by the O'Connells.'

Prudently I said nothing. She fumbled in her bag and found two pence.

'Slip down to Scuffle's an' get some broken biscuits an' you're not goin' over the back wall either!'

'I'm not, Mam,' I said.

I went across the square, watched by the O'Connells, whistling carelessly and ignoring the glare of the malignant Linda. I felt like giving her the raspberry, for I had one of the filthy rubber contraptions in my pocket, but I refrained. I had won a great victory. These fellows, who were outgrowing me would think twice before taking me on. Miss Linda would leave me alone in future and 'Son' would keep his place.

On the way back, Eileen O'Connell passed me on the pavement, smiling. She was not smiling at me, just smiling and I knew she must be going to see her fella tonight. Jimmy Kelly was the fortunate man. He worked up in Keegan's, the butcher's, alongside Sloppy Molly, the proprietor's daughter. Eileen was mad about him and there was no doubt he was a fine cut of a young man. He had the 'Blarney' too, by the bucket full all the way from Killane, County Wexford. Not surprisingly, his name being the same as the immortal hero of Killane, all the women used to pull his leg, calling him 'the boy from Killane', him giving back as good as he got, smiling, with perfect white teeth, set in a sunburnt manly face and to add to Eileen's sorrow, a cleft chin and a head of blond, curling hair. Six feet tall with cold blue eyes, that nobody seemed to notice except me. I did not like him. I was sharp enough to notice that the 'oul' wans' never got the best of him for all his repartee. With them, he was as tight as a tuppence. But if Sloppy Molly was not in the shop, that was when any good-looker, who knew her onions would pop in and get the best bargain in town.

It was widely known among the observant women that Sloppy Molly was nuts about her father's new assistant. Nobody ever caught them acting the linnet or anything like that, but it was the very lack of any bit of flirting in public, that put them on to Molly.

She was a rawfaced woman of about twenty-six, without wiles indeed, her cheeks were as red as the raw steak she was so fond of eating. Someone must have told her at some time, that she had a lovely complexion, for she never attempted to tone it down a bit by the use of powder. The same went for lipstick, although her lips were red enough, in all truth. She had obviously never heard of a bra, for her overlarge breasts hung pendulously under her white smock. She was the typical product of a small poverty stricken Irish town, where her family was prosperous and always well fed. She was full of silly airs and graces and thought herself above the people she served. She was Keegan's only child and would inherit the business. Since the advent of Jimmy, he had rarely been seen in the shop. It seemed he had a farm adjoining a widow's farm down the country and a cattle jobber from the Barn let it be known that Keegan had matrimony on his mind. His daughter had the same complaint. So it was surmised and correctly, that he was just waiting to get Sloppy Molly off his hands before he handed over the shop.

Of the five O'Connell sisters, Eileen was the acknowledged beauty. All her sisters were worth a second look, but Eileen was really something. And besides, she was gentle too, a quality not much in evidence around her. She was tall for a Dubliner of that day, five foot six and she had not had her hair bobbed, when the women decided to have their hair off. She had, wisely, not followed their fashion. She had a heavy pile of deep brown hair, naturally wavy and a flawless complexion. But the most striking feature about her were her eyes. They were a lustrous golden brown with long black eyelashes and all the boys my age were mad about her. Puppy love, but thrilling and real enough to us. And she had the best pair of legs outside the Theatre Royal.

This was the 'smasher', whose heart Jimmy hd captured and this was the smasher, whose heart he would break. Everybody knew she was wild about Jimmy. Everybody knew they went out together. But nobody could claim ever to have seen them.

'Very strange,' said my shrewd mother.

'Do yeh think so?' said Mrs Keirsey.

'I do. That get is only usin' Eileen. If he wasn't he wouldn't be afraid to be seen with her.'

'Maybe they want to keep it a secret for a while, not let it out for their own reasons.'

'An' maybe the sly get wants to keep Sloppy Molly from knowin'. Might spoil his chance a' takin' over the shop!'

'You never liked him, did you, Missus Redmond?'

'No, he's too bloody freemakin'. I soon cut him off the day he tried his oul' shinanickin' with me! I never deal there now.'

She did, but she did not know it. Keegan's was the nearest butcher and when I was sent for meat I did not go further. I stood now for a moment and watched Eileen walk away. No doubt, she had a lovely pair of legs, I decided. I was starting to take an interest in such things as 'gams and knockers' – legs and breasts. But I had no way of knowing then, that soon I would see more of Eileen's legs than even her mother did, now.

It came about this way. It was the season to go blackberrying and Tom, Bay and me had been looking several times, but like the apostles had fished all day and caught nothing. The bushes just outside the city were kept stripped by the hordes of youngsters who descended on them every weekend. One had to go a long way out in order to fill a can full or to get enough to make jam. And, for some reason this was not a good year for blackberries.

This afternoon, Bay was the bearer of good tidings. He had been sent up to his aunt, who lived just over Dolphins Barn bridge up Rutland Avenue, on some message and on the way had managed to squeeze through an old corrugated fence. It had been there for years and he had always wondered just what lay over the other side.

What he found had opened his eyes. An old Georgian manor stood in ruins, surrounded by quite a large area. The place was a wilderness, overgrown with nettles and docks and blackberry bushes.

Hordes of youngsters passed quite close to the fence on their long walk for blackberries, but it had never occurred to anyone of them to turn left and try behind the fence.

'Janey Mac!' said Bay. 'The bushes are drippin' with berries.'

He swore Tom and me to secrecy and the following day after school, we set out. We had already hidden sweet cans on the way the night before, for if we had been seen going off together with the cans, we could have been followed. So we slunk off singly and met on Dolphins Barn bridge.

In a few minutes we were squeezing through the iron fence and silently went to work. It was blackberry wonderland, a sanctuary for fruit, an elephant's graveyard of treasure. None of us had ever been in a place before, where the bushes had never been picked and were easy to get at too, for they straggled across the overgrown lawn, taking over from all before them.

It did not take us long to fill our cans. We hid them under a bush and being full up with 'blackers' – one for me, one for the can – we decided to explore the house. We took off our shoes for this, for we were trespassing and we knew it. The hall of the great house lay open to the winds, the huge front door lay on the floor, hinges broken. Broken windows let in sunshine to once gracious rooms. Crumbling, ornate cornices spattered the rotten floors and the beautiful, wrecked old staircase was almost unclimbable because of the heaped plaster from the ruined ceilings above.

We stole upstairs and crept across the main bedroom to look over the garden. We were all carrying our shoes in our hands and our feet made no sound.

Suddenly we froze. From outside, quite close at hand, had come the sound of a woman's laugh, then the lower tone of a man, laughing with her. We exchanged horrified looks, but said nothing. Together we looked out the window. Below us lay the garden with its jungle-like overgrown lawn, its barren, lichen–covered apple trees and the marauding blackberry bushes, taking over the whole place.

A man was laying his raincoat on the ground. A woman stood beside him. They lay down together and in a second were locked in each others arms, the man half way on top of her, his right hand caressing her thighs, showing the blue satin knickers underneath.

It was Eileen O'Connell and Jimmy Kelly! So this was where they came. This was the reason no one ever saw them together. They met here and parted here, after he had parted her legs, which he was doing now. Gently his hand was easing her knickers off, she raising herself to help him, her beautiful thighs flashing white in the autumn sunshine. And then the man's trousers slipped down, covering her with his body and the moans of ecstasy floating up to us.

All around them, I noticed, the grass was flattened, so they must have been here many times and with the accustomed readiness of practice, had begun to make love right away.

There had been no long drawn out petting session. The woman had been mad for him and he for her. We could see her frenzied, tearing hands clawing his back, pulling him into her as if she could never get close enough to him. And all the time her moans . . .

'Janey,' whispered Bay, 'how are we goin' to get out a' here?' In the gloom of the old bedroom, his face was white and strained. At close hand we had seen a man and woman couple, had heard the sounds of lovemaking and it was arousing sensations in us with which we were not able to cope.

We had all to confess to the 'terrible sin', the one dreadful act that sent boys into the depths of hell, and the thought terrified us. The dark, shut-in confessional, the voice from the void behind the wirescreen, probing, helping the shame.

'How many times did you do this thing, my son?'

'Three times, Father, I think.' Do not commit another mortal sin by telling lies to the priest, leave a little loophole.

'Three times, I think.' It could have been six times or sixteen.

The voice from the black void, gentle or angry.

'Don't you know if you had died in this state of mortal sin, that you would have been hurled into the depths of hell for all eternity? Have you no shame, wounding God like that, God, who sees your every action?'

'I had bad thoughts, Father.'

'Such as?'

'I was thinking about girls' legs, Father.'

'Anything more, my son?'

'When their clothes blow up . . . ridin' a bike.'

'But after all, my son, they are but legs. What is the difference between a girl's legs and a boy's?'

Silence in the confessional. Jasus, if he didn't know, I wasn't going to tell him.

'Well, my son?'

'I don't know, Father.'

'Of course you don't know, my son. They're but legs, the same as your own.'

'Yes, Father, of course.'

'Your sin is very grave, my son. Say six Our Fathers, and six Hail Marys in this church, every day after school for a week.' The voice intoning the prayers of Absolution, walking out into the chapel gravely with a soul as pure as an angel's, all care gone, close to God – until the next girl's skirt blew up and you could see the lovely softness and the gentle curves that drove men mad. And you were back to square one, bashing the bishop and the dread of another confession facing you.

'Let's see if they're finished. Maybe they'll go now,' I said.

The three of us were very dejected. All joy had gone from the sunny afternoon. Our lovely Eileen, who passed us by in a fragrance of perfume and walked in beauty, had committed the ultimate sin before our very eyes.

We could have made a run for it easy enough, but strangely and without discussion, we had opted to go quietly away. Not because we had done anything ourselves, but because we did not want Eileen to know we had seen her shame.

We looked out the window again. All was quiet below, passion spent for a while. Jimmy still covered Eileen, but now he was gently opening her blouse and began kissing her milk white breasts and she covering his face with kisses, eyes closed, transported with joy. And the lovemaking started again.

'C'mon for Jasus sake, they won't see us,' whispered Tom. 'Let's get out of here.'

So we came noiselessly down the stairs, out the back way, circled the house, collected the cans of blackberries and were outside the fence in jig time. They had not seen us, being away together in some place we had yet to find. On Dolphins Barn Bridge we stopped to put on our shoes.

'Don't say anything to anybody about this,' I said to the others.

'No,' said Bay. 'I won't anyway.'

'Neither will I,' said Tom Horan.

'They'd all be talkin' about her,' I added.

'Yes,' agreed Bay, 'she'd be shamed in front of the whole square.'

'We'll swear by God,' said Tom Horan, 'that we'll never tell another soul as long as we live. If we do, we are to go straight to hell.'

Solemnly we took the oath, the most fearful oath ever heard of. If we ever spoke of what we had seen, we were automatically damned forever. We never did tell, so we were never damned – for that anyway.

But we came to know who was – Eileen!

About a week after the events in the tangled garden of the old Georgian house, the butcher's did not open for business. There was no notice in the window stating why it was closed, that some relative down the country had died, or that they were going to alter the shop. It was just closed and that was that.

For me it was a minor inconvenience, as I had further to go for meat, but this I did not mind. I had already decided never to buy in Keegan's again. I had always disliked and distrusted Jimmy, the boy from Killane and now I hated his guts.

The shop did not open the following day either, nor the one after that. In fact, it remained closed for a full week and the square was buzzing with rumours.

Eileen, as she came and went to her job, was carefully scrutinised from behind every curtain as she passed. She knew where her Jimmy was and why the shop was not open, but she was not telling. Whatever Jimmy had told her, she believed and waited for him, counting the minutes. She seemed serenely unaware of anything wrong and still walked in cloud cuckoo land.

A week to the day it had closed, Keegan's re-opened. Sloppy Molly stood behind the counter with more affectations than ever. She sported a wide band of gold on the third finger of her left hand and underneath it an expensive engagement ring. Not one person from the square commented on her new status. They bought their meat and left – forever! Sloppy Molly and Jimmy were married. She was Mrs Kelly now.

'It's true, all right,' Mrs Keirsey told my mother. 'I've just left the shop and I've seen the wedding ring for myself.'

'Did you say anything? Congratulate them or anything like that?'

'I did not.' Mrs Keirsey's eyes were full of angry contempt. 'I'd like me job, congratulatin' that plattherfaced bitch an' her sly bastard of a husband. I never liked that fella; maybe Sloppy Molly is what he deserved.'

'What about Eileen O'Connell? How will she take it?'

'I suppose she doesn't know yet, Jesus help her.'

'Yes,' said my mother. 'Jesus help her an' the whole family this day – I'm sorry now we had words.'

Her voiced tailed off, as the singing came to us. We all knew Eileen's lovely voice, for she sang in the church on Sundays. She was the star of the choir and often sang solo, her voice pouring over the congregation below like a benediction.

'Come on, Missus Keirsey,' said my mother swiftly, 'into the parlour an' we'll see.'

Together they made a dive for the front room, peering through the curtains. I quietly went down the hall and stood outside in the sun.

Eileen O'Connell was walking slowly along in the gutter past her own home. She walked with her head down and she was singing.

'Paaanis Angeelicusss . . .'

Eileen's voice rose flawlessly on the air and the whole square was full of song. Never before had she sung like this. Had she been able to do so, she would not have been too long around the Barn. Places like La Scala in Milan or the Metropolitan in New York would have embraced her. Now she sang, heartbroken, as she had never sung before.

She seemed to sing in a great silence. Even the roar of the traffic in Dolphins Barn seemed to have died, muted, before the exhibition of such grief. She sang, gloriously, the long 'Amen' that comes at the end of the hymn. And she did not lack an audience. People had followed her in from the main street, for she had come down it, singing, past Sloppy Molly's, staring in pity at this lovely girl driven mad by love.

The hymn came to an end and she shuffled on in the gutter. At the door of her own house her mother had appeared, face bloated from crying. She had got the news of the marriage a long time before Eileen. I heard afterwards, that when Eileen had been told, she had quietly switched off her machine, gone to the cloakroom and left the tobacco factory, singing.

The fact that she had destroyed ten thousand cigarettes was never mentioned by her supervisor. It was not worth mentioning in the same breath as 'Eileen O'Connell'.

Beside her mother came the tigerish Linda, her face all broken with grief, so much that I pitied her. I should not have kicked her. After all, she *was* a woman.

Then, running, came her two sisters. They must have knocked off work and followed her home, for they all worked in the same place. They stood talking to their mother and came to a decision. Slowly, they converged on Eileen. As she passed our door, Eileen raised her head and paused, looking at the tranquil autumn sky that had lost its sun forever.

'Oh, my beloved father,' she sang. 'I love Thee well . . . Too well . . .' and as her voice rose gloriously to the top note, it cracked, broke and a scream of anguish rent the air, that I will never forget. Nor will anyone else who heard it, not until their dying day.

I went in quietly, closing the door and up to my bedroom.

I was crying. Thank God there was no one to see me. Downstairs I could hear Mam and Mrs Keirsey weeping unrestrainedly. It had been a sight to bring tears from a stone.

We often heard Eileen sing afterwards. She would open the top window of their house and sing until her voice broke and the terrible scream we had heard that first day would come again and the weeping that followed.

The boys would stop playing football. The girls, playing 'beds' with old polish tins filled with earth for weight, would stop and stand in groups, looking towards the O'Connell window. The women would come to the doors and we would all be called in. The Square, like the Liberties had, at the back of all the toughness, a kind heart. There was something indecent about witnessing sorrow on such a scale.

And in the street called Dolphins Barn, a man, whose newly acquired gravity of manner told you he was the boss, would gravely cut a sirloin steak, weigh it and wrap it for some customer with a smile.

Life went on. Tragedies were two to a penny in the teeming streets. Every day young girls, like Ginny Lynch, went off to Mount Jerome cemetery, drawn by four black horses with tossing white plumes. Went off with a bit of style, a flourish and a little panache. They went off. Eileen did not.

I watched her over a period of a year grow slowly back into sanity. She took up her job again in the factory. If her old machine had had eyes, it would not have recognised the woman who operated it now. Her hair, her gleaming brown hair, had turned grey in a couple of weeks, then white. She had lines of pain about her mouth which would only grow deeper with time. Her colour, her roses and cream complexion was gone with the wind. She had contracted, as if she stood in a freezing fog, gone smaller.

And she sang in the choir no more. She was a scald and a hurt to my heart every time I saw her. She would be better off dead, of that I was sure.

11 *Panis Angelicus*

Sometime, along the early years of my boyhood, I rescued a dog from the canal. I was strolling under Rialto Bridge, peering into the water, looking for fish as always, when the dog surfaced beside the bank, feebly treading water. A rope around its neck told the whole story. It had been thrown in to die. The rock that held it under had slipped lose and the unfortunate animal, more dead than alive, rose from the depths. She was a half bred collie, black as coal and I called her Nigger. In fear and trembling I took her home, but something about her made my mother love her at once and that made two of us. I adored her and to her, I was God.

When I was in trouble in the house – and that was frequently – Nigger was there to comfort me with a lick and a tail wag. When some quarrel with 'the gang' had put me in the wrong and left me lonely, she was beside me. When there was no one who wanted to ramble the fields of Crumlin with me, she was glad to come and off I went with my dog, no longer alone.

We never had any spare money in our house, so any idea of buying meat or dog biscuits was out. Mam would have regarded such waste of money as sin. Dogs, in her books, were fed on scraps which, I suppose, is all right if there are any scraps but no invasion of locusts ever left a rice paddy as bare as our family left the table. Nigger was fed mostly on tea and bread, a not very sustaining diet, but there were plenty of people around us, who were trying to live on the same. Mount Jerome was full of the ones who failed.

'That dog is not well,' said a man on the towpath of the canal one day. 'Her coat is too dull.'

'Maybe it would brighten up if I let her in for a swim, mister?'

'No,' said the man, 'she needs a few good feeds, she's too thin.'

'What'id be a good tonic for her, mister? To buck her up, like?'

'Well, I suppose be the look 'a yeh, yer father is not a butcher. Meat or dog biscuits,' said this honest man, 'if yeh can afford to buy them.'

He left me with flaming cheeks and a resentful heart. My summer shorts and gansey were worn and I had scuffed plimsolls on my feet. Anyone could see at a glance where I came from! Anyone with an eye in their head could see my dog was undernourished. Something drastic had to be done, so for Nigger I became a thief.

The Blanchardstown Mills shop was bursting at the seams with dog biscuits and some of those would soon be missing. Beside the counter there was always a sack of them, big, thick squares that dogs loved. I robbed them at every opportunity from then on. I felt bad about this, for the lady behind the counter was gentle and sweet, but so was my dog and for Nigger I buried my conscience.

The lady, whose name was Marian, was short sighted which made my task easy. Knowing her sight was bad, I would wait beside the door until she went to the back of the shop and then I would dart noiselessly in. It was the only time my smallness served me well. I would squat beside the sack, tight against the counter and there, hidden from Marian, I would hold my jumper to form a carrier and fill it with biscuits. I hated to rob Marian, for I had a schoolboy crush on her, but I loved Nigger more.

This went on for weeks, Nigger dining on the best. Her coat glowed with health and when I went up the canal now, she jumped in by herself, swimming and barking. She needed no encouragement from me. She was usually a very nervous bitch and my pugnacious little heart used to rage at the sight of her running before some little scruff-bag of a terrier, half her size. That was the way it was until she got dog biscuits. All my theft was amply rewarded the day she went after the Alsatian. On this wonderful day, Nigger was happily swimming when up ran this big Alsatian, who stood on the bank snarling and waiting for Nigger to come out. She did not hesitate. Out she came, went straight for the bigger dog's throat and took hold. The alsatian got such a shock that she turned and fled, yelping, dragging Nigger along until she lost her grip, then being chased over Dolphins Barn bridge.

I went home aglow, telling all and sundry about my dog's magnificent moment. No boy was ever prouder, no dog patted so much. The supply of biscuits must be kept up at all costs. Of course the day had to come, when I would be caught. Squatting beside the sack one morning, stealing, an 'oul' wan' came in to the shop.

'Yeh get,' she screeched, grabbing me by the collar and boxing my ears. 'Yeh get! Marian! Here's where yer biscuits are goin'!'

Panic-stricken, I twisted out of her grip and spilling biscuits all over the floor, got away. After that, the sack was removed behind the counter – but you could still rob, by leaning over it. Marian had not clearly seen me on that fatal day, so I took to going messages for two 'oul' wans', who kept hens between them and went often to the Mills on a legitimate errand. I nearly always managed to steal biscuits.

The Dog Show, though only on once a year, was another important source of supply. On the last day I would go and beg the men in charge for biscuits. They always gave me all I could carry, recognising in me another dog lover. I would stagger home, bent double with the sack, holding two months' ration. Bringing my pal biscuits was nearly as good as winning the exams and taking Mam home money and cakes. Nearly, but not quite. I developed a taste for dog biscuits myself and often took a couple on a walk with my half-collie, one for her and one for me – well, a half one, anyway. They were *her* biscuits.

About this time, the open fields between the Back of the Pipes and Cork Street were invaded by the Dublin Corporation. First to go was a small cabbage patch with a hawthorn hedge, that bordered the actual street. It should have gone a century before. The convulsion of building, that had followed in the wake of the Huguenot silk empire had ground to a halt, and ribbon-built Cork Street had degenerated in to a slum, a slum with its feet in the country and incredible farms trapped behind the tenements.

In a few months, the cabbage patch was built over and was called Huxley Crescent. Very shortly afterwards, men with wooden pegs, sledge hammers, tape measures and dumpy levels appeared at the top of Emerald Square. The fields were marked out for houses, the lovely old Tudor house demolished, the great orchard destroyed and my wide prairie built over. This was called Maryland.

The vast market garden, that lay at the back of Reuben Street on the far side of The Backers still remained, but its days were numbered. The oasis of the country side which had survived till my time disappeared under a deluge of Dubliners, all needing a house.

Our gang, in the square, had always hated the Cork Street gang, the true denizens of the slums, whose rickety tenements, houses of incredible squalor backed on to the ancient farm. Formerly, the vigilance of the owner, one Buggy Boylan and a few wicked dogs had kept them at bay. Now, with Maryland almost linked to the square, they decided to invade our territory.

We had been waging war with them ever since I could remember and long before that. We just perpetuated an ancient dispute and the war had never ended. It was now brought back to me just how much things had altered in the last two years. The crop of boys that had filled the square, were no longer with us to fight off our enemies. As they had reached fourteen years of age, they had been absorbed, one after the other in to various trades. Those, who had not, had gone to Guinness's.

We had always been the smaller gang in numbers, but had made up for that with fearless leaders like my brother, clever planning and sheer ferocity. That day was gone and the Cork Street gang knew it soon. Beaten back by a hail of stones, only five warriors left to defend the square, we retreated stubbornly. We would not run for cover. The final indignity would be if we had to run for our homes and the Cork Street gang walked through the square, back to their own terrain.

This was all out war. We loved it, lived for it and none of us, miraculously, until this day had been badly injured by the stone throwing. From behind the buttress of the square wall, safe from being hit, I scored heavily. I had hit at least three and they were wavering when I had to jump from cover to gather more stones. I was just straightening up when a lump of concrete from the Maryland building job hit me full in the face. It was a dreadful blow and even after all these years I still cringe at the memory.

I gave one heart-rending scream of pain and collapsed in the shadow of the wall, blood pouring from my mouth and nose. Dimly I remember my mother picking me up and carrying me home. I was in bed for a month. I had two black eyes and a nose swollen to three times its size. I was very sick indeed, so sick that I was taken, hardly able to board the tram, to hospital the second week.

I was given some drops and a small glass tube with a rubber teat. You filled the glass tube and forced the drops up your nose by squeezing. Nowadays, I would have been hospitalized at once, but in those days the working class died at home. Except, of course, when there was a war on. Hospitals throughout the British Isles were places where the wealthy went and poor children had to be at death's door to be admitted.

The few inadequate hospitals the British had left behind them were good enough for the Irish. They were in a deplorable condition – dirty, damp and cold. They were also filthy with fifty years of grime on the walls of the out-patients clinic and pitifully devoid of equipment even for those times and under-staffed. They were always short on money and long on patients.

My recurring bouts of illness since I was a baby could be chalked up to one of these hospitals and dirty surgical instruments. I still remember freezing waiting rooms, the cold hours before your turn came, then from the doctor to the dispensary and afterwards the humiliation of going before the Lady Almoner, who usually was no lady, handpicked for the job, a brazen-faced, overfed bitch of a farmer's daughter.

'How much does your husband earn? How many children have you? What rent do you pay? Have you anyone working in the house besides your husband? Yes . . . yes, you can afford to pay five shillings.'

'But I've only got three shillings.'

'You've no right coming here with that amount. Give it here and be off.'

The confusion, the shame of being poor, the resentment, my mother's uncontrollable temper.

'G'long yeh bloody Culchie bitch, up here to bully the Dublin people!'

'Be off, I told you!'

'Yeh platther-faced bitch!'

'Go now, or I'll call the porter.' The fruity country voice loaded with authority and contempt.

'Try actin' the lady an' no one 'ill know yer from the bog!' I continued ill. Day by day I grew worse. The doctor came and went and where the money to pay him came from, I will never know, or what sacrifices my mother had to make. And I did not care. I was dying and dying hard. Sometimes, I would have moments of lucidity, between raving, and came to, surprised to be talking so silly. And I would see my mother's stricken face, as she stood her ground before the advance of the Old Reaper with his scythe, for he was very close. Apparently, I had developed some kind of brain fever. I had the back bedroom to myself, my brothers and little sisters having to sleep on the floor in the kitchen. The neighbours lit candles for me in the chapel and did the Stations of the Cross. They stormed heaven with prayers. All to no avail. I had the whole square in turmoil.

On Wednesday of the third week, the doctor told my mother that the crisis would come that night. I would start to recover – or die. One way or the other. If I lapsed into unconsciousness she was to send for him. Not otherwise. I would then be rushed to hospital.

Some time in the small hours I woke and sat up in bed. I was very alert, frightened for some reason. From below in the kitchen, I could hear voices as Mam and our neighbour, Mrs Keirsey kept an all night vigil. The rest of the house slept. Dad, the work horse, who stood between us all and destitution, God love him, had to get his sleep.

My bedroom door was slightly ajar and through the opening the gas light from below found its way and lit up a four inch band on the wall. There were some coats and school bags hanging on the back of the door. I remember every tiny detail of that night, branded on my mind forever.

I rubbed my eyes, about to call out for some water, when I saw her. She was a woman about Mam's age with long, black hair hanging down her back. She was clothed in a brown kind of cassock, that I had never seen before but which I afterwards came to know as a death habit, used to clothe a corpse when on public view. She knelt quietly on the end of the bed, hands joined in prayer her face raised to the night sky. In silhouette she looked like Mona Lisa, but I knew she had come from another world. Through the window a crescent moon made the night light and a lone, pale star shone far away.

A scream congealed in my throat and my mouth opened, but no sound came. For all eternity, driven mad by terror, I tried to scream and when it came it was heard all over the square. I woke every family in it.

Dimly I could hear the stumbling feet of my mother as I gave my long cry, the lady in the habit taking no notice of me at all, continuing to pray. How long can a second be? It could not have been more than three seconds before Mam was in the room, yet it seemed like all eternity. The apparition was still there, as the door flew open and I remember thinking Mam would see it as well but as the light from the opening door hit her, she vanished.

My mother, distraught, threw herself on the bed, holding me in her arms. I was sobbing with terror.

'Mam . . . Mam . . . She was here . . . on the bed . . . Mam!'

'There, there, child, she's gone. Your mother has you now.'

'She was going to take me away.'

'Jesus, child . . . stop, love . . . Can't yeh see it's me has yeh . . . Jesus, she's gone . . . There, child, there . . .'

She has only come for me once since and that was in Australia where, dying beneath the Southern Cross, she tried to take me. I had had Extreme Unction and as before, she had come for me. But I would not go, *could* not go. Truthfully, she came as a friend and I would have been glad to leave with her, but I was a man now and had a wife and five children to provide for in an alien and hostile land. She did not try me too hard, seeming to understand and allowed me to defy her.

Next time she calls there will be no reprieve, nor do I want one. I am no longer young, my seeds have grown, there will be little reason not to go 'gentle into that good night', for all my friends, who had gone before me, will be waiting.

And so, my childhood crisis passed. Next morning I was on the mend, a slow and painful journey. Nigger stole into the room and was allowed to stay. The danger was over, but for the rest of my life I would know that I had been within seconds of death. The Old Reaper has received scant respect from me ever since.

It was a month before I was on my feet. It had taken me days to learn how to walk again. Every morning my nose would be blocked with congealed blood. I must still have been bleeding internally. I could no longer speak properly, but only through my nose, a snuffy, nasal sound that made people laugh so I spoke as little as possible.

Several of my friends from Clarendon Street Choir came to see me. I was to have sung solo there on Good Friday, the day after I was struck with the concrete.

That was all over for the present at least. I tried quietly in the bedroom one day to sing, but my lovely voice came like our gramophone, tinny and scratchy. I cried a little that day because I was still weak and sick and the honour of singing solo in Clarendon Street chapel, one of the three great choirs in the capital city had gone and a bright light taken out of my father's life. He detested priests and the Christian Brothers and with good reason, but for all that he had been born a Catholic, he was counted among the flock, branded for life and his pride that his son should sing, solo, in one of the grandest churches in Dublin, knew no bounds. All the men in the Carpenters Union knew about the son, who was going to sing solo. Dad was Vice-president and he let them all know.

'Your father doesn't say much, Lar,' my mother once told me. 'But he's proud as a peacock over you goin' to sing solo.' One more time I had disappointed him.

Uncle Pat arrived now from Wexford. He was fond of me and regarded me with some concern.

'Dolly,' he told my mother, 'you'd better get that boy away from here for a holiday or he'll go away in a box!'

'Jesus, Pat,' said my mother panicking, 'don't say that. He's gettin' better all the time.'

'Dolly,' said Uncle Pat in his slow Wexford brogue, 'he needs some country air. There's a big, empty house in Gorey an' I have two sisters who would be delighted to have him. Sure, Lil and Mag would be over the moon to have someone to care for. Will I drop them note?'

'I'll talk to Laddie about it when he comes home from work.'

Mam, Irish mother, too many children by far, but she would not willingly part with one. However, that night my father decided that when I was strong enough to travel I could go. I had been there once before, when I was about six years old and I had a confused memory of a snug town and two gay women, who told me they were my aunts. I dimly remembered a lot of kisses and loving and that was all. I had only been there two hours but the memory was enough to spark me off to get well enough to travel.

The nasal thing continued, however, I could still no longer sing or speak properly.

'It will go, Lar,' my mother would say. 'The doctor told me it would.'

But it did not and six weeks after I had been hit with the concrete the condition persisted, making my life a misery. I would not go outside and play any more. I knew I would be jeered unmercifully and I was too sensitive to take it and too weak to fight. Bay, my friend, came to our house after school and we played draughts for hours. But inevitably the day came when it was decided to send me off.

One blessed Friday morning, when Barn Street was full of horses and lorries I boarded the new bus that ran down the street and paid the fare to O'Connell Bridge. I took the back seat in the bus so I could watch Dad. He was coming along on his bicycle, close behind, to see me off. Sometimes he would disappear behind a cart or truck, but always reappeared, weaving through the traffic, keeping the bus in sight. At Christ Church we lost him. He could not climb the hill as fast as the bus and I panicked a bit, but soon cooled off. It was only weakness that did that to me. I was a city kid, I was not lost. I knew every street we passed through and it was not until I stood up to get off at the Ballast Office that I felt the movement at my feet. Nigger!

My heart contracted. Here was trouble and loads of it. Dad would have to take the dog back, walking. He would lose half a day's pay at least. Maybe he would be sacked, for these were days when the employers rode high, work was scarce and men were expendable. Nigger cowered at my feet, afraid of this big, new street. I made my decision quickly. She would have to be carried.

Staggering across the street with my dog and my parcel, I reached the Wexford bus. I was nearly crying with weakness and fright for I dreaded my father's displeasure. I knew the trouble this would bring him. Woefully, I staggered on to the bus.

'Aye . . . aye,' said the driver-conductor. 'No dogs allowed on the bus.'

I burst out crying.

'Aw, now, there's no need for that!' The driver was upset.

'I never said a word teh him,' he told the other passengers defensively.

'Wait a minute, me oul flower,' he said to me, 'hold on, it's not that bad. Tell us what's wrong.'

I told him my story. I was a sick-looking kid and the whole bus was on my side. The driver too. So, before Dad caught up, Nigger was safely under the back seat and all was well. Dad came, the amiable driver got out to talk to him. I saw Dad's face drop then light up and I went off the bus to him. He gave me a great hug and I knew he loved me.

And with my young heart singing, off to Wexford we went. This was better than all my dreams put together. My beloved Nigger lay at my feet, cute as a fox, knowing when to keep quiet. She lay behind the little bundle I had with me, weekday trousers, a spare pair of shoes, soled twice, a couple of pairs of socks and a gansey. It was nearly summer and it was hoped I would not need a heavy overcoat. Anyway, I didn't have one so that was that.

I was going away with my pal on a great adventure. This was the first time I had ever been on a long distance bus. Indeed, I had rarely been on any kind of bus, shanks mare and the nineteen tram serving my needs. The bus was full now, it was nine o'clock, so away we went. On the only occasion I had been to Wexford before we had gone by train and for a while I thought I had been cheated, but as we threaded our way through the traffic I could see that this really was a more interesting way to go than by rail.

But a lot of the excitement and ceremonial had been taken from the departure. There was no steaming monster panting on the rails, mad to be off, barely held. There were no whistles shrilling, no uniformed guards waving flags, no ear-splitting blast from the engine, as we chuffed savagely out of the station, past the waiting-rooms and toilets . . . no anything, but the bus was still a more intimate way to leave. And we went through all the villages and townships instead of just stations, that looked all the same.

We followed the tram lines until we came to Blackrock and then we swung onto the Bray road. Soon we were truly in the country and in half an hour passed through the town of Bray, penetrating deeper and deeper into the countryside. Kilmacanogue, Newtown-mountkennedy and Ashford, where we stopped for fifteen minutes which I spent looking into the Vartry at the trout leaping for flies, beauty and peace all round. The trees starting to burst their buds and daffodils watching themselves in quiet backwaters. The Sugarloaf mountain we had lately passed, coloured like cigarette smoke, pluming into the sky. Such magnificence I had never seen before.

This was far wilder country than the fields around Crumlin, the mountains higher than those surrounding the capital. This was the real McCoy, racing rivers coloured like strong tea from a bog brew, dashing over rocks to get to the sea. Thick forests, dark and mysterious looking. There could be wolves in there still, living on rabbits and pheasants and deer. Who could say with certainty what such forests could contain? There could be . . . I heard the noise of the bus revving up and made a run for it.

'Janey,' I panted to the driver. 'Yeh should have sounded yer horn. I nearly got left behind!' He grinned.

'No fear a' that, son. I'm watching you. Yer not in Dublin now.'

No I was not. With every yard we left Dublin further behind and it got better all the time. The very bus seemed to relax in this God-given place. The people in the towns and villages seemed at ease and smiling. Nigger, cute as ever, lay quite still under the seat, head on paws and looking up at me in silent adoration.

And so we came to Arklow, the town where Uncle Pat worked as a barman. The bus stopped in front of his pub and he came out to meet me, striding across the gravelled front, a handsome Wexford man aged twenty-five with dark brown hair, ruddy faced and healthy, like a bit of the open sea and country all about him.

I hero-worshipped Uncle Pat. He was everything I admired – easy-going, smiling, good natured, not one blemish could I see in him. He brought me into the pub, sat me on a stool and treated me to a glass of lemonade and biscuits. I was in seventh heaven with all the passengers around, suddenly important.

'Sure, Lar,' said Uncle Pat when we were leaving, 'you look tired but Gorey is just down the road. You'll be there in fifteen minutes.'

It took us a little longer. 'Just down the road' was ten miles with the first stop half way there at a place called Inch. It was not much bigger than its name suggested and half the passengers got off. Between Inch and Gorey it was all stops at tiny lanes where a pony and trap would be waiting for a loved one. The Dublin bus driver knew them all and barricked them. 'Puttin' on weight, Pat. It's a wonder yeh don't do a bit a' work on the farm.'

'An' why should I? An' the likes a' you sittin' on your backside all day. D'yeh call that work?'

And behind him Tara Hill, with yellow gorse on its slopes, puffy white clouds scudding across the blue sky and I wanted to get out and run and jump with my dog for joy. Summer had come earlier here than in Wicklow. The hedgerows were covered with mint fresh foliage. Laburnum and lilac bushes were drooping with blossom at every cottage we passed, the country was flatter, not so wild as the tumultuous slopes of Wicklow. For all that, I had an impression of deep countryside, rich and fertile with an unending variety of woods and fields and glens, happy streams where trout lay under stones.

At last we came to Gorey. The bus lumbered up a small incline and suddenly we were in a wide street, the Main Street of the town. It was open and clean and breezy and at the bus stop two young women were standing. One, Mag, was buxom and bouncing with rosy cheeks. The other, Aunt Lil, was taller, slighter, better looking with regular features, a nice, pale complexion with just a touch of pink, cooler than her sister, more ladylike than the scatter-brained Mag.

In a second I was on the pavement, smothered with squeezes and kisses, such a fuss that I could feel myself growing red.

And then I had to confess about Nigger. She was still under the seat, the bus driver grinning, waiting to see what would happen over the half-collie lying quietly at the back.

'Sure, it's all right, Lar, don't be worryin', sure he'll be company for you out in the Park Woods . . .'

'It's a *she*, Auntie Lil.'

'No matter, love, it's your dog and welcome.'

I gave Nigger a whistle and out she bounded, knowing that

all was safe, dancing, barking, jumping up on Mag and Lil, making friends all round. Everything was great. I was very happy. The sisters swam in a golden haze before my eyes, Nigger became a moving dark blur. I just knew I would be happy here.

'Jasus,' I heard Mag's rich brogue say quickly. 'Catch him Lil, he's faintin'.'

I came to about five minutes later. The first thing I saw was the two sisters' faces. I was lying with my head on something soft which I later found out to be a bale of cloth. The Buckleys, who owned the tailor shop opposite the bus stop had seen me faint and Jack, the eldest son, had carried me across. There seemed to be a sea of faces around me, all strange. I was lying on the tailor's work platform which was built directly behind the shop window where the Buckley boys sat crosslegged, stitching all day and the life of the town passed by. They saw everything, missed nothing. It was as good as looking at a silent movie.

But such a fuss and all over me. I had an overpowering sense of being wanted, loved and tears came to my eyes. I was still weak, easily moved and tired out. The bus journey had done that. So much to see, so much to learn on my magical journey from Dublin. Five and a half hours it had taken us and I was worn out.

Mrs Buckley, a lively, wrinkle-faced widow, was smiling at me.

'Is there anything I could get you, Lar?' she said.

'I'd love a cup of tea, Missus, if it's not too much trouble. I'm dying for one!'

'Well,' said the widow cheerfully, 'we can't have a death in the shop-window, can we! I'd better get the tea right away.'

'The funny little voice of it,' said Katie Buckley, the eldest daughter. I felt my face grow red and I wanted to die of shame.

'He has had an accident,' said Lil swiftly, 'to his nose. He will soon be speaking normally again.'

'Oh,' said Katie quickly, 'I wasn't remarking on that. Just the nice little accent of it . . . You're all right, Lar, aren't you?'

'Yes,' I said faintly. 'I'm all right, thank you.'

Already with the lightning perception of youth, I had sensed the absolute change in my environment and I would be my father's son while here. Or, put another way, the son my father had always wanted. There was no need for fierce struggle. I could relax now, walk in woods and listen to what the wind had to say. I was all on my own with two lovely aunts to spoil me and the Buckleys lived next door. They all seemed so genuinely glad to have me with them. It was only in later years that it came to me that the two houses in Main Street had not had a child around for many, far, far too many years. The boat to America had stolen the young men of this town, the ones who stayed behind were in many cases too poor to marry or too frightened of an uncertain future.

I was special around here. This was not the Liberties where every cul-de-sac was full of children. I would sing for these people. Wait till they heard me sing. None of them knew that I could . . . and then my face dropped, as I realised that I could not sing any longer.

Mrs Buckley came in then with tea and soda bread smothered with butter and honey and I ate and drank quickly, feeling the strong tea and bread and honey giving me strength.

'You're getting a little colour back into your face,' said Aunt Li quietly. I smiled at her. Already she had captured my boyish heart with her good looks, charming quiet manner and cool hands. It was the same for her, I knew. Something about me had made her love me at once.

'I think,' she said now to all the Buckleys, 'it's time I took him home. He has been very sick and come a long way. Say good-bye, Lar, until tomorrow.'

'Yes,' said Mrs Buckley, giving me a hearty kiss on the cheek. 'A seat by the fire and an early night, eh, Lil?'

'I think so,' said Lil. 'And he has yet to meet the man of the house. That's your Uncle Mike, my father,' she told me. Although I called her Auntie Lil she was really my second cousin.

We went home and I met Uncle Mike. He turned out to be a small man, leaning on a walking stick, shiny bowler hat on his head, briar pipe jammed in his gob, incredibly old to me. He was about sixty-eight I found out, but looked older.

'Bet from the drink,' Mag whispered. He did not drink much now because he had no money, but he was bet anyway.

He was affable enough for a minute or two and then forgot about me. From then on, with a single exception – and that a memorable one – I might have been one of the hens that rambled in and out the kitchen door. That suited me fine for I did not like his brusque manner. I had nothing to say to this old fossil who must have played pitch and toss in the shadow of the pyramids, when they were being built.

The house was quite large to someone used to an over-crowded artisan dwelling. It was sparsely furnished, due to Uncle Mike's having sold most of the furniture on various sprees. I had a large bedroom all to myself. It contained nothing except a wardrobe and a bed. Before going to sleep I would imagine myself afloat with my bed as a raft in a sea of dun coloured timber, for there was no covering on the floor.

There was little work available in those days and what there was, was beneath my aunts. They lived on Main Street, there was no shop in town good enough for them to serve in. A factory job, had there been a factory, was beneath them and they had no skills that would qualify them for a job in an office. They lived on the money their brother sent them from Dublin and Uncle Pat in Arklow, who always had a few pounds to throw away. I believe he dabbled in cattle on the side. Anyway, who had ever heard of a barman stuck for the price of a smoke or a drink or even a pub, come to that?

It was my first encounter with the dreadful pride of a small Irish town. Living there for three months I came to know, that if you did not live on Main Street you did not exist. People from Main Street went to England and America and gladly took work they would have died of shame to be seen doing at home.

However, on this my first day I knew nothing of this. The kitchen was a delight to me and a cause of sorrow to the sisters. Electricity had come with the advent of the Shannon scheme, the first hydro-electric venture and Ireland moved into the twentieth century. The 'model county', as always, went forward quickly.

The town soon had facilities for cooking and lighting that were clean and smokeless. Out went the open fire with its peat or timber fuel, glowing twenty-four hours a day. In came the electric cooker and an Aga range. Out went the oil lamps, stone age things to be cast aside, beautiful lamps with glazed roses on their bowls, elegant shades shedding soft light. And with them, the stools that stood in the inglenook of the open fire with the bar across for hanging pots. Out went the smoke blackened pot oven that made lovely soda bread for decades and, of course, the side of bacon up the chimney curing in the smoke, turning dark brown. You never got bacon like this in the Liberties. An old way of life died swiftly in Gorey. The people of Wexford, progressive as always, had moved quickly with the advent of electricity. Thank God, my relatives had not had the money to follow their example. Everything in the kitchen was as it had been for two hundred years.

The huge fireplace, that I could walk into, always had a fire. Being summer it was allowed to die down in the day, but at night it spread its heat and light and above all, lent itself to conversation. There was a wheel in the corner that turned a belt, that in its turn revolved a fan under the fire and if the fire died down, I would be asked to 'give the fanner a bit of a turn' – a job I loved.

We had many people, relatives mostly, I had yet to meet. To my amusement they were referred to as 'country people' by my cousins as they were all farmers, but they kept the sisters supplied with many a meal and one supplied turf, another logs and the pigsty always had a pig in it. They saw to it, that the sisters and old Musty Mike did not go short. And there was one special distant relation, Caroline, the same age as Lil, twenty, who always came loaded with gifts.

She brought homemade farmer's butter and apples in season, rabbits the brother had shot, pheasants poached from Lord Courtown, a flitch of bacon, a boiling fowl! The sisters thought of themselves as poor. Jesus, they didn't know what poor was! I did.

Down the country, no man need never starve if he is in good health. Here is everything needed for survival, from the nettles in the ditch to the watercress in the streams. Not to mention mushrooms, blackberries, brown trout and white trout, pheasants and rabbits galore. All in their season, of course. It was a poor specimen of a man who could not get himself a plot for spuds and cabbage and he could get all the firewood he wanted by trimming a farmer's hedge or felling a dangerous tree.

These easy-going people mostly thought of themselves as poor, even desperately poor and grew up, sighing for the plenty of London or New York, followed their brother or some relative who was doing great . . . and woke up. You could eat concrete in the Liberties if you were able but I have never heard of a rabbit being snared there. The people were about four centuries too late for that.

If you were stuck for a bob in Dublin, you were stuck for the lot. No money meant no fire, no rashers, no rabbits, no light, nothing. It was as simple as that. In many ways I could have bought and sold these people, for I had come through a hard school and would go back to the same. I dreaded the thought of it. Already, my heart had been taken by this town and its citizens and the obvious lack of fierce struggle which I regarded as normal. Now *they* could teach *me* something. How, for a while, to be easygoing and gentle, to leave the bold four letter word out of your mouth and fall in with the slow tempo of the country. I never wanted to see Dublin again. These were my golden days, before the all-conquering desire for sex took over my being, bringing its own heaven . . . and hell! These were the days of my innocence when I rambled the woods and fields around Gorey, no more lonely than a tree or a flower. A dandelion with its golden, sunny face turned to the sun knew nothing about loneliness. Neither did I.

Loneliness hates children. They are immune to its poison. Only when they become old and vulnerable does it attack, doubly distilled in the Vat of Frustration, powerful enough to kill. But the Lar Redmond, who roamed free as a breeze that rustles the rushes around the marlhole knew nothing of this.

The one big black spot on all this happiness was my accursed speech. The Buckleys did not know what to make of me for I stood, when late evening came on in their shop by the hour saying nothing, *me* that the Liberties said had verbal diarrhoea! They thought me a silent boy whereas I was the greatest chatterbox for miles. It was crucifixion for me. I could not tell them, only smile when they asked me if the cat had got my tongue. Lil was the only one I told about my humiliation.

This morning, washing under the pump in the yard, old Uncle Mike approached me. I had learnt he was nick-named Musty Mike and I was ashamed of him. But many years later with my boyhood over, I was told *why* he was called Musty Mike. It had nothing to do with his appearance. It was because he told all and sundry what to do. 'Yeh *must* do this' or 'Yeh *must* do that' – hence Musty Mike. Now he beckoned me to come to him.

'Come over here, you,' he growled in his voice of a lion. I went over, drying my face with a towel.

'Yes, Uncle,' I said.

'Kneel down there,' he told me, ''an I'll bless that nose a' yours with holy water. This water is from Lourdes in France an' blessed be the Gorey priest as well.'

'It must be powerful stuff then,' I said, trying not to sound sarcastic. He gave me a hard stare.

'This'll cure you,' he said.

'Thank you, Uncle,' I said civilly. I stood there, looking from him to the dirty cobbles with hen droppings everywhere.

'Will yeh kneel down when yer told,' he said on a rising note.

'Where? Here?'

'Yes! HERE!' he roared in the voice of a bull. 'Are yeh too good to kneel in teh yard!'

So I knelt down and got chicken shit on my knees while the old man stood over me. His walking stick was held between his legs as he unscrewed the top of the bottle. Making the sign of the cross on my nose, he sprinkled some holy water on it and said a Hail Mary and an Our Father in which I had to join. When we finished the Our Father together I rose to my feet.

'Kneel down,' he roared. 'I'm not finished yet!'

So down into the chicken shit I went again, while he said his own beloved prayer. 'Matthew, Mark an' Luke an' John, God bless this bed that I lie on . . .' he droned on interminably while I shifted uneasily in the shit. At length he came to an end.

'Yeh can get up now,' he said, 'an' stan' there while I make the sign a' the cross on yer nose again.'

Lil and Mag were watching from the door of the kitchen, but did not answer my smile. They were as deadly serious as the old man. Very quickly I learnt not to scoff at religion while down the country. They were not as progressive as Dublin, I thought. They were priest-ridden.

I forgot the many times I had had to fight over slagging Father Cleary, the priest in Dolphins Barn, fight boys, who came from *good* Catholic homes. I cast into the back of my mind the thousands, who thronged into chapels on a Sunday morning. I forgot the dealers, who despite their coarse language and fondness for a ball a' malt would tear the face off you if you said a word against Father Flash or any other priest either.

The ritual finished, I made for the water pump and started washing my legs.

'Thanks Uncle Mike,' I said.

'Ye'll be cured in the mornin',' he said.

'I hope so,' I said in my nasal, tinny voice.

The fields were lovely that day. I came home tired out. I had overdone it a little but I was growing stronger. My face had some colour in it now and my nose was freckled.

Falling asleep in the inglenook that night, Lil gently woke me and put me to bed. I must have been very sleepy not to mind her undressing me, for I was very shy in matters like this. But I allowed her to do it and to tuck me into bed. I felt warm and loved. My poor mother had to spread her ration of love out too thinly and sometimes when I was bold – and that was often – there was none left over for me at all.

'Do you love me?' said Lil coaxingly.

'Oh, Auntie Lil, I do. And I never want to go back to Dublin again.'

'Hush,' said Lil, 'you mustn't think that way. What would your poor mother say if she heard you talking like that?'

'I'd like her to come here every week, but I don't want to go back to Dublin again, ever!'

The noise, the congestion, the beggars, the characters, the poverty and the kindness, the cruelty and the wealth – there was too much of everything from where I came from.

So Auntie Lil kissed me, tucked me into bed and went away delighted because this little get had told her he loved her. The first of many women destined for a similar fate!

'Good Night, Lar,' she called from the doorway.

'Good Night, Auntie Lil,' I called in my tinny voice and promptly fell asleep. Nigger slept at the end of the bed. God was in his heaven, and the world all right.

Whit Sunday started with two momentous events. Speaking to Nigger as the sun came over the roof tops, I realised that I could speak normally again. The old man's Lourdes water, despite my derision, had worked the small miracle and while I slept, Matthew or Mark or Luke or John or the whole lot of them together had put things right and my gramophone voice was gone forever.

It was only seven o'clock in the morning and this household, country style, did not get up too early. So I quietly dressed in my best clothes, cleaned my shoes in the kitchen and went out in the back yard to say good morning to the pig which, grunting with delight, came up to me. She knew me well for I was always finding tit-bits for her and now I ran down Esmond Street where there was a potato store and sure enough, I found four spuds in the gutter.

I took them back to the pig, Nigger barking with delight, and fed her. She snorted and grunted happily while I scratched her head, laughing. Never was there a happier Whit Sunday morning. I felt I would burst with joy. I loved this town and its people. I loved Lil and Mag and Nigger. I loved the family of tailors next door. I loved this old pig I was feeding.

And suddenly, I remembered I could sing again! My voice was back! And I started to sing softly, at first to the pig trying things out and then really singing as before. I sang *Panis Angelicus*, the beautiful hymn I was to have sung in Clarendon Street, but never did. I sang from pure boyish happiness, from love of this sunny morning and these sunny people I was among. And most of all I sang because my voice was back and I *could* sing.

Leaning over the wall of the pig sty, I finished my hymn and feeling eyes upon me, turned suddenly around. The top windows of the tailor's house, our own place and the bootmaker's next door on the other side were all full of faces, listening to me and in utter confusion I turned and fled.

So, in one song, in a flash, my reputation as a singer went the rounds and from then on I never lacked anything a boy could desire.

Back home, in the Square, it was accepted that I had an exceptional voice and I would be asked to sing on special occasions, but that was all. Down here in Gorey, where the pace was slow, they had time to knock off any old tick off the clock to listen to a song. I was treated like a king. As I ran down the lane at the back of our house, I heard the chapel bell ring for eight o'clock Mass and I decided to go. Nigger could wait outside and by the time I came home, things would have died down.

Mass in this quiet country town was very different from Mass in Dolphins Barn. Here, all the people seemed to be pious, or at least God fearing, perhaps *priest* fearing would be more appropriate.

There was an enormous red necked one saying Mass, a huge man, grossly overweight, who looked more like a three hundred acre farmer than a man of God. Every time he genuflected, the collision between his knee and the wooden dais before the altar boomed through the chapel like thunder. His sermon was a beauty and interested me very much. It was all about his brother priests who, according to his Lordship were being reduced to the level of an Indian Untouchable by the non-payment of last Autumn's dues! '*Last Autumn's dues*!' he roared again, in case we had not heard him the first time. He then went on to say that although his brother priests were suffering, they had decided in their infinite compassion, that they would not read the names off the altar *this* Sunday, it *would* be done and the offenders made publicly known next Sunday if the dues were not forthcoming.

'Regretfully,' he added softly. For Mother Church loved her sons and daughters but could no longer endure the tithe dodgers . . . Mother Church needed money for many things . . . the millions in Africa . . .

This was the gist of the sermon, if one could call it that, and I left the chapel without putting one penny on the plate, although I had six, due to Uncle Pat. I sauntered home with Nigger, pondering the tirade I had just heard.

Deep down in the hearts of the people of the Liberties, their religion lies like buried treasures. But there was no way, I knew, that they would stand for this type of bullying. If this Gorey priest had chanced his arm like that in Francis Street or High Street or in Dolphins Barn, the reaction would have been immediate and derisive. He would not have received much in the way of dues in a long time.

As I came into the kitchen for my breakfast there was a delicious smell of frying bacon and eggs and something else that made my mouth water in anticipation. Boisterous Mag threw her arms around me as soon as she could.

'Jasus,' she said in her strong but musical Wexford brogue, 'the lovely voice of it. Didn't I tell yeh,' she screeched, hugging me, 'that the Holy Wather 'id fix yer nose! Now, do yeh believe me?' I nodded and extricated myself with difficulty from her embrace.

'Lil, hasn't he the darlin' voice?'

Auntie Lil quietly left the pan and knelt down before me, the better to look into my face.

'Lar,' she said softly, 'you have a God-given voice. May the Lord leave it with you. You'll never know what a hard day's work is.' And she kissed me and back to the pan. But the Lord did not leave it with me and I came to know only too many hard days work.

'I have a special breakfast for you,' said Lil. 'Guess what?'

Hafner's white pudding and sausages,' I said. She smiled.

'Too smart by half, though you're right. Your mother sent some down on the Wexford bus.'

'We'll see now if they're as good as he says,' Mag interrupted. 'He's always boastin' about them. I bet they're not as good as the Wexford ones.'

But at breakfast both my aunts had to agree that Dublin sausages and white puddings were really something. I was proud as a peacock. What a day this was turning out to be. My voice back, my favourite breakfast, the sun shining outside and the Liberties so far away that I could barely remember it.

After breakfast, the young women went off to mass. Uncle Mike never attended, being of too delicate a constitution for the rigours of early twelve mass, though he could drink like a fish and did. And roar like a bull and did. Especially when he was drunk. He had to be watched every Friday. If one of the girls was not with him when he collected his old age pension, he went on a spree. His daughters, waiting at home for the badly needed money, would never dare to go to the pub to collect him. It was not done. The town must never know how much it meant to them.

Mag would tell him off when he came home broke, screeching at him, but very careful to keep her distance. He would stand, head down like an old bull, roaring, stick raised and frighten the bejasus out of her. Lil never said anything but the old man feared her disapproval much more than he feared Mag's screeching tongue.

I went for a walk, but made sure to be back before twelve thirty. The tailor's shop, I had discovered, was great gas after last mass. It would be full of people – farmers, life-long customers, relations, friends of a lifetime and a couple of young farmers in their late thirties, with an eye on the two Buckley daughters, Katie and Bridie.

This morning the place seemed to be more packed than usual and I inched in as quietly as possible. Nobody would ask me if I had lost my tongue any longer for they would soon get an answer. There was a bit of a hush as I came in, for which I could not account until Mrs Buckley, coming out of the kitchen and into the shop stood looking and smiling at me.

'I was woken up this morning,' she told the crowd, 'be a lad singin' to a pig. An' such singin'! Where did yeh learn to sing like that?' I felt myself go red. I must have been the shyest city kid ever born.

'I could always sing,' I said.

'Not to sing *Panis Angelicus* the way you did,' said her son Eddie. 'I'm a member of the Gorey Church choir an' that was trained singin'. Who taught you?'

'Mr Sheen. He's the choir master at Clarendon Street. I sing solo there! Every Sunday morning.' There. The lie was out. But I felt it to be only a white lie. But for the Cork Street gang it would have been true.

'Begob,' said a farmer.

'Be the hokey,' said another.

'Is that a big choir?' Eddie asked.

'It's the biggest and best in all Dublin. Ask anybody up there.'

Yes, ask anybody except the parishioners from White Friar Street, or Marlborough Street, deadly rivals. But there was not anyone from there, only me from Dublin and I sang in Clarendon Street.

And here came another momentous event of that eventful day. In to the crowded shop came a slightly built figure with a heavy untrimmed black beard that merged into a head of curly hair, black as a crow's wing except for one narrow streak of silver straight through the middle. He was, for all his shabby coat and baggy trousers, a figure it was impossible to ignore. There was a chorus of 'Good morning, Dinny,' from all.

'Good morning,' he replied in an educated accent. It was Dennis Coyle, son of the biggest grocer's shop in town, scion of a wealthy family, educated at University College, Dublin and Lil whispered to me that he had had a nervous breakdown, there was a 'little want' in him. Where I came from it would have been said that he was 'a ha'penny short of a shillin'.' He was not more than twenty-eight, though I thought him old.

'Sing us that hymn again,' said Mrs Buckley to me. I hung my head. My accursed shyness stopped me in everything.

'Come on,' coaxed the widow. 'Sure, you've no excuse now. Your talkin' is all right again, I'm told.'

After a little pushing I agreed. But it was Aunt Lil who made me overcome my bashfulness. Her plea was my command. I adored her. I would do anything for her. Singing was nothing, if it gave her pleasure.

On this blessed Sunday morning a small miracle had happened despite my scoffing at the Holy Water and I was walking on air. So away I went, not a sound in the shop, not even a head scratched until I had finished. And then the applause! The praise! The innocent pride of Aunt Lil! It was worth all the weeks of agony, when I was ashamed to speak with my tinny voice, to see their faces and realise I could sing again at last.

'You've a lovely voice,' said Dinny Coyle, who was close by. 'I've seen you walking the fields a few times. Have you ever been in the Park Woods?'

'I found a wood, all right.'

'Yes, I saw you that day,' said Dinny. 'That's not a real wood, only a copse. I'll show you a big wood, one you can walk through all day. Would you like that?'

'Yes,' I said eagerly. 'When?'

'Tomorrow morning. I'll be down about ten or eleven.'

I felt strangely attracted to this man, even though he was supposed to be 'not all there' and through this meeting I would have a soft spot for 'God's children' for the balance of my life. Dinny was by no means mad. It was just that the hand of the mighty Potter, who lives in the sky, shook a little when He made him. There was a little something missing in him, that was all. And besides, even had he been the full shilling, I suspected that work was a four letter word in his vocabulary and a dirty one at that.

'Sing them another song,' he said quietly. They were all clamouring for more, so I obliged with my favourite ballad.

'There's a sweet, darlin' cratur
Called Kitty O'Toole
She's the lily of fair Tipperary
With cheeks like a rose
And eyes like the sloe
And a figure as neat as a fairy.'

Three verses in all, sung in dead silence and the uproar when I had finished. I had to sing again. I did not mind now, the shyness gone, delighted to please these Wexford people, who had been so kind to me. Anyway, my grandfather had come from hereabouts and the county was close to my heart. And destined to remain so, always.

These were the halcyon days of my boyhood, my all-too-brief boyhood. Here was my Island in the Sun, my Tir na n'Og, Celtic Land of Eternal Youth, where a part of me would always stay. This was my Hy-Brasil, Isle of the Blest, destined to flicker and fade and drown in the waves of time, too soon!

12 *Merciful Artane – Hardline Glencree*

The following morning Dinny called for me. Not for many years did I figure out the reason for his sudden adoption of the 'little city lad'. It was simply that I represented a meal ticket, in brief, my soprano voice. With me beside him, all farm houses welcomed him and kitchen cupboards flew open at his gentle touch. Unlimited loaves of soda bread, smothered with butter and honey, not to mention soft boiled eggs stretched before him. Dinny was a son of Wexford, these were his people and he knew them. They loved singing. It was as simple as that. With a lead soprano from Clarendon Street he was made.

It was almost uncanny the way we always emerged from Park Woods with a farm house beside us. My small fame had gone the rounds quickly. We would be invited in and in five minutes I would be singing. They were kindly, simple folk and their love of music was as deep in them as their hatred of the English. Their bitter defeat at Vinegar Hill a hundred and fifty years before had never for a moment been forgotten. My rendering of the Dublin song, *Kevin Barry*, brought rapturous applause, seeing as it was about an Irish rebel hanged at eighteen years of age in my native city.

The trade was not all one sided. Dinny repaid me more than he knew. He knew the Park Woods like the back of his hand and he opened a world as wonderful to me as the Black Forest must have been to Hansel and Gretel. Composed of beech, oak and chestnut trees, there was the occasional soaring Douglas pine, lording it over the rest. Monkey puzzle trees, spikily unclimbable, tall as an ordinary pine lined the mile long avenue, a few dead from old age, the rest still alive and flourishing, the largest of their species I was ever to see.

The Park Woods was vast, but the summer I came to know it had seen the tree fellers move in, axe and crosscut saw in hand. In a few years, all the leafy monarchs would be gone, but I have never been back. I do not want to see the farms and grasslands where they once were. For me they still stand, indestructible.

Dinny, on this first morning, introduced me to his rounds. He simply went into a shop and engaged the shopkeeper in casual conversation. Grocers gave him damaged fruit and broken biscuits and by request a few lumps of sugar. Confectioners would contribute stale or crumbled cakes, sweet shops sometimes came up with a mass of boiled sweets, all welded together from being left in the window in hot sunshine. We usually did well and then it was off to the Woods for the day, to wander at will among the glades, free as the breeze.

After the first morning we made an extra call at my suggestion, to the butcher for Nigger.

Beside a stream full of fat trout, Dinny showed me how an orange should be eaten, while Nigger enjoyed a bone. Deftly, with a penknife, he cut a small square out of the skin, forced three lumps of sugar into the hole, put it to his mouth and squeezed it. I copied him and found it delicious. Dinny was also adept at sucking a raw egg, but I had no stomach for this game, or perhaps I had too much.

He showed me how to set a night line for trout, but that was as far as his lore went. I knew more from the fields and ponds of Crumlin than he ever would. This would constantly astonish the farmers, the amount of real knowledge I, a city kid, possessed about badgers, rabbits, foxes and stoats, the smaller cousin of the weasel. In a moment of insight the Kipper had once informed us with a hard grin, that there were no weasels in Ireland except in Leinster House, which was where our parliament met. The point was not lost on me and I often corrected the farmers and, much to their amusement, passed on the Kipper's comment.

Dinny prided himself on being a 'townsman' and felt himself

above and apart from the farming folk. As, I supposed, he had a right to do, seeing he had been college educated and had gone on to university. He knew a lot more about Gilbert and Sullivan and the opera than pigs or work, both equally offensive to him. It took a while for the distinction between a townsman and countryman to sink into my mind, for as far as I was concerned they were all countrymen and Gorey just a village.

I, who had first seen the light in a Georgian house with its high ceilings, ornate centre pieces, from which a chandelier was meant to hang and its beautiful cornices, its wide, sweeping staircase, that had echoed in my time to the thunder of Black and Tan boots, was unlikely to be impressed by this little town. Compared to my city it was a mere skidmark. But I loved it far more than I ever would love Dublin's towering Georgian tenements, for on the north side of the city they had been invaded by the swelling hoi polloi. The beautifully laid out squares were a hazard to cross, especially if you were small like me. One was likely to be intercepted and beaten up by the resident bowsies.

However, the same vintage squares on the south side were still places of dignity and wealth. Being shabby, I was uncomfortable and out of place in them. 'Back to your Liberties' they seemed to say, 'back where you belong. You are better suited to your small houses and fetid lanes than you are to this. Get thee gone to thy Dutch Billys.'

The park in the middle of Merrion Square was closed to people like me. Sometimes, in summer, having gone to Merrion Strand, made ravenous by sea air, we had unwisely spent our pennies on fruit cake and had to trudge disconsolately all the way back to Dolphins Barn. On the weary journey we passed by Merrion Square and could see, through the railings, the elite playing cricket on the carpet of Axminster grass. They wore their school caps differently from us, those of us who had ever been lucky enough to have one. Whereas we wore it straight on top of the head or carelessly on the back, these Cromwell's bastards wore theirs with the peak resting on their noses, so that they had constantly to elevate it. It was a very real example of looking down the nose at one's fellows but these young gentlemen did not even glance at us. We were not worth even that much, even though we effed and blinded them and called them Cromwell's bastards and 'prods'.

For all that, I secretly envied them. It was easy to sneer and eff them, but at the back of it all I knew I should have been the equal of the best. My father had not deserved his fate either and the evil that had been done to him, lived after him.

When his patrimony had been robbed by his sister, he had come down in the world with a bang and his children were people of the streets. We had nothing except the two hands God gave us and, of course, our stinking Norman pride that no vicissitude in life would ever conquer.

One day out in the woods, with Nigger and Dinny, I told the story. My father had never directly informed me about the loss of his fortune but I had pricked up my ears the first time I heard it discussed by Dad and his brothers openly. I was supposed to be too young to understand. Sometimes, when Uncle Morrie would come to take me fishing, he and my father might discuss some other facet of the thing and I would add another little bit to my story.

The tale I told Dinny was largely filled in with surmises of my own, but essentially the facts, as related by me, were correct. Years after, my father told me the whole sorry story and I found little alteration to the tale I had confided in the woods. When Dinny and I fell out – and that was often – he would refer to the Coombe and Dolphins Barn with contempt and I think I told him the story to impress him, to let him know that I was every bit as good as him, or better. Neither of us came from landed gentry, not in this century anyway, but if things had been right, I would have gone to college too and university if I felt like it. And I would have felt like it!

The story was terrible enough. To begin with, one must go back to the turn of the century. The Edwardian world was dying and with it a woman called Mrs Redmond. There the tragedy started.

My grandfather had been the second son of a prosperous

farmer with no right of succession. But he had been armed with a college education, a good business head, some capital on attaining twenty-one and unlimited ambition. He came to Dublin and began his assault on the city. He was a big man, described as majestic in a tall silk hat, for he stood over six feet barefoot. In ten years, he had become the owner of a large city centre public house with an off licence, and a butcher shop. He had shares in a lot of companies, like the old Mountjoy Breweries and Dublin Whiskey Distillers. In other words, he quickly became a very wealthy man. With his education, he could hold his own with the best and was accepted as a gentleman. And if he was anything like my father, then he *was* a gentleman.

When he married, he married for love, a barrister's daughter named Keogh and he adored her. She had been a native Dubliner and if the old photograph I once saw half did her justice, then she was very beautiful indeed. She was a tiny creature, 'just up to my heart', the grandfather used to say. From here on, the Redmonds, who had all been big Wexford people became small Dubliners, small in stature and smaller in prospects.

Just before his marriage he purchased a Georgian house and to this he brought his bride. It was an 'Upstairs-Downstairs' house, as all prosperous houses were then and in the basement toiled the servants, who lived in the attic. My father had had a pony and a governess, no less, and for a few years had been brought up as a gentleman.

My grandmother produced a huge family, for the outrageous fact was that she had been pregnant twenty-three times and had died on the birth of the last baby. Some of them had been swept away by the rampant diseases of the time, some had been delivered only to die within the hour. Some had been lost through premature birth. One, Peter, who had been dropped by a careless servant, who never reported the accident, had been a hunchback and died at the age of twelve. The family who survived my grandmother and grandfather were: Cissy. The eldest, who married beneath her, was totally under the control of her husband, a scoundrel, who destroyed the family through his wife's power of attorney. Michael, the eldest son, drank, swindled and was destined to die alone in America. May, Edward, Morgan, Laurence (my father), Nan and Babs, who died at fourteen. She had fallen off the White Rock while on holiday in Dalkey and had been taken from the sea as dead. However, somehow she rallied and lived another year before death claimed her. She never got over the accident.

Nan took up holy orders and became a nun and spent most of her life abroad. As family, she lived on the perimeter. The ones who survived the holocaust were my father, Auntie May, Uncle Morris and Eddie.

Along with amassing a fortune my grandfather had also become a Justice of the Peace, a Custodian of Workhouses as well – a blond viking in appearance with, I was told, a heart of gold. But then, so had Cromwell . . . for his own! To my derisive Liberties mind, my grandfather was suspect. A Justice of the Peace? A Workhouse Custodian? A Castle Catholic? Lickspittle of the Brits? And guilty of being wealthy? To flourish in his day, you had to walk the tight rope between two camps, Irish and English. There was no in between!

Anybody I had ever seen in the Liberties, who was wealthy, was a grabber, like Kelly, the boy from Killane. With the solitary exception of Mrs Byrne, the moneylender, they were all from the country like my grandfather. Was he another from the bog with 'the little divil dancin' in his laughin' Irish Eyes' while he sold a naggin to a brasser? I suspected him but it was one thought I never, naturally, voiced.

Anyway, the scene is set. The year 1907, the place a Georgian house on the north side, where Mrs Redmond is dying. The British Empire is dying too, its sun has passed its meridian, though no-one has yet noticed. The gathering rage and jealousy of the German Kaiser is ignored. England has never been wealthier, her workers never poorer. Brittania ruled the waves and poverty ruled the masses except, of course, for people like my grandfather who lived 'upstairs'. Life for them was precious, death an outrageous intrusion. To the poor he came as a friend, to the wealthy a foul pestilence, who stalked them relentlessly, something to be warded off by the waters of Baden-Baden or Royal Leamington Spa for as long as possible.

Despite his wealth it seemed it was not too hard for my grandfather to slope off, for he lived only a handful of years after the death of his wife. He moved, I was told, like an automaton through the time left to him. I have never found out if he drank or not but this, too, has become suspect in my mind, for why then did he die on the sunny side of fifty? And how did it happen, that a businessman so smart left his young family completely unprotected so that his eldest daughter, who had brought him no honour by marrying beneath her, could get hold of all his wealth and hand it over to her husband, whom he knew to be a cunning scoundrel? How?

Shortly after the death of his wife, he had sold all his business interests, retaining only stocks and bonds. He bought a small grocery and packed his three boys off to boarding school. Above the grocery shop he lived alone, a daily woman providing his meals. I have a notion he bought the shop in order to prove he was still alive. Like all his enterprises, it turned out to be a goldmine . . .

Sitting under the chestnut tree, Nigger panting beside me and the hum of countless flies above me, I told my story to Dinny. Grass green and the buttercup gold fields were all around us, for we lay on the edge of the wood. Dinny listened intently. He should by law inherit his father's large store when he died, but that, of course, would never be.

It was clear that he would never be able to cope with life on a working basis. Yet, he was far from mad and bitterly resented the shabby clothes he wore.

It was Auntie Lil and the Buckleys, who looked after him. His brother did not give a Highlanders' if he walked around nude. Lil, with much effort, kept him in boots, the Buckleys in jackets and trousers, cast-offs of the three sons.

But Dinny must have been the only tramp in Ireland who, when in residence, would have his own room and be served breakfast in bed by Molly, the maid. It was the only meal he ever received at home. His father, though not dead, lay somewhere at the back of the house, bedridden from a stroke. The second son, a grabber, had the field to himself. With three assistants he ran the large store. It was the only shop in town we never entered, the only one that paid no toll to our passing.

One day when our rounds had been unprofitable and we had no biscuits, Dinny set his lips and came to a decision, my one and only glimpse of the man he could have been. He walked boldly into the family shop and calmly helped himself to a packet of biscuits. An assistant, who made a feeble effort to stop him, was boldly stared down.

'How dare you!' Dinny hissed and walked out.

'What happened to your father's family when the old boy died?' asked Dinny. We were lying with our backs against a tree, lazily at ease. We had provender in plenty today and like the cows around us, chewed desultorily.

'The girls were allowed to stay on for a while at the convent. Auntie May was never allowed to go back after she came home for holidays. She was only twelve but she was put to work, fourteen hours a day behind the counter of the shop.'

'And the other sister?'

'She was placed as a draper's assistant a couple of years later, but she had a vocation and the nuns took her back. Not as a lay nun either. She became high in the Order, Din, she must have been very bright.'

'And the three boys, Eddie, your father and . . .?'

'Morgan,' I told him.

'Yes, that's right. Well?'

'Eddie was found a small permanent job in the Dublin Corporation, the other two . . .' I trailed off. I took so long in answering that Dinny got tired of waiting.

'Don't tell me if you don't want to,' he said sulkily.

'No, it's not that, Din. I just want to make sure I'm right. They were sent to an orphanage, I'm trying to remember the name, but I can't.'

Bloody well I knew the name of the place and the circumstances, but I could not tell this man. He would repeat what I told him, the tale would be distorted in the telling and the town would have a field day at the expense of the proud Redmond sisters. For the place they had been committed to was as evil as the salt mines of Siberia, a hell of cruelty.

'And presumably to a trade from there?'

'Yes.'

'And your father never found out how they got their hands on the money?'

'No. He once said that they had probably torn up the will. They were too young to do anything. The only one who stood between them and the world was their sister and she turned out to be a monster.' Dinny fell silent, closing his eyes.

I knew by the time my father thought of taking action, that it was too late. The Four Courts, which housed the archives and land deeds of three centuries had been burnt down, gutted. Their slight chance of doing anything to right their wrong had gone up in smoke. And these were frenetic years for my father, always on the run, a guerrilla fighter, a fugitive in his own land, taking on the British Empire with a Colt .45. So much for that.

Dinny selected a banana with black skin, peeled it carefully and lay back, eating with voluptuous content.

For me, the summer's day had gone and I stared unseeing at the leafy tent above me. I was back in Georgian Dublin, the Dublin of James Joyce's boyhood. I had, over the years, eavesdropped to some purpose and of all the family, excepting Mam and Dad, I knew the most.

When Eddie was found a job, the next item on the agenda had been my father and Morry. They were at boarding school and costing far too much money. At home they were underfoot. They had to be disposed of, that was number one. Number two was to make sure they did not get too much education, perhaps become solicitors or barristers. Both these objectives had been achieved on the second attempt.

'Cissy's husband took us for a drive in a hansom cab, the first time,' my father told me years later, 'gave us a penny each somewhere in the city, where we had never been before and then disappeared in to a pub. He didn't come out again.'

The children had waited on the pavement, gradually

growing frightened by this strange and rough Dublin they had never known, which in fact was the Liberties, and started asking people going into the pub questions. 'If you see a tall man in a blue suit in there, sir . . .' And then a member of the Dublin Metropolitan Police, no doubt bribed, had arrested the two kids for begging.

They were jailed overnight, and the following morning appeared before the magistrate. Their nightmare had started. But for that day they were safe.

The children were well dressed, well spoken and could clearly state where they lived. The magistrate threw the case out of court and administered a bollocking in legal terms to the copper.

This first attempt to put the children away had been stupid and clumsy. The second attempt was much better and succeeded. From the first, there had been no effort at concealment by their sister, that they were not wanted. The two brothers lived in terror and their terror was well founded.

One morning when they woke up, their clothes had been removed from their bedroom and ragged ones subsituted. They were made to dress in them and this time as before, were driven to a strange part of the city, Ringsend. They both remembered the gasometer. It was their sister, who had elected to do the dirty work this time. Again they were given a penny each, left on the pavement for a couple of hours and trying to locate their sister, who had gone into a shop, were again picked up for begging.

Next morning, dirtyfaced from crying, in rags, hungry from a day with little food, they were again arraigned before a magistrate. He was a drunken old brute, well known for corruption and in jig time it had been established that they were orphans without a home, a pair of artful dodgers, who lived by begging. Two pennies were produced as evidence. They were ordered to be detained at His Majesty's pleasure in an Industrial School or Reformatory where in due course, having reached the advanced age of thirteen, they would be sent to a trade.

They were to be committed to Artane Reformatory, a name

in itself to strike terror into the heart of a child, to be guided and cared for under the discipline of the Christian Brothers. A place of detention for miscreants, most of them for stealing. They stole precious things like bread and meat and potatoes, even had cultivated a taste for oranges and bananas, no less. They were not to be trusted. They had adopted a preposterous life-style, eating without means to support the habit. There was little to be done with them; they had, for the protection of society to be put away.

In the next four or five years the good Brothers took pains to break them of these sinful and lustful tastes. Bananas and oranges, indeed! Plenty of stick, a little bread and copious quantities of water were found to be very efficacious in curbing their foul appetites, most of the water being used to wash blood from scourged backs.

For someone had made a mistake, for them a terrible mistake, because they were sent to Glencree, the Alcatraz of the juvenile correction system in Ireland. Here, all the hard liners who had caused the good brothers of Artane much distress by the ability to absorb punishment and still remain defiant, were sent to be broken. And broken they were. When their mentors had been really successful, they re-entered life mentally bankrupt, morally ruined or physically crippled in some way.

To this dreadful place, deep in the heart of the Dublin mountains, a full day's journey by coach from the city, came the two children.

The fire and brimstone of the Catholic church lay like a pall over the land. There were, however, men in the Liberties, 'hard chaws', who were not afraid to speak their minds. Men, who had had the terrible truth presented to them in the person of a broken son. Knowing the score from the inside, through my father, my rebellious little heart rejoiced to hear some Liberties drunk give vent to his feelings. 'Them crowd a' fucks . . . Them shower a' whores' bastards up in the mountains!' I hated things clerical for what they had done to my father and my little trout-fishing Uncle Morrie.

Only a year previously I had had at first hand an experience of Glencree and the hatred and fear it engendered in my area.

Kit Byrne was in our class in school. He was a wild, feckless poor devil of a boy, whose mother had died having him and whose father was too fond of the drink. But he loved his only son and was good to him in his own rough fashion. Kit was not too keen on schooling and with no mother to guide him, went astray. He had inherited his father's love of, and knack with horses. The blacksmith in the Barn even gave him money to be around the forge.

Kit saw no future in maths, which was of little assistance in handling a fractious horse. He took to going 'on gur' – playing truant – and eventually ended up in Artane. The harsh treatment he received in the place drove him to escape. He was brought back by the police, savagely punished but this only drove him to escape again. Sent back once more he was beaten stupid and when he was able to walk, went over the wall. This time, when he was caught, he was sent to be broken on the wheel of Glencree. He escaped from there, too, and met his father in Dolphin Barn Street, eyes rolling in terror like a frightened horse, spirit broken, sobbing, out of his mind.

Jem Bryne took his son home. Kit told him of the mandatory flogging he had received in front of the whole school on entering. He also told why he had escaped once more. One of the Brothers had taken a fancy to him. It was Brother Damien, he of the silver locks and he invited the boy up to his study for tea. The other lads told him what would happen. So Kit fled through the heather and gorse and by night found his way to the tenement where he lived, on the fourth floor.

As Jem and his son went up the stairs the first copper took up position opposite the house. They were trapped! The policeman sent for reinforcements and they soon arrived to take the boy forcibly.

The tenement house had to be stormed, like the Bastille, many times before it could be taken. Jem Byrne was a hard man. He had survived the trenches of Flanders and was a noted gutter fighter. He feared neither God nor man and although not big, could take on any country man within four stone of his weight and beat the shite out of him. Jail did not frighten him. He had been there before. But the sight of his son's rolling eyes and cringing gait drove him to madness. He had a bottle of whiskey in the top room that he proceeded to demolish before the fight began. It would be a long time before he drank again, but the coppers who came for him would pay dearly.

Six policemen went up the stairs the first time to be met by Jem. He defended the top landing like a Spartan defending a pass. Mad with rage, sorrow and whiskey, he took on the combined police force of Newmarket and Kevin Street, Newmarket having been decimated before Kevin Street was sent for.

It was a marvellous sight to see the police charging into the tenement, ten at a time and come staggering out, blood pouring from split heads, limping, some of them crying with rage or hurt, me looking between the legs of two Barn bowsies who stood there, roaring encouragement to their embattled friend.

'Lurry 'im up, he's no relation!' and the gathering crowd, hostile, effing and blinding the coppers, knowing full well they were afraid of them.

There were too many tough men in that mob for the police to handle at present. But they were taking note and in due course every man there would be made to pay for today's incitement. It is the way of the police the world over.

Jem, on the top landing, had torn the iron leg from the brass backed bed, a fearful weapon and stood there, taking them on, exacting a fearful toll. In the end, the police lost face by having to send for the Fire Brigade. The siege lasted just over three hours, from eight that night to eleven-fifteen, for I got a hiding for being there when I went home. That is how I remember it so clearly. But it was worth it.

The fireman stood on top of the tall ladder, directing a jet of water into the room. Jem slammed down the windows, but the force of the water broke the glass. The fireman narrowly avoided being decapitated by flying plates and saucers, but the combined assault with water, plus the police, was too much even for Jem. Kit went back to Glencree and another ceremonial flogging and his father to jail.

The Justice observed the condition of Jem in the dock, drew his own conclusions about police revenge and a merciful man, took Jem to his heart, for he had a son himself and knew how he would have felt if his own boy was sent to Glencree. Jem got eighteen months, but with time remission for good behaviour, he was released in a year. This boded ill for someone. Jem had never, in four previous jailings, ever got time remission, in fact, once he had received an additional three months for 'inciting to mutiny' and attacking a warder.

Jem, a violent man always, now nursed a homicidal hatred for a silver-haired satyr, who lived at Glencree. His old room in the Barn was waiting for him, the rent having been paid by his pals. He got himself a job handling horses in the Dolphins Barn brickworks, kept sober and saved his money. Revenge, a revenge that would leave its mark on Glencree for many a year to come, was in his mind.

He went there once, on a horse borrowed from a Crumlin farmer, to visit his son, but was not allowed to see him. Kit was well and happy, he was informed and turned away. He thanked them civilly and walked off. The horse he had tethered in a wood half a mile away, overlooking the reformatory. He had brought a supply of tinned food with him, a tin opener, a tommy can for boiling water and, of course, a quarter pound of tea. These he buried in the wood and rode away. He would return.

Two Saturday mornings later he did not report for work, but a workmate brought up a note to say that he was ill. By the time the note was delivered, Jem was hidden in the wood with two horses. He had set out late Friday night and ridden to Glencree, arriving just before dawn where the food was hidden. He had a pair of field glasses with him, borrowed from the local bookie and from the heather above it, he spied on the reformatory all day, with little result.

He went back to the wood, lit a small fire, made tea and ate beans from a can, wrapped himself in a horse blanket and slept through the night. The empty can was carefully buried. When he left on Sunday morning, he made sure there was no trace of his sojourn there. Sunday was another boring uneventful day and another night in the wood. There was grass in the open spaces and the horses were content enough. On Monday morning Jem saw the detainees being led out to work, trimming hedges around the fields. His son was among them. Silent as a ghost, Jem appeared in the ditch below his son's feet.

'Ay, Kit,' he whispered.

'Jasus . . . Da,' said the boy, looking down.

'Tell the other lads teh move away from yeh. I don't want teh get them in teh trouble.'

'Yes, Da.' Kit spoke quietly to the other boys, who moved away quickly. They did not want to *see* anything. They were terrified they would be involved. The boys worked steadily all day, watched by a Brother, who smoked one cigarette after another, bored. He would have no trouble from this lot. They were all well and truly broken on the wheel of Glencree.

No food was provided for the boys for this was a punishment detail. At one o'clock the bored Brother was relieved by another, equally bored and the winter afternoon dragged on. Jem lay doggo in the ditch, waiting for Brother Damien to appear.

'He'll be here all right, Da, don't worry. He always comes so he can get a belt at me for nothin'.'

Around three thirty, with the sky darkening already, a middle-aged Brother came into the field. It was Damien! He was alone and made straight for Kit, who was working apart.

'Stop workin',' Jem hissed from the ditch. 'Get the fucker over here quick.' Kit stopped. The Brother advanced towards him, smiling wolfishly. He had never forgiven the boy for reading him correctly.

'I see we are not inclined to work today,' said Brother Damien.

'No, Sir, Brother.'

'And, pray, why not?'

'I just don't fuckin' want teh,' said Kit with the last of his nearly extinguished spirit. The Brother produced the long, heavily weighted leather he always carried and smiled.

'I see we need our manners brought up to date. This,' he promised, 'will be a lesson you will never forget!'

As he was speaking, Jem, Flanders fashion, was bellying through the grass behind him. The Brother had no warning. The heavy oak club which Jem had fashioned and whittled over three days of waiting, descended on his skull and he hit the ground without a sound. The other boys in the field kept clipping and sawing at the hedge in a fury of activity. Not one of them glanced towards the fallen Brother. They were terrified that they might see something. It did them no good. Each and every one of them was afterwards flogged for *not* seeing.

Jem had the unconscious Brother's trousers down in a flash. He produced his penknife, that had gelded many a stallion and now he emasculated the man on the ground with expertise and dispatch.

'That fucker,' he told Kit, "ill never meddle with another mother's son.'

They made off then, found the two horses and were miles away before the alarm sounded in the reformatory. There was no telephone communication between Glencree and the outside world and Jem came by a route that it would be impossible to follow. It was miles longer than the only road and that much safer.

He turned his horse off the Glencree road, left down towards Gleann na Smol, The Glen of the Thrushes, went over the tiny bridge that spanned the River Dodder which, in turn, filled Bothar na Breena water works. Bothar na Breena, which meant The Road of the Ghosts, was a fitting place for them to be, for they carefully kept to the grass verge, silent in the winter mist. They stole up Ballinascorney Gap, past the granite cross which marks the spot where a shepherd died in a snowstorm long ago and turning right, over a trail known only to Jem and the sheep went over the small green mountain of Killinarden, down through Jobestown, which was only a pub and a name and rode fast towards Tallaght. This was the only dangerous part of the journey, for it was the main road and the village of Tallaght had a police station. Three hundred yards outside the village, they turned left for the village of Clondalkin, but only a few hundred paces along they turned right at the terrifyingly life-like crucified Christ, that had been erected the top of Ballymount Lane.

From here on it was a cake walk. They had been fortunate, for no motor car had passed in all their journey and they were soon in the fields of Crumlin, beside Dolphins Barn.

Jem left the horses and his son with a farmer, a war time pal and was well and truly home when the police came looking for him. In fact, he was treating himself to a whiskey, chased down with a pint when the police entered the pub.

Everybody in the bar knew where Jem had been, even the publican. Every man in Dolphins Barn knew what he had set out to do, and approved. The only ones who never knew, or could prove the crime against Jem, were the police. Not then, not ever. This was Barn business and nobody else's. A copper was a copper and they could see little difference between the Irish and the late, unlamented English, Dublin Metropolitan Police force. Poverty remained the same, whether it was under the Green, White and Gold or under the Union Jack. Patriotism, like love went out the window when poverty came in by the door.

One sergeant and two gardai came in to the pub, looking for Jem. Jem was offhand, barely civil. No, he did not know anything about his son's escape. He had been here most of the day, on and off. The gang around murmured assent and the publican backed them up. He knew better than to tell the truth.

'Why weren't you at work on Saturday?'

'Sick, the 'flu . . . Saturday and Sunday. Never even went teh Mass. Wasn't even in for a drink, was I mister?'

'Begob, ye were not,' said the Mayo publican heartily, glad to be telling the truth. 'Sure, didn't yer man there, Bock, take him up a naggin' a' Power's whiskey yesterday an' he sick in bed.'

'Why weren't yeh at work today?'

'Didn't feel like it. It's still a free country, sergeant.' The sergeant scowled.

'Yeh must be very flush with the cash,' he said slowly. 'No work an' drinkin' whiskey with a pint.'

'I am. Have a ging.' Jem produced a handful of notes, mostly fivers. The sergeant's eyes popped.

'That's a lot of money for you to be havin'!'

'Yeah, isn't it? That's what comes a' livin' a clean life. Should try it, sarge. Haven't touched a drop since I came out a' jail. An' I got this honest, burstin' me bangers up in the brickworks. Drink for the shop,' Jem told the publican grandly. 'Leave the coppers out. They're on duty. Mustn't upset the law.'

The sergeant glowered and the young guards were tight-lipped. They had all suffered at the ungentle hands of Jem during the siege of the tenement.

'Watch your tongue!'

'De yeh mean this way?' said Jem, sticking it out and looking down his nose. There was a rumble of laughter around the shop. The sergeant was fit to be tied.

'What's the celebration for?' he demanded.

'Why, sergeant,' said Jem, surprised like, 'for the good news yeh just brought me . . . Me son's excaped, isn't that what yeh said?' Red faced, the sergeant and the guards moved towards the door.

'An' fuckin' glad I am he is,' added Jem. The sergeant grinned. This was better. He moved towards the bar and Jem.

'Garda Murphy?'

'Yes, sir.'

'Profance language, you all heard him. Book him.'

'Yes, sir,' said the young garda, whipping out his little book.

'But you said "fuck 'im" yerself,' said Tucker Fogarty.

'I said "book him. . . . buck him", that's what I said.' The sergeant was losing his temper.

'That's not what it sounded like to me,' said Tucker sorrowfully. 'How about you boys? Did yez hear the same?' There was a murmur of assent around the shop.

'I said "buck him",' the sergeant roared.

'So yeh did,' said Spider Edwards unexpectedly. 'I'll back yeh up on that.'

'Thank you,' said the sergeant, 'I didn't expect *you* to help me, but I thank you for it.'

'Any time,' said Spider cheerfully. 'I'll go fuckin' witness.'

'Can't yez talk in front of the sergeant wit'out fuckin' cursin'?' queried the Growler Doyle.

'Listen, Growler,' said a hard case from Reilly's Avenue, 'if yes don't like the way we speak, why don't you an' the sergeant an' the other two nice young chaps . . . why don't yes fuck off?'

The sergeant and the guards moved slowly towards the door again. There were hard men in the bar that night. Ex-Irish and British Army types, Sinn Feiners, Republicans, who had kicked the Brits out and fought each other in the Irish Civil war. Some there had fought in all three wars, deserting the British Army after 1916 to fight for their own country, training the rebels with expertise learnt from the British and taking one side or the other in the Civil War. There was hardly one of them, who did not carry a grudge against the police, any police – Irish, English, French, Belgian or American. The Yank, lately returned from New York, had been in all five jails.

Discretion, thought the sergeant wisely, was the better part of valour. And the Kerry sergeant could not cope with this crowd, who were openly defying him, jeering him, calling him a culchie without saying it.

'There'll be another day,' he promised them.

'I hope teh Jasus there is,' said Tucker fervently, 'for I'm up teh me bollix in mortal sins. I'd like teh get confession before yeh catch up with me, sergeant dear.' There was a roar of laughter from the crowd. The red faced policemen moved off.

'Little apples 'ill grow again,' Jem roared above the noise.

Lying here in the grass, in this quiet corner of County Wexford, so different from the turbulent Liberties, I thought it all out. The rumour of what had happened in Glencree could not be contained in the Barn. Soon the whole city knew about it, but the papers reported nothing. The silent censorship operated well.

Emasculted was the word the Kipper used to the other school master, Gleeson. 'I believe he was emasculated . . . the Brother.' They moved off, quietly discussing this horrendous event. I could not wait to get to Thomas Street and the library after school and get hold of a dictionary. I soon found the word 'Castrated' – 'to make feminine' it said. Castrated? That did not help all that much. I looked that up too. 'To deprive of the testicles'. Ah! So that was it! For gas I looked up 'testicles'. 'Male reproductive glands' it said. So now I knew. Your bangers!

The whole school was buzzing with the story of Kit Byrne and his father. Everybody knew except the police it seemed. And they knew too, but could not do anything. They had not one iota of evidence to bring against Byrne. Ernie Mountain was well up in the story and like me, had ear-wigged on the Kipper.

'He said,' Ernie told us, 'that the Brother was em-em-as-skullated,' he finished triumphantly.

'That's right, so he did,' I said, backing up my pal.

'An' what, may I ask, is that?' asked Deasy, the thick.

'You may – it's debollicked, knackered, gelded,' I told them. I was delighted, in my element.

'Yeh mean,' said Ernie, 'in plain English he had his balls cut off?'

'Exactly so, both of them,' I said. The 'exactly so' bit was taken from *Alice in Wonderland*. Exactly so, said Alice.

'What'll happen to him now, I mean, will he die or something?' said Deasy.

'He won't die,' said young Perry from the field of Crumlin, 'but he won't be able to have a proper ride. Me father is a horse dealer. I know a stallion is no good after that's done to him.'

Dinny was quietly snoring now. He must have been up all night, I thought. My aunts told me he got funny moods when the moon was full and he wandered the roads, upset.

'Sure God love poor Dinny, there's not a bit of harm in him.' We were so quiet in the shade, Dinny snoring away that a sudden snort from him sent a red squirrel, hunting on the ground hurtling up a chestnut tree from where he surveyed us with large lustrous eyes. I was spoiling a beautiful day with my thoughts, but this time I felt I had to face them. The bits and pieces of information I had collected over the years I had brought together at last. Subconsciously, I had resented the fact of my family's poverty. I should have been better dressed, lived in a bigger house, gone to college instead of a national school.

The whole rotten story had coloured – or discoloured – my whole life, and today I might as well think it out to a finish and have done with it. I was twelve years old, a dreamer in a world of brutal reality and now I had to face the truth. No more fairy tales.

More than once I had imagined, by some twist of fate, that the truth had reached an Irish court and that my uncle – by marriage only – had stood in the dock and received twenty years hard labour. I had imagined the Judge giving back to my father all the money he was due and his property. No more last year's school book, patches on trousers, canvas school bags, no more indignity.

And that robbing bastard breaking rocks while I went to college like Harry Wharton. Jesus, would that not be great!

At the point where my thoughts had wandered off my father and his little brother had been taken to Glencree. By some malignant twist of fate they had been sent here instead of Artane, itself a dreadful place for the correction of boys, but Glencree stood for terror. To this place, these two little gentlemen had come. For the most part I think they went comparatively unpunished, by the standards of the place but there was one incident I overheard that I never forgot. Uncle Morrie and Auntie Maggie had come over to the Square on a Christmas visit. A few bottles of stout and a drop of the hard stuff loosened their tongues and they forgot about me.

It seemed, that shortly after their arrival at Glencree – many years before poor Kit Byrne – a young Brother with a beautiful and revered name, had approached them. 'Ah,' said this smiling man, 'you've just arrived, haven't you?' The Brother chatted with the children for a while and asked my father, who he said was a nice little chap, to come to his room next day. Warned by an instinct of evil, he did not go. The day after Brother Damien caught up with him. 'And why,' he asked, 'did you not come to my room?' My father hung his head. A hard box on the ear sent him flying. His little brother began to cry. 'Come,' said Brother Damien, 'I have a job for you.' He walked them along a hedge and gave my father his pocket knife. 'Cut down a good stick,' he told him, 'for if you don't I'll pick out a better one.'

The Brother finally agreed with my father's selection. Dad was made to strip naked. The punishment about to be given, the assembled boys were told, was for the cardinal sin of disobedience.

Then the beating began, stroke after stroke, until my father's body ran red, he screaming, his brother in hysterics. The louder he screamed, the harder the Brother hit. Here in Glencree, the clock had stopped about the year 1785. No wonder my uncle and father hated the church. They had good reason. Old ways, long discarded elsewhere by an outraged society lived on at Glencree. Oliver Twist would have felt quite at home here, Charles Lamb would have bent to his studies and shivered.

* * *

Christs Hospital, five and thirty years ago, in the city of London.
(*The London Magazine*, November 1820)
By Elia. (Charles Lamb.)

> . . . I was a hypocondriac lad; and the sight of a boy in fetters, upon the day of my first putting on the blue clothes, was not exactly fitted to assuage the natural terrors of initiation. I was of tender years, barely turned of seven; and had only read of such things in books, or seen them but in dreams; I was told he had *run away*. This was the punishment for the first offence.
>
> As a Novice I was soon after taken to see the dungeons. These were little, square, Bedlam cells, where a boy could just lie his length upon straw and a blanket – a mattress, I think, was afterwards substituted – with a peep of light, let in askance, from a prison-orifice at top, barely enough to

read by. Here the poor boy was locked in by himself all day, without sight of any but the Porter who brought him his bread and water – who *might not speak to him*; or of the Beadle, who came twice a week to call him out to receive his periodical chastisment, which was almost welcome, because it separated him for a brief interlude from solitude: here he was shut up by himself *of nights*, out of reach of any sound, to suffer whatever horrors the weak nerves and superstition incident to his time of life, might subject him to*. This was the penalty for the second offence.

Wouldst thou like, reader, to see what became of him in the next degree?

The culprit, who had been a third time an offender, and whose expulsion was, at this time, deemed irreversible, was brought forth, as at some solemn auto-da-fé, arrayed in uncouth and most appalling attire – all trace of his late *Watchet Weeds* carefully effaced, he was exposed in a jacket, resembling those which London Lamplighters formerly delighted in, with a cap of the same. The effect of this divestiture was such as the ingenious devisers of it could have anticipated. With his pale, frighted features it was as if some of those disfigurements in Dante had seized upon him.

In this disguisment he was brought into the hall, (L's favourite State room) where awaited him the whole number of his school-fellows, whose joint lessons and sport he was thenceforth to share no more; the awful presence of the stewards, to be seen for the last time; of the executioner Beadle, clad in his state robe for the occasion; and of two faces more of direr import, because never but in these extremities visible.

*One or two instances of lunacy, or attempted suicide, accordingly, at length, convinced the Governors of the impolicy of this part of the sentence, and the midnight torture to the spirits was dispensed with; this fancy of Dungeons for children was a sprout of Howard's brain, for which, saving the reverence due to Holy Paul, me thinks I could willingly spit upon his statue.

These were the Governors, two of whom, by choice, or charter, were always accustomed to officiate at these *Ultima Supplicia*; not to mitigate (so at least we understood it) but to inforce the uttermost stripe. Old Bamber Gascoigne, and Peter Aubert, I remember, were colleagues on one occasion, when the Beadle turning rather pale, a glass of brandy was ordered to prepare him for the mysteries.

The scourging was, after the old Roman fashion, long and stately. The Lictor accompanied the criminal quite round the hall. We were generally too faint with attending to the previous disgusting circumstances, to make accurate report with our eyes, of the degree of corporal suffering inflicted. Report, of course, gave out the back knotty and livid. After scourging, he was made over, in his *San Benito*, to his friends, if he had any (but commonly such poor runagates were friendless, or to his Parish Officer, who, to enhance the effect of the scene, had his station allotted to him on the outside of the hall gate.

Charles Lamb

13 *Glimpse of Paradise*

That night I had a dreadful nightmare. I had stayed out too long in the woods, I had thought too deeply about things past, I had fretted too much about things present. After my own fashion I had faced up at last to the events that had shaped my life, over which I had had no possible control. It all came together in dreadful confusion of a dream, in which I was pursued relentlessly by the dreaded black cassocked keepers of Glencree, running, running, running . . . until I woke up screaming, sobbing, nearly demented, half out of my mind.

My aunts, awakened by my screams came rushing into the room together, loving me, holding me, comforting me, bringing me back to my senses, kissing me, until I left the terror behind.

However, it was decided between them, that I should share their enormous big bed for the balance of the night, in case I had another nightmare.

In the morning, when I woke up, I was surrounded by soft, feminine bodies. I rose on my elbow, trying to sneak out without waking them up. These female cousins of mine were arousing the strangest feelings in me. I felt ashamed. Mag stirred sleepily and enfolded me with a soft arm.

'Ah, Tommy,' she whispered passionately and drew me close. I tried to push her away but my hand landed on her breast, which fluttered like a bird I had caught. I lay still and my hand, without any direction from me, caressed her. I knew what I was doing was wrong, but I seemed unable to stop. Mag woke up, I knew, for her hand found mine and squeezed it hard into the softness of her. I could hear her breath coming in short gasps like my own and we both pretending to be asleep. In the distance I could hear cattle bawling and then there was a crash against the front door, for the street was full of milling cattle.

It was fair day in Gorey and hordes of cows, bulls and bullocks and calves were invading the main street. Lil woke up then and we all tumbled out on to the floor. Fair day was not to be missed.

'Are you all right again, Lar?' said Lil. 'You had a very bad nightmare . . . frightened us all.'

'Yes,' I said. 'I'm all right,' and gave her her good morning kiss. I avoided Mag and she me and it was a couple of days before we could thrust what had happened between us far back, into the recesses of our minds, back so far as to believe it had never happened. After that was done, all was well between us again and she could ask me to sell her my eyelashes.

' 'Tis not fair, Lil,' she would say, 'would yeh look at the eyelashes on it. Should belong to a girl.'

But it was fair day in Gorey now and looking down from the front bedroom window, I could see that the street was a milling mass of cattle, bawling, scuttering all over the road and pavement. Carts with red painted creels on them, timid calves peeping between the bars, men with peaked caps and ash plants, bartering, buying, selling, spitting on the hand to close a bargain, farmers all in to buy and sell.

I had never seen a fair before, held, as it was in the Main Street of the town, which smelt of cow dung and piss for days afterwards, a dirty, filthy way of conducting business, tolerated from time immemorial. Fetid, flyblown, it is impossible to imagine it happening now, but it did then and I had never enjoyed anything like it. The air was vibrant with the excitement it generated. Beside it, the hay auctions at Smithfield in Dublin were staid and gentlemanly affairs. Here you walked the street at your peril, for sometimes a bullock, half mad with fright would bolt, and if you were small like me, you had to be quick.

Never had I spent such a morning. Breakfast gulped, I flung

myself into the day with wild gusto. For I had something to forget, something to hide, a thing so terrible that the thought of making my next confession to the priest, hung over me like a sentence of death.

I had knowingly, and taking pleasure from it, felt my cousin's breast. I had sinfully taken carnal joy from its sweet softness. I had had a premature glimpse into the world of women. I had, in a couple of mad moments, been shown the terrible beauty that belongs to the world of women, their infinite power over men, their ability to build or destroy. All this I vaguely felt.

I had not meant to caress her breast, something stronger than me had directed my hand and when I allowed myself to think about it a sudden elation would come over me, *all* over me and I knew I stood on the threshold of unimaginable joys.

I was growing up. Behind the saintly, boyish face, the long lashed eyes and the angelic voice, forces were stirring in me, that did not plague other boys so soon or so intensely. I had been born highly sexed. From this day on I would be after girls, not just kissing them but kissing them with passion and feeling their womanhood as often as they would let me.

There was a whole undiscovered world before me on a fair day in Gorey, this fair day when my manhood, like a sleeping tiger had come to life and claimed its quarry. The thought of what had nearly happened that morning was to haunt me for six unrequited years and then let loose in a flood of passion that swept all before it.

By three o'clock the street was empty, hardly a thing to show that there had been mayhem there that morning. The only sign was the shopkeepers, brush and bucket in hand, washing the pavement outside their premises. If the shop had gone broke, it announced its presence doubly, once by the shutters and twice by the cow dung that remained outside its door. This was no man's land, untended even by the Council road sweeper, for his business, as he saw it, was to sweep the street.

'I'm not here teh swape the bloody paths for the bloody shopkeepers,' and in this easy going town it was let go. So over a period the cow dung was walked off, dispersed, gone with the wind like the fair that caused it.

I was exhausted, the fair done, and I went home. I came into the kitchen, shivering, although it was not cold.

'You look tired, Lar,' said Lil.

'I'm all right, Auntie Lil,' I said. She gazed anxiously in my face.

'No, you're not, you're worn out. Will you lie down in bed for an hour?'

'An, no. It's too lonely. I can lie down here in front of the fire.' She fetched a blanket and a pillow and I lay down on the long stool before the glowing turf fire and in a moment I was fast asleep. It was dark when I woke up, the oil lamp was burning brightly but I was still tired, spent from the passions and fears that had assaulted me early in the morning of this long day, now nearly over. Sleepily I ate a boiled egg and a slice of soda bread and stumbled up to bed.

When I woke it was morning, the sun was blazing and I sang my way through washing my face, and going down to breakfast, the past behind me. The sisters were already at the table, listening starry eyed, as they always did when I sang. There was another woman with them, of whom I had often heard them speak, Caroline from Castletown. She was about twenty, a very distant relative and she told me to call her Carrie.

'Yes,' I said shyly, 'good morning, Carrie.' They all smiled upon me. Lil said suddenly:

'Lar, if I put you in for the Gorey Feis, will you go in for the singing competition?'

'Would I have to sing in front of a lot of people?'

'You would, this is the Gorey Show. You'd have to sing to a whole field of them.'

'Through a microphone,' she added.

'No,' I said. I was still painfully shy.

'Oh, Lar, don't refuse me this,' said Lil. 'You'd beat the lot of them. You'd make me so proud.'

'Would the little Harper girl be up against me?'

'Yes, it's for under fourteens, boys and girls.'

'I wouldn't stand a chance against her.'

'WHAT?' The concerted shout came from the three young women at once. Then they informed me, in answer to my question that they had all heard her sing many times. Did she not sing solo in the chapel choir? I would wipe the floor with her. This made me reflect.

A couple of weeks before, out walking the Arklow road after a night of rain, Lil and I met another woman with a little girl. They stopped to have a chat on the road and something the other woman said about the young girl having the finest voice in Gorey made Lil spark up.

'She has not,' she contradicted firmly. 'This lad beside me has. He'd show them all the road home!'

And there and then on the spot the bet was on. The little girl sang on being asked in a lovely clear voice that I knew I could never match and I hung my head and blushed, and did not sing. I had disappointed Lil, whom I loved but at the time I had thought it better to be silent than to let her down by singing, shame her in front of this little girl, who I could not match. And now, here were three women, for I had seen Carrie briefly one Sunday morning when I was singing in Buckley's next door, all of whom had heard the Harper girl sing and who all were very certain that I would lick her. I must really have a good voice, I thought.

'I will, then. I'll go in for it, Lil, but don't blame me if I get beaten.'

'You won't get beaten,' they said together and laughed. Aunt Lil's eyes sparkled and her face was flushed with pleasure and I thought once again, how pretty she was. Caroline came over then and kneeling down on the floor before me, looked into my face.

'Your Aunt Lil and me were talkin',' she said. 'She'll let me have you for a week or so, if you're willing. I've been telling mother about you, she's confined to a wheel chair, she'd love to hear you sing.' I looked at Auntie Lil. She nodded.

'Only two weeks though, at the very most.' I was not very enthusiastic and showed it.

'We have a sheep dog named Patton, he'd get on well with

Nigger and we have a glen with a little trout stream in it.' That did it. I was sold.

'Yes,' I said. 'That would be nice. A *real* farm with no houses around, way out on its own in the country?' They all laughed. Carrie remarked, rather grimly I thought, that it was too bloody far out in the country. Cows and dogs and horses were all she ever met. She would love to live in town, but only got in about twice a month when she bought flour and poultry feed and the things the farm did not produce.

So that afternoon saw Nigger and I sitting up grandly in Carrie's trap with a small powerfully built horse between the shafts, which she informed me was a cob, a small farm horse, for times were tough and her family could not afford a smart trotting pony. She seemed to me to be excessively sensitive on the issue, for I felt like a king riding in a gold coach as we left town. Cob or pony, it was all one to my uncritical Liberties eye. The bloody animal could walk, trot or do the charleston as long as it got me to a farm with a glen and a trout stream.

The farm was not too far from Curacloe, we went on about a mile and then turned right down a tiny lane where the hedges made us duck our heads, neglected and overgrown as it was. We went a quarter of a mile down it and there was the farm. It turned out to be all that Carrie had promised, with a glen and stream, that flowed across a golden sandy beach in a cove and although the sea was so near, one would never have known this from the farmyard. There was no sign of it and they told me that only on very stormy nights, when the wind was on-shore, could it be heard.

Patton, the sheep dog, was friendly right off, but Nigger showed her teeth at him, I suspect because I made too much fuss of the big dog, but before night was out they slept together in the corner by the chimney. Auntie Sarah turned out to be a postcard Irish mother, silver haired, rosy cheeked with a flawless complexion sitting in her armchair, a long hazel stick from the glen in her hand, occasionally poking the fire, in the corner her wheel chair. That is how I remember her, long after she has gone.

Although she was Carrie's mother, it was plain that poor

Carrie had not inherited her mother's good looks. She had a wide, square, plain face, honest and smiling with good strong teeth, set in a firm mouth, a strong peasant body, moulded by heritage and toil and big, soft breasts that would suckle big children mostly for export. Her best friend could have made no claim on her behalf to good looks, though she attracted by her warmth and obvious good heart, especially when she smiled. She was loved far more than her mother had ever been for all her good looks.

I settled down in the farmhouse as if I had been born there. Nigger too. The brother, Seamus, talked to me sometimes in his rough, kindly way but most times he was too busy or too tired.

I had the run of the meadows that swarmed with life as they no longer do. Cutting grass twice and sometimes three times during summer has killed off the corncrake. My meadows were not complete without two or three 'craking' away and at least one cuckoo, gone for the same reason, nowhere to shelter. In my boyhood the countryside echoed to their delightful call from morning till night. And butterflies. There were hundreds of different varieties then, and I saw one once, that I have never forgotten. It was four inches from wingtip to wingtip with a blood red circle on each, surrounded by leopard spots and gold flecks that dazzled the eye.

In my efforts to capture it I went far across the fields, lost my way and floundered, panic stricken until I remembered that all I had to do was to follow the sheep dog home. When I stood up from resting in the long grass, Patton and Nigger made off together and I came home to find Carrie frantic with worry and Seamus, the brother, getting ready to launch a search. There was a deep marlhole filled with water a couple of fields away. There always is near any mud built house, for it was from here that the yellow marl clay was taken to construct the building.

Carrie grasped me in a vice-like grip and held me close outside the half-door of the house and again I felt the softness that lay under her woolly jumper on my face and did not resist. In fact, from my experience the morning of the fair I could never get too much. Carrie kissed me all over the face, half crying, half laughing and it took the voice of her mother, suddenly sharp, to bring her to her senses. She let me go then and I went inside. Aunt Sarah's silver hair gleamed in the firelight as always, her flawless face smiling, though she was not upset.

'Can you swim, Lar?' she said.

'Yes, Aunt Sarah.'

'I told them so,' she said serenely. 'But you worried them sick.'

'I couldn't help it. I lost my way chasing a butterfly.' She laughed, a soft knowledgeable laugh that I never forgot. She had observed something through the half-door when poor Carrie was kissing me.

'You'll get lost chasing many another butterfly, Lar,' she said, 'although if you keep your long eyelashes you won't have to run too far.'

Carrie came in then, avoiding her mother's eye but smiling, overjoyed that no harm had come to me.

'He'd make a lovely priest, mother, in a few years, wouldn't he? The sweet little face of him,' Auntie Sarah, crippled in her chair, laughed softly again.

'He'd *look* like a lovely priest, Carrie,' she replied, 'but he'll never make one, not Lar. He lets on he has no interest in girls, but I know better. He loves them!' In the darkened room with the tiny penal days windows that the family had grown used to and never made bigger , I grew scarlet. So she had seen me nuzzling into Carrie. I would have to be more careful. These Wexford women seemed to be inordinately fond of young boys. It was only years after that the truth came to me, that most of them were sexually starved, their young men gone off to America. Sometimes they made good and sent for them. Mostly they did not, so that good looking women like Auntie Lil with no dowry, were left unmolested, never aroused by a male, a woman who, in a different society, would have been plagued to marry. Farm labourers belonged to a different world, and farmers' daughters did not marry with them. Nor did women like Lil, whose father had drank a business out but who regarded themselves still as the town society.

The Carries of Wexford married another farmer, brought their dowries with them and settled down with the blessing of the Church to produce children for export. They were usually widowed before they were fifty, their husbands being old enough to be their father, but as the saying goes, he had a 'quare puck left still in his hurl' and usually fathered a lusty brood before shuffling off his mortal coil.

And strange young boys from Dublin with long eyelashes got smothering squeezes from the most unexpected quarters and the quarest ideas took root in their minds. I swear to Jesus, had I been on that farm two more weeks, I would have lost my virginity at an unseemly age. Carrie, bursting her blouse at the seams, loaded with love and feminine lust, breathing fast when she brought a cow to the bull. Anything in male form was bound to be squeezed! I squeezed her well enough a few years later. But at the time of which I speak, the disparity in ages was too much, though I was not lacking where it counted.

I had strayed too far on my first day at the farm. That night Aunt Sarah had sat in her chair, answering my questions, telling me about her childhood spent in the Curacloe of long ago. In fact, just like her mother before her, she had never set eyes on her husband until she stood before the altar with him. The match had been made and settled by her parents. I was struck dumb by this revelation. I had heard of it, but in my mind it was some ancient custom that had died out long ago. To meet a woman, who had been the victim of this monstrous practice was a shock, for it was obvious to everyone that my father and mother were in love, you could not be in our little home without being aware of this. Here was love. But now, looking back on a lifetime of marriages, my brothers' and sisters', my friends', my own, it was clear that my parent's coupling had been ordained in heaven and that most were not so lucky.

Aunt Sarah was in no way disappointed with her life, and said a sensible marriage to a good man with the bride bringing her dowry was the only way to marry, the only *sensible* way to marry and that she and her departed had never had a cross word. Privately I thought it was because they had nothing to say to each other. But I kept quiet.

She did not ask me to sing on that first night, but let me go to bed and settle in. The following morning I was awakened by the bawling of cows waiting to be milked. Carrie and her brother were already working in the cow shed when I came down, though nearly finished and then it was breakfast and off with Seamus to Inch Creamery with the milk, bringing back the 'skim' after all the cream had been taken from it, to feed the calves. This was my job, feeding them from a bucket. I was in my seventh heaven. Nigger too, had settled down.

This night in the fire light, with her silver hair gleaming, Aunt Sarah asked me to sing. I was anxious to please her, for she seemed to love me and I sang her song after song, ending up with the *Dear Little Shamrock*. Of course, from then on, I could do no wrong.

After that it became a ritual and my pleasure, to sing a couple of songs for Aunt Sarah and Carrie and at the end of my first week on the farm we had collected a few visitors, who began to drop casually in, so quietly and gradually that I never noticed the kitchen becoming crowded and so was never shy. I came to know these men one at a time and on the fifth night of my singing, a grown man, twice as shy as I, Linnet he was called, brought his fiddle and made it sing in the voice of a Celt. I have heard many fiddlers since, but never once to match him. His fame should have echoed round the world but he had rarely been out of his own parish. He had a magic touch that made the violin sing and cry and when the Linnet accompanied me as I sang *Panis Angelicus* we nearly brought the thatched roof off the farm house. Such applause, such praise . . .

'Damn the chance,' said a local farmer, 'of any Wexford gassoon batin' the Dublin lad. He'd sing the trousers off any a' them.'

The Gorey Feis was only a few days away. My time in this farm house was nearly up, my long holiday in Wexford coming to a close. So soon! I hated the thought of going back. Here, life was gentle and kind. Here, the struggle for existence that I had witnessed every day of my life in the Liberties was not so bitter. Here, I had been able to become the gentle dreamer of a boy that God had meant me to be, wandering the fields and the woods, becoming freckle-faced and sunny with my dark brown hair shining with sun gold streaks, reflecting the health inside me.

In all my life I had never been so well or happy. It was not to last. The days were flying, flying and I could not hold them back. On the morning before I was to leave Carrie, she found me crying in the orchard. Patton lay in the long grass, nose on paws, Nigger stood beside me, whining. Well, she knew I was unhappy and Carrie, hanging out the clothes to dry heard me and found me, when I thought I was hidden from the whole world. She had held me close and kissed me and tried to comfort me, talking.

'Is it, Lar, that you don't like Gorey? Are you not happy there?'

'Oh no, Carrie, I love Lil and Mag, they are lovely to me, the same as you. I could be happy in Wexford forever.'

'Well, what's wrong then?'

'The letter I got this morning. I met the postman up the lane. It was from my sister. She said I would have to go back to Dublin next week, the school holidays are near and I have to pass my exam or be held back in the same class for another term!'

The sands of time, the highlight of my boyhood were running out. The coming night was the last I would spend under this kindly thatch, for many a year. That night a few of the farmers brought their wives, an unprecedented happening. They had been invited by Aunt Sarah, no doubt, to hear the little Dublin lad and the Linnet make music together and I sang to a rapt audience.

These Wexford people had taken me to their hearts, they would be clapping for my side at the Feis for was not the lad's grandfather a Wexford man?

Surrounded by my friends on my last night in Castletown, I sang my little heart out to please them. The Linnet was there, he played an old Irish air from Fenian days, 'Mise Eamoinn an Cnoic' – I am Eamonn of the mountains, or litterally a fugitive on the run – and I joined him and sang it in the old tongue. And brought the house down.

They had all gone by eleven for the milking in the morning had always to be faced. They would all be in Gorey on Sunday to see me win the singing competition.

Carrie came to me that last night, kissed me and held me close. She was in her nightdress, it was nearly one o'clock in the morning and she was crying.

'I'll miss you Lar,' she said through her tears. 'Your lovely little face and that blessed voice of yours. Never was a boy born with so many gifts.'

'Hush, Carrie,' I whispered, for I was afraid Aunt Sarah would find out. 'I'll come down here again. Maybe soon.'

'Promise me you will.'

'I promise I will come back one day.'

'Don't say it like that, Lar. You make it seem so far away.'

'Next year,' I said. 'Or maybe Mam will let me come again this year.' I might as well rave here as in bed if it brought her comfort.

An Irish mother guards her chicks well. I could not see this happening. None of my mother's chicks would be fostered out, even to close relatives. For I loved Wexford and Lil too much and my mother, fey like me, could sense this, all these miles away from Dublin. I did not, of course, raise these fears in front of Carrie. She held me close in the dark and again, ashamed, I felt the gathering manhood in me surface. I was filled with wild desire, a longing and wish to snuggle into her naked body and go to sleep with my head on her ample bosom. I think that was the night our pact was made and that when I came again, things would be different between us, that it was inevitable that she was the one who was destined to open the world of women to me. Carrie felt it too but in the end, giving me a passionate kiss and a squeeze, she fled.

The next morning, early, Lil arrived for me. She came in Buckley's borrowed trap, for she was piqued with my long absence and a little jealous that I could be happy away from her. Besides, she missed my singing, the Sunday mornings in Buckley's and the times at home in front of the turf fire, when I told her stories of fairies and giants and witches, for I had been born with an urge to invent tales where my imagination could run riot. And finish off our evenings with a song.

All this was to cease at the end of this week. Sunday, the day of the Feis, would be the last day of my stay in Wexford. Nigger too, was strangely quiet on the journey to Gorey and whined occasionally.

'She misses Patton,' said Lil softly. Nigger had mated with him one day when I was fishing and no one had told me, so there were two sorrowful beings in the trap, not counting Lil, who would miss me when I went and that was soon.

Just then I hated Dublin with a bitter hatred. I knew only too well what I was going back to, the struggle to survive, the relentless pressure of the seething Liberties, the poverty, real poverty not this sham country brand, a lot of it due to laziness and pride. Back to real suffering, starving poverty with sallow faces and wizened bodies, permanently contracted from the cold of this world. The wild roses that bloomed all too briefly on the cheeks of a Liberties child before galloping consumption galloped it off to Mount Jerome, free at last from pain like Jinny Lynch.

The countryside rolled past on this saddest and most beautiful of all July days. The furze no longer bloomed on Tara Hill but crops of oats and wheat waved water green on its lower slopes and broke a fragrant surf against the hedge cliff. It was all spoilt for me. Already I was back in the artisan dwelling on the edge of the fetid slums, my Wexford existence over, done with and an icy premonition came to me, that I would never know another holiday here, that this golden time would have to be paid for dearly. Already, so young, I knew this, that great happiness is paid for with great sorrow.

On the floor of the trap, Nigger whined again and I absentmindedly patted her on the head. Lil smiled at me a little tremulously.

'Are you so sorry to be coming back to me?' she whispered.

'Oh no, Lil, I have to go home,' and I fumbled in my pocket

and found my sister's childish scrawl that spelt out my doom. I handed it to Lil and wept, with my head on the side of the trap. She read the letter, stroking my head.

She did not know me, I thought. If only she had known the things this little Dublin child knew she would have recoiled in horror. Behind the long eyelashes and saintly face was a boy who knew too much for his years, far too much. I could have told her things she did not know or would ever wish to know. I could have told her in detail how the sexual act was performed, either lying down or standing up against the brewery walls, a 'knee trembler' we called that. I could have told her about gonorrhoea (the clap) and about mercurial ointment (Navvy Blue Butter) for the treatment of crabs or their more fearful cousins, 'the Brophy's', who not alone bit a piece out of your balls but ran up your arse to eat it.

I could have told her all about 'the pox', Liberties style for syphilis, about the way all your hair fell out. Down in Dr Steevens' Hospital beside the railway station, the nurses kept an eye on you and when your hair could be pulled out by the handful, you were shifted to that last of all horrors, the Lock Hospital down near the Pigeon House and the sea, as far away from the city as they could get you! It was goodbye for you. You had 'siff'. It was whispered, that the nurses, when the patient was in the last stages of the disease, could take a piece of his stomach flesh in her hand and pull it off, so rotted away was he.

And the cruelty of Steevens' Hospital and the Lock made death desirable. The doctors and nurses hated the dirty patients they were over and had no pity. They were in hospital dying, making a nuisance of themselves. For they were guilty of a terrible sin, here for doing the filthy Thing! The Thing the priests were always talking about and anything was good enough for them. And we all knew their bodies were thrown over the wall into Dublin Bay, never to know the solace of a consecrated grave, condemned to the everlasting fires of hell for all eternity. Yes, Lil would never speak to me again if she knew half what I knew!

I watched my tears fall on the white gravel road as the pony trotted along and Lil sat staring unseeingly over the countryside. She wept quietly, silently and I knew at this moment Carrie would be doing the same. Aunt Sarah, however, would be dry eyed, poking the fire, still as the eye of a cyclone, for I had found out that behind her beautiful, unlined face and waving silver hair, she was a tyrant over her son and daughter and ruled the farm with a rod of iron. She brooked no refusal or contradiction. She was the law. She dominated Carrie and Seamus so that it never occurred to them to rise, go their own way and shake off the yoke of tyranny. I had discovered this bit by bit, but it did not stop me from loving Aunt Sarah, for to me she was always kind. But I knew, where I came from, if she had tried this on her old guitar, she would have been told to fuck off pretty quickly. A couple of days neglect in the wheelchair would have cured her. But of course, Seamus and Carrie would do her bidding until she died. She would dominate them until she went. They would do nothing about it. It was the way of the land and they knew no other.

So, on this day that I was to refer to in later life as 'Sorrowful Saturday' we came back to Gorey. Dinny was waiting for me. He had forgotten a quarrel and so had I. We played draughts all evening. The following day I would win the Gorey Feis for singing. I did not feel very much like singing now that my time was up, but I knew I sang better when I was sad, so the contest would get my best.

Mag cheered me up a little at the prospect, squeezed me in a hurry and ran off to meet her Tommy. And so Sunday morning came. I went out, as I had once before, found a few spuds and fed the sow. She was fully grown now and carrying a litter, but she knew me and gave me an ecstatic welcome. Very softly I sang to her. All was well. I had never been in a better voice. Lil came quietly up behind me then and gave me a kiss on the back of the neck.

'All set, are we?' she said. I nodded.

'As set as we'll ever be, Lil. If we don't win today, we'll never win.' She nodded confidently.

'You will,' she said, 'but no singing after Mass this morning in Buckley's. You have to save your voice for the competition. Anyway, they'll all be there to hear you.'

'What time does it start?'

'Half three. You are number eight out of fifteen. What are you going to sing?'

'*Panis Angelicus.*'

'And when you win, what will you sing?'

'*Kitty O'Toole.*'

'Lovely. Come on now and have your breakfast.'

It was Mass for me after the meal and seeing there was no Buckley's this morning, I sat watching old Musty Mike being shaved by Mag, grunting like the sow outside.

'What's for dinner today?' he growled.

'Bacon and cabbage, your lordship,' said impudent Mag.

'Did yeh get a piece a' the lad?' 'The lad', I might mention, was cheap, fatty American bacon, heavily salted to keep it from going off and imported because it was dirt cheap. It seemed, that under the British we had export choice Irish bacon and lived on American rubbish. Uncle Mike had never had anything else in his life and prefered it to anything else on God's earth. Its import had ceased abruptly with the advent of an Irish government. To Uncle Mike this was a major tragedy.

'An' where would I get a piece a' that? Sure, you're dotin'. It's not allowed in the country any more.'

'God's curse on them,' said Musty Mike. 'But it was good an' chape, dirt chape compared to our stuff.'

'Compared to our stuff it was chape dirt,' said Mag, imitating him.

'They knew how teh salt it anyway,' roared my uncle.

'There was nothin' else to it except salt. Can't yeh put all the salt yeh like on it. There's no one stoppin' yeh.'

' 'Tis not the same,' roared the epicure. ' 'Tis never the same.'

'Hold still, for Jasus' sake,' said Mag crossly. 'You and yer bloody oul' lad. Filthy oul' salty bacon.'

'T'was great!'

'Great, me arse,' snapped Mag.

'Lovely,' said my uncle, 'lovely talk from a daughter on a blessed Sunday mornin'.'

'If it's that blessed,' said Mag tartly, 'yeh might make your way down to the chapel and get Mass. It's six months surely since you were there. Hold still, blast yeh, yeh bloody oul' heathen.'

'You've bloody cut me an' me not bad enough with rheumatism! Are yeh finished, yeh bitch.'

'You'll do . . . Don't forget the pubs open at half twelve. Don't be late.' She bolted then as the old man reached for his stick. Another who ruled with a rod of iron. And he had got his maulers on the pension this week. I could see that.

At three o'clock I went to the fair ground outside the town, so called because the circus used the field when here. The place was crowded and sporting events were taking place all over the field. The long jump and high jump, egg and spoon races, and sack races for the little ones, all kinds of events.

At a quarter past three, I made my way over to the stage where the singing competition was to be held. To be the father and mother of the best singer in town brought great honour to a family and already a large crowd had gathered before the microphone. Promptly, at the fixed time the competition got under way.

I stood there listening to the first six before making my way round to the back of the stage. Number seven was the little girl Harper, who I feared and I paid great attention to her singing. Although sweet as a blackbird, she had a slight tremulo that the microphone showed up and to a trained singer or judge it would not go unnoticed. I was home and hozed. There was nothing here that would beat me this day and Aunt Lil would be proud of me.

'NUMBER EIGHT . . . LAURENCE REDMOND. BOY SOPRANO,' said the voice over the microphone and I stepped on the stage. I was nervous and shy, always the bloody shyness and today it might undo me. But then I thought of Clarendon Street in the five hours singing on Good Friday, with all the statues draped and the light shut out. From the choir, way up at the back, one could see the flash, brilliant as lightning, as some woman with diamond earrings moved her head. I sang in Clarendon Street Chapel and this was, after all, only a small town with no voice so far to beat mine. And so, talking to myself I overcame my fear, waited until the man adjusted the microphone to the right height and then . . .

'Panis Angelicus . . .' Floating over the crowd. I had never in my life sung better.

I thought of the coming parting with this place I loved and knew it would put depth and pathos in my voice. There was a few moments silence when I finished, and I knew I had won. Then the storm of applause! Lil met me with eyes shining with tears. She was in her seventh heaven.

We went then and got an ice-cream, ate it and wandered back. We had not been out of the range of the microphone. What came after me was nothing to be ashamed of but they did not win against the like of me. I knew one other boy in our choir from the slums of Golden Lane, who I was glad was not pitted against me. He would have shown the road to anyone here, maybe even me.

The result of the singing event was a long time coming. There seemed to be consternation behind the scenes and the agitation spread to the crowd. A Kilkenny man had the deciding vote. This in the interest of fair play as a Wexford man might be related in some way and be partisan. He forced his way now through the crowd; red of face, excusing himself and the whole crowd turned to look as he strode swiftly across the field and out the gate.

Head down, one of the other judges, for there were three, came on stage.

'The result of the soprano competition is,' he shouted, 'number one . . . EILEEN HARPER!' There was a surprised buzz of disapproval from the crowd, but the judge ignored it. He was not relishing what he was doing and only wanted to get to hell out of it.

'Number two . . . SEAMUS KAVANAGH! Number three . . . HIS BROTHER SEAN.'

'Oh my Jesus,' said Lil softly. There came an angry roar from the crowd.

'WHAT ABOUT NUMBER EIGHT, THE BOY WHO WON IT?' The roaring gathered momentum and a couple of sods of grass hit the stage. Helplessly, the announcer shrugged his shoulders and walked off. Then came a fusillade of grass sods and the angry roar of a crowd that meant business. It ceased abruptly as the paunchy figure of the parish priest came on stage. Contemptuously he surveyed the crowd.

'You can quit the sod throwin' as of now. There'll be no more of that! The boy yez are creatin' about was here under false pretences. He had no right to be up against Wexford children, a boy who sings in wan of the biggest choirs in Dublin. He was disqualified. He was not from Wexford.'

'Show us the rule that ses he has to be! Show us!' This from a man called French, a Protestant who feared neither God nor man. A hard one.

'Show us the rule,' he roared, 'or did yeh just make it up?' The priest squinted his eyes at the man, trying to identify him.

'Here,' shouted French defiantly, holding up his hand. 'I'm the wan. Here.' The parish priest looked at French with assumed pity.

'I might have known without lookin',' he said contemptuously and he got off the stage quickly just the same.

And that was the end of my day of glory, a white-faced aunt trying not to cry and an angry heart from the Liberties with a little added contempt for priests, especially Wexford ones. A contempt that was to last for the major part of a lifetime, lead me into trouble around the world, for I had confused an ignorant, bigoted country priest with a loving God.

There was much head shaking in the town over the priest's decision, the crowd who had heard me sing saying the priest was wrong, but softly. The rest of the town said 'Well . . . I dunno maybe he was right, an' then again maybe he was wrong . . .' non-committal remarks, frightened remarks, afraid of the priest. You did not criticise the 'sky pilot' in Gorey in 1931. Maybe now, not then!

These people were the prisoners of the Church, the same Church that had refused my father absolution because he would not stop fighting the British. He and twenty-two thousand others had spit in the eye of the Catholic Church, risked damnation and fought all the harder.

It was our new freedom, bought at a great price, that the Church was turning against the people, the attempt to rule. They still had it all their own way down here. Not, by Jasus, where I came from!

I would remember this long holiday all my life, but now the time had come to go. I did not want, nor did anyone ask me to sing a farewell song the following day. That department had dried up, it seemed. I went into Buckley's to say goodbye, told Kate to give my love to Aunt Sarah and Carrie and left the next day with less heartache than I should have. The priest had saved me a lot of that.

'Is this the little lad that was barred the other day in the singin'?' said the guard to Lil as we waited on the platform for the train.

'It is,' said Lil evenly.

'Isn't it a pity now, that he was not from Wexford. I'm told he would have won hands down.'

'He won hands down anyway,' said Lil, 'it was supposed to be a singing competition, nothing else. He won it!'

'All the same,' said the guard, 'if the rule said . . .'

'What rule? The one that priest made up on the spot?'

'I dunno about that,' said the red-faced guard, getting a shade redder. 'Maybe so . . .'

'No, you *dunno* . . . everybody *dunnos*.' Lil was turning vicious. I felt a little sorry for the guard, but he was just another lick-spittle. I looked him square in the face, an unusual thing for me, for I had been brought up to respect my elders and this man was old enough to be my father twice over.

'I won the singing fair and square. Everybody knows that.'

'But lad,' said the guard, who I am sure was sorry he had opened his mouth, 'it was only for Wexford lads.'

'No. The priest made that up to stop me. I'm not from Wexford. I'm from Dublin, the Liberties, and we wouldn't do to a country lad what you did to me.'

'Wait now,' protested the guard. 'I didn't do it.'

'You all did,' said Lil bitterly. 'You're all afraid to raise your voice because the priest is involved . . . Ah, don't be annoyin' me.' And she took my hand and we walked to the far end of the platform until the train came. To be truthful, losing the competition meant nothing to me. It was Lil I was sorry for. She loved me and hated to see me slighted or hurt. I was neither! Only resentful that the ignorant priest had cheated me.

I held Lil through the carriage window and kissed her and loved her until the train pulled out and left her weeping behind me. Nigger hid herself under the seat, whining softly from time to time, as the smiling fields flew past. Soon we were at Arklow and all the other bloody stations on the long way home we stopped at too. Today everything was wrong. How different the bus journey had been. But then it was all before me and now it was past.

Nigger never shifted the whole journey. Like me, she knew her carefree days were gone. She looked well. Her coat gleamed, though come to think of it, she had had no dog biscuits since we left Dublin and had only been fed on scraps. The other dog, Patton, had only been fed on scraps too, mainly mashed potatoes and milk and Nigger had eagerly adopted his diet. Both dogs looked a picture of health and Nigger, I noticed, was fatter too.

We had boarded the train at five o'clock in the afternoon and it reached Westland Row at nine. This arrangement had been made to give Dad time to eat his dinner, wash and change and come to meet me.

He was standing on the platform, smiling, as we steamed in after our long journey. I thought he looked older by far than when I had last seen him. He wore his trilby hat as usual, for he had gone bald while on hungerstrike in jail and was selfconscious about it. He had a white bandage round his neck, but I had seen this before. He had broken out in boils again, working in pain through the day for some builder on his first million. He was only thirty-six but looked fifty. Ironically, when he was fifty he looked forty, for he had made it by then and life was easier. Some other poor bastard was doing his work for him then and making him wealthy. All this was less than four years away, but greeting this shabby man at Westland Row station it was difficult to visualise that in such a short time we would have escaped from the Liberties for ever.

'Hello, Dad,' I said. He embraced me awkwardly. 'Well,' he said, taking my little bundle from me, 'glad to be home?' I had a strong piece of rope and was busily putting it through Nigger's collar. She gave me trouble and I had to slap her. She, like me, no longer liked the big city and its stonewalled streets.

'No,' I said truthfully.

'Christ, boy,' he said resentfully, 'you've had a great holiday. Couldn't you be grateful for that much, at least?'

I sullenly finished fixing Nigger and stood up. She jobbed a little, but the vicious tugs I gave her made her see reason quickly. We walked from the station in to Westmoreland Street and got the tram at the Ballast Office. It was the number nineteen from Nelson's Pillar to Rialto. We would get off at the Barn chapel.

I sat silent on top of the tram and looked at this, my native place. It looked shabbier than I had remembered it, though cleaner. The dealers were being hunted off the streets, kerbside selling was banned nearly all over, though here and there the odd heap of garbage told where some stubborn harridan of a Molly Malone still carried on. But her days were numbered.

The headlines on the news boards outside the shops told of soup kitchens and bread lines in New York. Another said trains were being fired with wheat mixed in the coal while half the world starved. Brazil had a mountain of coffee rotting in railway sidings. And half Dublin was living on bread and tea.

'You're very quiet,' said my father. 'What has the country done to you?'

'Nothing, Dad, it's just that I miss it. I loved it down there. It was so peaceful and Lil and Mag and Carrie were lovely to me. Carrie had a sheep dog named Patton and he and Nigger got on great.'

'Obviously,' said my father dryly. 'You'll be in trouble with your mother. That dog is going to have pups.'

'*What!*'

'Yes, she's going to have pups alright. As if we didn't have enough in the house.'

'That's not my fault,' I said sullenly.

'Christ, you're not even home and the trouble starts.' I looked out the tram window, trying not to cry, but the tears came anyway. I heard my father give a gusty sigh of impatience beside me and knew he was finished with me. For a while anyway.

I dried my tears quietly and was all right again when we came to the Barn chapel. We went down the Back of the Pipes and so home to the Square. The family was playing around in the long summer evening, there were ten of us now, all crowded into this small artisan dwelling and Mam was calling them in for bed. They came, one by one, all younger than I, except Sean, who was off on his new bike. Mam gave me a brief kiss and a hug, told me I looked well and to get ready for bed.

'Bed early for you every night,' she said. 'We can't have you sick on our hands again.' Jesus, I was sick now! So, it was a slice of bread and jam and up to bed. I told the others about Wexford, the woods and the rivers, the farm with all the animals and the guinea hens that laid eggs with thick shells so that you could drop them on the ground and not break them and the way they called 'go-back, go-back' all day. Well, I was back. When they dropped off to sleep, I stole down to the kitchen, Dad had gone to bed so I sat up with Mam telling her everything that had happened to me. Everything I wanted her to know. Not about feeling Mag's tits. She would have been disgusted about that.

At last we went to bed, Mam kissing me good night on the landing. Poor Nigger was forcibly ejected to sleep on a sack in the lavatory. It was a big change for both of us, Nigger alone, me surrounded by too many arms and legs, kicking, tossing, rolling over, Jesus, would I ever get used to this again? If I ran away, would Auntie Lil take me in? She would send me back, there was no solace there. I sighed and went to sleep.

When I awoke in the morning the sun was blazing, it was ten o'clock and those of the family who went to school had gone. Incredibly, I had slept through it all. I went down the stairs. The little ones were playing outside in the sunny square, safe with no through-traffic. Mam was up to her arms in tub washing. It was Monday morning every day in our house now. 'Dolly's Squad', as we were referred to, was large and lusty and could make dirty clothes faster than she could clean them. It was hard, heartbreaking, never ending work.

She pushed her brown hair off her sweating forehead, kissed me with sudsy arms around me and said:

'Lar, make a good cup of tea, like you used to. None of the others has the knack.'

'Yes, Mam,' I said, pleased.

'I thought I'd let you sleep on today, give you a little time to get used to things, before tomorrow.'

'Thanks, Mam. What did Dad say?'

'He was worried, but in the end let you sleep. He's afraid you'll be kept another year in fifth class. What do you think?'

'He's wrong. I won't be. I had Uncle Pat's school books in Gorey, from the time he went to school. I did a bit of studying.'

'But that won't be much good to you, will it?'

'It should be. He was in a higher grade than me and I could do his work alright. The history and English and Irish and geography were easy. What's for breakfast?'

'There's two slices of Indian Meal on the pan. Look after yourself, child and don't be too long with the tea. I've been at this since nine o'clock.'

Indian Meal was the staple diet for our breakfast. How Mam discovered it I never knew. I think Mrs Madigan with the big diddies from Kerry told her about it. But whoever did, it was great stuff and cheap. It was of course meal made from Indian corn, maize and when boiled in a pot and left to cool it set like a jelly. You could upend the pot on to a huge plate we had, cut slices from the set meal and fry them on the pan. With milk and sugar, it was a good meal to send a boy to school with. Our family was reared on it and, besides, I thought it delicious.

While Mam drank her tea, I got my breakfast ready and sat

opposite her. She was pensive this morning as she let Nigger in. The dog made her way slowly over to me, wagging her tail feebly. And her nose was dry . . .

'Mam,' I said, 'Nigger isn't well!' She got up and squatted in front of the bitch.

'Did you miss me, Nigger?' she said. The bitch licked her face, quietly walked away and lay under the table.

'See if she'll drink some tea, Lar.' I gave her a cup of tea in a saucer with plenty of sugar, the way she liked it, with some bread broken in. She eagerly lapped up the tea but left the bread and, going to the back door, whined to be let out again. She was going back to the sack in the lavatory. I let her go and turned a scared face to my mother.

'Now, Lar,' she warned me, 'don't start worrying. Nigger is a little bit off colour, maybe the travelling upset her. And she is going to have pups.'

'What'll we do when she has?'

'Find homes for those we can. The rest . . . into the canal they go,' she said matter-of-factly. I was home all right. That was the way it was here. Life was lived with death never far away. You were supposed to become hardened to it. I never would, but that was the way it was.

'No fear of bringing any fancy cakes home from the exam this year,' Mam said, 'and a few bob. I used to look forward to it.'

'I'll pass anyway, Mam, I think. When does the exam start?'

'Wait now, let me think. Tomorrow is Wednesday, you go to school. You have two weeks to catch up, tomorrow fortnight is exam day. You go on holiday the following Monday.'

'OK,' I said off-handedly, 'but don't lose hope of the cakes entirely.'

'Entirely!' She laughed. 'You speak like a country man, Lar. Anyway, there's no harm in dreamin'. You might as well rave here as in bed.' I grinned. She was right, of course. I had been off school three months. I would be lucky to pass at all.

I went back to school the next day. Colin was there as always. Ernie Mountain, wiry and tough as ever, the class with one empty desk, mine. The dear old Kipper was glad to see me I knew, and gave me his hard smile, a reluctant token to a soft heart. There was no betting on me for the exam this year. Freddy Dunne, a quiet hard-working boy was making his name; Branwell, as always, was there and the betting was mostly on these two. Colin was too easy-going to attract. He never appeared to do anything except chew sweets and smoke on the sly. Yet he was always in the first three. I spoke to him before the exam, not for the first time.

'Janey, Colin,' I said to him, 'if you'd only try a bit harder, you could . . .' Colin just smiled and told me he had found a new quarry, deep in the fields a mile past the Half Way House pub, a fearful journey, but the quarry we knew was doomed, our little stream all being piped.

'The perch are big in it,' said Colin and that was that.

I was an 'also ran', said the class. Three months spent in the country had slowed me down. The terrible truth was that what they said was true. I had grown lax and lazy while in the sleepy countryside. Out in the school yard I was slow, could not hold my own and was thrown in wrestling matches by boys I would have mangled a year ago. I was all washed up, said the class, quieter, easily got at. That week back at school opened my eyes. I had become a pushover – and they did not survive long here.

On the evening of my third night home, I stayed out late with the gang, until it was dark. We had a pile of grass sods gathered and lay in wait where the Square meets the Backers. Soon, a gang of big fellows would pass this way, headed for the Fountain Picture House in James's Street, also known as the Bowery. We were sure of some fun. Within five minutes our scout came running, panting that about ten fellas were slingin' along, smoking. As they drew level with the Square, we let fly, belting them with a storm of wet sods – some of our crowd had pissed on them – good suits getting plastered and their owners with the lugs nearly knocked off them. Of course, the whole thing about an attack on young men, say from seventeen on was that we relied on speed to save us from their wrath. Mostly by the time they were seventeen they were shortwinded from smoking, grown slack from lousing at street corners and this gang was no different.

We flew before their pursuit and then a terrible realisation came to me. I had no reserve of speed. Even to avoid being caught, I could not keep up with my pals. Kevin O'Connell passed me with a delighted grin. He would be looking for more fight soon. And all the rest as well!

Hearing the feet of vengeance upon me, I ducked and barely missed a punch behind the ear. I received a slight blow from the other side not hard, and ducked and swerved, receiving another blow across the head. Ducking and weaving, more by instinct than anything else, I collected many a box, none of them heavy but the shame of being the only one who could not outrun these bowsies, who held up street corners all day. In the end a few women came to my rescue and the big ones fled. I had gone soft. There was no place for me here, that was clear. Something had to be done. In the next few days I regained my fleetness of foot and in a hurry. O'Connell had taken to running beside me if he saw me and passed me, grinning. He was working up another scrap and he was a hell of a lot bigger now. Maybe he would take me.

I started training. I ran everywhere – to school, on messages, to Thomas Street library. After the fourth day O'Connell lost his grin. I let him keep running alongside, pacing me and when he began to pant I grinned, put on speed and left him behind. He never came at me again.

I flattened Paddy Holihan in the school yard the next day. Normally, he would have been afraid to ge. fresh with me, but the word had got around. Redmond had gone soft, anyone could take him. I felt ashamed it took me so long to burst his snot and send him back to class, crying. This would impress nobody. But the next day I flattened his pal, who chanced his luck, in a few seconds of ferocity and things were being put back in their place.

The three days of the exam caused me no worry, but even I was surprised when I tied with Branwell for first place. The old order was now restored. The class was flabbergasted. The Kipper gave his hard grin and brought Gleeson in to observe the Order of Merit line-up. Gleeson smiled.

'The same old faces in the same old places,' he said.

'Redmond was not a fancied runner this time, Ned,' said the Kipper. 'He was supposed to be out of condition, but it seems he didn't know that.' Gleeson looked at me with affection.

'The same swift throughbred, Red,' he remarked. 'Never say your mother . . .' he paused.

'. . . reared a jibber,' I finished for him, grinning. And my pal Colin was smiling too. He was the only one who had laid odds on me and in his loyalty had pawned his all. Now he collected his bets with interest. He won five complete sets of cigarette cards, two seasoned chestnuts (future havoc) and five pence. He had come second himself, with Dunne third.

Had I known it, this was not the day for rejoicing. This was my swan song. Like Samson, with shorn hair, I had shot my bolt. From here on in the balance of my school days would become an increasing nightmare. But I had no premonition of this as I went down the South Circular Road that morning. It was Monday, of course. They had a funny way of bringing you in to school just for one day in the new week before the holidays.

The lady in the confectioner's had come to know me over the years. She was a Scot and spoke pleasant, fractured English.

'Really,' she said smiling, 'You're not tellin' me you've won again?'

'Yes,' I said grinning from ear to ear as I gave my order.

'And,' she said, looking at me intently, 'lookin' so well. The girls 'ill be after ye, you're gettin' to be a bonny boy. I do believe you've grown an inch as well . . .'

Jesus, how good could you get it? To be one of the fleetest, to burst snots in a hurry, to top the exam and now this! I could not wait as I flew home to stand against the wall, where my height mark had remained unaltered for centuries, it seemed.

Nothing had changed in our house. It was still Monday, wash day, there was a small mountain of clothes to be done, with mini-washing during the week. Mam nearly collapsed when I came in, grinning from ear to ear. She had had no hope this time, neither had I, but I had known since Friday that I was in the running. I had said nothing to anybody. As always, her lovely brown hair was stuck to her forehead as she tunnelled her way into an alpine range of dirty clothes. The place was full of steam but everything was dropped now as she kissed me and held me close.

'God bless your brains, boy,' she said smiling. 'It must be from your father you got them, it wasn't from me.' And that, too, was correct. But she did not need brains. She was fey. She could look through people. Her instinct was never wrong.

'Mam,' I said, standing against my mark on the wall, 'look, am I growing?' She took the ruler I gave her and held it on my head, standing sideways to see that it was held level. She smiled, took the pencil I handed her and put my new mark on the wall.

'I've put on nearly an inch, Mam.'

'Great, Lar, it must have been Wexford.'

'Can I go back again to Lil this year? She would love me to go.' She regarded me through narrowed eyes. She had a habit of giving this penetrating stare when she wanted to know the truth.

'You're very fond of Lil, aren't you?'

'Yes, Mam, I am.'

'Love her more than me?'

'Oh Mam, you know I don't. I love you best in all the world.' We settled down happily then to our strong tea and cakes. Mam said she would keep the big one I had bought for her, to split between herself and Dad as a surprise before he went to bed.

'I don't think, Lar,' she said at length, 'that I should let you go back to Gorey, at least not so soon. It's not right that you should have all the holidays and your brothers and sisters be left here, is it?'

'Maybe not, Mam. I'm not taking anything away from them. Lil doesn't want them. She doesn't know them. She wants me.'

'Well,' said this very Irish mother, 'she's not going to have you. A boy's place is with his parents, even if they are poor. He belongs with his family. Never to get too far away from them. Why, Lar,' she said softly, 'you're only coming back to me now.'

And that was true anyway. Soft country voices and softer hearts had nearly seduced me from her and that would have broken her heart. In one blinding flash I realised just how much I meant to her and I felt ashamed of my temporary treachery. But it had been lovely in Wexford. I told her then about the singing competition and the priest disqualifying me and the rage of Aunt Lil. I also told her the people of the town seemed to be afraid to talk about it.

'Ach,' she spat with contempt. 'Them bloody culchies think the priest 'id turn yeh into a goat, the bloody oul' bitter get.' It was the only time in my life I ever heard her come close to cursing a priest.

We finished our little feast, I gave Mam a few bob and she resumed the assault on the mountain of children's clothes. I volunteered to clean up the back yard. Mam was right. A boy belonged with his family. I had gone far away, nearly too far, ever to come back, really to come back. My brother Sean had only gone next door years ago, but that had effectively alienated him from his mother for the balance of his life. He had never come back.

Mam had sensed with her infallible instinct that she had nearly lost another son and this one part of her. And I had nearly lost a family. It would have hurt her more than me for I was far away, I realised that now. Except for her, there was little around here to compete with Wexford. I loved my father now and then. There was little communication between me and my eldest brother. The rest were all younger and I loved them after my own fashion, but we were all too busy growing up to be really close. When I thought of my family in total I loved them. It was all very confusing, for when I thought of them individually I could sometimes detest them. And I had not missed them when in Wexford. Truthfully, I had been glad to get away. So had poor Nigger, who was lying sick now on the floor of the lavatory. I patted her head and she waved her tail feebly.

I did not blame her for being sick. She had loved the woods

and fields and Patton. The fields that had been around here were gone. Maryland was complete Buggy Boylon's Orchard and fields and streams now lay under a tide of houses stuck, like new plaster, on the scabrous face of the slums.

The canal no longer defied the city and kept it at bay. The marauding army of house builders could no longer be contained. A mile up the Crumlin Road, Dad was working on a new building project for Guinness's men. Well constructed brick houses, semi-detached, far out in the fields like a parachute drop of men and materials behind the enemy lines. Nearly opposite to it and up Windmill Lane, Wills Tobacco Factory workers, many of them English, had another estate built for them and these two outposts were, for a few years, the high tide mark of the houses. There were many acres between them and the dark lanes still. Economic ups and downs, wars and building shortages due to them would interfere with the forward march of the houses, but the end was inevitable. It would be an Irish Waterloo for the fair fields of Crumlin.

Known as 'the English colonoy', Wills's houses were a fair target for us on Guy Fawkes' Night when the English boys would light a fire in their playing field and set fire to a made-up figure, chanting 'Guy, Guy, stick it in his eye . . .' and we would open up with a volley of sods, but it was poor sport and not worth the journey. They were too easily routed.

And now the lovely sparkling quarry, where I and Colin and Ernie fished the summer's days away, was being used as a dump. They had begun filling in at one end. The quarry was seventy feet deep in places and the filling would take many years. But Dublin, I figured correctly, had enough dirt to fill anything.

Along the dark lanes men were moving with wooden pegs and theodolites. Sundrive Road was being built over the ancient lane. Thousands of people who lived in the festering slums of the Liberties would find a house here. Crumlin, as I remember it now, was finished! Very few of the first generation found a home. Home was The Coombe and they went back there to get drunk.

At fifteen minutes past five every evening now, Dolphins

Barn Street would be jammed with hundreds of men, all pouring off the massive building schemes that spelt ruin to me. I was being built in, the fields going fast. Still though, I thought, they would never get as far as Crumlin village, the estate Colin and I raided for walnuts was still intact. That was some small comfort.

I finished the yard by throwing buckets of water all over it and sweeping it down the shower. Nigger needed dog biscuits and although I had four bob left after giving Mam seven and splurging the rest on fancy cakes, I had no intention of buying them. Dog biscuits would set my pal up again. The fair Marion was about to be honoured by a visit from me after a long lapse. I was home!

I would go up for Colin. He was off school too and we would go for a walk in the fields. I would nick a few biscuits on the way out, hide them and pick them up on the way back.

'Come on, Nig,' I said. 'I'm going for a walk.' She made no attempt to join me. Instead of barking and dancing, for she knew all my words, she lay there, feebly thumping her tail. If Colin did not come, I would walk alone this day.

Care, like a dismal fungus, took hold of me and spread. Suddenly, looking at my dog, my heart was down in my boots. I was home! That much I could be sure about. If it was the only thing in the whole empty universe I could be sure about it was that! Home, sweet fucking home!

14 *Moira Leddy*

Few children in The Liberties reached fourteen years of age, without experiencing some personal tragedy, a father or mother, brother or sister taken swiftly, or bitter slow, by 'the Con'. Then there was diphtheria, that pounced like a tiger on the swarming slums, scarcely leaving a room without sorrow.

It was then the schools closed, to try and contain the epidemic, and a pall of fear lay over the narrow streets. Cork Street hospital would be packed to overflowing, even the corridors having beds in them, and the bell in Dolphins Barn chapel tolled to offer up prayers for the repose of the souls just gone to Heaven, and black veiled women wept openly. Now on my first week back at school it struck with a vengeance and the black crepes, with the mourning card appeared on the doors of all too many houses. It struck at children mostly, and ignorance, crass brute ignorance, played a major part, and helped empty many a cot.

It seemed to be a more virulent variety than usual, the nurses in Cork Street hospital were reported dropping, literally collapsing from fatigue. Besides, a few of them had contracted the dreaded scourge, leaving the already exhausted staff to cope with the avalanche as best they could.

Coming home from school, I saw Mrs Fox, who lived a few doors from us, stand smiling in her doorway, while her child shared a lollypop with Keven Stacey. Mrs Fox already had one child in Cork Street hospital.

I watched the kids in horror.

'You shouldn't let them do that,' I told her. 'You see, Mrs Fox . . .'

'G'wan you,' she snapped. 'Feck off, head a' sense, an oul' man cut short!' So I departed with flaming cheeks, while she indulgently encouraged the children.

'Lovely teh see them sharing with each other, that's what I say,' she told Mrs Mongey. 'God's will. If they're goin' teh get it, they're goin' teh get it.'

Kevin Stacey was taken to hospital next day, and died that week. Mrs Mongey, who had listened to Mrs Stacey with compressed lips, but said nothing, must have told the stricken child's mother, for on the night Kevin died, she went berserk in the Square, screaming, battering the Fox's door, 'Yeh killed me child . . . yeh killed me child . . . yeh bitch, the curse a' God may light on yeh, yeh Culchie bitch . . .'

She had to be forcibly hauled off the door knocker. As for the Fox children, both of them survived the disease, though the family fled the Square within a couple of weeks, where to, no one knew. Or cared.

For Mrs Stacey had temporarily lost her mind, and daily we were treated to the sight of her assaulting the Fox's door. Mrs Fox must have done her shopping very early or in the dark, for she and her children were never seen. One morning the curtains were down, gone from the windows, and the Fox's with them. And following close on their heels, the sulphuric curses of a Liberties daughter gone mad.

'May the Curse a' Jasus folly them teh the doors a' Hell!' All of this, however, passed over me like a dream, for I had my own sorrows. Nigger was in trouble, real trouble. There was a smell in the lavatory where she slept, even with the door open you could smell her. Her nose was dry, she only drank, and daily got weaker while her belly grew bigger.

'Lar,' said my Father one golden summer evening. 'You'll have to do something about that dog. We can't have her here like that, among the children. There's a smell in the toilet.'

Jesus, the toilet stank to the high heavens, it had to be bad if he could smell it, for his olfactory sense was nearly dead.

'What do you want me to do, Dad?'

'What do you think yourself, Lar,' he said gently.

'There's a vet in Harcourt Street. He's open every evening

for a couple of hours, for people with no money, or not much anyway,' I quickly added, for I well knew my father's pride.

'And have you any money?'

'Yes, Dad. I've still got four bob . . .'

'Shillings,' he corrected.

'Shillings, from the exam.'

'When will you take her?'

'Now, Dad, tonight. She's bad.'

'But how will you get her there?'

'I'll carry her up the Backers, and get the nineteen tram at the chemist's corner.'

'But you are hardly strong enough for . . .' Mam quietly put her hand on his shoulder and gave it a squeeze. He stopped speaking abruptly.

'All right, then, but try not to wear yourself out. We've had you sick long enough.'

'Don't worry, Dad. I'll be all right.'

Half an hour later, dressed in my best short trousers and jumper, I struggled on to the tram, carrying the dog. I made it to the top, staggering up the steel stairs, for Nigger stank. Downstairs I would have been put off, but there was no one up here.

At Harcourt Street I staggered off with my burden, and found the vet. He was a quiet silver haired man, in his late forties, and I have always remembered his extreme good looks, and his kindness. He examined Nigger briefly. She seemed to be half asleep, almost in a coma, though as always she was gentle. She was dying, and wanted to die in peace, but I would not let her. My love was so strong that I believed she could not leave me, and would not leave me, because she loved me too much.

'I want you to give her these two pills tonight when you go home,' said the vet.

'Will she be all right, sir?'

'Yes, she'll be all right. In the morning you will find that you have no more need to worry.'

'How much are the pills, sir?'

'How much have you got?'

'Three and eleven pence, sir. I'll need a penny for the tram. She's too heavy to carry all that way.'

'What's your name, sonny?'

'Lar Redmond, sir.'

'Well, Lar,' said this smiling man, 'I'll charge you eight-pence for the pills. We can't have you walking home.'

'And the rest, sir? The examination?'

'I do that at night for nothing. Like yourself, I love dogs. You're a good kind lad, God bless you. Now, don't forget. The minute you get home, if you love her, give her the pills.'

I was tired when I reached home, and it was twilight. It had taken me a long time to carry Nigger down the back of the pipes, but my heart was singing.

'Well?' said Mam anxiously, as I came in.

'She's going to be all right, Mam. All I have to do is to give her these two pills now, and put her to bed.' I carried Nigger outside, and gave her some lukewarm tea, with plenty of sugar to give her strength, and managed to get the pills, one a really big one, down her neck. She obeyed me, swallowed it, and feebly licked my hand. And smell and all, I kissed her goodnight, and went to bed exhausted, for Nigger weighed at least a stone, and although I was made of whipcord, still, it had been a long carry. But I dreamed the dreams of the innocent that night.

I woke the following morning rested and excited. Maybe Nigger would be able to come for a small walk today. Everybody in the house was still asleep. It was six o'clock on a beautiful summer morning, as I crept downstairs in my shirt, for we did not live in the world of dressing gowns and pyjamas. I quietly turned the key in the back door. It opened out, and sometimes, Nigger, in her eagerness to see me would be scraping her paws on the door, and we would have a little shoving match before we met.

She was doing that this morning, for I could feel her holding back the door, although funnily enough, I did not hear her whining with eagerness. I shoved the door firmly, but hard. It opened, and I saw Nigger's backlegs and tail protruding around the door. I jumped outside, and my heart nearly stopped. My pal was dead, had been for hours, for she was stiff, and had died trying to get to me.

I do not know how long I stayed there, staring. Presently, Mam came down to get Dad off to work, found me kneeling beside the dead dog, and burst out crying. As for me, my grief was too deep for tears. They would come, later, floods of them, but not now. I was stunned, mind frozen, only able to realise one thing, that my dog was dead. Never again would I walk the fields with the closest companion I was ever to have. For Nigger knew everything about me. When the whole world was against me, she was there, with a bark and a lick to comfort me.

When I was sunk in despair over some fight that a big fella' was seeking Nigger was there to tell me in her own way, that I would win. And although I never lost a fight, I always went in terrified, too proud to acknowledge that at heart I was a coward.

'Never say your mother reared a Jibber', the Liberties axiom I was to live by for the balance of my life, and dearly I paid for it.

But of all the vicissitudes in life, and it held plenty, there is no single event that had such shattering effect. It stood alone. For weeks after we buried her I would steal away into the ruined acres of the Dolphins Barn brick works, to cry. Nobody ever went there, except me in the spring for tadpoles, and here I gave way to my grief. I was inconsolable.

The epidemic abruptly came to an end. Our school had closed for ten days, and now it reopened. We did not go back to the Kipper. He was finished with us, another blow for me. We now passed out of fifth class, into sixth, and were under the Head. This was *the* year, the year we sat for our Primary Certificate. I was confused and upset. With no pal to comfort me I was bereft, forsaken, heart-broken.

With my dog, I had lived in a world of make-believe. Sometimes I had been a Mountie, sliding on my snow shoes, through the green snow of some meadow, and Nigger, the last of my dog team, loping alongside, lean and starving, keeping the wolves at bay. We had four hundred miles to go to get to Fort McKenzie, we had no food, and only two bullets left which if we did not sight a deer or moose, I would use on Nigger and me. To be torn to death by the wolves was unthinkable!

At other times, I was Finn Mac Cúl, leader of the Red Branch Knights, with Bran, and Scolín, my majestic wolf hounds racing beside me. In Castletown this had always been the game, for I had Patton too.

The outbreak of fever which, always before had terrified me, came and went, almost un-noticed. But when I returned to school two desks were empty. Four boys had died, the first since Dessy Duffy. Three more, over the years had disappeared, Kit Byrne and the Mount Shannon gang had gradually faded away. The last, Branwell, was left now. In the beginning we had numbered fifty-one. We were now down to forty-two.

Ten years later our ill fated class of 1926 was decimated by the second world war. With no jobs to go to after they left school, they had gone the way of their fathers, joining the British Army, the Royal Navy, the Merchant Navy, and the Royal Air Force. Some went down with their ships before they were twenty-one, some mingled with the sandy beach at Dunkirk, some slept quietly in an English graveyard, having fallen out of the sky. A few lasted until the beach head at Anzio, in Italy. A couple more got their lot in the Battle of the Bulge.

But most of them slept forever in the sands of an African Desert, alongside the classes of '26 from Dusseldorf, Hanover, or Dresden, at peace at last, they who had never quarrelled, but who had killed each other.

So it was adieu to the Kipper, the only school teacher who ever taught me anything. Who persevered with me and my tantrums, who slapped me and corrected me and loved me. We were all set for our Primary Certificate, and for ninety-nine per cent of those with me, that was the end of the line. From here we were sent to work.

My elder brother had preceded me by two years, had been a favourite of the Head Master, and like me, had been Dux of class. There, all resemblance ended. Two brothers less alike it would be hard to find. Although never a big man, he had done all his growing by the time he was fourteen, and was by no means the smallest boy in his class. He could more than hold his own when it came to a scrap. He was a natural fighter, and was something of a legend around the district. He littered Dolphins Barn with fellows twice his size, with a mixture of cunning, science, and sheer ferocity. I could fight too, but compared to him I was an also ran. Besides, where he fought for the love of it, I only fought to protect myself. To my knowledge he was never defeated in the countless fights he fought. Even taking on seventeen year olds when he was only fourteen, he came out on top.

I knew his style, his tactics, and to my regret, his punch. I watched him one day correct the reigning champion of Cork Street buildings. This lad was mad to get at him. He was sick hearing about this Redmond fella' and so he issued a challenge. The fight was arranged for a lane beside the Woollen Mills at three o'clock on Patrick's day. All the Square gang turned up, as did the Cork Street Buildings gang, who outnumbered us by nearly three to one, I prudently selected a position on a wall of the lane, so that if general hostilities broke out after the fight I could get lost quickly. I carried two pockets full of stones as well, another prudent thought. The lad who had foolishly issued the challenge was feeling his weight, at fifteen, nearly a six footer, good-looking and lithe. His name was Devlin. Beside him, my brother, at five feet four, and at least a stone lighter, looked a poor prospect. He ran his fingers through his blond hair, grinning, in no way intimidated. He was used to fighting big ones. As for Devlin, one could see that he was sure of himself. In his careless attitude and arrogant stance, one could see that he had his mind made up not to give his smaller opponent too much of a thrashing. He would let him off lightly.

The fight opened with no preliminaries; they knew each other by sight, had had no quarrel, but had to prove something. Devlin belonged to Guinness's boxing club, he stood up straight, in classical pose, dancing forward throwing straight lefts the Marquis of Queensbury would have applauded, but then, the Marquis, as was well known, was mad. The cries of the Cork Street Buildings gang mounted as Devlin drove Sean back. My brother moved rapidly in a circle, and what the enemy was missing was the fact that he had not once been struck.

'Lurry him up, Jack . . . Bate the shite out a' him . . . show him what the Cork Street Gang can do . . .'

I sat on the wall grinning. I knew what was coming, it did. Suddenly Sean stopped, took a step forward, ducked under the surprised Devlin's guard, and then, a burst of power punching, rapid as machine gun fire.

One-two-three-One-two-three-One-two-three, nine punches delivered in two seconds, that left Devlin with a crumpled face, and a nose that poured blood. And then came the hiding, after a couple of seconds of grinning respite. Devlin, nearly out on his feet, courageous to the last, Sean dancing in and out, belting him in the guts, doubling him up, then straightening him with a few upper cuts to the face. The lad from Cork Street was a mess. My brother backed away, and dropped his guard.

'Fight on, Jack. Yeh have him . . . He's gettin' tired . . . He's afraid!'

Devlin came forward with a rush, unexpected by Sean, and managed to get a good punch in. It was the first and the last. My brother demolished him with unparalleled fury, picking him off carefully, belting him over the heart, punching him in the chest, until Devlin, eyes closing, went down to a punch in the stomach. A foul punch. But then, this was not the St James's Club in Pall Mall. This was a back lane in the Liberties.

The Cork Street Buildings gang slunk off, too dispirited to start a ruggy up the thing I was making sure I avoided. Sean was admired by our gang because of his fighting ability. He was admired by the Head Master for his clever brain, and fearlessness. And I, who had to stand outside the lavatory, while he went in the dark, had to follow in his tracks, a disappointment to myself and my new teacher every day I spent in his classroom.

I had joined the Head with a towering reputation, Dux of class. He had expected another one like my brother. Instead he got me and he was disappointed with me. I was much smaller. I was quieter. It took people longer to get to know me. It was a ruin and a wreckage for me in the Head's class right from the start.

For something had happened for which there is no accounting. Part of my brain went on strike, shut up shop, pulled down the shutters, and bankrupted the firm. I had never had to study hard. In fact I had never had to study at all. Knowledge was blotted up like a sponge, and retained. But now, past long devision and decimals, my brain knocked off. No more maths, it said. No more geometry! No bloody algebra, in any manner whatsoever. Never!

English, Irish, Poetry, Essays, Composition, all came as easily as before, but now I had to struggle fiercely to try and even get a foothold with algebra, battling to understand decimals, and the accursed Euclid . . . Jesus!

I tried. I fought. I floundered, although studying hard until eleven o'clock at night. Sometimes until I was ordered to bed. The maths went badly, the geometry was painstakingly done, the algebra a wreckage and a ruin. I had become a stumer, like Deasy and Kevin O'Connell and I could not take it.

The very first time I jumped up to answer a question, I got it wrong. The second and third time too. The fourth time I tried I was told, 'Sit down, you Mug.' Me, Dux of class, at the top for five years, now reduced to the lowly status of a stumer. It was too much. It broke my heart, and spirit, and I moved in a world that was suddenly filled with disaster. I had panicked and could not think clearly any more. To make matters worse, boys who up to this had just been average, suddenly displayed astonishing ability at the three subjects I could no longer do. There seemed to be less and less emphasis on English, compositions became minor events, poetry almost non existent. The whole living, breathing world became a nightmare of maths, a Dali landscape of geometry, a limitless desert of algebra.

I lapsed into sullen silence. I was afraid of the Head's

sarcastic tongue. I could not concentrate, and failed miserably at everything. I came in for the Head's biting humour. He was not a bad man. He had a family himself, and was no brute, like Yella' man, and a few more bastards I was to meet. Sarcasm was his weapon, and used against me, ultra sensitive, it was as bad as a flogging. Maybe worse.

For his part, I suppose he was puzzled and hurt by the fact that this boy, who had been Dux of his class was now doing so badly. From his point of view, it must have looked as if I was being deliberately obstinate. So he laid on with sarcasm, and crucified me. As I grew daily more sullen he took to asking me why I did not go to Donore Avenue School, or the Christian Brothers? I became the target for the odd witticism. He began to make me the butt of the class. I was often compared to my brother, to my great disadvantage. Something had to give. I could take no more.

I had passed into Oul' Paunch's class mid way through May. Two weeks later the Summer holidays came as a merciful respite, from the master's scalding tongue, but not from labour. For we had opened a shop! We took over the shop where Sloppy Molly, and the boy from Killane had presided. They had fled the wrath of the Square, and opened up on the South Circular Road. Besides, the shop had suddenly become accident prone. In three months the shop window had had to be replaced four times. They ran out of insurance companies before they ran out of customers. When that happened, they ran out of the Barn. And I did my small bit to help them on their way.

The first time the window went in, half a Dolphins Barn brick had been found among the chops. It was generally supposed that it had shot from under the solid rubber wheel of a passing truck. So it was replaced without much comment. The second time it happened was in the small hours, and lacking an explanation, was put down, by the gullible, to the same cause.

The third time old drunken Mrs Mahon did the job from the inside with a two pound weight. She had staggered into the shop, drunk, picked up the weight, and cursing like a trooper, flung it through the window.

'That's for you, yeh mangy fucker,' she told the boy from Killane. She left under the escort of two coppers and she got two months in jail. The last time the window went in was the work of the Square gang. We had hatched out the plot, practised carefully against the wall of the Backers, and were ready. Each of us, six in number, was equipped with a catapult. This took more time than it would have done two years previously. The hawthorn hedges were receding fast, and we had to travel further for timber forks. Suitable rubber had also to be found, not so plentiful then. The leather holder of the missile was easy. You just cut the tongue out of your boot. We practised for a week, perhaps a little longer, and were ready.

Practise took the form of running at full speed, and knocking a can off a post, from fifteen paces, the width of Dolphins Barn Street. As the appointed time drew near, we grew afraid. We could all go to Artane or Glencree for this. But we could not back off. The code of the Liberties was not to be flouted, and not one of us would say we had gone too far. So the night was set, and we practised away in fear and trembling.

The time came and we waited for a lorry, the noisier the better, to come along. We each had two lead missiles, made from an old water tap. It was the month of October, ideal for our purpose. It was dark by eight thirty, and most of us had to be home by nine o'clock. Just as if we had ordered it, a lorry, carrying empty tar barrels came up from Cork Street, going past Sloppy Molly's. The noise it made was appalling, solid rubber tyres bouncing off the cobbles, the barrels dancing and banging in the back.

We ran, like small Indians, in single file, alongside it on the pavement. As we came opposite the shop, one after the other we let fly, and ran on with the lorry. At the top of the Barn we crossed the road, and ran down the Backers into the Square. The catapults we buried on the waste lot, talking excitedly. It had been too simple. Not a sound had been heard over the clamour of the truck. Silently, large stars had appeared all over the window, and it was ready to fall out.

That was the final straw. The shop closed. A month later Sloppy Molly opened up again, on the South Circular Road. The name over the shop was still Keegans, not Kelly, so perhaps things had not worked out all that good for lover boy. The old shop remained idle for months, there was much whispering and consultation between Mam and Dad, and one night, just before our school holidays, Dad brought me up the Barn Street, and opened the former butchers. It was three years now since Mam had had a baby, and I suppose, God love them, they thought all that was over. Anyway, there was already a pile of new timber in the shop, and Dad started putting up a counter and shelves right away. He was an exceptional carpenter, accurate and fast, and the shop was ready in a week, working every night. Then Mam took over.

She must have had the courage of a tigress, an Amy Johnson, and an Amazon all rolled into one, for she had eight school going children, one going to work, and Dad to cater for. Nevertheless, she had it all worked out. I had nine week holidays before me. I would have to go to the market at least twice a week, for fish and vegetables, and take over in the afternoon when things were slack. She would go home at one, and so nobody would miss their dinner except me. I would have to wait until nine o'clock when the shop closed, but she would send up some tea and sandwiches every night at six.

Roughly, that was the way it worked out. Dad had made a little box cart and I would start off on Thursday morning not later than seven fifteen, to meet Mam in the vegetable and fish market. All the way down Cork Street, right along the Coombe, through Patrick's Street in the shadow of the mad old Dean's Cathedral, up Nicholas Street, under the arch that spans the road part of the beautiful Protestant Cathedral, known as Christ's Church. Down Winetavern Street, across the Liffey, and so, running into the market. Mam having got there before me, would be waiting, the stuff already bought. That was the way it worked. And then running all the way back through the heart of the Liberties, water streaming out of the cart as the ice melted on the fish, cauliflowers, cabbage and tomatoes piled on top.

When I got back to the Barn it would be half past nine and Mam would be behind the counter serving. We sold sweets and spuds, bananas and grapes, headache powders and brasso, fish and cauliflowers. In short we sold almost everything.

And then it was time to do my hated rounds, knocking on oul' bitches' doors on the South Circular Road, taking small orders, frostily given, to the 'vegetable boy'. 'The Vegetable Boy is here, Mammy,' and red faced I took the order, ashamed of what I was doing. I had more than my full quota of Norman pride. But I did it, Christ help me, I did it for Mam. Back I went to the shop, loaded up the orders, and delivered them with my little cart, no better than a Rickshaw Coolie in Singapore.

In some of the houses where I had to go lived former pupils of Rialto, now going to Singer (Synge Street Christian Brothers School) who remembered me as Dux of class. Most of them ignored me, or pretended not to know me. Revenge was sweet, and I stood no longer in front of them, in order of merit. I was finding out the hard way, that there was no order of merit in life. Outside of the classroom the world judged you for what you looked like, not what you were. If you were born poor, naturally you were shabby. If you looked shabby you received indifferent treatment in the shops and at the houses, even though your money was as good as the rest. The caste system operated well. One look and the world knew how to treat you!

Sometimes, when the shop was doing well, I would forget the ignominy of door knocking. Mam behind the counter, me helping her and the money rolling in. But these occasions became fewer and fewer, as the people of the Square ceased to deal with us and reverted to their old ways. We had been a bit of a three day wonder, and they rushed to help us, but seeing we were doing well at first, one by one fell away. To this day I am not sure of what went wrong. I think Mam had bitten off more than she could chew, and let the shop run down.

Our long school holidays were coming to an end and I would be going back to school. She would not be able to manage then, and she could not afford to pay anyone to run it. It did not make enough. Nevertheless I think it made a few bob before it closed. As Autumn came on I grew to detest the shop as the customers disappeared. I could see now it was going to fail. I was now going back to the Head's sarcastic tongue, going back to writhe again under its lash. I could hear him now, long before the event. I could see him, fat face grinning, advising me to go to James's Street or Donore Avenue. The diabolical part was that he never advised me to go to Synge Street. I was not good enough for that.

'Get yourself another job as a Messenger Boy. You seem to be cut out for that.'

It was all in my mind long before it happened, but roughly the projection was correct. The shop closed, the school opened, and I was back to square one. The final indignity came the day he checked up on school readers, our literary exercise for the year. I had not got one. Colin had not got one.

It must have been hard on the masters to teach a class when some of their number lacked even the basic things, but it was a bloody sight harder on the unfortunate pupils.

Oul' Paunch called us out and told us to sit on the hot pipes, screwed to the skirting. Rialto was a brand new school, one of the first in Ireland to boast a heating system.

'Now,' said the Head, 'cross your legs under you, and place your hands like so.' He held his hands at shoulder height, wrists bent backwards, palms flattened, in what is known as the lotus position.

'Now,' he said, 'say alms for the love of Allah.'

Grinning, Colin obeyed. It did not take a feather out of him.

'Say it,' said Oul' Paunch.

'Alms for the love of Allah,' said Colin grinning. It was different for Colin than for me. It was just laziness on his part that he had not got a reader. I had been persecuting Mam for three weeks for the money, without result. I had been belted out the door for refusing to go to school without money for the book. This was the finish.

I was too proud, too thin skinned. Why, I asked myself, could I not do as Colin did? I could not. The Head disliked me, made it plain, and in return I hated him. I was doing no good in his class anyway. Education virtually came to an end here. The Head was expected to run the school, and teach a class as well. It was too much for him. I was learning nothing. I would see if they had room in James's Street Christian Brothers. Bay McKay went there, and he never seemed to complain. It must be all right. They had changed a lot since Dad's day . . . I hoped!

That evening I told my mother and father I would go no more to Rialto. They were aware of my sudden rejection of the school I loved, and the reason, and attempted to bully me. I would not budge, not if I was killed. I would never enter the Head's classroom again. There was a furious row, and my brother helped things no end by saying that oul' Paunch was all right, that most boys liked him. I got a hiding from both Mam and Dad, but crying, sent up to bed, I shouted down the stairs that I would not go back. The following morning, Dad being at work, I refused point blank to go to school. They had to capitulate.

So, in due course I found myself in James's Street Christian Brothers. My father, over and over again, had warned me not to go to them. He had had a horrific childhood under them, and he hated their guts.

And I found out my mistake the very first day. This was an old school, dark and dismal, reminiscent of Dickens day. It was unheated and bitterly cold, and a wet Autumn was turning into a savage winter. It was in the shadow of Guinness's Brewery, and the air was laden with the smell of malt. The boys who went to it were cowed and spiritless, broken under a sustained reign of terror by the good Brothers, who kept themselves warm on the coldest day, beating the bejesus out of some poor little Liberties boy. For the rest of my life I would never forget the nightmare of James's Street under the ferrule of the most un-christian Brothers.

Too late I realised my mistake, and longed to be back with my pals, even with Oul' Paunch thrown in. I could have tried a little harder. In hindsight the Head emerged for what he truly was, a man with a sarcastic tongue, but a humorous and kindly man for all that. In no way could he ever be compared to the brutes who now stood over me. My stinking Norman pride had betrayed me again. I was so used to being cock on the dunghill that a reversal of fortunes was too much. I had no one but myself to blame.

One other thing, too. Not even at play time was there respite from tension, and the school yard was a concrete box, small, with high walls. Just that and no more.

In Rialto school the back of the play yard had been railings, and green fields all the way to the canal. There was no sense of being shut in. You could see the barges in the distance, and the horse on the tow path, slowly drawing its load. And beyond that was wide open countryside all the way to the Atlantic Ocean in the West. The air was fresh and lovely, not this soup-like miasma, larded with malt fumes that landed on the concrete box where we were supposed to play.

And the black cassocked figures of the Inquisition moving around, looking for an excuse to punish. Sometimes, standing miserably against the wall, I was told in a country voice like the late Yella' Man's to 'Move around boy . . . or ye'll feel this.'

They were all Yella' Mans in this dreadful school, young Brothers, fit and merciless in punishment. My particular savage was named Gallagher, aged about twenty-five. He ruled with a rod of iron. No sound broke the stillness when he taught. You only spoke when asked a question. If it was not answered correctly the silence was broken, by the sound of the leather being used by a man in his prime, on a boy. Sobbing was against the law. You had to cry quietly, or get a bit more that entitled you to weep aloud.

Gallagher was very keen on Irish games. If you went to the Phoenix Park to play Gaelic or hurling after school, the number of exercises to take home, might be reduced to two. If you chose not to go, you got the usual amount of home work, six or seven exercises . . . 'that'll teach ye, ye little Jackeen bastard, to play Irish Games.' For me it was dreadful. I never played games. Neither did Colin. We fished and rambled the autumn woods seeking nuts or swam in summer. But I scraped the money for a hurley, and tried, to escape, perhaps, a problem in maths! Most of my class mates lived near the school or near the Park, but for me it was different.

Run back all the way from James's Street to Dolphins Barn, choke down your dinner, and run all the way back, past the accursed school, still only half way there. Then trying to put up some show of joining the game, and at the end to face the weary journey home. After a couple of these marathons I hung up the hurling stick, and tried to do the exercises. And would go to bed crying, defeated by the maths, geometry and algebra, excellent in composition, geography, history, poetry, it did not save me the following morning.

First thing every morning one had to place one's exercises on the Brother's desk. The bell rang. Anyone arriving after the bell stood against the wall. They were first for punishment for being late. Any mistakes in their homework would bring more strokes. Gallagher usually had a warm up preliminary bout, beating this lot. Studying our readers, we waited in silence. One might have been in a vacuum. Not a sound. Another happy school day had started. Gallagher would have all the home work corrected by the time the Chapel bell sounded, at a quarter to ten, and as the oul' wans and oul' fellas filed into the Chapel, we, the guilty ones, filed out of our desks. I was always in the line. The rules were simple.

One sum wrong – one stroke. Six sums wrong six strokes. No one exercise attempted, eight strokes. It was the same for algebra and geometry. I rarely escaped with less than six.

Gallagher had a square butter box in class, on this he would stand, while the ones about to be punished filed around him, in a circle. As the leather rose and fell, your hand had to be there to receive the blow. He never missed a trick. If you were due to circle six times you did not get off with five. As the leather rose above shoulder height, he emitted through tightened lips, a long Mmmmm followed by, as the strap connected, a savage AAHH!

Round and round we would file, breath rising in the frosty

air of the classroom, hands pulsing with pain. It was our introduction to another day's instruction.

At the end of the punishment session, Gallagher would be red faced and glowing with health. And any time during the day he was likely to feel the cold, had he not the remedy for it? He had, and he resorted to it only too often. He had another little trick if he caught a boy whispering. He would start softly on the Mmmmm bit, and the AAHH came as he flung the wooden backed duster at the pupil, with all the force at his command. Usually the kid got it in the head, and went home with a lump the size of a golf ball. Sometimes one of them got it in the face, and was marked for a week. The boys were afraid to tell how they came by the injury. I often thought that it was a wonder he did not put some kid's eye out, but the likelihood in no way stopped Gallagher's fun.

He did not care. My companions in misfortune, I found, were a lot different from the boys who went to Rialto. James's Street was in the heart of the Liberties slums. Nearly all of them came from tenement houses, or tenement areas. They were lower down the social scale than the Rialto boys. In Rialto school a tiny minority came from the real slums, here, a few only, came from anything else. That was the difference. The good Brothers knew this, and beat the bejasus out of them for oul' divarsion. The good Brothers, celibates all, worked their warped and frustrated sex lives out on the kids. A good strong woman would have fixed most of their wants and desires, and given us a blessed respite from these monsters. My friend, Bay McKay, who had always gone to school here, and knew no better, moved quietly through all the mayhem, and rarely, if ever, knew punishment. He was an example of all that the Brothers admired. He shone at nothing but quietly and doggedly made progress at all subjects. The Brothers respected him, any one could see that. And besides, he was better dressed and fed than anyone else except Lanagan, Dux of class. He was a small comfortable looking boy, who was a dependable and reliable work horse. I envied him so much.

I could have left the whole class for dead when it came to

writing compositions, and I knew this, but no one else did. My compositions were quickly done, just good enough to protect me from the leather. All my time was spent trying to do the accursed geometry, algebra and maths. Oul' Yella' Man, and this bastard Gallagher must have gone to the same harness maker for their leathers, for they were identical. Heavy bludgeons, and this sadist could hit harder than ever pissy old Yella' Man could. He was younger and stronger, though no more vicious. That was not possible.

There was a boy in our class called Leddy. I never spoke to him in the nine months I spent in James's Street. I never saw him speak to anyone. He was a stocky, tough product of the slums. He never carried any lunch to school or played in the school yard. When twelve thirty came, he went out the gate. Sometimes he did not come back. The word was that he always had money, and went to the fish and chip shop for lunch. When one looked at him, at first sight he appeared poverty stricken. But on closer inspection his clothes were good, though untended. His hair was never combed. He was neglected more than deprived. He always looked unwashed, and probably was.

Gallagher hated him, and beat him unmercifully, but he could not make him cry. This boy had grown too tough for tears, and I believe he would have died rather than shed them. He was often absent for days at a time, and this time he was absent for a week before I missed him. I had my own worries. As the weeks slipped by I forgot all about him. Brother Gallagher did not. He had spies everywhere looking for him. It was Lanagan who carried the news of where Leddy hid out in the daytime. It seemed he was camping in a derelict house, quite close to the school. Lanagan went with Gallagher to show the way. They were accompanied by Johnny Flynn, the Brother next door, who also had a pupil hiding out. Flynn was even more ferocious than Gallagher. When he smiled, and that was often, for he smiled as he punished, his upper lip curled back, showing his teeth like a wolf with rabies. He was red headed and red faced, with red rimmed eyes. He was grinning his curled grin as the three of them went off.

Gallagher left us with six problems in algebra, enough for an hour's work, in my case, enough for a week. I was past caring now, so I simply copied off Bay, and relaxed. They were gone less than an hour, when the sound of strife came floating up the concrete stairs. The next thing was the classroom door burst open, and in came Gallagher, dragging Leddy with him. He was literally frothing at the mouth as he flung Leddy in to his desk and going to the door turned the key in it, and put it in his pocket. There was no escape for the boy. Along the passage outside came shouts and screams as the curly lipped one dragged his victim into his classroom.

Gallagher sat down on his desk, facing the class, panting. After a while when his breathing became normal, he lit a cigarette, a thing never seen before. He quietly smoked it, eyeing Leddy from time to time. Then he stubbed out the butt, while we waited with bated breath.

'Come here, Leddy,' he snarled. Leddy stared back at him, but made no move. The Brother had a smaller target if he stayed in his desk. That was the way he figured it, for I had seen him do this before.

'Come out!' roared Gallagher. Leddy looked back at him, but did not stir. He sat immobile behind his desk.

Gallagher left the table, picking up the strap as he went.

'Hold out your hand,' he snarled. Leddy did so. A terrific blow from the leather strap sounded like a pistol shot in the room, and another, and another and another, and another . . . 'Hold out your other hand,' panted the Brother. Again the pistol shot report, and again, and again, and again, I lost count of the blows. I was dizzy with fright, terrified beyond words. At last it ceased, and Gallagher, winded again, stood gasping for breath before the boy. Leddy was nursing his hands under his armpits, but he did not cry. He stared implacably back at the Brother, dry eyed. And then Gallagher went mad. He flung himself at the boy, tearing him from the desk, strap flailing like a threshing machine, belting the boy anywhere he could. This had gone far beyond the level of corrective punishment, even by the standards of those days. This was a physical assault by a grown man, on a young boy. He got him between the desk and the wall, and beat him until he could beat no more. Leddy was dazed, beaten stupid, and when it was all over, collapsed into his desk. But he did not cry. From the room next door came the screams of the boy who had been caught with Leddy. Flynn, of the curled lip, was doing better than Gallagher, and collecting his full quota of squeals and tears. It was the most terrifying afternoon of my life.

The following morning I nearly had to be beaten out of the house to go to James's Street. There was no sympathy for me. I had refused to go to Rialto, but I would go here. So my mother said. But she was wrong. The place had become a Dante's Inferno to me, a living hell.

Gallagher was subdued that morning, and punished with little zest for the job. I collected my usual quota of slaps, seven that morning. It was very cold and frosty outside, and the big Clydesdales were blowing like steam engines as they left the brewery. The cobbles had been white as I ran to school, and my hands were frozen. The accursed classroom was like an ice box, and the slaps, even though delivered with less force than usual, hurt more than ever. I tried not to cry, but the tears squeezed themselves out from under my eyelids, and I made up my mind. I could not stick this any longer. I would go sick tomorrow. Mam would have to take me to the doctor.

About eleven o'clock, the door opened. Leddy had not been to school, and I devined correctly why Gallagher was not his normal enthusiastic self. He was afraid he had gone too far the previous afternoon and was apprehensive as to the result. No boy could take a beating like that and not be badly hurt. Not even Leddy with his face of stone, and his refusal to cry.

'Brother Gallagher?' It was a woman's voice from behind me. I did not dare to turn around.

'Yes . . . what can I do for you, madam?'

'I'd like teh see yeh for a minute.'

It was a soft, common voice, coaxing now, a flat Liberties voice, with its own musical cadences, infinitely alluring. A wave of perfume assailed me as she went past. Gallagher stood waiting, smiling. She was dressed to kill. A good fox fur draped elegantly across her shoulders, a woman of twenty-eight or nine, quite tall, beautiful, and quite obviously a Brasser, a lady of easy virtue, a woman of the town. You would not find her kind at the back of Guinness's, not yet anyway, although that day would come.

But that morning she was enough woman for any man, and stirred me strangely. She walked easily on Spanish heels, her purple skirt moving from side to side as she jiggled past me, and I had a sudden, erotic vision of two peaches in a silk handkerchief. There was a peculiar tight look about her eyes as she confronted the Brother, smiling. Casually she placed her bag on his desk, and stood up on the rostrum beside him, still smiling.

'An' you're Brother Gallagher?' she said softly, as if she loved him. The Brother nodded, grinning, delighted. And then with a scream, she raked his face with scarlet painted finger nails.

'Got yeh, yeh bastard,' she shrieked, and as the Brother staggered back blinded, she tore at his face again and again.

Roaring, he covered his face with his hands, but she picked up the strap, the one he had used on her son, and gave to him full force across the hands, and when he dropped them, across the face again and again. Every time with all the force in her body.

Johnny Flynn came running in, but stopped short of the woman. The red headed bastard backed off, afraid of her. Gallagher, blood pouring from between his fingers was staggering blindly around as she walked back. She was still carrying the strap, and Flynn made for the door as she came near him.

'So this is where yeh work, Johnny,' she said reprovingly. 'An' yeh told me yeh worked in a bank.'

She stood there, watching Gallagher trying to wipe the blood from his eyes, and nodded significantly.

'It'll be a long time before that get forgets Moira Leddy,' she said. Sneering, she turned to Johnny Flynn, who was poised in the doorway ready to flee.

'I'm sure ye'll use yer good influence teh stop him prosecutin' me, won't yeh Johnny, Johnny the Culchie from Bally Slap. Yez pair a' bastards.' She glanced around while picking up her bag.

'There's a get here be the name of Lanagan,' she said, as Lanagan shot from his desk, and hurtled down the stairs.

'Ah,' she said softly. 'Never mind.'

And then she was gone, her high Spanish heels clicking down the concrete steps, growing fainter and fainter, and out of all our lives.

And that was a nice quiet satisfying kind of a Tuesday morning, the best I had ever spent in this dreadful hole. Gallagher was away for the rest of the day, and we were supposed to be studying our readers, to read on and progress on our own. I had read the shagging thing from cover to cover the first day I got it, and kept busy all right, talking. Jesus, the relief of this barbarous day, with that misbegotten cunt out of the way. That night I put on my act and went sick. Mam took me to hospital. I convinced everybody I was sick, and I *was* sick, sick with fear. I studied diligently at home, getting nowhere with maths, and no help from my brother, just the big shot stuff, jammed in between coming and going, standing there on one foot, telling me 'you just do this and that, anyone can figure *that* out.'

Dad tried to help me, but I'm afraid his intelligence did not run to higher maths, or algebra, though he was good at simple geometry. But really I was past help. My mind simply refused to deal with these subjects. My history and geography improved greatly, and my knowledge of literature came on apace! Now, when I went to the Library, I wrote myself out a note in my father's absence, for I had induced him to join when I found out his weakness, French history. He was entitled to borrow two books at a time. The second one, concealed, was for me, for there was no way a librarian was going to give a precocious little get like me a hunk of Emile Zola, or a Guy Du Maupassant.

I was in and out of school like a yo-yo in the next ten weeks; my Father told me frankly I was faking, and that there was nothing wrong with me, which was untrue. I was *frightened* sick. But after this confrontation back to Jambo I went. There was only three weeks left before the Primary Exam and then it was the nine weeks holiday. That would bring me within two months of my fourteenth birthday, and no school attendance officer was going to bother me. Especially if I got the Primary Certificate. Honour would be satisfied. The State education system justified. Another thick to hump and haul; another sow's ear made out of a silk purse!

On the whole, considering the brutal kip I was returning to, I was of good heart. Frankly, I had little hope of passing the exam at all. One way or another I had spent five months dodging the column. I had resorted to every trick in the bag, even going on gur for two whole weeks, and forging a note in my mother's poor writing to get me back. I had fooled them all, my mother, my classmates, my father for some of the time, but I knew I was not going to fool the examination papers *any* of the time. My friend Bay was quietly confident about the exam. I had lost all hope. But I had no anxiety either. All I wanted to do was to sit for the bloody thing, and get it over with. And leave this malodorous kip forever.

I found the classroom a changed place. The fearful grind of the earlier days was gone, for we were only doing revision work. Home exercises, too, were fewer, and the leather was scarcely used these days. Moira Leddy, had, as she would put it, softened Gallagher's cough for him. I have never forgotten this ill-starred creature, who put manners on at least one most un-christian Brother. He would never beat another boy like that again.

May the merciful God, who looks after this world's Mary Magdalens, love her, cherish her, and take her into Paradise forever. If this was the only good morning's work she had ever done, she deserved to sit on the right hand of God, who loved little children. Let her not come to know the dark shadows of Guinness's Brewery in the twilight of her beauty. Take her before then, I beseech thee, Oh Lord. Amen.

Leddy's desk remained empty, but, like the song, the

memory lingered on. Gallagher still wore the marks of Moira Leddy's finger nails in white lines across his face, and his left eye was covered. He had nearly lost it, and it was still weak and under treatment. Rumour said he would have to wear glasses for the rest of his life.

'A bloody pity,' said Frank Payton to me, 'that she didn't put out both his lights.'

A sentiment heartily endorsed by me. Lanagan, the pimp, who seldom spoke to me, told me off-handedly one day, as one speaks to an inferior, that the lady in question had not been prosecuted. Brother Gallagher, he informed me, forgave her and her son, and had refused to drag them into court. Lanagan was coming back from the head's room where he had been sent with a note. The Head was a surprisingly gentle old man named Jock. At least that's all I ever heard him called. Something had come up that gave Lanagan a chance to open his big mouth.

'She should be sent to jail, sir, for what she did to our Brother.'

'No,' said old Jock. 'Brother Gallagher, though grievously injured, had elected to forego a prosecution. He had chosen the Christian way of fortitude!'

'If yeh believe that, y'ill believe anythin',' I said coarsely.

'Why shouldn't I believe it?'

'Because it's a lie. The bastard wouldn't like teh meet Missus Leddy in court, not if she'd taken Leddy teh the doctor. It'd all come out, an' a bit more about Johnny Flynn . . .'

'D'yeh know what,' said Lanagan superciliously. 'You're a real little fuckin' smart aleck. Who told you all this?'

'Nobody, but you'd want to be dopey teh believe Gallagher 'id forgive anybody.'

'Are yeh callin' me dopey?'

'If the cap fits, fuckin' wear it.'

Lanagan stood there glaring. He was head and shoulders over me, stronger, with every advantage, and I waited for him to attack. I was ready. Somehow, I thought Lanagan all piss and wind, like the Barbers cat, and I was in no way afraid of him. Besides I was intensely jealous of him. He was King of the class. He was where I used to be, and deposed kings do not take kindly to mingling with the common herd.

'You better mind yourself,' he warned.

'What'll I mind meself for?'

'Because I'm tellin' yeh.'

'Tell away. I don't fuckin' care.'

I knew I had him. I was not usually that brave, but I sensed Lanagan was a coward. And he was. Only the school bell saved him, and we trooped inside, Lanagan glad to have saved face, me wildly elated, for there had been, for a couple of minutes, signs that the old Lar was not dead, after all.

That night, I got talking to my father, the first time for a long time. I told him about Gallagher, his beating of Leddy, and the Mother's revenge, with the Brother still wearing an eye patch. He was vastly interested, and I innocently, had dropped the woman's remark to Johnny Flynn.

'Ah, yeh told me yeh were a bank clerk, Johnny the Culchie . . .'

'Dear me,' said Dad smiling, and muttered, 'that's an improvement, they're going for women now.'

Gallagher informed us that we were for the Primary Exam the following morning, and told us to go home. With a gleeful heart, I departed early. The idea was that we would have time to browse through any work we were shaky on, but I no longer cared. I went for a ramble by myself, and looked in still water for fish.

The next morning we were marched down the echoing concrete stairs, and across the yard to where a timber building served as a babies class. A different teacher took over from there. He was not a Christian Brother, he did not wear the dismal black gown of pain. He wore a Donegal tweed suit, and reminded me of Gleeson, the cheerful, Oxford Bags teacher in Rialto. There was a paper on each desk. Arithmetic.

I looked over the paper. There were three easy ones. I picked them, did them, but made a mess of the others, I think. I got three right out of six, I know that. The geometry paper was not as tough as the stuff Gallagher had been dishing out, and I got a couple of easy one's right. I got one out of six in algebra. It was one that the dear old Kipper had taken extra trouble to teach me, nearly a year ago. Was that all? Jesus, it seemed like a century. Then came the lunch break. All the boys filed out to play in the concrete pit in different moods. Some were delighted, some apprehensive, some down right despairing. I was surprised. I had always thought I was the only one with problems but if that was so, who had been my companions in the circle of pain each morning? I had never thought of that.

Lanagan was disporting himself like the show off he was, but he kept clear of me. I was waiting for him, and would have crippled him with a kick as soon as look at him. It was obvious from his carry on, that he was flying through the exam, and the big act now was to show us all how simple it was. Me, I did not give a damn. I was doing my best, and I could do no more. I was quite satisfied that in my long lay off from school, I had missed nothing, only slaps. I had progressed at history, geography and English far in advance of the class. If I had gone to school I would have learned nothing. My mind stopped functioning when Gallagher started the Mmmmm-Aahh-bit. We did geography after lunch and then it was home.

At nine the following morning, we attended the same room, for the last three subjects, Irish composition, English composition, and history. I would enjoy myself today. This was for me. I flew through the Irish, and sat back watching Lanagan work. I caught his eye, openly grinned to show him I had finished with it. I put him off. I know I did, I saw him start to flounder, get muddled, half turn to the boy behind him to ask something . . .

'You boy, turn around!' The Examiner had been right on him. I watched his face go fiery red, and chuckled with malicious satisfaction. This was a great exam. I was having a ball.

History came next, that was no bother, and last of all, like good brandy or port after a meal, came English. We were to write a composition on the following subjects:

A day in the country
A day at the seaside
On going fishing

There were a half dozen or so crappy subjects one could go for. But for the fact that a lot of boys would go for the 'Fishing' I would have gone for it myself. Every Sunday now was spent with Uncle Morrie on the Knocksedan stream out Swords way, and I knew more about fishing than anyone here. But there was one stated subject that I knew, from its starkness, that no one, except me, would chance. It simply said: 'My uncle', and that was for me.

We had an hour for this subject. I sat at ease, thinking, looking at Lanagan. He looked up and grinned a couple of times, seeing me not working. He was King of the class at composition too. Well, he'd get a run for his money today. I started off, I was certain I was the only boy who would attempt this subject. Slowly I gained momentum as my confidence grew. Jesus, wasn't this my subject? I loved it!

I put my heart, and all the acquired skill I could muster into this one. Inside me, something was singing. I was doing what the dear Jesus had created me to do. The sums, the geometry, the algebra were all behind me, and I could let my imagination soar in the dreamy realms of fancy, and the result came out at the tip of my pen.

Then the Examiner gave us five minutes warning, the bell went, and it was over. My school days were done, I knew that.

Slowly I walked back to the Square with Bay. He was tired. Today had taken a lot out of him. Today's subjects had not been his best ones. Imagination was not his strong point. But I was elated, not in the least tired. We had just over a week left before the summer holidays. I was wildly exhilarated by the fact that this time next week I would never again have to cross the threshold of James's Street, never go round the circle of pain again, to be free of Christian Brothers for evermore!

I did not care if I had passed, failed, scraped through, or

dazzled them all. I was too small to be sent to work. I would go to Bolton Street Technical School for a year, and hopefully I'd be big enough by then. Of all the boys around there were only three left who were under five feet, Colin, Bay and me, but before the autumn came I was all alone. The other two had started to shoot up.

In the week that followed Gallagher relaxed all discipline. It was either a feast or a famine with this bastard. He spent a lot of time away from class, attending the Eye and Ear hospital, and as long as we kept quiet we were safe. The red eyed Johnny next door was keeping a wolfish eye upon us, but I think Moira Leddy had frightened him too. He was not so ready with the cane, and practised some restraint now.

The exam had been held on a Thursday, and our holidays started the following Friday, but one. It was like being on holidays already. I kept quiet, read a lot in my desk, and remember Gallagher being somewhat surprised to see me reading Somerset Maugham, but he did not correct me for doing so. Probably the Culchie bastard had never heard of him, I thought. For the first time in months I was happy.

The last day dawned bright and fair, and for the second last time I went over the little iron bridge at James's Gate. The last time would be this afternoon when I went home. I had joined Kevin's Street Library, so as I would no longer have to pass the accursed school, such was my hatred of it. My footsteps rang on the metal and I paused, as I always did, to glance into the still water below.

In the class all was excitement, as the results of the exam had to be read out on this, my last day in school. The real excitement was confined to a few, but the other poor bastards, who were leaving forever, and did not care, put on a bit of a show, just to be in it. But I did care. It mattered to me, even though I was leaving too. This was the day I fell down, and I could see my brother's covert grin, and hear his, 'Aw . . . sure it doesn't matter, Lar . . . forget it.' But he would not forget it, that I knew. Bets were taken on the boy who would be second to Lanagan, for it was already conceded that he would take first in everything.

It was my sorrow that he was as good as he was at all subjects. English was his special, he being the best in class at writing, for I had never really tried. However, no one expected me to beat him, least of all myself. My morale had taken a terrible beating in the past nine months. At half past two, Gallagher went out and came back immediately with the result.

Lanagan: Passed with Honours.

McKay: Eamoinn: Passed with Honours.

Nulty: Desmond: Passed with Honours.

O'Driscoll: Patrick: Passed with Honours.

Redmond: Laurence: Passed with Honours.

There was a surprised buzz in the classroom. As for me I was stupefied. It had never in a million years occurred to me that I would attain honours.

'That's a quare one for you,' said Gallagher, grinning. 'An outsider from Rialto.'

He grinned at me and I tried to grin back. I was not very successful. I hated the bastard. It was no thanks to him that I had passed. He had taught me nothing but fear and hatred. This result was the dear old Kipper's doing, his and nobody else's. He would be proud of me when he heard, and I would make very sure he heard. Gallagher went on to read the rest of the results, and his face slowly grew black with rage. Nine boys in his class had failed. That was almost twenty-five per cent, and I watched him grow livid as he reached for his leather. He was going to do something unprecedented, he was going to punish the nine who had failed on their last day in school. For not one of this lot would ever go on to secondary school. At that moment the door opened, and old Jock, the Head, came slowly in. He came down between the rows of desks to join Gallagher on the rostrum.

'Brother Gallagher,' said the old man distinctly. 'Call out Laurence Redmond. I want to see him.'

Holy, sweet mother of Jesus, but my heart nearly stopped. Two weeks on gur had come to light . . . letting on to be sick . . . copying other fellows' exercises any chance I got . . . all had been found out. I felt the apprehensive stare of the class upon me. Something of grave import had brought Old Jock here. I was going to be publicly flogged, and on my last day, too. Old Jock rarely entered the classrooms. I had gone as white as a sheet, glancing right and left in pure terror.

'Come up here, Redmond,' Gallagher said tightly. I stumbled out of my desk and approached. Old Jock placed his hands on my shoulders, and gently turned me around to face the class. I could see Lanagan grinning behind his hands. He'd get a bit of his own back now.

'Class,' said Old Jock slowly. 'It is my pleasure to tell you that one of your number has brought honour to the school. This little chap has written a composition, in fact an essay, that could not be matched by any pupil in this school. I have read it out from the top Intermediate class down the line, and now I come to the boy who wrote it.'

I listened, the world spinning, stunned, but I saw the smile go off Lanagan's face.

'This effort,' resumed the old man, 'is so far above one's expectations of a boy, not yet fourteen, that the Examiners, in their wisdom, have given him the ultimate in marks, fifty out of fifty. This, in the history of the Primary School Certificate, has never been done before, and I want you, on behalf of the school, to give three hearty cheers in Gaelic . . . Dimly I heard the abū . . . abū . . . abū given with gusto especially by those unfortunates who were about to feel Gallagher's leather. The balance of the Class were glad to see Lanagan's light go out.

When you are at the top there are always those who are glad to see you tumble. I knew that better than most. This was Lanagan's first taste of defeat, not that he had really been beaten, for he had not. I think in the overall tot of marks he was still at the top. But there was no way the class were going to give him a hearing. He had been big-headed and boastful. Now he would pay. It did not matter a damn if he had twice as many marks as me, he had broken no record and I had. I felt sorry for him, but he had made too many enemies. The grinning faces around him told him that.

Dimly I remember being paraded from one class to

another, by the proud old man, right up to fifth year where the boys were all men. Then five minutes before we broke for the holiday, I found myself back in my own classroom. The boys who had failed had not been punished. After all, Gallagher's class was the one that had produced the small record breaker. He was in great form, and thinking of the dear old Kipper, I hated his guts more than ever.

'That's a quare one for you, Kevin,' he jeered at Lanagan. 'You didn't expect that!'

Lanagan's face was a rosy red, and I suddenly felt intensely sorry for him. He said nothing, just tried to grin it off.

'The favourite,' said Gallagher, 'not pipped on the post . . . slaughtered. And by an outsider from Rialto at that,' he continued, watching Lanagan's face. 'I got top marks anyway,' said Lanagan, suddenly furious.

'Drop it,' said Gallagher. 'You got a hiding, didn't you.'

It was some perverse streak of nature in this bastard that was making him torment Lanagan. It was not fair. Even I could see that! But at the back of it all, deep inside me, was a fierce and savage delight that I had taken the lustre from the Dux of class. And I think, to the present day, that someone who loved the English language as I did myself had been over kind to the balance of my papers. With honours? I had my doubts but I kept them to myself.

I avoided Bay on the way home. It was no trouble, as he ran on ahead to give the good news of his pass with honours. Bay would go on to secondary education, and was destined to join the Dublin Corporation, a good steady job for a good steady man. His ship was going to sail the mill pond that was Dublin, while mine, not so sturdily built, had to face the four winds and the seven seas . . . and survive!

I had a lot to think about. There was no doubt in my little mind now that I could become a writer, and that is all that I had ever wanted to be. The desire had crystallised at a very early age, so far back I had no memory of it. I had proved that I could beat Lanagan, and the Old Head had said I could beat anyone in the school. I pondered all this and for the last time went over the little iron bridge that spanned the Canal, and on to home.

Sometime, towards the end of the holidays Old Jock paid Emerald Square a visit. He stood at our door and asked for Mam. They spoke for a little time, then she called out, and I joined them.

'I've been telling your mother,' said Old Jock, 'that you have a wonderful future as a writer. Will you come back to school, Lar, after the holidays?' I looked at Mam. I knew she could not afford to send me, but anyway I was too terrified of the Christian Brothers ever to go back.

'No,' I said quietly. 'Never. Not ever!' And sealed my fate, in a few words, for a lifetime.

15 A Taste of Wild Cherries

So now, at the end of my thirteenth year, I was finished with school. This holiday meant nothing to me and had no end. I was all grown up, four feet eleven, round–shouldered and skinny. I was lonely and I missed Nigger a lot. Our gang was broken up as more boys went to work and I went to Nigger's grave almost daily. It was on a waste lot at the end of the Square. I would have been desolate except for my books and Phyllis. I do not know how long we had been falling in love, but now it was becoming obvious to us and, unfortunately, to her sister as well.

Phyllis was a redhead with a pert nose, covered with tiny freckles and a cupid's bow mouth meant for kissing. She was the girl who had kissed me gently on the day of my confirmation and I had been kissing her ever since, every chance I got. My kisses were not all that many, for Phyllis was a Protestant and past the age of ten, she was no longer allowed to mingle freely with the other girls. She wanted to, we all knew that. Sometimes she would wave wistfully from the top bedroom window and the girls would gather around, but usually that ended with the window being slammed down by her much older sister.

I was daft about her and she about me. In the 'slanguage' of the 'twenties, she was my 'big moment' and I was hers! And anyone who says that children aged twelve and fourteen cannot know love must be mad. I was to love many women during the course of my life but none better than her. I was thinking of her this morning, and whistling, I went around to her house, and stood in the back lane.

I knew, if she heard me whistling, she would, if she could, open the back gate a little and speak to me. And that is precisely what happened. She was sweeping the backyard and I stood close to the wall so that Lorrie, upstairs, cleaning and keeping a vigilant eye eye on Phyllis could not see me even if she tried. Phyllis tarried by the gate, sweeping as we talked.

'I haven't seen you for ages,' I whispered through the crack in the door. 'When will I see you again? You're never let out now.'

'No,' Phyllis whispered. 'Lorrie knows you're after me and she keeps me in.' I felt my cheeks redden.

'I'm after more girls than you. Does she know that?'

'Maybe, Lar, but you're not in earnest.' She paused.

'Lar,' she whispered.

'Yes, Phyllis?'

'Lar, are you fond of me?'

'You know I am, or I wouldn't be here.'

'Do you miss me, Lar?'

'You know I do. When can I see you again?'

'Tomorrow,' came the swift reply. 'Saturday. Lorrie will be gone all day, she's going to Belfast and won't be back 'til late.'

'What about Billy and John? They're worse than Lorrie.'

'I don't care about them. I'll see you at the top of the Backers at one o'clock.'

'I'll bring some bread and stuff and we'll stay out for a few hours.'

'Not too long,' said Phyllis, 'not long enough for me to be in trouble.'

'Course not, Phyllis. I have a skylark's nest to show you.'

'Have you? Where is it?'

'Phyllis!' shrilled Lorrie from the top floor. 'Will you get on with sweeping the rest of the yard, or are you going to sweep that patch all day . . . is there someone talking to you through the gate?'

'No, Lorrie,' Phyllis's voice came back to me as she moved away. I heard Lorrie bang down the window and her feet running down the stairs, but I was long gone before she reached the back gate.

Phyllis's mother had died three years before and Lorrie watched over her with biblical severity. Her father, a quiet man, who kept to himself, a stranger by choice in his own country, was to die two weeks to the day I spoke to Phyllis. But nobody at this stage suspected he had a weak heart. He was only forty-nine and could easily have married again.

Saturday morning I was up at cockcrow, buttered a few slices of bread and hid them. Maryland housing scheme now stood where I had watched the thundering herds of bison a few years before, but the plots at the back of the Woollen Mills were still there and I raided them now and back to bed with a bunch of nice scallions and radishes, hidden as well.

Promptly at one o'clock I waited at the top of the Backers and as soon as I saw Phyllis coming, moved ahead. I kept in front of her until we came to the Dark Lane. The place was devastated. I no longer recognised it, hedges gone, trees down, sewage pipes and timber shoring all over the place, as Sundrive Road got under way and the last of the countryside near the Barn was buried under an avalanche of houses. From now on the slum area, where I had grown up, with one fetid foot in the green countryside, would be gone forever. Dolphins Barn would look properly placed, part of a crumbling inner city.

The cages on every tenement window, each with its feathered prisoner would grow scarcer, thank God. It would be a good slog now, uphill, on a bike before wild birds could be netted, although the Bird Market beside the Lousy Acre appeared to thrive as well as ever. Sunday morning, on the way to Clarendon Street Choir, I would check, only to find it unaltered and my heart would go out to these other songsters, who unlike me had to sing, or die!

It was only after we came to the Brickworks that Phyllis joined me. We were safe at last. We ducked under the fence wire in to the city refuse dump, where rats lived in numbers, but beyond stretched the ruined fields that the Brickworks had left behind, with their pools of water, waving thistles and dog daisies. And further on again, the green fields of Crumlin, not yet despoiled, went all the way to Wexford and the sea.

'Hello, Lar,' said Phyllis shyly. And I was suddenly shy too, realising that this was our first date, that we were in earnest, that we had met on the sly, that we were growing up, that we adored each other and were kept apart for reasons we did not comprehend. Or ever want to!

It meant nothing to us that she was Protestant and I a Catholic. All I could see was a lovely girl with Titian red hair, a pert nose covered with tiny, brown freckles like a bird's egg and a mouth made for laughter and kissing. She was Phyllis Halloway and I was Lar Redmond and we were mad about each other and that was all there bloody well was to it. Bugger the Protestants and Catholics, kick them all to hell or Connaught and have done with it.

'Hello, Phil,' I said. 'Did you find it hard to get away?'

'No . . . Lorrie was gone away, Billy is working all day and John will be home about now. I left his lunch ready – cold salad.'

'Won't he be wondering where you are?'

'Let him. We won't spoil today thinking about tomorrow.'

'No,' I agreed, as we clambered over piles of stones, heading for the fields. At one pool, a late hatch of tadpoles were swimming around, mad tadpoles born out of season and we lay down beside the pool to watch them wriggling around with their big heads and tiny tails. The Brickworks was a dangerous place for kids, for between the piles of stones left behind when the yellow clay was dug away, were pools up to four or five feet deep with treacherous sliding banks and still, deep pockets of water. These pools were alive with life.

Beetles hunted the small depths like marauding submarines, water spiders skated merrily on the surface and sometimes a dragonfly landed like a small sea-plane, before taking off again. We lay, me talking, telling her about the miracle of life and struggle for survival in these watery jungles and all the time I was watching her bewitching face in the water with a white cloud scudding overhead and the innocent reflection of the golden eyed dog daisies, nodding beside her with petals for eyelashes, longer than her own. One of the striking things about this Liberties beauty was her black eye-lashes, startling against the Titian red hair and her green eyes. Quietly I turned to her as she turned to me and we exchanged a kiss as sweet as honey. 'Chomh milis le mil, chomh bán le bán', in Gaelic; 'As sweet as honey, as pure as purity'.

'Oh, Lar,' she said breathlessly, pulling away from me, but a second later we were kissing again.

'Dear Lord,' I said to myself, 'never let me be more than fourteen, never let this day end. Never let Phil or me grow old.'

All around us the dandelions competed with the dog daisies and threw their yellow shawl over many an ugly heap of stones and we were two kids, wandering in fairyland, not in a devastated area of shale but in some enchanted place where the outside world could not enter. All the day long I had this sense of being isolated from everything, within some magic circle. I was in love for the first time and the overwhelming joy of loving and being loved made me dizzy. And Phyllis, with her green eyes and flaming hair was Eve and this was the garden of Eden.

After that we had wandered hand in hand through the fields and I found the meadow where the skylark's nest had been. It had gone. Only a few bloodstains and feathers marked the spot where a rat or a fox had found a meal. Her eyes filled up and she was pensive until I found a blackbird's nest in a bush and she dropped tiny breadcrumbs into the ever open beaks. The mother blackbird, sensing we meant no harm, rested quietly on a branch overhead and swallowed the worm she had been saving for her voracious brood.

So we wandered through the afternoon, deep in the fields, further than I had ever penetrated before, until we came to a small wood. There we stopped and shared the bread and scallions and radishes and I had thoughtfully brought some salt. The sun was shining hotly, but here in the dappled shade it was lovely, the shifting light through the waving leaves making play with her red-gold hair.

She sat on a stump of some fallen monarch of the woods and I lay back against it, stealing glances at her, for she had never looked more beautiful. We finished eating and in the languorous heat of the afternoon, I was in one of my daydreams when she leaned over and kissed me full on the lips. And I put my arms up and around her and gently pulled her down to me and the growing passion of our first real kisses was something I had only imagined in a passing erotic dream . . .

Did you take sinful pleasure in your thoughts, my son? Did you abuse your nature? Say ten Our Fathers and ten Hail Marys and do the Stations of the Cross twice . . . Flee, my son, for you are in great danger, Lucifer has marked you out for his own, do penance, my son, repent. Repent, me arse! I would dare the gates of hell itself for anything so sweet as this. Death and eternity were a million light years away and old Nick himself counted little in the balance against Phyllis. He would have to wait awhile and in the meantime, my hand, the one that had fondled Mag's breasts was caressing Phyllis, who was budding fast.

She moaned with pleasure, then went limp in my arms and her breathing came faster and faster and she held me, squeezed me so hard it hurt and suddenly we were two wild young things, clinging together in wild abandon and reached a climax as one. And for the first time in my life I had drenched my trousers and realised the thing I had heard the other, bigger, better developed boys speak of, had come upon me, puberty. And although still with the stature of a boy, I was a man at last. Phyllis had precipitated adulthood upon me in some unmeasurable time, in which all the clocks in the whole world had stopped and our young hearts with them.

So now we lay quietly, breathing hard, looking into each other's eyes, until she kissed me again, gently and I answered her gently, and like the lock gates on the canal when they opened and the released water gathered momentum and thundered into the lock, our passion gathered again and now I was caressing her unresisting thighs and it was all here for me, the beauty, the love, the passion and the terror. Terror of the confessional, terror of Phyllis having a baby, but no terror was going to stop me from having what I wanted, what we both wanted. It was Phyllis, God love her, who, trembling and shaking, saved us both that day.

'No,' she panted, 'no . . . no . . . we can't . . . Pity me!' That did it. I loved her too much to bring shame upon her and besides, I was only a confused boy, who had just attained manhood. So we lay in each other's arms, quietly looking at the waving tree tops and high overhead, puffy little clouds scudding past. Presently, Phyllis broke the silence.

'Lar,' she whispered, 'do you see what I see?'

'Where, love?'

'There. Will you get me some?' She pointed upwards. We were directly under a wild cherry tree and there were still some cherries left.

'Yes, Phil.' I rose, ashamed of the dark stain on my trousers and jumping high, caught a branch and held it down for her. The danger was over, the spell broken. Only the love remained now. A part of Phyllis would always be mine and a part of me, hers. This day had marked a milestone for us both. Neither would ever forget it and sometimes, in the years ahead, remember it in tears.

'Pick them now, love,' I said for I had unconsciously adopted the speech of the Liberties for your sweetheart. And so my redheaded rose filled her hands with cherries and we ate them together.

'They're lovely,' she said, 'and sweet. It's a pity there are no more.' I studied the tree. There were no more.

'Yes,' I agreed, 'but not so sweet as your kisses,' and kissed her cherry red lips again. Like most shy people when the dam of shyness has been breached, I gave myself into her keeping with simple abandon. All or nothing! It would always be that way with me.

'You,' she said when I released her and her eyes were moist, 'you say lovely things and Lar . . . you're so gentle.'

'Me! Gentle! Ask Kevin O'Connell or some of the others how gentle I am. They'll tell you.'

'Ah,' said Phyllis with womanly wisdom, 'that's only boys fighting. I know you're pretty good at that. But, Lar, I know something else too.'

'What?'

'It's only an act. The girls can see through it. The girls know you. I hope none of them know you so well as me.' She blushed.

'Yes, I know what you mean. None of them will ever know me like you do. Not after today.'

Suddenly we both realised that the sun was low in the sky. We had done it now! Somehow this lovely day had flown away, like the birds in the sky going home for the night. Lorrie, the sour faced bitch would be back from Belfast. We had been missing for hours and hours. She would make her tell who she had been with.

'Run!' said Phyllis frantically. 'Oh, Lar, I'm in terrible trouble.'

We ran all the way to Dolphins Barn and split there. Phyllis lived at the end of the Square, nearest the main street. I could get home by going over our wall from the Back of the Pipes. I would be in no real trouble, but I knew Phyllis would. That marked the end of our love affair. Never again was I to be alone with her. Never again were we to wander the lost fields of Crumlin. A hundred thousand Dubliners were living in squalor with one backyard toilet to serve a whole house and ten people to a Huguenot room. In the Liberties the narrow streets swarmed, like the tadpoles in the pool, on top of one another.

These were the pressures that spelt death to the fair fields of Crumlin, and one by one, like green lights at night they went out, and with them went the enchanted Grove where my fair Protestant and me had found love. I never saw her again, for within two weeks the family moved. In the fretful days that followed I went back to fishing, and discovered a fundamental truth, that fishing and love have something in common, and it is this: THE ONE THAT IS REMEMBERED FOR A LIFETIME IS THE ONE THAT GOT AWAY!

16 The Calm Before . . .

About that time the exodus from the Square started. First of the very respectable families to move, were the McKenzies, who, with three daughters working and the collection of a large insurance policy on the death of their alcoholic father, bought a new house up Herbiton Lane.

Next went the McKays, my friend Bay whose family fled to a new house near Rialto bridge, the very last bit of the South Circular Road to be built over. And, quite suddenly, with the heart attack of Mr Halloway and the collection of another insurance policy, Phyllis's family moved away from the near Liberties, where they had never belonged.

Things were changing, and changing fast. The native government's subsidy towards house ownership was paying off. The vast Kimmage housing scheme that had obliterated the Dark Lane was half completed, people were moving in and the pressures of the Liberties were easing. Not much, just a little. Further up the Crumlin Road the impossible had happened and Drimnagh housing scheme had outflanked the Brickworks and cut off the supply of clay. It died quite suddenly. The works that had made the bricks for the Georgian squares and the artisan dwellings of Dublin had spilled its guts, given up the ghost and passed into folklore.

Within six weeks three families had gone forever and I was attending Bolton Street Technical School, not for carpentry and joinery which were after all creative and at which I would have done some good but at Architectural Drawing and Quantity Surveying, which I needed like a man eating sour apples needs a dose of jalap.

The days droned by in a weary succession of boredom. The Master, who taught us each morning was in a twilight zone, not quite dotage but a deposit on same and he would soon realise his capital. In the meantime he gave us something to do about every three days and then nodded off to sleep in his chair. No one cared whether you learned or not. One was never corrected – caned. The inquisition of James's Street at least was over. In the afternoon we were, twice a week, turned over to another nut, where I learnt about the Doric order and the Corinthian order and they might as well have been an eviction order for all I cared about Roman or Greek marble cornices. I sat in class, like a small ghost, dead with disinterest, browned off with life and more aware than ever that I was a square peg in a round hole. But there was nothing I could do about it.

Sometimes I would be writing a composition or reading a book when I was supposed to be browsing over the mysteries of foundations, hipped and valleyed roofs and the quality of gravel and washed sand.

We had an Irish cement factory by now, but this fossilised old refugee from Glasnevin was specifying Portland cement, which no decent Irishman would buy. For the Irish government, under de Valera, had decided to pay no more land annuities to the British. It had been part of the Treaty we *had* to accept, but now we decided to pay no more money to England for Irish land that was ours.

They replied by locking the English ports against Irish cattle and brought our Free State to its economic knees. From that position, from which we had always fought, we battled on.

The hardship and waste was dreadful. Calves were killed for their hides and the carcase buried. The towns and cities lived on the skin of a rasher, while daily, herds of cattle were butchered and left to rot. One more notch in the Irish hatred stick and one the British would pay dearly for in the coming war. And I was one of the ones who exacted tribute in British lives, for I was an Irish soldier and guarded the ports the English so desperately needed to combat the U-boats.

Anyway, at this time I did not give one damn if the foundation rested on yellow marl or shit, if it was Portland cement or Chinese clay and the stupid old bastard in charge of the class, still specifying Dolphins Barn brick, when they were building houses where the Brickworks used to be – concrete houses!

Another screwball, the maths' master, drew hieroglyphics on the blackboard and talked about something called 'pie R squared' and vainly tried to teach me how to find the area of a truncated pyramid or cone. In the name of Jesus, what would I want to know that for? It nearly drove me mad.

All in all, if it had not been for Uncle Morrie, a trout rod and the Knocksedan river, I think I might have gone simple! But at the end of every weary week, there came Sunday, and every Sunday morning now saw me lower the saddle on my father's bike, so I could reach the pedals, tie the rod to the crossbar and away with me, across Dublin to meet my little uncle on Binns Bridge. I would have sandwiches and tea and sugar and milk and together my uncle and I would spend the day. God rest him and be merciful to him. It was not his fault he did not believe in You. His faith was beaten out of him by those who professed to walk in Your footsteps. He gave me the happiest days of my life and died on me, too soon. But not before he had taught me to be a fisherman and a good one. He was the young brother who had faced the Calvary of Glencree with my father. This gentle, little Christian, who had been scourged at the pillar, who should have grown up, bitter and savage, but by some miracle of good nature had not. I adored him, loved the ground he walked on.

To me he was the fount of all piscatorial knowledge and to my mind he bestrode a trout stream like a king.

And when winter came, unlike other trout men, he did not hibernate, miserably waiting for the spring. That was the time, he said, when the perch and pike were at their best. He taught me the charm of still, deep water in lakes and abandoned quarries and stretches of the Royal Canal, far out from the city. He introduced me to frost whitened fields and banks and taught me to appreciate cold days and savage pike. And made me responsible, in no small measure, for killing the thing I loved – him!

Uncle Morrie was sick, had been ill for three weeks now and the reports were not reassuring. I was very worried and constantly asking about him, though forbidden to visit him. He was *that* sick. Now, this cold Sunday morning, my father spoke to me.

'Lar,' he said gently, 'I think you should go and see Morrie . . . today.' His face was grave and anxious and my heart contracted.

'Is he that bad?' I whispered.

'He is . . . Lar, don't be surprised . . .' His voice trailed off.

'Can I borrow your bike, Dad?'

'Yes, Lar,' he said quietly. 'Take my scarf as well. It's very cold and give Auntie Maggie my regards. Tell her your mother and me will be over tonight.'

Within half an hour I was on the other side of the Liffey, where my uncle lived. On the North Circular Road in Dublin, if it is winter and you live in a basement flat, the morning comes late and the day dies soon. For my small uncle on the bed it was all one. His day was nearly over.

It was all my fault, I knew. His lungs had never really recovered from that second onslaught of pneumonia and I should not have coaxed him out into the bitter weather with tales of enormous pike to be caught at a quarry beside the canal. I sat in the dimly lit bedroom, telling myself he would be all right.

His wife, my Aunt Maggie, sat pale as a snowflake beside the bed. For her he had already gone and I raged in my heart at her silent resignation. The door bell rang and she was there before I could move, a tiny flitting thing, white hair, white face, surrounded by a quiet white silence.

The priest entered, a big man, content. For my uncle was one of the Godless ones and in all his days in the parish had never gone to Mass.

'Don't worry about me,' he had once told this priest when they had quarrelled. 'I won't be sending for you when I'm crossin' the Jordan.'

And now the priest was here, triumphant at last to cleanse a soul black with sin and help it on its last journey. He the only one who stood between all eternity in hell and the everlasting joys of heaven.

'Ah, well,' he murmured sententiously, 'this moment comes to us all.' He lowered his great bulk into a chair. My uncle said nothing. He was past speech. The priest accepted a cup of tea from my Aunt, delicately placed a wafer biscuit on his plate and nodded his dismissal. She, poor thing being an English Protestant and intimidated by Ireland, withdrew.

She had come here, thirty years before and had loved my uncle and Ireland ever since. They had been married in a registry office in England, a measure of my uncle's implacable hatred for all things clerical, though a better Christian it would be hard to find. I knew where his hatred stemmed from – Glencree. He rarely spoke of it, but his whole life had been coloured by the experience and I, who was closer to him than most, knew the depth of his bitterness.

'Boy,' said the priest, 'fetch me some matches.' A Martian to an Earthling!

'Yes, Father,' I said meekly and with murder in my heart stole from the room.

In the kitchen, although it was only early afternoon, twilight reigned and my Aunt, quietly weeping with her head on the table, looked like a little polythene ghost, manufactured in some sunless English factory. It was this appearance of fragility that had captivated my uncle, her and her wafer biscuits, her transparent china and her porcelain paleness that hid an English strength of steel. And by Jesus, us Irish knew all about that.

I wanted to put my arms around her and comfort her. I wanted to tell her that she did not need to have this priest in the house, that Uncle Morrie would not have wanted it that way. To remind her that he had lived his life without benefit of clergy and reckoned to die that way. She knew all this, but how could I, only fourteen years old, tell her? She had lived in Ireland since she was twenty and she knew the score. No Catholic died without benefit of clergy.

'For what,' the old ones would say, 'what way did that English wan bury her husband!' And they would not *see* her any more. She would be crucified in a vacuum of silence for the few short years she had left.

I returned with the matches and silently handed them to the priest and maybe he felt my resentment, despite my downcast eyes, for he abruptly told me to leave the room. I tiptoed towards the little front parlour, opened the door and closed it softly with me still in the room. There was an alcove on my left with a curtain across it and I swiftly stepped inside. I instantly regretted that I did, for I was among other mourners there, five to be exact, standing in their worn canvas cases, waiting to be picked up by a near dead hand, Uncle Morrie's fishing rods.

Beautiful, old-fashioned Greenhearts, a nine foot fly rod, another ten foot one and one, eleven foot six that was kept for clear water worm fishing. Standing apart, another nine footer, a Hardy's split cane and fit for a king. Seldom used, it had been cherished against the day he could afford to go West, to the country he had only read about where the rivers shouted their way out of the mountains, where the sea trout in their tens of thousands swam in from the Atlantic and forging inland, quivered like reeds in a wind of water.

A Swank rod, given to him by a boozy, old English toff, out Ballsbridge way. He had been rewiring his house, for the uncle was an electrician and a good one, and the old sassanach had taken a fancy to him after hearing he had married a girl from Cheltenham.

'I never told him I was in the Troubles,' Uncle Morrie would say and he would give his little heh-heh laugh, not loud but an enormously enjoyable sound, so that one had to smile with him.

For the uncle's association with the rebels had been harmless. He had only donated a few bob to the cause.

'We were only kids,' he told me one day, 'and we wanted the glory without the danger. Your Dad, laddie, is four years older than me, an' was in the thick of it.'

We were standing on the banks of Knocksedan river, out Swords way and both of us putting our rods together as fast as we could. There had been a couple of hours rain that had kept us under a beech tree and now the river was in small spate and we were mad to wet a line.

'Well,' said my uncle as he picked a worm from a tin of moss and at least four moves ahead of my trembling, impatient youth, 'one day a fella took us out to the country. We were supposed to learn how to march, form fours, stuff like that an' the best part of the whole thing was sneakin' across the fields to this old worked out sandpit without being seen. Mick O'Riordan was one. You met Mick with me, didn't you?' He put a tiny split lead shot in his mouth, bit it tight on the gut, never taking his eyes off me. I thought he looked like a very intelligent little otter!

'I did, Uncle Morrie,' I said, raging inwardly as I tried to unsnarl my line. A tall man I remembered with heavy glasses and a stoop, a man who appeared older by far than my small Dublin uncle but who, I knew instinctively, was not.

'Well,' said my uncle, experimentally wetting his line in the river, 'poor Mick's eyes were never the best and doin' watch out, squintin' Indian fashion at far horizons, the Tommies jumped out of the hedge and caught the lot of us.'

'I suppose,' I said as casually as I could, for I was within a second of cutting the bloody line, 'I suppose you all hated him after that!'

'Not at all, me dear boy. Hated, indeed! Sure, half of us could have got away if we had wanted, but it was an honour to go to jail in them days.' My uncle measured the distance across the pool with his eye, swung the eleven foot Greenheart slightly and placed the worm about seven feet above a current that ran under the opposite bank. Still battling with my gear, I watched him enviously.

The pool was already spoiled, for I had stood in full view of the trout and they would touch no bait for half an hour. The water was only slightly discoloured, not enough to hide us from view, but trust Uncle Morrie to go after the only trout that could not see us.

'And did you go to jail?'

My uncle remained silent and together we watched the line run with the current and disappear under the opposite bank. Suddenly he spread his hands, fastest and best way to hook a trout and his rod bent half over as a three quarter pound brown trout left the stream and landed plunging on the bank.

'A daisy,' said my uncle reverently, 'a daisy of a trout. Yes, Lar,' he went on, 'I spent the night in jail but the British were fed up filling the jail with boys of no consequence and the following morning they gave us a kick in the arse and sent us home.'

And all at once I was confused, for this was the first trout I had ever seen caught, caught by a man I adored, a small God-like figure who could whip a trout, a three quarter pound beauty out of a river with skill and grace and in the next breath tell me about being kicked in the arse by the British and sent home! My uncle gently disengaged the trout from the hook, knocked its head expertly on the heel of his shoe and told me: 'Never leave a fish to gasp out its life on the bank. Never do that!' A gentle one, my uncle.

He pulled a couple of handfuls of juicy grass and spread it on the bottom of his fishing bag and placed the still form of beauty inside. I can see him yet, standing quietly, shaking his head, suddenly very serious.

'It wasn't the same with O'Riordan, though,' he said softly. 'Bad eyes or no bad eyes, they had bloody good reason after to be sorry they didn't keep him locked up. Sure, poor Mick did terrible things then, an' in the Civil War afterwards. It's made an old man of him.' He nodded to himself, lit a Woodbine and came across to me.

'That,' he said, 'is no way to start a day's fishin'. Impatience without skill is a desperate way to start a day. Now . . . watch me.'

And so started the lessons that were to make me a passable fisherman in three weeks, a good one in three months and a boy who could hold his own with the best before the season ended. I learnt how to fish wet fly and dry fly, why you fished into the wind on a lake shore, instead of taking the easy way and sending out your line with expertise.

'For what the hell,' said my little uncle, 'would the trout be doin' there, when all the flies are blown to the other side?'

I learnt how to fish the backwaters of a stream in flood, and how to fish a mountain river when it was low on a hot day, with your gut stained in strong tea and the lightest of tackle. How to open the first trout caught, to see what they were on. To roll over a stone at the edge of a river in mid-summer and pick off the cor-bait, the larvae of a water fly stuck to the underside in their stony cases. For these grubs formed a granite home around their bodies from tiny particles on the stream bed. And my uncle once showed me a fleck of Irish gold, glinting in the cor-bait case and I had often seen it since. How to catch cowdung flies and how to fish with two of them on the hook, never one. How to trap minnow in a brandy bottle and how to salt and dry them for future use.

And in winter, for he and I were born with a lake and a river just behind the eyes, he showed me how to spin for pike. 'Joe Pike' he called them and he hunted them without mercy.

'Trout killers all,' he would say and when fishing for pike he always carried a stick, a 'priest' it was called because it administered the last rites, as this one was doing now. 'Even a pike,' my uncle would say, pounding its skull, 'does not deserve to die, gasping on the bank.'

And dear, sweet Mother of Jesus, wept my despairing heart from the cupboard, why was he left to die gasping on the bank from double pneumonia? Why? Sure, if the dear Jesus had any compassion, could he not have killed him with a train or a tram or a bus . . . or a stroke? What about a nice little stroke? Could he not have arranged that? Dead easy, said my young mind and I fell out with God that day and I did not make it up with Him for a long time.

Outside the curtain the priest was finishing the prayers of Extreme Unction, the Church's last concession to a Catholic, who is dying in sin and poor Uncle Morrie was lousy with sin.

Even I, who adored him, knew that. The way he never went to Mass, but went paganly fishing instead. The way, when a Church Retreat was on in his parish and all the men came rushing into the pub for a couple of quick ones when it was over, Uncle Morrie would be there before them, propped up in a corner, quietly sinking a godless Guinness in solitary splendour. And it was not until the pub was well aired, as you might say and the ghosts chased out with talk and smoke that they would notice him and include him in their conversation.

All the crowd who knew him were fishermen and he, like the St Peter he denied, was the greatest fisherman of them all. Yes . . . I knew his sins, but black and all as he was I did not think he deserved to die, gasping out his life on the bank from double pneumonia.

The bedroom door opened and the little, brittle shell that was Auntie Maggie came into the room followed by the doctor. The priest looked at the doctor and shook his head. The doctor, a young man with a kind look about him which he was still practising to smother nodded.

'I'm afraid it's nearly all over,' he said and led my aunt to a chair.

'It's not, it's not,' I shouted in my mind, 'he's not sixty yet . . . he's still the best fisherman in Ireland!' And I stood there among his fishing rods and willed my uncle to give a sign, to sit up in the bed and defy the priest as he had done so often before. I could see him in my mind's eye, throwing a fly across the pool below a waterfall and in the maelstrom of foam, catch a trout and fight it . . . and beat it . . . and land it. And him standing on a lone rock, in midstream and no landing net! Sure, the man who could do that could do anything!

And I never stopped my willing, until I saw the doctor gently draw the sheet over his face and the sobs burst out of me. They came and found me then and told me to go home. And the priest, suddenly gentle, gave me a tuppence and a pat on the arse and, like Uncle Morrie, I went home.

Two days later I stood in Glasnevin Cemetery with my father and watched his brother laid to rest. I did not cry. The death of my dog had been such a traumatic experience and so recent, that somewhere along the line I had come to realise that to die is as natural as to live. My beloved uncle would never be dead as long as I lived.

But I would never fish the Knocksedan again. That would

be trying my luck too much. And, anyway, it was on the North side of Dublin where the Georgian houses I hated still dominated the city and where the county around it was flat. It was like a stage without scenery and my kind of country was mountain country. Two things I grudgingly conceded. That the trout on the North side of county Dublin where the land was fat, were infinitely superior to mountain trout in weight per size, though not in flavour.

The second concession took much thought, but in the end I figured it out. There was a sense of being in deep countryside on the North side that could not be denied. A charm in high hedged country roads, an enveloping sleepy peace that one did not find in the mountains. For here, one had only to look and see over three counties. There was a sense of security and protection in the lush meadows of North county Dublin and Meath, but us South-siders preferred our mountains. And, anyway, it was well known that over the Liffey they ate their young!

Auntie Maggie, true to race, kept a stiff British upper lip as far as she was able. There was no Celtic scene of keening or wild scenes of screaming abandon as the coffin was lowered. Just a quiet welling of tears that might keep flowing from some deep spring and easily outlast the Celtic deluge that was taking place at the graveside next to us. The uncle's daughter, Maureen stood weeping beside her mother. She was about the same age as me and now it came to me how utterly incomplete they both looked without him. And so vulnerable!

We had come in a hansom cab and went home that way too. It was the last time I was ever to travel in one and the last funeral I remember that was horsedrawn. After that it was all motorcars.

Walking back from the graveside to the cab, a friend of my uncle's turned me aside away from the crowd.

'Lar,' he said, 'I want teh show yeh somethin' . . . Yer Uncle Morrie showed it to me the last time we were in this place at a funeral. It won't take a minute.'

'Right-Oh,' I said and together we left the crowd and cut

through the headstones. Within a minute we were before a mausoleum type building. It had a door with a letter-box in it. Your man, the uncle's friend, was grinning.

'De yeh know who's tomb that is?' he asked me.

'No . . . why?'

'That's Matt Talbot's tomb, the one they're trying teh get made into a saint. He was a great friend of your uncle's . . .' I smiled. Uncle Morrie's pagan comment on the saintly Matt Talbot had been, to say the least of it, derisive. Poor Matt, it seemed, had been a drunkard until about thirty years of age and then a spiritual experience had changed his whole life and to the end of his days he had lived a life of sacrifice and self denial. He was regarded by most Dubliners with tolerance and not a few with reverence. The uncle had not belonged to the latter few.

'Open the letter box,' said this friend of Morrie's. I did so and gaped in astonishment, for the tomb, which was below ground level, was full up with letters from the faithful with requests for help from above. So full was it that when the letter box was opened the banked up mountain threatened an avalanche.

'What,' I said to Morrie's friend, 'in the name of God is this?'

'That,' said your man, 'is his feckin' fan mail! At least that's what yer uncle told me when I asked.'

I burst out laughing. I could see my uncle, hear his little heh-heh-heh laugh and quite suddenly I was crying and it was funny no more. I was glad there was only one there to witness this. Paddy Kinane, who became a friend and fishing companion from that day, put his arm around my shoulders.

'Don't be ashamed, Lar,' he said softly, 'let'er go. I don't blame you. He was one of the best.'

I went back to Bolton Street but not for long. Within three weeks I started work under my Dad, who had become a foreman on the Crumlin Road. A year later he was building his own first two houses. Mam had accomplished the miracle, saved a hundred pounds (ninety-eight to be exact). Dad had met a man while he was foreman, who liked his honest ways.

This man had sites he wanted developed and he gave them to my father on a 'build now, pay later' basis. This man was no fool. Within eighteen months Dad was building a row of six houses, starting on six more. His credit was unlimited. The world seemed to be coming out of the torpor of the 1929 Wall Street crash, builders providers were anxious to sell, glad to help with a sound bet. Within his building career, my father was known as a hard but fair man. He built good houses. He held his head high. He owed no man anything he could not pay.

Within eighteen months of the Halloways fleeing the Square, we had also fled. Nothing was moved from the artisan dwelling except the piano. All the rest was taken away by one of Dad's labourers, who was getting married. Old lamps for new! Old furniture for new marriages and the furniture would look at home where it was going, deeper into the Liberties, near Pimlico.

We now lived in one of Dad's houses in Raphoe Road, but only for two years. After that we moved into the country altogether, Dad building a fine ten roomed house in Walkinstown on two acres, planting an orchard, hiring a gardener. We had a brand new car after a couple of bangers, a large house filled with good furniture and the cuckoo and the corncrake in summer filled the meadows around the house with their calls.

The winter before we moved in, an old house had got in the way of a Redmond development and we knocked it down. It had a fine orchard and a few of the trees were of recent origin, apple and pear trees about eight years old. Gardening was one of my interests so I advised Dad to have a dozen of the youngest dug up, roots, clay and all. It was a fifty-fifty chance of them surviving, but we moved them and planted them around the new house that was just being built. Every last one of them thrived so that when we moved in in summer, the house was surrounded by fairly mature trees and our house looked right at home from the moment it was finished. It had an established air about it right from the start, lacking that lean, famished look that new buildings have for the first few years. For three quarters of its total height built with dark, red, rustic Courtown brick, the last quarter topped with colourful dry dashing, which is marble chips and coloured small pebbles mixed. It blended in with the lush countryside around.

Crumlin village, with Ireland's smallest chapel, was a mile away. The nearest bus stop was three quarters of a mile off. The Tallaght bus, the number 77, went by our door three or four times a day, a real country bus. It was lovely to come home on its last run at night. One soon grew to know everyone, it was like belonging to a family, even though I only knew them to say 'hello'.

Things were happening to the Redmond family . . . but oh, my Jesus uprooted so late in life, torn away from the Liberties, my life guillotined, friends gone, here, where I loved the loveliness I was lonelier than I had ever been before, in some limbo where all had stopped until I roused myself to make new friends and rejoin the ranks of life again.

Things were happening outside the Redmond domain, too. Hitler had rocketed to power in Germany, self propelled and was making what the English press, by and large, regarded as silly noises. Their Sunday papers were full of hilarious cartoons about him and his sidekick, Mussolini, the sawdust Caesar.

America, that land of the free, was coming off the breadline. The millions who had starved for years were shortly to be called upon to defend that right! Franco, that misbegotten son of a bitch, was giving the German Luftwaffe some practise in precision bombing on Spanish cities and allowing them to perfect the technique of dive bombing and terrorising civilian populations, gentle arts that came in handy a few years later from Warsaw to Dunkirk.

Mussolini had driven the Lion of Judah off his ancient throne and annexed Abyssinia while his aristocratic son-in-law, Count Ciano wrote poetically about bombs bulging from the womb of a plane, opening on impact like red flowers, one after the other, a sight bewildering in its beauty! From the plane, that was! It was not so hot if you happened to be on the receiving end. All us young men, working for my father, regarded war as inevitable.

My father and his generation argued and speculated for hours about Hitler and Germany. The Germans had been shamefully treated. They would, however, be satisfied with the return of the disputed provinces of Alsace and Lorraine plus, of course, the Ruhr. But us young fellows, who haunted the picture houses and saw the Movietone News every week thought differently. At a fleeting glance, Hitler provoked laughter, for he was the spitting image of a Hollywood comedian named Charlie Chase, but on closer inspection the laughter ceased abruptly. His hypnotic hold over the German masses was frightening

Vast squares, jammed with people, banners hung with the crooked cross of coming crucifixion flashed across the silver screen week after week. Rally after rally, some a quarter of a million strong, soon convinced anyone with a brain that these people meant business. The scornful terms offered them in a railway carriage in France after the First World War would be avenged twice, thrice, aye . . . ten times over. The same carriage would be used in cruel irony and revenge on a France laid low. Us young Irish boys knew the score; our English counterparts seemed blissfully unaware how near the holocaust was. They had no idea it was only half time. The football match played in 1914 with cannon balls to a packed field had been declared 'a foul'. The replay was about to begin. None of us lads had any doubt and made the best of the time left to us.

My cousin Stephen went to Paris in the summer of '37 and brought back news that the French expected the battle for the conquest of Europe and then the world to begin when the harvest was gathered in '38 or '39. It would not be long anyway. They were better aware than England of the menace Hitler posed. Stephen reported that the French seemed listless, apathetic, accepting it as a fact of life. Of course they would fight, he was told, but this was said with a Gallic shrug.

Their generals felt slightly differently about it. France was safe behind the impregnable Maginot Line, their indestructible underground fortifications stiff with long range artillery, machine guns, Bren guns, mortars and generals bristling with eagerness for the stupid Boche to have a go at their impenetrable defence. Manned by half a million bored young Frenchmen, who had grown up on the skin of a rasher, their fathers' reward for the Calvary of Verdun and the sustained lunacy of Flanders, young men who soldiered indifferently, played cards indifferently, even made love indifferently. Death had been staring them in the face too long and they were well aware of just how their generals regarded human life – indifferently – as they had regarded the lives of their fathers. And for the most part, these old bastards were still in command.

There was a malaise, a sickness abroad in France. This was the twilight of a great nation that had never really recovered from the bloodletting of the Napoleonic wars, that had been bled white in the last conflict, whose women wanted live men, not dead heroes. It was a nation that had lost its way. They had forgotten, as us Irish had not, how precious freedom was. The bored troops of the Maginot Line had never known foreign domination. Few of them believed Hitler was the anti-Christ, the Devil Incarnate, the Spirit of Evil abroad.

In England, a few courageous politicians spoke out against Hitler and warned of the coming holocaust but went unheeded. In Ireland we believed nothing the English news media reported. They had cried 'wolf' too often here to be regarded as anything but liars and devious ones at that. We had nothing against the Germans. They had never done anything against us. But our bloody neighbour still occupied six counties of our ancient province, Ulster. After five years of guerrilla warfare, from 1916 to 1921 during which my country had been subject to hangings, torture and rape, they finally had to face the fact that this tiny population could not be subdued, not even after seven hundred years of bludgeoning and brainwashing, not ever!

The scum of British jails had been unleashed upon us, the Black and Tans, who were paid well and received a bonus for a year of service in Ireland. With their contract went the unwritten lines of licence, that you may rape and loot at will. They did that but a lot of them never took home their loot. And if the British expected any help from us in the coming war, they had another think coming. That was our attitude then.

At home, here in the Free State, we had our own troubles. We had just signed a treaty in another war against us, an economic blitz by England that had brought the infant state to its knees.

We had decided that we had paid enough money in compensation to England for repossessing our own land and had ceased to pay. In revenge, they blocked the sale of Irish cattle and broke us. Perhaps in their own bumbling way they thought we would cry 'enough' and invite them back. For the Brits had never really believed that we did not want them. They made the mistake of swallowing their own propaganda that the Irish could not rule themselves.

They had forgotten that law and order prevailed in this island when the native Briton was running around daubed in woad, one degree removed from a savage while across the water another island was the light and hope of western civilisation.

In Europe shirts were all the fashion. Mussolini had his blackshirts, Hitler had his brownshirts and here in Ireland we had our blueshirts. They went off at the North Wall, headed by General O'Duffy, blessed by the clergy, hundreds of them to batter the people of Spain into submission in the name of the Catholic Church. Good, fascist defenders of the faith.

From Liberty Hall, the Labour headquarters in Ireland, hundreds left too, though unblessed, to fight for the Workers Republic in Spain. The people of that sad country were challenging the men of property and the Church. They were destined to loose! Everywhere, and all around me was strife that would soon turn to horror.

But all that I and my friends were interested in was getting some little colleen's knickers down as soon as possible. We were all virgins except one, who had dared the risk of a dose of the pox and paid eight pence for a ride up against the walls of Guinness brewery. He was lucky. He did not get a dose, but he was strangely reticent when questioned about the mysteries of 'it'.

My own private opinion was that he had paid his eight pence for nothing, that he had 'trousered off in his cambers' before he got near it. That it was a non-event. But your man persisted without much conviction that it was lovely. And me? I was going mad for a woman.

17 *Growing Up*

In the Irish Free State all types of contraceptives were banned. It was a criminal offence to be caught in possession of one. Once or twice I came across a reckless spirit who carried a 'French letter' in his pocket, but not often. The Catholic Church still maintained its iron stand against birth control. The eleventh commandment said that 'if thou dippest thy wick, thou must do so with the firm intention of reproduction' – the last thing any of us wanted.

The girls were too frightened to open their legs and the boys resorted to masturbation, or what was known as a 'dry ride', like I had with Phyllis. There were no state brothels of course, but if you had the money, you saved up and went to Paris for a holidays like my cousin Stephen. But once there, he found himself powerless to overcome the brainwashing he had received at school. The Church with its terrible hell and eternity had triumphed and he returned without knowing the comfort of a woman.

The fellow he was with was different, and told me he had a couple of bangs every day at least and ended up with the Madam of the brothel, a favour reserved for the very few.

'Ere are ze girls, M'sieur . . . which one you like?'

'I want you,' said this chap whose very apt name was Ryder.

'Oh, non, non,' chided the buxom Madam although not displeased. 'I am not for sale.'

She was forty and ripe and succulent as a plum. Ryder had to be content with one of the girls. But twice a day he repeated his request to the Madam, who was after all only a woman and flattered that a handsome young man of twenty-three should want her. So on the last night before the holiday ended, she succumbed and Ryder rode again. The Madam, so pleased was she with his performance that she made no charge.

On the day of departure Ryder, who had stayed there the night, did not bother to leave, but did a Toulouse Lautrec and stayed in bed all day with the Madam, barely arriving in time to catch the Calais train. He looked exhausted, but not as exhausted as Stephen, still a virgin boy.

It is wonderful what a good Catholic education at school and chapel can do to keep a young man pure, guard and shelter him from the temptations of the flesh and send him home from Paris unsullied, something as unnatural as a foreskin in a synagogue. They both arrived back in Dublin, Ryder looking the picture of health and poor Stephen close to a nerve breakdown. But there was only an odd one, like Ryder, who had the moral courage to spit in the Church's eye and do his own thing.

'Only there's a war comin', I'd chance me luck at livin' in Paris,' he told me, 'an' the Madam 'id make it easy for me to get started . . .'

'What's her name?'

'I dunno. I called her Jiggy-Jig, it made her laugh. I'd no time teh find out her name.'

No time to find out her name! Jesus . . . would I ever be so lucky? Would I ever have the money to go to France before the war started, or would I die a virgin boy, fighting for his onions in this sexual desert or be driven to getting across one of the girls I fancied and having a shotgun marriage? Or worse, try around Harcourt Street or Leeson Street and end up with a dose?

Often I went, solitary, to the Theatre Royal and saw the show and the lovely legs of the chorus. Often I went in the Lounge Bar, never too sure of being served for although I was nineteen I looked sixteen and drank gin and tonics and hoped one of the 'brassers' would approach me, but none of them ever did. Perhaps they would be ashamed to be seen with someone who looked like a school boy. None ever came near me, although I would have ignored the risk of a dose I think, if one had!

The reason I was so often alone was simple. I had no friends. At fifteen years of age I had been uprooted, torn from the Liberties and transplanted out to the fair fields of Walkinstown, where there were no boys or girls. The break-up when we left the Square was total and for me, devastating. My friends had been scattered in all directions by the new houses. Colin still lived on the South Circular Road, but I was working while he went on to school and for five years we did not meet.

So I was lonely and sex starved, and without direction. It was work and then home to our big, lonely house, busy with the footsteps of our large family, a crowded house but a lonely one to a sex starved boy. I was only too well aware that a night in bed with a good, strong woman would fix all my frustrations. And I was willing to sin, my Jesus, was I willing! Mortal sins or venial sins were all one to me in this context. Just so long as I got a woman and found the key to their world. When the opportunity did arrive, like most treasured things, it came unexpectedly. One day I overheard my mother talking about buying turkeys for Christmas.

'Why, Mam,' I said, 'sure that's no bother. Can't you drop a line to Caroline? She always has turkeys for sale at Christmas.'

'Which one is she now?'

'Caroline Kinsella, where I stayed out from Gorey, where Aunt Kinsella and Seamus lived.'

'Oh, yes, they were very fond of you I remember . . . when you were sick, years ago. I suppose you could get a couple of birds there for me.'

So it was – years ago! I was nineteen now and had never had a chance to get back to Wexford. Life had come between me and it. I felt a rising sense of excitement and determined to go.

So Caroline was written to and and a week later came the answer, yes, she had turkeys for sale, what weight would we require? She had cocks up to twenty-eight pounds and hens up to eighteen. Mam decided wistfully enough, I thought, on two about eighteen pounds each for ours was a large family. I sat down and wrote to Caroline at once to seal the deal and Mam in silence made a cup of tea.

'What's wrong, Mam?' I could read her like a book and studied her closely. She was forty-one now and her brown hair still had no fleck of grey. She had put on a little weight lately, but she was still a fine woman, fresh faced and virile, expensively dressed in middle age as she never was in the flower of her womanhood. She sighed.

'Nothing, Lar,' she said. 'It's just life is so easy now, just order two turkeys for Christmas, no bother. But I remember a few years ago I'd wait until Christmas Eve night and chance getting one cheap off the dealers. It was great . . .' Her voice tailed off.

'Miss the old days, Mam?'

'Yes, I do. I was more important then, struggling to make ends meet, to rear this squad . . .' Her eyes suddenly filled with tears.

'I miss the old days, the neighbours and the Square . . . although, mind, I wouldn't like to go back there.'

'Neither would I,' I said, 'but I miss it too. The Barn was great gas then, there was always something going on and I was never lonely.'

'Are you lonely here, Lar?'

'Yes, Mam, I am. There's no one to make friends with.'

'You should join some club, a tennis club or concert party, something . . .'

The only tennis club I knew within a mile of us was Wills Tobacco Factory Club, for employees only. They were not a particularly sociable crowd who stuck together and kept strangers at a distance. Except when they ran a dance to raise funds, then one could buy a ticket, but they still tended to keep to themselves. And I was too bashful to get going in an atmosphere like that.

In the desert of my loneliness I was looking forward to going to Wexford, my old oasis. My memories of it were gentle and I would love to see Lil again. Mag had long since flown to England and old Musty Mike was dead, with only Lil left, still unmarried at twenty-nine. Now and again I corresponded with her.

All was unchanged at Buckley's except that the younger, prettier daughter had gone to the United States of America and married a childhood sweetheart. Katie was engaged to be married to a farmer and would be when the leisurely formalities and customary assumed indifference had been overcome. I found their method of mating hard to understand. Where I came from, people married for love or at least thought they did. Also, I had been schooled well by Hollywood, passionate close-ups in the kissing, the American dream – whippoorwill fed on slush and romantic nonsence that had no basis in fact, though, of course it appealed to me no end.

In the country, every single contingency had to be considered and the bride's dowry was of paramount importance. To me it was a cold and inhuman affair and smacked of the Gorey fair but the fact was, that if a girl did not have a dowry, she had no chance of making a 'good marriage'. Poor Mag had been as pretty as a picture, in a chocolate box sort of way, blooming, even slightly overblown, but a fair armful for any man in bed, as my little left hand could bear witness to. But she had to go to England to find a man.

Sassanachs were overfond of Irish women, with their lovely soft brogues and coaxing ways. And usually they were gentler than their English counterparts, who were used to mixing it in the factories, well up in sex and so forth, and how to prevent a baby, rarely virgins over eighteen. So the English married their Irish colleens and mostly got a good wife, though I doubt if Mag's husband got a virgin.

Still though, Katie Buckley would have been hard put to get a husband without a dowry and the system worked in her favour. The farmer who took Katie had to be paid a large dowry to compensate for a plain wife. She was small, sallow faced, tiny breasted, brown eyed and lovely inside. The farmer got a bargain. No doubt, in time, observing some neighbour's once pretty woman turn into a shrew, he would come to count his blessings.

'What are you dreaming about now, Lar?' Her standard of speech had improved over the years and she made less grammatical errors.

'I was thinking of Wexford, Mam, looking forward to seeing them all again, Lil, the Buckleys . . .'

'Aye,' said my mother firmly, 'you'd have stopped down there if I'd let you and missed all this.'

She waved her hand round the well furnished room, deep in carpets with a coal fire burning in the most expensive of fireplaces. I thought of the old open turf and log fires of Lil's kitchen, the one she was so ashamed of . . .

'It's come a bit late for me, Mam.' The words were out before I even thought. She looked startled.

'Why, Lar, what do you mean?'

'I mean, all the younger ones are going to college and it's wasted on them. The three eldest of this family would have loved to have had that chance, but we never got it. I've no education to go with all this. The others will all have been to college. That's what counts.'

'You could have gone back to school when the old Christian Brother came to the house for you. It was your own decision then.'

'No, Mam, it wasn't, not quite. We had nothing. Even if I had wanted to go I could not have done so. The money wasn't there!' Mam sighed.

'I suppose you're right, Lar,' she said, 'but you could always go to night school now.'

'I don't even know where there is a night school.'

'What about Bolton Street? Isn't that a night school and you won't go.'

'That's a bloody Tech for carpenters, plumbers, bricklayers. I want a school that teaches advanced English. They don't teach you that there.'

'Watch your language, young man. Nothing suits you. Other boys go to Bolton Street.'

'I'm not "other boys",' I shouted, suddenly very angry that she could not or would not understand and flung out of the room. I stormed up the stairs and sat down in my bedroom, my mother's voice angrily following me.

'There's Mass this morning,' she reminded me, 'and I'll be watching.'

'All right, Mam,' I said, suddenly contrite. 'I'll go to twelve in Tallaght.'

I had no intention of going to Mass, I had not been there for four years, give or take a couple of times when I had to attend a funeral or a wedding. I had no intention of ever going again. Not to Mass, not to a Protestant church service, not to kirk, chapel or synagogue. Religious orders I detested, like my father. And although my experience had not been as bitter as his, my brutal handling by the Christian Brothers had left me hostile to religion of any kind. The nine months of unadulterated hell I had gone through in James's Street were with me yet. The slights of the snob priest of Dolphins Barn, who ignored me in the classroom had not been forgotten. Four years ago, my dislike of the clergy had hardened into hatred and for many years I would be an agnostic. J.C., the carpenter in the sky still got through to me somehow, but formal religion was out.

My father was the same and only suffered the weekly Mass to keep the peace. He detested all clergy and with far better reason than I. But it was the death of my mother's friend Mary, that finally put me on the wrong side of the fence and charted my course for years. Mary lived in a squalid two-roomed artisan dwelling, that had been designed to accommodate two adults and two children at most. In nine years of marriage she produced nine children. To my mind she looked like the Blessed Virgin, for facially she had that gaunt prettiness and haggard beauty that is portrayed in paintings, she at the foot of the cross weeping, hands reaching up to clasp her dying son's feet, white face, distraught, in hopeless resignation. Mary was like that. She had the same expression as the Madonna and her troubles after their fashion were no less.

Sometimes, between pregnancies – or rather in early pregnancy, for she was nearly always in the family way, she came to our little house in the Square. I always got out of the way when she came with her growing tribe of snotty nosed children. The children spoke fractured English. 'Giz a piece a' bread an' burr,' meaning a request for bread and butter after the fashion of their father, Harry, who was an ignorant thick.

He was unemployed half the time, but when working was hardly better off. He worked spasmodically in a laundry and when laid off, sat at home. He never made any attempt to find oher employment, the laundry would be busy again soon. In the meantime, the family starved, or half starved, for the dole money of the good old days was death postponed.

To my derisive mind, had he been born on the subcontinent of India, he would have been an Untouchable, the lowest caste. I was young and merciless and things then were either black or white. No shade of grey crossed my mind to temper my judgement, though even now I would hang the jawbone of an ass over his door. But here, in God fearing, Catholic Ireland he had the Church's blessing to give his wife a baby a year. Had contraception devices been available, he would not have used them and as he had been taught he was right. Had he not the Church behind him, from the lowest acolyte to the Pope of Rome?

'On this rock I will build my church', said that great fisher of men, Saint Peter. And his church was the only *true* church. Increase and multiply said the Bible and replenish the earth!

This, Harry gladly did, for it was his favourite occupation and carried no twinge of conscience with it. It had never occurred to him to abstain. How could it, when he was only consummating the holy bond of marriage? And even my biased mind had to agree that he had been taught nothing else since he was born.

The tenth child died and Mary, bled white, died with it. In her coffin, which had been brought to Harrington Street chapel, I saw her for the last time, one summer evening as the sun went down.

We still lived near the Liberties then, but were preparing to move. I cycled over to the chapel and locked my bike to the railings. I dipped my hand into the lukewarm holy water, made the sign of the cross and entered. On one side of the church were all Mary's relatives and friends, respectable and hardworking folk, on the other a motley collection of underprivileged rabble, who resembled the stud who had married Mary and sent her to an early grave.

'Do not go gentle into that good night.' Jesus, what else could she do? Mary shuffled off this mortal coil without a fight, innocently killed by an ignorant ram, who had the moral blessing of one of the world's greatest churches.

'Well,' I thought bitterly, looking at the drained, white Madonna-like face, she would get all the priests' blessings in a few minutes to help her on the way to heaven, she who deserved it so much, who all her life had unquestioningly accepted the Church's teaching and had, underfed and half starved, borne crucifixion ten times before going to her just reward. Surely, she would sit on the right hand of God? I looked long and hard at the alabaster face and hands and my gorge rose. I went and knelt down and started to say a few prayers when there came a crash that made me jump. So loud was the bang that for a moment I thought a truck had run off the South Circular Road and crashed into the chapel. However, as it turned out, it was only the sacristy door being hurled shut by a strong and enraged priest.

He had been called out to bless this corpse, the mother of a poverty stricken family who lived on the perimeter of his wealthy parish, to send her on her last journey and she with no fare! There was no money in this rite, not this time for the whole ignorant downtrodden clan of them had not a ha'penny to rattle on a tombstone. Yet, they could force him to perform his duties and not a sixpence change hands.

I watched him carefully as he charged out of the sacristy, big man, bullnecked and virile, stamping angrily over the floor. In the late evening sunset, the multicoloured light from the huge stained glass window in the gable sent soft, delicate colours over the pews, the coffin and Mary. The blessing was brief, holy water was literally hurled over the corpse, the whole scandalous, sacrilegious act taking no more than half a minute, before he flung away and another resounding crash of the sacristy door announced his lordship's displeasure.

There was a stunned, stupid silence in the chapel before

the people started to move away. The rite had been swift and merciless. The message was there for all to see, but of course none of them would ever mention it, much less speak out. Sneering in my mind, I left the chapel. I never again attended Mass if I could help it. The memory of Mary's shameful demise was made all the more bitter, because she was blameless. She had died doing what that rednecked priest had told her to. 'Obey your husband and multiply in the sight and love of our dear creator.' He had been taken at his word, and she had left him to find orphanages for five boys and four girls and no money to pay for it. I sat in the bedroom, now remembering . . .

'Lar? It's twenty past eleven. Time to go!'

It was my mother reminding me, so I called back that I was going now and left the house with my new bike. I rode up Fox's Hill, past Killnamanagh and Allenstown with the Bona Fide pub, the Cuckoo's Nest on my left. Riding through the vilage of Tallaght, I turned left unconsciously for the river and Old Bawn. The chapel bell was ringing to tell the few people around that it was time for Mass, no more lingering in bed with sinful temptation at your side, that the afternoon matinee could take care of that, but to hurry, hurry, all eternity yawned before you and the gates of hell were open, like the Marys of this world, gams agape, ever ready to receive the sinnèr.

The river Dodder ran brown and strong this morning. The fishing season was well over and the trout were increasing and multiplying too under cover of the peat-brown flood. I sat on my bike, wishing it was spring, for I was now an expert fisherman, wet fly, dry fly, clear water worm fishing, it was all one to me, taught well by a gentle little genius, who fished elsewhere now. Sitting on the saddle of my bike, I gazed in to the puddle at my feet. It had rained hard into the early hours of this morning, that was why the puddle was so deep, but unlike the brown river, clear. I studied myself dispassionately. I saw an oval shaped face, topped by thick, gleaming brown hair, slanted grey eyes set far apart, with the long eyelashes I hated so much, a straight nose and a cleft chin.

The girls said I was good looking, though that did nothing

for my ego. One of the ungliest bastards from our class at school had been dipping his wick for over two years now with a servant girl from the South Circular Road and another one from the Barn. I knew this lad well and knew he was not lying when he told me.

What was wrong with me? Nothing, except I was too shy, too afraid of the consequences. In two weeks I was going to Wexford. My memories of the too close holding and kissing when a boy were vivid in my mind. The reflection in the pool was not that of a boy but a young man, who looked deceptively slim, but had big muscles developed by long hours of hammering and using a jackplane, a stripling hard as iron from working like a horse, for my father was just the boss on the job and wanted his pound of flesh. Those were the times that were in it and though he was not unkind by the standards of yesterday, he would never have got away with what he did, today.

These were the hungry thirties and they called for tough, hard men. My father was one of them, who had clawed his way up the bloody cliff-face of success and I had a fine body to prove it. He was never going back to the jungle he had escaped from. I had grave doubts about his moral honesty, for one year he was Vice President of the Irish Carpenters and Joiners Union, fighting a bitter strike and a couple of years later was fighting the men he had fought with so lately.

My mother surprised me too, by her sudden change of attitude, for I had been reared on the diet of the 'unfortunate men' and the 'bloody employers' and now it was the 'ungrateful men' and the 'good, kind employers', who made work for them. No talk of sweated labour any more. No talk of men working like horses so that we suddenly got rich!

I was cynical and outspoken about this and it got me in plenty of trouble. But I did not care. I was sacked about once every month, usually through some quarrel with my brother, who was self assertive and arrogant, but then, so was I with him. I was, it seemed, always wrong, and my father showed me little justice or kindness at this period of my life and looking back, I really cannot blame him. But I knew how to hit back.

The truth hurt and there was always an element of truth in what I said on the subject of employers and employees. One of the smart cracks I used with great effect was 'yesterday this family advocated profit sharing and today won't even pay the men what they ask, a family of strike breakers!'

My record for being sacked was seven times in one month. I was a good worker and if requested *properly*, that is civilly, I worked cheerfully. But in no way would I take the eldest son bit, the arrogant assumption that he would inherit the earth, that the sons who came after were minor constellations compared to his star. When my brother ordered me, I effed him from a height in front of the men. I would not take it. I, too, was the boss's son, but I got fired anyway.

When off the job, I did not pine. I was too interested in literature for that, but that week Mam got no money. When Mam applied pressure on Dad to take me back, she was not going to keep me for nothing, back I went. I was a bloody good carpenter, fast, willing and neat. By any other employer I would have been treated with good natured humour. Not here. But it had always been that way between me and my brother, there are people born this way who cannot be in the same room without quarrelling.

If I had been Stanley and he Livingstone, after the famous 'Doctor Livingstone, I presume', and the answer in the affirmative, I would probabaly have said: 'Just my luck, to meet a bloody louser like you out here.' And it would have been on for young and old in seconds. That is the way it was between us.

So, letting the peace that only a mountain stream can bring to my soul, steal over me, I pedalled to the far side of the bridge and listened to the thunder of the waterfall below, shutting out the noises of the world. Elbow on the granite bridge wall, I pondered many things.

There was a day during the building strike when I asked my father straight out how he felt about being a builder, when his old mates were going short, on strike for a couple of pence extra an hour.

'Why don't you give them tuppence an hour, Dad? That's not much and they need it.'

'When it's your money you're talking about you can be as generous as you like. In the meantime . . .'

'Mind your own business,' I finished off for him. I was a young man now, not a child and I could go to England and get a job easily. I was through – or thought I was – taking crap from anybody.

'That's no answer,' I said impudently. 'I asked you why you did not give the men the lousy tuppence.'

'Because I'm a member of the Irish Housebuilders' Federation. That's another kind of union, an employer's union. I'm not going to be the one who breaks ranks. I'd never be able to hold up my head again.'

'Why not? Maybe not among the employers, but the men would respect you. You're not getting respect from either side, using your sons to break a strike!' For the fact was, that Dad had his three sons busily employed making door frames and doors for future houses. That did it. He was suddenly coldly furious.

'You needn't do it if it hurts your conscience,' he said bitterly.

'What do you expect me to do? Starve with the workers? I've no option, but I don't like it. I'd sooner be with the men you used to be with, the carpenters, your old friends.'

'Are they? I didn't see many of them ever coming to help me. All I ever got from the men, my friends as you call them, was abuse. I remember during the last strike I was in, a bloody big drunken thick wanted to beat me up because I said "accept the terms, we're licked, we've no more money for strike pay, we're broke" . . . and that idiot wanted to fight on! On what? There's too many like him and you, singing *The Red Flag*, wanting Moscow in Dublin.' He was growing very angry now, I noted with satisfaction.

'And if you got that tomorrow, you'd be singing *Faith of our Fathers* and dying for a Catholic Ireland and Rome.'

'Not me,' I said impertinently, 'not for the two things you mentioned anyway.'

He flung away, restraining himself with difficulty from striking me. And here it was, the visible evidence of his background. He had never belonged in a trade union hall. Never! It was only his superior common sense, good literate speech and undoubtedly above average brain that had brought him quite naturally to the top of the union heap. But he was top of the wrong heap. By tradition and training he belonged to the opposite side.

His 'upstairs' childhood had marked him for life, just as my shabby 'downstairs' childhood had marked me for life. Father and son, we stood on opposite sides of the barricades. Let it be so. But he was learning this day, that I had a mind of my own, that he did not own me and that I would only do his bidding as long as it suited me. I think we understood each other, for once. At the doorway he paused and glared at me.

'You're lucky to have a job to work at,' he told me.

'Am I? I have to work hard enough for what I get. You don't give me anything for nothing. I *earn* what I get, twice over. But I don't like being made to work during a strike. I wonder what your old pals think of you today! Does it never worry you.' I must be out of my mind, I thought. I had never talked to him like this before, never stood up to him.

'Worry me!' Turning again to go, he laughed.

'Worry me,' he repeated on a rising inflection. 'Jesus Christ, you must be out of your mind. Every one of those men you refer to would walk barefoot on broken glass or in hob-nailed boots on a baby's face to get where I am. Worry me?' He laughed again.

'Grow up, Lar. The world is a tough place. You've got to face it yet. Stop bloody dreaming.'

He walked out of the half-completed house, a stocky, blond, good-looking man in his early forties and left me furious. But there was damn all I could do about it. Had I not faced the world, running with my little boxcart all the way to Christ Church and beyond? Had that not been facing the world? Going around, begging orders from old bitches on the South Circular Road? Dragging smelly fish all the way from the Dublin Market and me only a kid? Was that not facing it? Going to school to get slapped, because your mother could not find the money for books? What the hell did he call that?

But the real difference between me and my father was one of class. He stood for law and order, the establishment, an instinctive identification with the upper class, while little Liberties me identified with and loved the characters I had been reared alongside. 'Spacers' they call them now, but I preferred one spacer to a dozen of these college types, who picked their words with a tooth pick, a bit at a time. They used a lot of stalling devices like 'er' and 'aw'. A Liberties boy would say more in an hour than one of these things would say in a day and have more wit and sense to it. Whether it was because they liked their own accents or because they were naturally slow brained, I do not know.

There was a cottage up the road where I left my rod during the fishing and paid the woman with a few trout for minding it. She supposed I had got to early Mass before I got there, my mother supposed I got Mass in Tallaght, so it was a thoughtful arrangement which hurt nobody.

On this cool autumn morning, the river tore under the bridge as it had less than a hundred years ago, bearing a corpse or two from the famine of 1847, when Marys all over Ireland were being put down in numbers, though hopefully with a bit more respect than my mother's friend, who had crossed the Jordan in a bitter hail storm of holy water! Ballinascorney Gap lay before me, leading to the heart of the mountains and on the sides of the gap one could still see the unbroached potato drills.

These starving ones had run up the hills to escape the scourge, but the blight had kept easy pace with them and they died anyway. The green cloaked drills marked their end.

Winter was near that Sunday morning, sitting on my bike, but the sun was up and it was mild and warm. Trout had started to rise in quiet backwaters, out of the main flood to a late hatch of flies and the water dashed headlong over the fall below. The air around me was singing and the river Dodder raced to the sea, twelve miles away.

I had come to know rivers and each had a soul. Like my own, I could not touch it or smell it, but I knew it was there. The placid rivers of the plains were not for me. I could not identify with them. The mountains I loved so well were all about me. The brown peat water, that raced down their sides was wild and tumultuous and some of that wildness lived in me.

The mountains and rivers had been there for a long time. Measuring my own life span against them, why, I had scarcely time to get to know them! The years were flying and I had never yet been to bed with a woman. Not yet! Even the mountains, I reflected, measured against eternity, would last only a little while. The ancient Celts had known this and I knew it too. It was knowledge I had been born with, a racial heritage I would have been better without, perhaps. When life was so short, why not live it to the full? Eat, drink and be merry, for tomorrow we die. The careful road trod by my father was not for me. His one deviation had been his involvement with the struggle for an independent Ireland. That achieved, as far as it could be, he dropped politics and settled down to work. That would not do for me, his son.

Dying in bed, after a fruitful life – whatever the hell that meant – was not on. I did not give a tinker's curse where I died, as long as I did not live long enough to grow old. And there and then, sitting on my bike above the roaring deluge, forty was decided upon as the last birthday I would like to see. Racing across an open plain, John Wayne style, dying in the saddle with my boots on. That was the way to go. Charging a battery of cannons in the Valley of Death, blasted out of the saddle by a cannon ball, shot from one world into the next with the reckless abandon of the water below, crashing, uncaring to its end. Yes, I could identify with this river.

18 Nae Gentlemen

As my father's building firm grew big, my lonely days came to an end. Auntie Nelly's sons, my cousins, joined me on the job, Freddy, the younger one as a late starter apprentice. We hit it off at once, he was about my own age and we became inseparable companions. God rest him, he died too young and took a part of me with him. But on this day both of us only nineteen years old, death was as remote as the farthest star in a lost constellation, light years away.

'Tell us, Lar,' he said to me at the bench making doors, 'why did you never see that little mot, Phyllis, again?'

'I don't know where she lives. It's somewhere on Herbiton Road, I know. I'm sick and tired trying to see her. She plagues me. I love girls, as you know, but she keeps coming between them and me . . . Know what I mean, Freddy?'

'Maybe it's just as well, Lar,' said Freddy, 'she being a Prod an' all.'

'What the hell do I care, I don't care if she is a bloody hotten-tot, she is the one I want.'

'Well,' said Freddy, who was a far gentler young man and better balanced than ever I would be, 'all I know is that it takes a lot of trouble to marry one and makes a lot too.'

'How?'

'Well, if she "turns" with you, she'll lose her family an' if you "turn" with her you'll lose yours. How would you like that?'

'I wouldn't. I don't see any reason why either of us should change our religion as long as we loved each other.'

'What about kids, Lar?'

'Ah, I don't know. All I know is that I'd like to see her again. Maybe it would be different if we saw each other again. Maybe we wouldn't love each other any more. That would settle everything.'

'Well, in that case, did you ever think of standing on top of the Barn bridge on a Sunday morning? Sure, if she goes to church she has to pass that way, hasn't she?'

'Thanks, Freddy, I never thought of that.'

'Well, think of it now and you can tell me about it at the dance on Sunday night.'

Lord God, the times out of number I had tried to catch a glimpse of her, cycling all the way from Walkinstown to Loretto College, turning down Herbiton Lane, which had now become a half built road, searching for my lost love. I saw her brother once coming on to the Crumlin Road, but he pretended not to see me. He had no idea I had come up in the world a great deal further than he, or maybe he knew, but the fact remained that I was a Catholic and he did not want me around his sister. And then, I was a reminder of the near Liberties, which he and my father never wanted to remember.

I put on a cream coloured shirt with a wine coloured tie, in which a gold pin gleamed. I wore a rust coloured jacket with light gabardine trousers, both well cut and I cycled carefully that morning not to spoil the knife-edge crease. Brown brogue shoes, shining and fawn socks completed the outfit, a summer one.

I told my mother I was going to Mass in Crumlin village and at twenty to ten I stood on top of Dolphins Barn bridge. It was very quiet then with little Sunday traffic and two swans preened themselves in the harbour that used to be on the Sally's Bridge side. I kept a close eye on my watch. At ten minutes to eleven I crossed over to the other side of the bridge and looked up towards Herbiton Road. Two figures were quite close and I instantly recognised the sour-faced Lorrie.

She was wearing a 'poke' type bonnet, Salvation Army style and the long blue skirt and clothes that go with it. Beside her, dressed the same, Phyllis walked in durance, like a convict, escorted by her biblical warder. Her head was down, bent forward in feigned humility, her eyes were downcast and for one terrible second I thought she had not seen me.

But she had! As she passed me, her green eyes flashed upwards and she smiled. I was transfixed, torn apart by a wild storm of love. Phyllis, the same and yet so changed. She was a woman now and even the drab, Quakerish garb could not conceal the beauty of her face and form. As they came past, I involuntarily took a step forward, but the bitter bitch of a sister turned a look of unadulterated hate upon me and stopped me in my tracks.

At the same time she pulled Phyllis roughly across, so that she was away from me and together they walked rapidly out of my life. It had all happened so quickly and with such terrible finality. I would never have the chance to go out with Phyllis again! Lorrie had delivered the message with brutal clarity. That night, for the first time, I took a bottle of port to a dance, drank half of it before I went in and had a ball. Shyness had gone with the wine. The hurt of the morning forgotten in the swirl of skirts and the Haymakers' Jig. Then it was ladies' choice and a girl who was crazy for me took me up and we danced a slow waltz together, bodies close, passion in motion, for this girl loved me and I did not give a damn about her. I liked her as a girl, that was all I had to give. But she wanted me and I could have had her outside in the grounds when she clung to me, voicelessly pleading with her young body that I, the boy of her foolish dreams would take her and love her and be one with her. But of course I was afraid, afraid of putting her in the family way, of having to marry someone I did not love. But, even so, it was hard to resist – now, if it had been Phyllis! Poor Maureen held me like she would never let me go, she had nothing to lose but her virginity and what was that measured against the young man she wanted? For women, I was discovering, were in no way like men, nor did they think like a man.

When the natural habitat of all the wild creatures on earth has been destroyed and their convict descendants live by consent of the urban society, there will still be two things abroad on the face of this planet, free as the wind – women and cats! That is, domesticated cats and domestic women, who are no more domesticated than sabre-toothed tigers. But this knowledge was not to come to me for many years, was bought dearly in sweat and tears and savage feline maulings!

On the night in question I was saved only by an orgasm I could not control. Saved from what? I could have married worse than Maureen, but that night it was wet pants and shame all over again.

'You're looking very peaky this morning,' said my mother when I slumped down at the breakfast table. 'What time did you get home last night?' I smiled.

'You know, Mam. You heard.' She always did. She had ears like a fox.

'You shouldn't be out so late when you have a day's work to face, Lar. I hope you weren't drinking.'

'You know I don't go in to pubs.'

'Who were you with? Tell me your company and I'll tell you what you are.'

'Yes Mam an' no Mam, an' Mam, if you please, will you serve the brekker' quick. That old so-and-so Dad took on will be waiting with his watch and I'll be short of money again this week.'

This was the latest idea adopted by my father in his never-ending battle with his sons and apprentices. He had fifteen carpenters now, five lads serving their time, five bricklayers, three plasterers and about twenty labourers. He was getting to be a big builder and quickly. Apart from me and my brother, relations between me and the other lads were great. Friends and first cousins, we were real pals, Auntie Nelly's boys.

We never found out exactly how my father found McAlister, but one morning there he was, granite faced as the city he came from, Edinburgh, watch in hand, inexorably taking the time of our arrival. Five minutes late equalled quarter of an hour, sixteen minutes late meant half an hour stopped from your pay. The first week we were all short in our wages. Which in my case meant being short in the pocket. Mam had to receive her tithe, stoppages notwithstanding.

McAlister was a house painter and while with our firm, he combined painting with the time keeping. We hated him and he returned our regard with interest. We discussed our misfortune one day at lunch hour, sitting around a timber fire in one of the incomplete houses. Kevin, the youngest apprentice, who was only paid ten bob a week, had been short three shillings. I was down twelve shillings, the brother and first cousin, almost on full pay, were down nearly a quid each.

The 'oul' fella', my father was laughing his head off, for he had us at last. This war had raged for four years now. The iron discipline my father had known all his life he now brought to bear on his sons and workers. Just because he was unfortunately related to us, was no reason why he was going to pay us for being late. He would break us. He forgot we were his sons, that it takes a diamond to cut a diamond! And to add insult to injury, McAlister often blew the whistle at ten minutes past five, ten minutes over the time.

'He'll have to go,' said my brother savagely, for although he was only twenty he was foreman on the job. McAlister, however, was not under him and served only Misterrr Rrredmond, this said with venom and rolling Rs.

'Yes,' agreed my cousin Paddy. 'But how?'

'What about sticking his new bike to one of the partitions? With scrim?' Scrim is a hessian-like material about four inches wide which, when dipped in liquid plaster is used to cover joints in ceilings. It sets like iron.

'Right! Kevin, get the bucket. Lar, get the plaster . . . Paddy . . . the water!'

The plaster was ready in a few minutes; in to the slurry the scrim was dipped. McAlister's new bike, the pride of his Highland heart, shining like a Rolls Royce stood against the timber studs of an unplastered partition. The scrim, carefully wound between the spokes, around the saddle through the timber studs, through the forks, over the mudguards was done well. This plastered sack would set like concrete in fifteen minutes and the machine would literally have to be hacked off the partition. Old Mac did not learn the fate of his bike until he knocked us off at ten past five, almost dark. He was reported picking pieces of plaster off it under the street light at half past seven. One up for us!

We were all early the following morning. Not one of us dared to say good morning to him. We went past with grave faces, convulsed laughing under the shell, crab laughter, for his granite face had taken on the bleak aspect of Ben Nevis in a snow storm. The following morning we lapsed, were all two minutes late and were stopped half an hour. The fact that the road was like a skating rink meant nothing to him. Slow buses or walked bikes were all one to him. He could be on time, so could we! Half an hour stopped the next morning, too. This time we were not late. He had put his watch on three minutes. Two up for him! Lunch hour again, a week later. Five desperate young men. It was to be all out war now. McAlister was winning every round now.

'He's got to go.'

'What'll we do to him this time?'

'Where's his bike?'

'Beside him. He never lets it out of his sight now. He even works beside it.'

'There's one time it's out of sight,' I said.

'When?' An eager chorus.

'When he stands there, holding his watch, waiting to blow the whistle.'

That was when he would be off his guard. He stood on a heap of gravel, watch in hand, looking out for those who had stopped work, for even though the time was past, if he caught you idling you got time stopped. And with no court of appeal. The boss refused to listen to complaints. Why should he? He was getting something for nothing! It was a sign of the times, that he was no longer 'dad'. The 'oul' fella' was good enough these days. He had ceased to be our father and become our employer. We had ceased to be his sons and become employees, a sad exchange for both sides. We waited until Mac took his stand on the gravel. We already had a rope up in a roof. This was now dropped into the hall, lashed to McAlister's bike which was hauled up the stair well, through the ceiling joists, one being left un-nailed and left in the roof.

The rope was hidden in the chimney, the last joist nailed as the whistle went. Two up for us!

We sidled past him the following morning with obsequious 'Good Mornings' but no answer came from the stone face of wrath. We all expected him to report this latest atrocity to my father, but he did not. His Scot's pride would not let him. He would beat us on his own.

The time stopping now reached Cromwellian proportions of vengeance and we had no redress.

Sent up to the office one day – yes, we had an office, a clerk, a phone and a joinery shop now – I found my father and his clerk there.

'By the way, Tom,' said the Oul' Fella'. 'I found out it's Mr McAlister's birthday on Friday. Put a fiver in his packet for a job well done.' This was said in front of me to let me know who was the boss. I felt myself go red with rage. He thought we were licked. Maybe I should give him something to put the grin on the other side of his face! I told the lads. 'Jasus, a fiver, more than a week's wages!' Next morning I came up with a fiendish idea. It was lunch hour the following day. The same weary question.

'What are we going to do to get rid of that oul' bastard?'

'I have an idea,' I said.

'Let's have it.'

'We'll send him a birthday present, too.'

'Well, yeh crawlin' little . . .'

'Shut up, you.' This to my brother, who as usual had opened his mouth too soon.

'We'll send him,' I said clearly, 'a little box . . . a little box of shit.'

There was a roar of laughter and assent. There and then the draw took place as to who would fill the box. The five of us drew lots. Poor Kevin, as usual, lost. We found a box that had held three inch hinges and was ideal in size for what we had in mind. Kevin reluctantly made his way over to the dry lavatory, us following but keeping back from the toilet. It was a place to go only in emergency. It was simply a trench with a plank over it, surrounded by a few sheets of corrugated iron.

It was malodorous, buzzing with flies in summer, filthy in winter, dank and mucky.

Kevin went inside and presumably dug in deep, for we could hear him gagging, all of us outside falling around laughing. We had ceremonially presented him with a wooden spoon, made specially for the occasion, eighteen inches long, sandpapered and well finished, to be used only once. He came out retching to more howls of mirth. He carried the box in to the lunch room, put it on the bench and went out and got sick. We carried on, delighted. After a short birthday speech by the brother, the box was capped, wrapped in brown paper and neatly tied with a string. It was sealed with red sealing wax, for nothing had been overlooked.

Kevin, recovered, was immediately sent to the Post Office to send it by registered post. It would arrive in my father's office about four o'clock the following day, when McAlister was picking up the wages. He would pick up our present as well.

Four o'clock next day came and McAlister came back on site with the wages. He also paid them out, and added insult to my brother for it was not, of course, fair. The foreman or boss always paid out. This was the unwritten law of a building job, broken only at peril for it demeaned the foreman, who after all had to command respect. A stranger would not have taken it. My brother had to. And, disgracefully, my mean little heart rejoiced to see him taken down a peg by a father no less arrogant than himself. The pair of them gave little consideration to me. I drew the wages of a senior apprentice, but did the work of a man. It seemed to be a silent conspiracy between them, however much they fell out over other matters, never to praise me no matter how much I did and I bitterly resented it. I was delighted to see them at each other's throats and had a ball every Friday when the painter paid out and I watched my brother's murderous face.

This Friday, McAlister's face was something to behold. His cold, grey eyes glittered with malice, his granite jaw set in rocky mould. It was a very mild winter evening, but around him it seemed to be freezing hard. We collected our assaulted pay packets one by one. The following morning he stood on his heap of gravel as if he had never gone home and did our coming wages a mischief. Monday morning was the same. On Monday evening, at half past four, nearly dark, I slipped into the house where McAlister was priming doors. His bike was in the room and he was working by the light of a carbide lamp. I slipped off my shoes, silently shoved a handful of shavings, which I had thoughtfully lit, under his arse. I was back next door when the roar came. Kevin, who was sand-papering timber looked up.

'What was that, Lar?'

'Oh, some of the lads tricking, Kev. By the way, what time is it?'

'Where's your watch, Lar?' It was in my pocket but I told him a lie.

'I'm leaving it at home now, Kev. All that hammering is ruining it.'

'About half four, I think,' said Kevin.

'Why don't you ask old Mac next door. He's in there.'

'Not me! That oul' bastard is going to do something terrible on us before long. Yeh don't think he's forgotten the shit, do yeh?'

'Oh, I don't know. I think he's beginning to thaw out. He said good morning to me this morning.' Another lie!

'Did he?'

'Yes, he's not a bad old devil, Kev. It's just that he's too fond of the boss. Slip in and ask him the time. After all, we've got to make it up somehow. We've failed to run him off the job.'

'I suppose so . . . I'll chance it.' I watched poor Kevin approach McAlister's room, saw him stick his head around the door and heard him respectfully address the Scot.

'Excuse me, Mr McAlister,' said Kevin, 'but could you tell us the time, please?' There was a long pause. Then . . .

'It's aboot time ye got this,' snarled the Scot and threw the contents of an almost full gallon of undercoat over the unfortunate Kevin. It covered the door, the floor, splashed the ceiling and windows. Kevin was the best primed apprentice in Ireland with stark white hair. Even the precious bike was covered. Kevin fled. McAlister, having gone too far, destroying the Boss's property, left in seconds and I watched him cycle out of our lives through the window. We never saw him again.

We had finally made it, got him off the job and bested the Oul' Fella'! He would be unlikely to look for, or find another Mac. It was an hilarious incident in our lives, that got better in the telling after years, but for me it has always carried overtones of sadness. It marked the final confrontation between my father and myself that was not healed for many, many years. It came about the same night McAlister got his birthday present.

That evening my brother and I had remained unusually silent at tea. Inside we were laughing, but at the same time were a little apprehensive about meeting the Oul' Fella'. The grapevine had carried heartwarming news of McAlister and his present.

'Anotherrr grrreat surrprrise, Misterrr Rrredmond,' he had said joyfully after receiving five pounds extra. 'Aye ken nobody who wud send me a prrresent.' He had opened the box and the smell had nearly lifted the roof off the office. Once or twice Mam glanced curiously at us, for she was accustomed to the never ending feud between us, but she probably decided that we had called a truce. She was wrong. For once we were brothers in spirit. We heard Dad's key in the front door and he entered the dining room. He kissed my mother and said: 'Ah, cold evening, Dolly, what's for tea?' We hurriedly finished our meal and, as one, rose to go.

'In a hurry, boys?' he said chattily.

'Yes, Dad,' we chorused together.

'I have to see the girlfriend,' Sean volunteered.

'The same one?'

'Yes.'

When he first came in he had been nursing a little smile. This was over our revenge, for he had an excellent sense of humour. But he was saving his tongue for the present. Sean left the room.

'Any timber arrive on the job today?' he inquired.

'Not as far as I know.' I turned to follow my brother.

'Come back here, you,' he said sharply. 'I'm talking to you.'

'I know. I'm off work now. Your foreman has just gone upstairs. Maybe he'll know. I'm finished for the day.'

This was the worst I had ever answered him, but I was sick of his job, sick of him and sick of not having a normal home life. No other lad I knew was badgered with work twenty-four hours a day and got paid for eight, if you were lucky.

'So,' he said bristling, 'we have a good trade unionist on our hands, have we?'

'Yes, we have. I joined the union, *your* union this week. The one you used to be Vice President of . . . and I'm finished with work for the day.' I stood there defiantly. He had taught me well in the hard days and now I was expected to forget about the hardship strikes brought to working class homes. The grinding poverty that came with the strike, the fight for better conditions, no security from one end of your life to the other, the pawn shop, the years it took a worker to get over the financial wreckage of a strike if he ever did. The effect of a lock-out.

'Laddie,' said Mam softly, 'you know I asked you not to bring the job into the house again.'

'I only asked him a question.'

'It only starts trouble and he *is* off work. Why can't you leave him be.'

'Am I not allowed,' roared my father angrily, 'to ask one of my sons a question in my own home?'

'No,' I snarled, 'you're not! Ask your foreman upstairs or oul' McAlister.' And I flung out of the room. I was becoming a man. Fuck him, he was not going to grind me down, ever. I was not going to stick his job much longer. Anywhere would be better than here.

'Stop . . . stop!' said Mam softly as I turned in the door and suddenly, to both our surprise, she burst out crying. She stood there, she who was as tough as they come, sobbing helplessly.

'I wish to Christ you had never become a builder,' she wept. 'There's no happiness or home life since you did.'

And that was right, anyway. Money had walked in our door and polluted our home. My father had died and this arrogant boss taken his place. I closed the door quietly. He could comfort her, it was his fault. He treated us like workers eight hours a day and then expected us to take an interest in the job after hours, for free. During the day we were just beasts of burden along with the rest. Apparently, at home, we suddenly became what it said on his sign . . . 'AND SONS'. The boss's sons. Big deal!

Outside in the hall, I suddenly stopped. There was something vaguely familiar about Mam, something pitiful and in a flash it came to me. She was pregnant! She was going to have a baby. Jesus Christ, she was forty-two and had had nine. The boss, as he was now, was touching fifty and he was going to be a father again. We would number collectively twelve now, a soccer team with its own hard coach. Jesus, would they never stop? Would her babies and mine play together? It looked like it.

The Square and the Liberties were unexplored mysteries to the last six members of our family. The brothers went to Terenure College, the three girls to Loreto Convent where the nuns taught them religion and how to ostracise the girls in the national school next door, and little else. The Commandments were drummed into them. 'Honour thy father and thy mother . . . love thy neighbour . . .', but for Christ's sake do not carry it too far. Keep away from the hoi polloi in the national school.

This child, who was coming would have no conception of the way it had been with me. Boy or girl, I wondered if we would ever be able to communicate? I suddenly felt ashamed. From where I stood, my mother's heartbroken crying came to me. Jesus, it was she who had to face the old ordeal again, not me, smart bastard! I softly opened the door. Dad was standing with his arms around her, her crisp, permanently waved hair touching his chin.

'Oh, Laddie,' she wept, 'I hope I am able to . . .'

'Shhhh, Dolly,' my father warned. My mother lifted her head and gazed at me with brimming eyes. She could still see through me. No amount of tears was going to alter that.

'I'm very sorry, Mam . . . Dad.'

'That's alright, Lar,' said the old boy gruffly. My mother turned her face away from me.

'Go on, Lar,' she said. 'I'm alright.'

But would she be? She knew that I now knew. She knew that I would worry. Hence the added 'I'm alright'. I had a sudden compassion for my father and what he would go through in the coming months. And my poor mother! Was not nine enough? Compassion for both of them flooded over me, for it was the way with them as it could have been with Phyllis and me. Their love for each other had never flagged either. She was still in my father's eyes the Belle of all Liberties belles, he was still the handsome gentleman's son come down in the world and now, with her help, gone back up again. And he had brought her up with him, a willing pupil, prepared to work to be his lady. They were the two closest people I have ever known. They loved forever on the first day they met. Just sometimes, not often, a marriage is made in heaven. In a week, came the sudden thought, I would go to Wexford, away from the bloody job for a few days. A memorable day indeed, McAlister's birthday.

Monday came cold and grey.. McAlister stood exactly where he had stood at twenty to one on Saturday. It was as if he had taken root. Nevertheless, before this day ended he would be gone forever.

'Good morning, Mr McAlister,' said cousin Freddy. No answer.

'Good morning, Mr McAlister,' said Kevin, sloping past. No answer.

'Good morning, Mr McAlister,' said my brother civilly. A stony stare for reply. I looked him over coolly. No surrender, no truce with me! I hated his guts, not just for the money he cost me, but for his dour, ignorant ways. And then, he had said something so true, that I would never forgive him. He had said: 'The fetherrr is a gentleman, but the sons . . . I nae ken them. They're nae gentlemen or everrr will be! A crrrowd a' skunnerrrs . . .' – the Glasgow equivalent of a Dublin gurrier, 'a louser, 'a corner boy . . . 'nae gentlemen!'

19 *Caroline Shows Me How*

Christmas week was a lousy cold darkest week of the year, which we worked through cheerfully enough. McAlister was gone, the sun shone over our lives again, and all was well. Despite this my brother and me found time to quarrel. It was a vicious enough affair while it lasted, one of only too many. And there was little reason for it, except a bitter determination to best each other.

On Saturday at three o'clock we headed for Wexford. We had, at most, two hours daylight in which to get there, and this was soon to be cancelled by a dank fog which rolled in from the sea and enveloped the car. Sean, peering through the windscreen, groping his way along as best he could.

In hindsight, looking at these two young buckos I see little to like about either of them. They were both arrogant, conceited, and jealous of each other. They had come up in the world too fast, and lacked the balance of their gentlemanly father, who had, after a long twilight, come back to his inheritance. This had never been more clearly demonstrated than the previous summer, when the whole family had booked in to Kilmaccuvagh Park Hotel, in Wicklow, and the 'oul' fella', much to our amusement had appeared from the stables, riding a fiery hunter and rode off, very much at home, and wiping the grins off our faces.

And it did not take long in the fog for hostilities to break out again. Sean, doing the best he could, narrowly missed a parked car at Blackrock. I, still smarting from another confrontation with my father over the latest quarrel, seized this opportunity to do a bit of back seat driving.

'Christ,' I said, as the car swerved, 'If you can't do better than that, shove over and let me drive.'

'Since when can you drive?' said the brother, with a laugh.

'Since before you, Mr Big Fella,' I answered coolly. 'And I can drive a car better.' And the stupid quarrel started all over again, neither giving ground.

'I'm responsible for the car,' he snapped.

'Then drive the bloody thing right.'

Actually there was nothing wrong with his driving, the near miss just gave me an opportunity to get at him. I blamed him for the breakdown of communication between my father and me, and looking back I can see I would have managed that for myself anyway. He had been working on the north side of the city, bringing in a much needed few bob, while Dad and me struggled with the first two houses. But I had held the first foundation peg for my father as he drove it home, and made a claim on a fortune. I had been there first, so that when Sean came to us, aged nineteen and took over as foreman the trouble started. No doubt my nose was out of joint, no doubt either that he acted the bully, ordered me, like the men, which I would not take, and also, no doubt that he had had the burden of responsibility thrust upon him.

Always we had been like a pair of fighting cocks, sparring with each other, fiercely competitive, both Dux of class, until the mathematical part of my brain closed up shop, but nothing so traumatic ever happened to him. He remained what he had been born, top of the heap. Once, when he was sixteen, somebody in Oxford University had split something called an 'Atom', and I had listened stupefied as he explained in detail to an equally stupefied father, what an atom was. I would never admit that he was cleverer by far than me, never until I grew up, and in my case that would take a long time.

That he loved me, at the back of it all, I knew well, for he had always come to my rescue when some big lout terrorised me, and had burst snots galore on my behalf. That I loved him, at the back of it all I also knew well, but in the car going to Wexford there was only two young stags, antlers locked, playing a deadly game for no reason.

At Ashford we ran out of the fog, and from there to Gorey was quiet enough. We arrived there about seven o'clock, with frost already sparkling under the street lights.

'We've no time to call on Lil,' he told me. 'I want to drop you and get to a dance tonight.'

That suited me fine, of course I started another row over his presumption that he was calling the shots. I did not want to go with him to a dance, for I had other things on my mind – the promise held out by Caroline years before.

Looked at correctly there had never been a promise, merely a hunch on my part, but I had learned to trust my hunches. The 'fey' part of me was never wrong. The only time I was wrong was when I brought cold logic to bear on a given situation. The only time my brother was ever wrong was when he did not!

We entered the labyrinth of lanes leading to the farm, still sniping at each other. Then Sean lost his way. The hedges slipped past under a cold moon, anonymous as the fringe of an African jungle. We stopped many times at roadside cottages to ask the way. He made wrong turns and ended up in strange farms. We were re-directed and got lost again. I sat quietly in the back, refusing to get out and ask for guidance for I knew the way. I had told him in Gorey I knew the way but of course he was not going to hand over the car to me. I clammed up, afer telling him that he was of course the foreman on the job. He told me to shut up.

'O.K, Meester, me take orders, no give them,' I said in servile fashion from the back seat, where I was lolling, blowing smoke at the roof. All my grievences against him were with me, and Jesus, I swore to myself I'd make him pay now. I lay back, enjoying myself. Finally, after wandering around for nearly an hour, he pulled up at a crossroads, hopelessly lost. I was in my seventh heaven, for I recognised the crossroads straight away. We were a hundred yards from Caroline's farmhouse.

Sean pulled up and got out to look for a signpost. There was none. A pale winter moon, weary old corpse of our night sky, reflected pallid light on the mysterious landscape. Knowing his fear of the dark, a legacy of the terrible Gardiner Street days, I stuck my head out of the window.

'Kitty the Hare country,' I told him. 'Why don't you ask the headless coachman when he passes by?'

He glared. 'In the name of Jesus,' he said viciously, 'where are we?'

'Get out from behind the wheel and I'll show you.'

'Why can't you show me now?'

'What do you think I've been doing since we left Gorey? No more, know all. Move over and I'll show you!'

Fuming he got behind the wheel and off we went again. Another crossroads. He was licked! Time was running against him, and there would be no dance tonight if we did not get to Caroline's soon.

'Right,' he said at length. 'You drive and I'll watch genius at work.'

'Fair enough,' I told him. 'You might learn something.' I was paying him back spitefully for the sorrow he had cost me in the past week. I could afford to be confident, for I knew this maze of roads like the back of my hand. Nigger, Patton and me had roamed them together, in the shabby long ago. I got behind the wheel, smoothly reversed, and went down one of the roads. If I had gone straight to the farm, there would have been a punch up, and I would have lost, for he would have known that I had been playing our dangerous game of besting each other, and it would have been too much. So I thought it expedient to go for a little drive, for we were on top of the farm.

'I hope you know where you are going.'

'Shut up . . . I do.' Eventually I entered the little lane that led to Caroline's. I watched out carefully for the gate, for there had been one. It was still there. I pulled up.

'What's wrong now? Lost?'

'The gate has to be opened.'

'Open it your bloody self.' I sat quietly behind the wheel, with time on my side. 'The least you can do, Sean, is to open it,' I said reasonably. 'For I did get you here.' He got out, and opened the gate, flinging it back against the hedge with venom! 'Lovely,' I said to myself. 'You've more coming.'

He flung himself back in the car, I drove through, and pulled up again. 'Jesus,' said the brother through his teeth, 'what now?'

'The gate has to be closed.'

In deadly silence he got out and closed the gate. When he got back I was sitting in the back again. Enough was enough.

'The farm is straight ahead,' I told him. I could afford to be magnanimous, for I had won the day. I had humbled him, and that was what it had all been about. Sometimes, with brothers, it is like this for a lifetime. Happily, there would be a day when we could meet as brothers, but that day was a long time away, and the world had 'put manners on us' before then.

Silently he drove into the farmyard and pulled up. By the wan light of the moon it looked no different from the last time I had seen it, but like most Irish farms it had become sadly run down. I was to find this out the following morning.

The economic war, settled at last, had crippled the farm, and drove Caroline's brother, Seamus to seek refuge in an English factory. I thought of the fine ruddy faced Wexford man, seeing him innocently standing in the cow shed when it rained, because he loved the sound it made on the galvanised iron roof. In no way could I picture him in a factory, any kind of factory, no more than I could picture an eagle in a cage, though that has been done often enough.

A dim light came from the kitchen window of the double story house, which told of an oil lamp, then a dog barked, the kitchen door opened, and Caroline came to meet us.

She had not changed at all in the years since we had last met.

'Welcome,' she said to the brother, and shook his hand. She kissed me briefly on the cheek, saying nothing, then led us inside.

'You'll think us very much behind the times,' she said, 'with no electricity.' She turned up the wick of the lovely old oil lamp, and gazed at us in wonder.

'So,' she said in her soft Wexford brogue, 'Lar and Sean . . .

all grown up and quite the city gentlemen. It only seems like yesterday since Lar was a boy . . . Come into the Parlour, you must be frozen. I have a great fire lit, waiting for you.'

And indeed she had, a *coal* fire which meant she had gone to Gorey specially, to spend her precious money on coal for us. The glen usually provided fuel for the farm house, there being no bogs around here.

I would have preferred to have had tea in the kitchen. The parlour was only used for visitors, and it smelt faintly of must and disuse. But the beautiful old treasures of the house were on display, and I remembered them all. Cut glass sugar bowl and milk jug, jam dish and cruet set, all from Waterford, handed down from generation to generation, the product of a factory killed long ago by the invader, but one that would rise again soon, phoenix-like from the ashes, under the more genial climate of an Irish Government. A snow white table cloth from Belfast, lace doyleys from Limerick, delicate china from Worcestershire, beautiful stuff, all of it, and for all our newly acquired wealth we had nothing to touch this in Walkinstown. Caroline was rather apologetic about it all, fussing over us like a mother hen, overawed, probably, by the gleaming new Ford in the yard. She obviously thought we dined off gold plate, instead of which, every week day we drank from a blackened Tommy can, and ate sandwiches in a half finished house. The English saying was true, where's there's muck, there's money.

Occasionally she glanced at me, but looked away when I caught her eye. She had scarcely said two words to me since I had entered the house, confining her conversation to Sean, discussing turkeys, but somehow I felt complimented. I was the special one, and knew it.

Sean quickly finished up a plate of rashers and eggs, paid the money for the turkeys, and then announced his plans for the night.

'Yes,' Caroline agreed. 'The dance in Gorey was a great one . . . half Irish . . . half Ballroom dancing,' great, altogether, she had been told.

Caroline showed him the bedroom where we were to sleep,

and then he was off, lights blazing on the frosty ground, glad to be away from me and a dull night in a country farmhouse.

After the noise of the car merged into the night, Caroline started to clear away the dishes, and I, silent, helped her. In the soft lamplight, coming into the kitchen, I almost collided with her, and stepped swiftly aside to save the precious Waterford glass. In the tiny passage formed by a three foot thick wall, she paused, and looked at me.

'Ah, Jasus,' she whispered to herself. 'Hasn't he turned into the lovely young man . . . Lar,' she said aloud. 'Is it really you! And still with the lovely long eyelashes.'

'Now you're making me blush,' I said almost angrily.

She followed me over to the sink, smiling. She knew she had me. Every woman knows when she is desired, and she read me like a book.

'Your lovely long eyelashes, Lar; you have the face of a priest.'

'Stop, Carrie,' I said. She moved closer to me and placed her hands on my shoulders. She was a couple of inches taller than my meagre five feet four.

'Shy but willin', like a cat in a dairy,' she murmured. 'Let me look at you, Alannah!' And somehow we came together, and I was kissing her passionately, and it was for real, there was no pretence with either of us, she wanted me, and I, with all the bottled up frustration of a sexless life, was mad for her. There, beside the rocking chair that Aunt Sarah used to sit in, I took her on the sofa.

It was a quick, too thrusting, too eager coming together, but there was no way it could have been otherwise, me doomed to spend my life in a sexual desert, afraid of the priests, afraid of a dose of the Johnny Rocks, afraid of giving a girl a baby, but this was a woman that was panting under me, a woman with ten years more sex starvation behind her than me and we were like a pair of wild things.

At the last second I tried to pull away from her, for I was well up enough in the theory of the thing, and knew that the withdrawal method was widely practised. One of my friends had gone into bad health doing it too often, and had ended up in a sanitorium with TB. Nevertheless I tried with all the willpower I had to leave her, but she pulled me to her with the strength of a tigress, a willing captive, and together we went into orbit around some unseen star that is the light of the world without which all would end.

And if this was what King Edward had just jacked up his job for it was well worth it, with him on the winning side. I lay on top of her, panting wildly. I thought my heart would burst, and I could feel Caroline's heart jumping under her blouse. There was no lamp lit in the kitchen, and I watched for a second the flames flicker on the smoke brown ceiling before I moved.

'Don't,' she whispered. 'Don't, Alannah, leave me so soon.' Leave her? Jesus, I never wanted to leave her, this was heaven on earth. And this sofa would be littered with mortal sins this night, if God gave me the strength!

The tide of passion had gone out for a minute, but only a minute, and now it came flooding back, and this time it took longer, she moaned under me as if she would die of happiness, and again we went spinning around the universe, in harmony with cosmic movement. It was lovely and peaceful then, in the kitchen, and we spoke softly for a while.

'Carry, what will you do if I've given you a baby?'

'As long as it's yours I'm happy, so don't worry.'

'But, Carrie, what will you do?'

'Shush,' she whispered. 'The brother will be back from England at the end of next week, to take over this farm, and pay my dowry. This time two weeks, I'll be married to a farmer from Woodenbridge.'

'Married!'

'Yes, married to a man old enough to be my father. A sound man they call him. He'll give me half a dozen children before he dies. 'Tis the way of it, down here. There's plenty of young widows around.'

'Christ,' I said, appalled, in the flickering darkness. 'Do you like him at all?'

'Yes, he's all right. He's a good practical man, who'll make me a good practical husband. I could do worse.'

'And you don't mind cheating on him like this?' She laughed softly.

'Maybe he wasn't always as correct as he is now. How do I know what divilment he got up to when he was young! Sure, maybe there a girl somewhere that has a baby by him. How do I know? He's twenty years older than me.'

'Have you had many men, Carrie?'

'What!'

'Sorry . . . I mean am I the first?'

'Wouldn't you like to know!'

'Yes, Caroline.'

'Why?'

'I wouldn't feel so bad if I wasn't. I would not have been the one to . . .'

'Make me sin?' she finished for me, and laughed throatily. 'Well, you *are* the first as it happens.'

'Really?'

'Yes really. 'Tis something I can't explain, from the first day I saw you, and you only a boy, I wanted you. I never wanted anyone else. 'Tis some kind of madness I can't explain, even to myself.'

'Somehow, I felt you did, but of course that was madness too.' Caroline sighed happily.

'I used to dream of a time like this, that somehow we would come together like this, and always, that I would have a child by you, and like you, and dream about you makin' love to me like you just have.'

'Are you telling me you love me?'

'No . . . although I do. What I'm tellin' you is that with me t'was only a dream. I knew I could never marry you or have you, so I dreamed of a time like this, just one short time in a whole life, when God would send me you to adore, for a little while. 'Tis no sin, no matter what the priest says for God to grant me my wish.'

So, this was the way of women! I was learning, and learning fast, that in most ways women were infinitely superior to men, and this confession of Carrie's had made me feel small.

'You are mad, you know that?'

'Yes, Alannah,' she smiled and bit my ear.

'Carrie, could I ask you another question?'

'Fire away.'

'Carrie . . . I thought . . . when a man went with a virgin that . . .'

'Alannah, you thought a lot of things, most of them wrong. You're talkin' about my maidenhead, I know, but I lost that a long time ago, riding a horse, I think. Anyway, women who do hard physical work nearly always lose it long before they're fourteen.'

So it was true. I was her first. She stirred under me and I responded at once.

'No,' she said quickly. 'Not again. We'll go to bed proper. Anyway your brother might walk in.'

And so, candle in hand we went up the incredibly narrow stairs of the old farmhouse. I lit a candle from her's and went into the bedroom where me and the brother were supposed to be sleeping. I undressed quickly, blew out the candle, and carrying my pyjamas on my arm, rejoined Carrie as God made me. She was already in bed, and only a patch of moonlight on the floor by the window lit up the room.

I slipped into bed beside her, and soon had the heavy cotton nightdress off her, and knew the inexpressible bliss of lying with a real, live, fully developed woman, with large lovely breasts, wide hips, and thighs as soft as silk, softer than the old fashioned feather mattress that we lay on. And the love making started all over again. Somewhere about three o'clock she woke me up. I had fallen asleep, and her heavy breast lay under my cheek, my arms still around her ample figure. She pulled me in to her, then released me.

'Get into your own bed quick,' she said. 'Here's your brother.' 'Hell with my brother,' I swore savagely, but I could hear the car in the yard below. I tore myself away from my new-found Paradise, went into the other room, and got into the bed. It was empty and cold, big and desolate as some undiscovered plateau near the South Pole. Presently I heard Sean stumble up the stairs. Carrie had put her nightdress back on, and was standing with a lit candle at the top to meet him. I heard him laugh drunkenly, saying 'sorry, Carrie, sorry . . . a few drinks too many . . . see you in the morning,' and he fell into bed clothes and all. He was asleep in an instant. And in another instant I was back in the luxury of Caroline's bed, had the night dress off her, and was with her again.

It just got better. I rang the bell with her every time, and I had to cover her mouth once with my hand, in case her moaning woke up his nibs next door. It was lovely. Somewhere about dawn, I stole back to my bed, satisfied at last, replete, for the present, a man! A man with a newly discovered world at his feet and young with it. So I fell asleep, surely the happiest mortal sinner in the Irish Free State.

The next morning the brother slept late, in fact it was half past twelve when he woke up, and came down the stairs looking a bit pale around the gills. He was jittery, and gulped down a cup of tea, grabbed the two turkeys, and was ready to go. He was frantic.

'Jesus,' he gulped, 'I have to be in Dublin by half past five!'

'Don't worry,' I said comfortably from the couch, 'There's plenty of time.'

He gave me a poisonous look.

'You mind your own business, and get yourself into the car. I'm leaving now.'

This was the foreman's voice, the one that never worked with me.

'Leave away,' I said, 'that doesn't suit me at all. I came down to see some friends of mine, and that bloody girl of yours is not running my life Peg ahead.'

'You mean you're not coming?'

'You catch on quick . . . that's right!'

'An' what do you intend to do?' He was livid.

'That's my business. I'll tell you this much. I'm going into Gorey with Carrie to see Lil this afternoon.

'We're going in the trap. I'll probably stay the night, with Lil.'

'And when will you be back home?'

'When I feel like it. In time for the Christmas dinner anyway. Why? It's nothing to do with you.'

'Now look, I brought you down here, and I'll bring you back. You're my responsibility.'

'Your responsibility?' I sneered laughing. 'Thank Christ I'll never want anything off you. Now, eff off, and leave me in peace. I'll find my own way back to Dublin.'

'Wait 'till Dad gets you,' he said between his teeth.

'Up you and Dad,' I thought comfortably, and blew smoke at the ceiling, 'and all his friends and relations in America, and if he has any in Ethiopia up . . . them an' all.' But I said nothing aloud. Just grinned.

Outside I could hear him talking agitatedly to Caroline. I rambled over to the door, and lounged against it.

'Don't take any notice of him, Carrie,' I said easily. 'Dad won't mind, and even if he did I do what I like now. It's just that he is trying to make a big fella of himself again . . . He's the foreman,' I added with a laugh. 'In case you don't know.'

I lounged back into the kitchen. Jesus, he was no match for me off his home ground. I was delighted.

Outside I could hear Carrie talking soothingly.

'It's just that he wants to meet Lil and the Buckleys. You know, Sean, he knows a lot more people down here than you do.'

'Any use in your speaking to him?'

The anxious brother bit.

'No, Sean, he'll stay in Gorey for the night. Yes, yes, but isn't there a bus and train? Off you go now, and see to that girl of yours. Don't forget to give my regards to your Mam and Dad.'

Next minute he was back in the doorway.

'Are you coming? I'm going now.'

'I told you,' I said softly so Carrie would not hear, 'Fuck off!'

'Jesus, wait till Dad hears this.'

'Dad won't hear anything,' I said blowing another smoke ring. 'Not if you know what's good for you.'

'Are you threatening me?'

'Not half!' I heard the car start up then, and waited for him to come back, as I knew he would. A minute later he was in the kitchen again.

'What'll I tell them about the car, the bursted headlight?'

'And the buckled mudguard,' I reminded him, for I had looked over the car.

'Well?'

His eyes were starting out of his head with rage, and I knew he was within a second of attacking me. But I did not care. To best each other was *all* in this deadly game that we played, all day and every day, and God alone knew when it had started, and how it would end.

'Tell them you got drunk, and ran into a bar,' I said judiciously.

'JESUS!'

'Look,' I said suddenly growing weary, 'you ran into a parked horse cart. It was upended in the fog, in a lane outside Gorey, got it? We both looked around but found no one. We're not sure where it happened. So we just had to drive on with one light. O.K.?'

'Right, thanks,' he added grudgingly.

I looked at him with contempt.

'Don't bother to thank me,' I said bitterly. 'You'll find a way to thank me on the job, I'm sure. Now, piss off. You look like something that was dragged backwards through a furze bush,' I added.

He flung away and a second later the car roared out of the yard.

'Nice bit of lying that,' I told Caroline, 'from the pair of us.' She sat down beside me on the sofa, smiling.

'I want you a little longer, Alannah,' she said, and in two minutes flat her knickers and my trousers were on the floor, and we were making love again.

Before we went to bed that night we lay in front of the fire on a blanket, with pillows, watching the shadow bats fly. The lamp was not lit, but we did not make love. The night was long. It would be all the better in the feathers.

'Sing me a song, love,' said Carrie dreamily. I shook my head. 'It's gone, Carrie, my voice, ever since I was sixteen, and it broke.'

'Will it ever come back, do you think?'

'No.'

'Can you sing at all?' She was silent then, and I knew she was a little misty eyed. No doubt, part of her dreams had been me singing to her.

'My singing days are done, Caroline,' I said regretfully. No one regretted the passing of my voice more than me. If it had stayed with me, I would never have known a hard day's work, never have known the crude animal brutality of the building line.

She sighed, and ran the back of her hand over her eyes.

'Such a beautiful voice to die,' she said. She was silent then, for a while. Presently I felt her stir, for I had my head on her heavy breast.

'Well,' she said at last, 'if you can't sing beautiful anymore, you've learned to speak beautiful.'

'And make love?'

'Beautiful!'

'Carrie?'

'Yes?'

'Will you let me know if I've given you a baby?'

'Only if you insist, Alannah.'

'Yes. I must know. How will you tell me?'

She thought for a little while, then came up with the solution.

'I'll send you a photo' of my wedding. On the back I'll write "every thing is beautiful" I'll underline the beautiful. That will mean you have.'

'And if I haven't given you a baby?'

'No photo . . . ever.'

'Carrie, come to bed now, love. I need you.'

'Yes, my bonny boy, oh yes!'

Of course, we had not gone to Gorey that day. It was two days later when we went, Christmas Eve, and Carrie drove the trap with the cob. The old horse was still sound as ever. I had an hour with Lil before the train went. I told her Sean and me had had a row, and that he had gone off without me, but that I had wanted to see her anyway, and was glad he had gone.

'That was a rotten thing to do,' said Lil. 'But wasn't it always the way between you two? One row after another.'

'And always will be,' I added cheerfully.

'Why, in the name of God?'

'I'm afraid you'll have to ask God. I don't know.'

'He shouldn't have gone off and left you, anyway,' said Lil. Having told him to eff off, I smiled. Poor Lil had no reason to disbelieve me. And at home I could talk about Gorey as if I had spent most of the time with her. The half truth I had found was best, the most difficult to refute, though I was an expert liar if driven to it.

'He has grown into a lovely young man,' said Lil to Carrie. She was starting to get that slightly faded look, that comes early to a woman who has never known a lover. She was still good looking, but gone off, dusted over, jaded about the eyes, like me. I had two blue circles from exhaustion under each eye.

'You still look delicate, Lar. Are you?' said Lil anxiously. Jesus, a Guinness's Clydesdale, a six meal a day blood stallion would be looking delicate if he had had as much of 'the other' as I had! They would have been forced to drag him out and use the humane Killer on him!

'No, Lil. I just have a cold and it's a cold day. I'm O.K.'

'It is a cold and bitter night, and I am all alone,' sang Caroline from the trap. 'But the Bonny Boy is young and he is growing.'

Lil glanced up sharply at the glowing faced Carrie who was singing. Caroline was flushed, her eyes glistened, her usually pale face had a nice tinge of colour to it. She looked away quickly from Lil's gaze, fiddling with the reins, then jumped down, abruptly, tightened up the harness, and turned to Lil.

'I'll be off,' she said. 'I have two cows to milk before dark. Goodbye Lar,' she said lightly, and hopped back into the trap. She paused, whip in hand, for a second.

'You know, you're right Lil,' she said. 'He's grown into a lovely lookin' lad, the Bonny Boy himself. Happy Christmas,' and then, with a flourish of the whip she was gone.

I had time for a cup of tea before the train left, and Lil showed me her new kitchen with pride. Her brother Pat, decent as always, had got the job done for her, and done well. He was a smart man, and made money besides pulling pints. He bought and sold cattle, pigs, anything he saw a quid in, and did well. And with it, remained a decent man, unpolluted by money, as my family were becoming now.

An Aga cooker stood where the turf fire had been, the floor tiled, the walls hacked off and re-plastered, and the small penal days windows* had been replaced by those of much larger size. The kitchen had a new false ceiling too, much lower than the old one, a double drainer board of stainless steel, built in cupboards, and hot and cold running water. There was little difference between it and any kitchen in Dublin, except this one was larger. When Pat did a job he did it well.

But I liked Caroline's primitive kitchen better, for primitive reasons, especially when the shadow bats, made by the fire, flew across the brown ceiling, and we made love. I had a sense of following directly in the footsteps of my race. All my people for centuries had sprung from this kind of farmhouse, this setting. How many Redmonds had been begotten in a setting like this? Before that, we had, as conquering Normans, raped and had our way beside turf or log fires. For the Normans were a practical and passionate people, who had tried to swallow the Gael whole, but had been seduced, and happily seduced from their purpose, by the sweet voiced Colleens of the Irish Race.

I kissed Lil goodbye, and told her I would definitely get down to spend a week with her the following summer. The train pulled out with me in pensive mood. As before, it seemed, when I left Wexford, I left half of me behind. I looked at Lil as long as the train would let me, sweet Lil, who had no dowry, and who was destined to go through life in the bitter Nunnery of Spinsterhood, without knowing a man. Destined,

* During the savage Penal Laws, enacted against Catholics only, an Irish man was taxed on the size of the pane of glass in his window.

because of her religion, never to have an affair, even one that would shame her and break her heart would be better than none.

Instinctively I knew this, but then, a lot of the things I knew were instinctive.

Someone had left the morning's paper on the seat, and idly I glanced at the headlines. There was a picture of the Prince of Wales, no longer King, and now the Duke of Windsor, and his bit of fluff, Mrs Simpson, standing beside Hitler in Berchtesgaden. Ribbentrop, Germany's Ambassador to England stood just behind, and despite the grin on Hitler's face, I knew it boded ill for England.

I had been thinking, for a while, of joining the Volunteers, the 11th Battalion, spare time soldiers, and now I made up my mind. I would join.

The respite between the two major wars was about to end, and it was time I was trained to fight. It mattered little to me who I fought. I had no special hatred for any of them, except England, who occupied six of our counties, and ruled with the boot and the bully boy. But anyone who invaded my country, under any pretext, was to be made accountable to me, even if I died for it. I was bred for the job. My father had taken his chance like a man, too. But I had no illusion about the forces that might be pitted against us. An Irish Army would not last a week in the field. It was bitter guerilla warfare I expected to be involved in.

The big news of that day was not in any paper. The 'stop press' was that I had slept (well, dozed off with) a real, big, well-developed woman, with soft spreading thighs, and an all embracing love of me. She had adored me, worshipped me, kissed the face off me. She had humbled me. I had always been over fond of the girls, but the reality had been more than even I could imagine.

This had been no Phyllis, slight as a boy, and just burgeoning. This was what Kelly, the boy from Killane, had had in Dolphins Barn, when he had got across Eileen Og, this was what men were powerless to resist, although I thought the Duke of Windsor's 'Mot' a bit on the slim side. I mean, if he was giving up a King's Crown, he should have got a bit more for his money. Not that I was looking, personally for a fatso, but my preference was for a bit you could get a good handful of . . .

I wondered idly if I had made Caroline pregnant. I could not imagine her in that state, yet it should have been easy for me. After all, I had never seen anything else except swollen bellies in the Liberties, and now my poor mother was going to go through it all again. A bit bloody embarrassing, when I might be a father myself, at nineteen, and my eldest brother twenty-one tomorrow, Christmas Day. But the thought of Caroline being a mother remained too big for my mind. It could not happen. After all, we had only done it a few times, well, maybe a little more than that, Jesus Christ, why not face the truth. It was twelve times in three days! There had to be something wrong with one of us if she was *not* bloody well pregnant twice over.

She had said she would let me know. She would send me a photo of her wedding, and it would say 'Everything is Beautiful,' and an underlined 'beautiful' meant she was to become a mother. Well, face that day when it came!

The train pulled into Westland Row about four o'clock in the afternoon. It was dark, the city lights blazed, shops sparkled with mock frost, and holly was everywhere. I headed for Henry Street to see the city decorations at their best. It was thronged, with city shoppers, and Holly and Ivy revellers, and Moore Street, the light of my Dublin heart, with its dealers behind their stalls, 'Tuppence a poun' th'onions . . . th' apples, th' oranges . . . Get yer Mickey Mouse, Donald Duck, or Pinocchio . . .' Jesus, some of them I remembered from my market and fish days, poor oul' wans, still at it, and I, the young toff on the pavement went unrecognised among them.

My Mount Calvary of Christ's Church, and the South Circular Road was behind me, they would die on theirs. This was the way of the world. Better get used to it. Unfortunately, I never did. Funny, here it was all Christmas and down the country there was no sign of it at all.

Opposite Todd Burns I went into a pub for a drink. I felt no doubt about being served now. I had suddenly grown up, long eyelashes and all. There would be no more lip from Bar men. I sat up on a stool, sipping a Jameson Whiskey, with a bottle of stout for a chaser, a fair dollop, but then, I intended to get merry in a hurry. After a minute Santa Claus came rushing in from Todd Burns, scarlet Robe, white whiskers, and all. He was a very Dublin Santa. He slipped down the false beard to reveal the red nose and face of a tippler.

'For Jesus sake, Willie,' he said piteously. 'Give us a double Jameson, them little fuckers over there are drivin' me mad!'

'Now, now, Santa,' said the grinning barman, 'suffer little children to come unto me . . .'

'Ay,' roared Santa, taking a gulp of the whiskey, which he drank neat, 'But it's me that's doin' the sufferin' . . . What am I goin' teh get for Christmas, Santa,' he mimicked in a high falsetto voice, 'I know what *I'd* give them for Christmas. A swim in the Fuckin' Liffey . . .'

'Tsk-tsk-tsk,' said the young bar tender, 'Such language on the Eve of the birth of Christ.'

Santa rolled up his trousers and put his right leg up on a chair.

'Will yeh look at that,' he bawled, showing his battered leg. It was bruised all over, but the most recent one was bleeding slightly. 'Just look at that! Little fuckers kickin' yeh teh see if yer real, pullin' the whiskers off yeh . . . bastards, I'd quit now only the Manager won't pay me off. Put that on the slate, Willie,' he told the young barman, 'until tonight, that is,' he added bitterly, limping towards the door. 'If I'm not in hospital or jail, for killin' one a' the little . . .'

'Now, now, dear,' said the Barman. 'Mustn't kick Santa must we? Make Mamma very angry an' Dada won't be let put anything in my stocking tonight . . . mustn't pull Santa's whiskers dear . . .'

'Fuck you,' said Santa, and left with a glare.

'If he slips in here for any more whiskey,' said the barman to me, 'he'll throttle one a' them kids!'

I was home. No doubt about that. This was Dublin, the place I loved. I went out again into the swirling crowds, and up to meet the gang in the Oval. We had all arranged to meet there Christmas Eve, and sure enough, Freddie was there, and Colin with him, Hughie too, and some more class mates who had got wind of the get together. In a moment we had occupied the bow window that overlooks Abbey Street, and we were all set to go on the tear.

Before the night was over we did most of the things foolish young men do, like climbing the O'Connell Monument, and puttin' a bra on one of the angels. I rode up Dame Street on top of a taxi, until a guard stepped out at Georges Street corner, and made me get down. I had only done it for a bet, and the gang were jammed in the taxi. The shy me had disappeared with the drink, and Caroline. I had broken the good news to our crowd, but said I had slept with a girl called Kathleen from Enniscorthy. They were all green with envy, except 'Nackers Clery', who had beaten us all in the virgin boy bit.

I arrived home that night after twelve. All the house lights were on and a large Christmas tree was lit up on the lawn. The house was packed with neighbours and relatives. Mam kissed me and gave me a bottle of stout, but little notice was taken of me. It was Christmas morning, and I had fleeting thought of other Christmas mornings, waking early, to find my way to Clarendon Street Chapel, through the heart of the silent Liberties to sing in the choir for seven o'clock Mass.

'Adeste Fideles' a pure young boy, with a voice to match, and now, a few years later, an experienced lecher, draped with mortal sins like a wrecked ship with seaweed, and uncaring. Still, though, the peace and holiness of the chapel were lacking this Christmas Morning. I sighed, and went off unnoticed to bed. Caroline would be yoking up the trap in a few hours to get Mass and spend a lonely Christmas on her own. The last lonely Christmas for her. This time next year she would be married and probably have a baby, maybe mine. And be the mother of another child the next year, this time by her husband. As the Bard said, 'It's a wise child knows its own father!'

I went to bed long before the others, and slept the sleep of the dead. It was a peaceful Christmas for me. Caroline had fixed all my worries for a few days. I was free from the torment of longing, though I would know it again only too soon. But I was grateful for a few days of peace.

We made merry that Christmas of '38. The clouds over Europe grew blacker by the week. Every day brought the inevitable nearer. I think we all, young and old, understood that by now. In Germany the harassment of the Jews gathered force, and was no longer, if it had ever been, a subject for a joke. Jews of international reputation, writers, artists, doctors, scientists with some German business men who had their ear to the track, and could hear the roar of the approaching juggernaut, were leaving the Fatherland in growing numbers, despite the vigilance of the SS to the great advantage of England and America.

Hundreds of Jews were disappearing every week, to where? It was only after the war, and the movie pictures were shown, that even the Irish had to believe the English for once. There was no disputing this evidence. But that was all in the future, though for the Class of '26 there was no future, except for the few.

It was all before me like the man with the wheelbarrow. But just now the world was my apple, and I would have my fill. I saw things differently now. There seemed some purpose to living since Caroline. Christmas soon passed, and spring came, the last spring before the horror descended on the world, out came the trout rod, and away with me to the mountains and their brawling streams. I had found a woman to replace Caroline, for my needs were explicit. Indeed she was a friend of my mother's, about eight years younger, and at thirty-four was as randy as myself.

I had had a suspicion for a long time that I could make her, and Carrie had given me the experience to do so. She had no children, she was married and she presented no danger. Life was great! Robert Louis Stevenson was right. Writing was a mighty bloodless substitute for living! Then why, I asked myself, was I torn with the desire to write? To regard everything else as subsidiary. Why in the name of God wouldn't the writing leave me alone. Why did I write all night in my sleep?

Why did I fling off to work in foul mood sometimes when there was no reason? Why was I so difficult? Why the hell couldn't I be normal, and enjoy life, instead of possessing a recording machine somewhere in my head, that recorded, drunk or sober? Why could I not make love with out the recorder working overtime, never giving me peace.

Damn the writing! That was past. I had no education, and no time to spare. There was a bucket of money in building, and I was becoming an expert. It was something I knew now. No starving genius in an attic act for me. I would be a builder, and wealthy. And one day live in a house even bigger than ours, and have a beautiful wife, straight out of a women's magazine, naturally!

And my whole nature cried out against the practical commonsense of my plans, and those of my father. It did not occur to me then, that if a horse was born in a sty that he never became a pig. I had not figured out that because Hitler would be dropping presents out of the sky, down half the chimneys of Europe, next Christmas, that he would never be mistaken for Santa Claus. Or that if I, in my lifetime, built another St Patrick's or Christ Church, in the Liberties, I would still not be a builder. So much to learn, and all of it the hard way. Those whom the Lord loves, he chaseneth! Well, behold the prodigal son!

My mother gave birth to a baby boy that Easter. She was in hospital three weeks this time, for it went hard with her. She was forty-two, had been having babies since she was eighteen. She had washed and scrubbed and reared a large family, carrying the next baby while she was doing it, working like a galley slave.

I went in, reluctantly, and under pressure from my sisters, to see her. I dreaded the womens' ward, and I was embarrassed by the fact that my Mam had had another baby. But when I inquired from my mother, a smiling nurse led me to a private room with deference. Jesus, a private room, and yet it was said that money did not bring happiness, nor did it!

But it brought respect, comfort, and it could buy service. With it one could arm oneself with all the treasures of the

Orient, but it did not buy love. Or happiness. I was painfully aware of this for since Dad had become wealthy, love and happiness had walked out our door. I knew that from the internal warfare in our home. But as I saw it, it erected a barrier between you and the world. People thought twice about affronting you if you were wearing a Grafton Street suit. It was as good as chain mail in deflecting shafts of ridicule.

A private room! This, more than anything else, impressed me with our new status in the world. And just a few years ago, this mother of mine had had a mid-wife, and last night's *Evening Mail* to have the baby on, the way you did not ruin a pair of sheets. I knew. I had come across a bloody newspaper once, forgotten in the rush, and I knew where all the gore came from. But of course, the young nurse, making eyes at the well-dressed young man before her, would find it hard to believe this.

My mother was sitting up in bed, breast feeding the latest when I came in. She covered herself up quickly, and then showed me my new brother, a wrinkled wizened caricature of a baby, I thought, and nineteen years between us. And then the thought hit me. I could have been his father! What about Carrie? She had never contacted me, and I sometimes wondered.

Mam had lovely brown hair, that refused to show a trace of grey, but today she looked every minute of her forty-two years, and more. She was never, after this last birth, to be the same woman again. I kissed her, looked with feigned interest at the little monster that had laid her low, determined to hate him, fell in love with him at first glance, and loved him forever.

We spoke for a while, and I arranged the daffodils I had brought her in a vase, under a shower of instructions as to what was to be done at home. I did not tell her that she had daughters quite capable of running the house, but it was so.

'Right Mam, I'll tell them . . . yes ma, I'll do that, no Mam, I promise I won't quarrel with Dad, yes, I know he is worried over you . . . yes . . . yes, Give us a kiss, I'm off.'

I got as far as the door when she spoke again. 'By the way,

Lar, I think I have a letter here for you . . . well, not a letter . . . a photo. Your sister Rose brought it in by mistake. I thought it was for your father. Here it is.'

I felt my face grow red, and avoided her eyes. 'Thanks, Mam,' I said.

'Funny remark that, written on the back.' I turned the photo over and looked.

'Everything is beautiful,' it said, the last word heavily underscored.

'Caroline must have got married,' I told my mother. 'It's her and her husband. I forgot, you have never met them.'

'Caroline who?'

'Mam, the turkeys . . . Wexford . . . the farm I stayed at when I went to Gorey as a boy . . .'

'Oh yes, of course. So that's Caroline. Let me have another look at her.' I handed over the photo, with my face on fire.

'Funny remark all right,' she said to herself. She gave it back to me without meeting my eyes.

'What's funny about it?'

'Oh . . . nothing.' Jesus! She knew! I knew she knew, and she knew that I did. Christ, what a thing to have a mother who was fey, and to be her son, fey like her, so that never could she have a secret from me, or I from her.

I do not remember leaving the hospital, or saying goodbye. I do not even remember unlocking the bicyle, for it was chained to the railings outside Holles Street, or pedalling away from the city. But I was instinctively heading for Old Bawn and the River. Peace was what I wanted, for I was in a turmoil.

I must have gone like the hammers of hell, for I was suddenly in Fir House, on the road to the bridge, and soon I sat on its stone wall, sweating like a pig, letting the roar of the waterfall blot out all thought. The turbulent river, crashing, fiercely brown, for it had rained most of the day, over the fall, was for me. I took the photo out of my wallet, and looked at it long and hard.

Carrie, with an old fashioned floral hat, stood beside a heavily moustached man old enough to be her father. A solid man, past all frivolity. A settled man, who would give her a family, and die twenty years before her. It was all as arranged. And suddenly my heart lifted, and I did not feel such a lousy little bastard after all. I had fullfilled all her dreams, the dreams she had thought would never come true, and remembering her words, 'Dreamin' that you were making love to me, like now,' I suddenly felt proud and humble at the same time.

And it occurred to me that there was more to a woman than a ride in bed. When a man was responsible for creating a baby, he moved into the realm of eternity, one generation following another, as far back as the human race could see, and on and on into a world without end, Amen.

Perhaps in Wicklow a gentle boy with a golden voice would surface, that the dear Jesus would let him keep it into manhood, and he would never come to know toil; a lyrical tenor, the me that never was, the gentle me that had been brutalised and hardened in the crucible of Gardiner Street and the Liberties.

Or maybe a lovely young woman's soprano voice would ring out from the Opera Houses of the world's great cities, and that woman would be my daughter. I looked down into the puddle at my feet, and saw a young man with a shock of gleaming brown hair, and an oval face with the far apart eyes of a dreamer, and a cleft chin. A slightly built young man who had a body as tough as old rope from hard work, youth in its glorious prime.

And then, as had happened once before, my reflection stepped out of the puddle, and stood before me. My other self, my Doppelganger was back! He stood there regarding me with some amusement, mixed with contempt.

'Well, Lar,' he said quietly. 'You're a big fella these days, aren't you? A great hand with the women!'

'That's right,' I agreed.

'You had a great time of it in Wexford last Christmas, didn't you?'

'The loveliest time ever!'

'Of course you know that Carrie will have your baby next August, don't you?'

'Yes I do, and I'm glad. She wanted it that way, something that was hers alone to love, a memory of me.'

'And you have it made now, haven't you?'

'Yes, I have. I know how to get around a woman now.'

'And have you figured that all the countries in all the world are full of women?'

'Thank God for that!'

'And you're going to make love to them all, are you?'

'It won't be my fault if I don't!'

I grinned back at him defiantly. He regarded me with pity.

'A little undignified, don't you think, your arse going like a fiddler's elbow from here to Bangkok? And you're going to be wealthy as well!'

'There will be plenty of women and plenty of money,' I told him. 'It's not hard to make money. I'll be rich while I'm young.'

'And where are you going to get all that money, you that can't save a ha'penny?'

'I'll be a builder, like Dad, only I'll be a real young builder, and the money will roll in.'

The young man regarded me sorrowfully.

'What happened to the writer,' he said. 'What happened to the boy who wrote a record into the Primary Cert! Where has he gone? I seem to remember a kid telling me he was going to be a writer, down by Guinness's harbour. What are you going to do with all the stories inside you, trying to get out?'

'I'll make the money, then I'll write. Ten years as a builder, and I'm set.' The young man shook his head and sighed.

'Sweet Jesus,' he said softly. 'Is there any sense to you at all?' He regarded me with sorrow, and there was no laughing now.

'What,' he asked me at length, 'did your Uncle tell you the other day when you went back to the Liberties?'

I had gone to Auntie Nelly's little place a few evenings ago, just jumping on my bike on impulse. All around me were the quiet fields of Walkinstown, too quiet for my mood just then. I'd go to see my cousins. When I got to the tiny artisan dwelling I was chagrined to find them gone to the movies, my Aunt out.

Uncle Fred was there, a small well-knit figure of a man, elbow on piano, demolishing a bottle of stout. This was his favourite position when he knocked off on Saturday, until Sunday night. He drank steadily all weekend, never drunk, steadily blotting up stout. He rarely drank whiskey.

It was a smiling early summer evening, and he had the back and front doors open against the heat. He was a renowned carpenter and joiner, never out of work. He toiled for a big joinery firm, rarely subjected to the broken employment that had once terrorised our home, and threatened us with hunger. I had a brand new pair of overalls on, for I had been polishing the bike when the fit of boredom hit me.

'The boys are at the pic's, Lar,' said Uncle Fred.

'Oh, I would have gone with them had I known . . .'

'That's the trouble with livin' so far out. Tell me, Lar, how old are you now?'

'Nineteen.'

'You'd never think it. Tell me, Lar, how long did it take you to put on those overalls?' I gazed at him, hard. No, he was not drunk. But it seemed a stupid question.

'About thirty seconds. Why?'

'Because it'll take you a lifetime to get them off.'

'Well,' said the other young man. 'I asked you a question?'

'You know what he said, but I don't take too much notice of the Uncle, not at the weekend anyway. He's always half twisted.'

'So would you be if you were growing old, and the work piled up on the bench from Monday morning until half past twelve Saturday . . . and never a sign of a rest. You think you know it all, but you've a hard and tough road to travel before you get sense, and start listening to people older and wiser than yourself. You have deserts to cross and mountains to climb, and tropical Islands to see, and you'll make it all the harder with your grá (love) for the women and the drink. Your Uncle was right!'

I grinned. Mountains and deserts and tropical islands were all right by me. And women! Why, there might be a dusky maiden waiting for me under a palm tree. He turned to go.

'I'll miss you Lar,' he said.

'Why? Are you going somewhere?'

'No, you are. You'll be quite old before you see me again. Goodbye, and the best of luck to you.'

He grinned. 'Never say your mother reared a Jibber,' he said, and was gone.

I gazed down at the white foam and brown water tearing off to the sea, to what? To rise again in vapour, and once more become a cloud, scudding over the face of the earth, until some cold air stream or mountain crossed its path and it rained itself away.

An Indian on the banks of the Ganges might purify himself in its water, or perhaps an alligator in the Everglades would bask in its warmth. Or maybe it would not get very far and come down this river again soon. Who knew? Only God.

Only God knew my fate, in this tumultuous year of '39. Uncle Fred and my Doppelganger might think they knew, but they did not. Unfortunately, as it turned out they were right.

THE END